Ancients

Faye Knightly

Acknowledgements

Where to start with this one. I'll certainly need to include my editor on the list of people I'm eternally grateful for. Without her gentle touch, encouragement, and heavy hand, Ancients wouldn't be what it is today. This story has been sitting in my head for far too long, and to see it finally become something sharable has been nothing short of magic. I'd like to acknowledge my friend Ambur Watt, who was the first and only person I told the story of Ancients to for many years. Thank you for listening and for not saying I was crazy to dream it up.

Thank you to my early reader team, especially Kari Robinson and Alysha Stafford who read Ancients in its very early form and still loved it. You have no idea how knowing it was moving in such an early stage helped fortify me for the very long process of taming this manuscript.

Thank you to my beta reading team for putting up with my incessant questions and need to just *talk* about these characters after keeping them to myself for so long. Now we get to talk a whole lot more. I have so much I want to tell you.

The truth is, I never thought I would write this book let alone release it. I dedicate this book to the spirit of believing in yourself.

Yes, you *can* write a book. Yes, you *can* paint a portrait. Yes, you *can* get up on a stage.

Your vision and your spirit matter.

Doubt is the dream killer.

Start today.

It's worth it.

FAYE KNIGHTLY

This book includes: blood and gore, a pseudo foster care system, and the discussion of emotionally abusive childhoods.
If any of these topics are a trigger for you, PUT DOWN THE BOOK! Your mental health is important.

Contents

CHAPTER I

SARAH

You're a hunter, Sarah. A predator. A part of me, of our family, and it's not something you can hide from because it's inside of you. The need to hunt, to tear, to kill. The sooner you give in, my daughter, the sooner you will be free.

"Sarah? Are you listening?" Nina huffed, and I brought my eyes up from the jagged crack in our linoleum table to meet my roommate's fiery gaze. My father's voice still pounded in my aching head, and of course it would come to me now when I was vulnerable. Lack of sleep and a mix of work and lectures had left me exhausted.

Nina's emerald eyes flashed with annoyance, her ruby red lips pursed as she cocked one perfectly manicured eyebrow at me, demanding an answer. Damn, what had she said? Nina's small frame quivered with annoyance, and I winced when I realized the hands at her hips were wrinkling the delicate fabric of her black dress. She was dressed for a date, the form fitting dress matching her slicked back hair, and giving the calculated impression of sleek perfection.

Nina put up with a lot, and my absences of attention weren't exactly rare. She certainly didn't deserve to have a roommate who paid her less attention than the voice of a man she was hoping to never see again.

"Yes, sorry," I replied wearily. "It's been a long day." The diner was short staffed, and I'd been forced to work a double. All I wanted was to be left alone so I could find something to ease the hunger gnawing at my insides and try to find a bit of sleep before I had to do it all over again, but then there was Nina. Sweet, patient Nina who kept the fridge stocked when I forgot, and reminded me to put on a jacket when it was raining.

"I need your help." A deep baritone echoed through the room, and I looked up to find Adam awkwardly sliding his large frame into the foldable chair across from me. When had he arrived? I held a hand to my head, uncertain how I could've missed the tall clan leader who so easily dwarfed the simple furniture in our small apartment. Adam settled into his folding chair with a creak and stared at me expectantly, his large hands folded on the table.

Short brown hair framed a narrow, pinched face that was paler than normal, and there was a hint of desperation in his eyes. While it was something most people wouldn't notice, I knew Adam well enough to tell that something was bothering him. It was there in the tic of his jaw and the stiffness of his shoulders.

A chill wended its way up my spine.

Adam didn't ruffle easily.

Tension settled between my shoulder blades. Clearing my throat and sitting up straight, I exhaled slowly, stretching my fingers out flat on the rickety table to brace myself. Whatever it was, however bad it was, I already knew I would agree to it.

I owed Adam.

Owed the clan.

"What do you want me to do?" My quiet tone sounded shaky even to me, and I cleared my throat to disguise my discomfort, fiddling with a thread at the sleeve of my sweater and ignoring the way my stomach clenched at the possibility of him requiring me to do something violent. As the strongest member of The Shades, Adam would turn to me if a show of strength was needed. Brutal fights with other clans played out in my mind as I waited for him to continue.

The Ghosts had been encroaching on our territory, just around the edges, and I knew Adam was concerned about them. Could they have tried something? Was everyone at headquarters okay? The thought of those outcast kids piled into our ramshackle old house on Kendall Street made my heart ache. I'd been just like them once, a weak runaway kid in need of protection, and the clan had done just that.

If not The Ghosts, then maybe this was about The Bones. I shuddered, hoping it wasn't. They didn't have the strength in numbers to challenge us, but maybe they were willing to risk it? What they lacked in numbers, they made up for in brute strength. The Bones were known for their brutal initiation tests. Only the strong survived long enough to join them, and those who didn't cut it were dumped in the harbour.

My empty stomach turned at the thought of them setting their sights on us, and I was in danger of throwing up bile. Not that it would get me out of this conversation. So, I swallowed hard and pushed down the panic, shifting in my creaky chair. There was a chance this had nothing to do with them.

"It's my new roommate. I put out an ad and I get this weird fucking guy."

A roommate? One guy? This was what had Adam shaken up? I'd seen him manage a mutilated corpse without blinking. It didn't make sense. Sitting back in surprise, I waited for him to explain. This wasn't like Adam, and one guy was something he could easily deal with on his own. So, why ask me?

Adam stared hard at our gossamer drapes for a moment. They moved with the breeze from a crack in the window our landlord had failed to seal. His eyes tracked the movement as he spoke. "There's something off about him. His heart rate is faster than a human. He smells supernatural, but I don't think he's a vampire. Maybe a werewolf? I don't know. If he was a vampire, he'd know he was in our clan's territory and he should have come directly to me, but he didn't. He acted like he was human and invited me out for a drink. I could've just sent him off and looked for somebody else, but an unknown supernatural in our territory? Sarah." Adam shook his head worriedly. "We can't take that risk." His anxiety was almost another physical presence in the room. He turned from the dancing drapes to me, and we shared a look.

A single supernatural wouldn't pose much of a threat on his own, but if this guy was working for The Bones or another one of our rivals, it would be a deadly mistake to ignore him.

Shit, other than The Bones, I couldn't remember what else had been happening with our borders. I'd been too busy, too sleep deprived to follow clan politics like I should. There had been meetings to reaffirm relations and borders, but I wasn't Adam's second anymore and my attendance wasn't required.

Truthfully, I'd been happy to distance myself from the clan, to pretend I wasn't a vampire for as long as I could before the hunger drove me out into our territory to hunt. But now that there was a threat, guilt brewed in my chest like a living thing. I tried to force myself to think like I once had, considering those who surrounded our territory and who might try to make a move on us. As Adam's second, this stuff used to come naturally to me, but not anymore. Not since Adam and I had gone our separate ways, and Nina had taken my place at his side and in his bed. I cursed myself for not paying attention.

Adam thought his new roommate could be a werewolf, but the packs preferred to settle outside of the city proper, their need for the wild places and lack of a demand for human blood making them reclusive. Then again, the occasional loner was known to come into the city, and they could be bought and used by a vampire clan if need be. The Bones certainly weren't above using whatever they could get if it meant claiming more territory for their ever-expanding domain.

They'd take the whole damned city if they could. The Temples had made the mistake of inviting them to their safe house for a territory negotiation. The Bones had been offering them an adult video store on Clareway—a spot that drunks frequented after the bar on fifth closed. It was a prime hunting spot, and had been an enticing enough offer that they'd agreed to the meeting.

They'd paid a terrible price for it, and I swallowed hard at the memory of the report on the six o'clock news. The anchor had claimed it was drug-related violence, but I recognized the house even if I hadn't been able to identify the torn-apart bodies.

It had been a bloodbath with no survivors, and afterwards, The Bones had advanced into Temple territory, easily dispatching the remaining clan members and claiming the area as their own—an area that now bordered our territory. Adam's eyes reflected the same remembered horror, and I knew he was thinking about The Temples.

We couldn't let that happen to us.

"I need you to find out about him. Get close to him, figure him out. I need to know if he's a danger to us and what his intentions are. I'm going to set you up on a double date with him, Nina, and I."

A date? My heart clenched, and I drew in a tight breath, slumping back in my chair and trying to come up with an acceptable reason to refuse Adam's request. But he held up a hand before I could begin.

"No, no complaints, Sarah, I need your help with this. You have a better sense for these things than I do. I want you to figure out what the hell he is. Use your magic." Adam waved his hand around. Magic was something he had never understood, and he gave me too much credit, acting as if my ability to get an impression of other people's minds and intentions solved every problem the clan came across. Very few vampires had a witch's magic. I was rare, and that made me a valuable resource. Of course, he wanted to use me as the tool I was, and he should. It was the smart thing to do.

The tension drained from my shoulders as I thought the assignment through.

One date, with Adam and Nina there for support. I just had to get this new roommate of Adam's to feel comfortable with me; to let down his mental guards. If I could get him to loosen up enough to give me a glimpse of what his intentions were, I'd know if he was a spy.

It wouldn't be an actual date where I'd be expected to open myself up. I'd just have to fake it for one night, put our minds at ease, and move on.

Adam was right, I could do this.

Blowing out a steadying breath, I reluctantly nodded. Adam tipped his head in thanks before bidding me goodnight in a clipped tone that would have made anyone else think he was displeased with our encounter. But I knew he was just eager to head out the door with Nina. He might be about as gloomy as I was, but there was no denying how much he loved her. Adam awkwardly extracted himself from the low folding chair, stretching out his long legs and turning to Nina. He dwarfed her by at least two and a half feet, a fact that had never bothered either of them.

"All set? The movie starts in twenty." Adam smiled down at her with a warmth he reserved just for her. I was Adam's ex-girlfriend. It *should* have been hard to see how easy things were between him and Nina, how apparent their love for each other was. Only, I didn't feel the slightest bit of jealousy, just a familiar dull ache in my chest reminding me how lonely my days were, how hard it was to let people in when my mind was haunted by the faces of my past.

I tried with Nina, I really did, but even she didn't know my history.

"Yes, let's go." Grinning up at him, Nina's eyes shone with affection as she wrapped herself around Adam's arm, molding into his side, and tucking under his arm. She steered him towards the door with a quick backward wave to me. I didn't know when, but she'd smoothed out the wrinkle at her waist from earlier. The thought made me chuckle. She'd have a lot more wrinkles to deal with after sitting down for a movie.

My stomach rumbled, reminding me I hadn't had blood today. I'd managed a few bites of a chicken sandwich during the lunch rush, but while it held off the hunger for a time, it couldn't sustain me. I probably should have planned to head out with the clan tonight to hunt, but the cow's blood in the fridge was convenient and unaccompanied by the screaming faces of my past.

Taking the two steps towards the refrigerator, I quickly located the hard plastic container of cow's blood. Not bothering to warm it up, I popped the lid and tilted the edge to my lip, determined to get my feeding over with.

Thick like honey, the blood slid down my throat, its rich metallic taste prompting my fangs to emerge—eager to pierce flesh, though there was none to be found. My mind flashed to the many nights I'd spent out hunting with The Shades, to the way a human's trembling skin gave way beneath my sharp fangs. My eyes squeezed shut as though doing so could stop the thrill of those memories brought—the excitement.

You're just like us.

A monster.

With a hiss, I slammed the now empty container down on the table and squeezed it as though all my pain and anger could somehow be channeled into that tiny plastic cylinder. But there was too much of it, and the cylinder gave way, cracking beneath my grip at the same time as whimpering cries and pleading eyes from the past flashed through my mind. My father was there, always there, in the corner, his boisterous laugh at odds with the pain and suffering of his—no, *our*—victims.

Sighing at the sight of the shattered plastic, I quickly cleaned up the mess with one of Nina's colourful dishrags, careful not to cut myself on the plastic shards.

I couldn't stand the sight of any more blood tonight.

It was past time for bed, and I headed to my room praying to whoever cared that the dream haunting my nights stayed away. The parts I could remember of my childhood were bad enough, but whatever had happened to me before the age of eleven was a blank, and the dream was all that remained. Whatever horrors lay in my subconscious from that time refused to let me rest.

I awoke in the dream, an icy shiver running down my spine. *No, not tonight. I couldn't deal with this tonight.* But there was no choice. The dream didn't care how badly I needed rest, that I'd worked myself to the bone and barely changed out of my grease-soaked uniform before falling into bed.

A wall of thick pines surrounded the clearing where I stood, broken only by a circular tunnel with branches twisted away from the opening as though moved by an unseen hand. The afternoon sun warmed the air, and I curled my toes into the thick, luxurious grass, savouring the softness against my bare feet. But I couldn't stay here for long. The pitch blackness of the open maw called to me as keenly as a siren waiting to dash its prey upon the rocks.

Quiet, it was so quiet in the clearing. Unsettlingly so. No birdsong met my ears. No wind ruffled the branches ahead of me. The path looked harmless, a simple way through the trees, but I knew the truth. As soon as I set foot on the dirt floor, *it* would give chase. If only I could stay here in this beautiful field until I woke, but painful experience had taught me the only way to awaken was to follow the path to its end.

A breeze flowed straight across the clearing, originating from the path and ruffling the springy green romper I wore. The small leaves sprouting from the strange moss-like cloth danced in the wind until the breeze blew more strongly and sent them rattling hard enough to blow a few loose and push my loose red curls over my shoulders. The thing that waited was done letting me take my time. It was insistent. Urging me onward.

Demanding my obedience.

With a shuddering breath, I fought through the unwilling clench of my muscles and forced myself to take a trembling step towards the path. The air stilled, as if pleased with my compliance.

Swallowing hard, I crept forward until the treed archway loomed overhead.

There wasn't any movement I could see on either side of the path, but I knew it was there. Watching. Waiting. The presence pressed in on me as I continued onward, far enough that the trees closed in overhead. Slowly picking my way down the path, I watched and hoped that tonight it would stay quiet, that tonight I would somehow pass unseen.

Quiet, quiet lest it hear me.

My legs shook as I scanned either side of the path for any sign of movement.

But even if I didn't see it, couldn't see it, some animal part of me knew it was there, that it was stalking me—wanted me. God knows what for. Fear pounded through my veins like ice, slowly consuming my system until it became a panic, but I held myself steady, sure the moment I ran, it would give chase.

Something rustled the branches to my left, and it was more than my tensed body could bear. My muscles released like a spring under tension, and I took off at a flat-out run, dashing through the tangled brush and down the winding dirt path, my feet following the twists and turns as though I had been down this path hundreds of times before. The familiarity of this place struck me, as it always did, but there was no time to think it through, no time to look more closely at my surroundings.

There was only the chase.

Dozens of tiny rocks bit into the tender flesh of my bare feet. It should've hurt, and I knew if I stopped to actually look at my feet, they'd be raw. The flesh torn and bleeding. But the pain didn't reach me. I barreled down the path. Pushing myself harder, unwilling to slow.

I ran. My breath coming in squeaky gulping gasps as I pushed myself to my limits and beyond. My feet flying across the rough terrain. My ankle caught on a lifted vine, and I had the strange thought that it should have been flat—had been flat until something pulled it upwards with the intention of tripping me. Stumbling, I hazarded a terrified glance over my shoulder and saw a shape formed of shadows. It looked almost humanoid.

Hot tears streamed down my face as I resumed my pace. There was no time to slow.

It was gaining.

My heart couldn't take much more. It pounded in my ears, one word screaming in my head until everything else faded away. My muscles were screaming, but I couldn't feel them, not really. I was outside of my body, desperately pounding down the path with only one thought driving me forward.

Run.

Finally, light appeared ahead of me—the end of the path was in sight. I broke free of the tangled brush and crushing darkness to emerge onto a pristine beach of pure white sand. Sparkling waters glistened in the bright sunlight stretching across the horizon. The soft sand was a soothing balm to my battered feet. But my pace didn't slow, couldn't slow.

A glowing figure waited for me at the water's edge as it always did, turning to me as I approached. Their arms lifted, extending out to welcome me into its warm embrace. The being radiated a sense of peace I was desperate for. Relief flooded my system, and I pushed through the last few feet to fling myself at the figure, clinging tightly to their torso. Their arms came down to envelop me, and I gratefully sank into their warmth, letting the peace it exuded work its way into me and soothe the fear and panic still pounding through my blood.

Here. This was where I belonged. Everything was okay.

I was safe.

The peace lasted only a moment before I awoke in my bed with blankets twisted around my legs like the raised vine from my dream. Crimson curls plastered to my forehead with a sickening amount of sweat. A wave of sorrow overwhelmed me and, sobbing, I rolled up to perch at the edge of the mattress on the floor I used as a bed, burying my face in my still shaking hands. The terror of the thing in the woods was bad enough—racing with it always one mistake away from catching me. But the figure at the end, the one who held me, who comforted me, who I felt safe with…

That was the true nightmare. Never in my life had I felt such a strong sense of belonging, and waking up to find it gone was the worst part. Like something good had been torn away from me. A piece of myself ripped cruelly away to leave me broken and empty—a shell of myself.

But it was that moment of pure love that had kept me from labeling the recurring dream a nightmare. There was no peace to my days, no rest, no sense of belonging. Only in the dream did I find that.

I felt terrible, as I always did. Not rested at all. I never woke up from the dream feeling like I'd slept. Grabbing the small towel I kept on my nightstand to wipe the sweat from my brow, I checked the clock on my nightstand. Five a.m. I'd slept for a paltry three hours, and I had a full day of work and lectures ahead of me.

Blowing out a breath, I sat forward to hang my head between my legs, the tangled web of my curls blotting out most of the room. I struggled to find some distance between myself and the emotions still lingering. Three hours of sleep, and it was going to be a long day.

It would have to do.

"Hey babe, could you warm this up for me?" A meaty hand slapped across my ass. Startled, I looked up to glare at the burly man just barely fitting in his booth seat, his plaid shirt bunched up against the table. But my rage at being manhandled quickly turned to hunger at his closeness. He was warm and soft. How easily I could sink my teeth into his ample neck and claim his blood. I stared at the spot where I would strike, at the pulse I could see beating there as the big man grew more nervous. There was a mole there, placed like a target just over the pulsating bulge of his throat.

Like it was placed there just for me. Hunger gnawed at my stomach. My lips parted. Just one drink, a quick one. Maybe no one would even notice.

"Hey, come on. I was just joking around. What? Do I have something on my shirt?" The folds of the man's neck undulated as he dropped his chin and began scanning his front. The coffee cup he'd thrust out at me forgotten.

No one here could stop me. My stomach growled loud enough to be audible.

"Sarah. Hey. Get a move on." Kim's irate voice snapped me out of the haze, and I met the blonde waitress' irritated stare with a blink of surprise. She moved on with a shake of her head and a flip of her ponytail, plopping down the three plates she carried without a backwards glance. With a shaky nod to myself, I moved away without a word, not bothering to pour the man a refill of his coffee, though I held the still warm metallic carafe in my hands. The carafe—I turned my attention towards it, trying to let the scent of stale coffee mask the humans in the room.

I couldn't put off hunting anymore. The miniscule amount of cold cow's blood I'd allowed myself wasn't keeping the hunger at bay and working at the diner was becoming dangerous—the craving for warm, fresh blood nearly intolerable.

Excusing myself to the break room behind the kitchen, I checked the time. There weren't too many humans roaming the streets on weeknights, but Adam always ran a hunt on Wednesdays. I should feel lucky a hunt was planned for tonight, but all I felt was dread. As much as I hated the idea of feeding off a living, breathing, scared human, I needed to join in tonight or risk losing control and exposing myself.

They're nothing to us, Sarah, just prey.

They exist for our pleasure, our enjoyment.

My father's words echoed in my mind, and I felt nothing but shame for almost attacking the plump man in his plaid shirt. I peeked over to see him laughing, his double chins wobbling harmoniously at something his equally overweight wife had said.

He was fine. Maybe I'd had the thought, the instinct, but I hadn't acted on it.

"Excuse me, miss?" I turned to find a young mother with a set of matching twin toddlers in tow. "Can we have more napkins, please?" The little blonde girl was eating spaghetti, and she gave me a toothy grin before taking a glob of pasta in her hands and smearing it across her face. A smear that perfectly matched that of her brother.

But I wasn't seeing her, not really. Memories of dead children heaped in a pile for burning threatened to pull me down to the place where I couldn't stop screaming.

No, no, that was over. I'd gotten away. Hugging my arms around myself for stability, I dropped some napkins at the mother's table before tracking down my manager and telling him I was feeling ill. By the way his eyes roved over my haggard, too-thin face, I didn't need to say more.

Shit, I must look rough, but at least this meant I could leave without attracting much attention. I punched my card with a satisfying clack before gathering my street clothes into my satchel and heading out into the night. This was what I needed, and I breathed deeply of the crisp night air, savouring the distracting sounds of street traffic as I navigated my way around a group of clustered tourists, pausing to snap a photo in the middle of the sidewalk.

The clan house was nearly empty by the time I arrived, and I hurriedly entered the brown brick two-story house someone long ago had gifted to The Shades. Whose name was now on the deed, I had no idea, but no one had ever come to interfere with our business. Stealing into the main floor bathroom, I changed out of my uniform and into the black leotard I kept permanently stuffed at the bottom of my duffel. The black suit hugged my willowy frame, showcasing the curve of my hips. It was a good lure, even if it made me feel like a piece of meat dangling on a fishing line.

With a sigh, I tugged my crimson curls free of my work bun, shaking them out across my shoulders, and enjoying the release of tension across my scalp. I just needed to get out there and get this done, rid myself of the hunger at least, even if it meant feeding on humans. The very thing that clenched my heart even as it made my empty stomach rumble.

I zipped my bag, leaving it in the corner of the bathroom and hurried out of the building, sidling past two youths wearing baggy pants and backwards caps, laughing and completely oblivious to the way they blocked the only hallway leading to the back of the house.

Stepping outdoors, I let the heavy door bang behind me and hopped down the short drop where our stone steps had broken apart, coming around to the alley beside the house to find everyone gathering for the hunt.

Eager, friendly faces surrounded me, but I kept my posture stiff and unfriendly, not wanting to encourage a conversation. There were so many of us now, nearly three dozen, but while we had the numbers, taking in whoever needed a safe haven had left us weak. Scrawny street kids lined the alley in front of where Adam stood on a stack of hastily stacked pallets. There were some adults mixed in, but too few. Much too few.

Adam's voice carried over the crowd as he neared the end of his speech.

"Tonight we'll be focusing on quad four. There's a Bears game tonight, and we're expecting the bar to be packed. Crowds will disperse when the game ends at eight. Remember to take your pick."

Always your *pick*, never your *prey*. I clenched my teeth.

Humans are our food, Sarah, our prey, and we, their natural predator. I shook my head to dispel my father's words, to remember that this was different. Adam was different. This *clan* was different.

We hunted to live, but we didn't kill.

"Somewhere secluded. Smile at them, woo them, take enough for yourself, but listen to their heartbeat and make sure it isn't under any true strain. Do that, and we'll all go home happy." Adam's smile faltered when he caught sight of my grim face. "Okay. Be safe."

His speech always ended the same: *Be safe*, like we were the ones in danger tonight and not the human prey we were set upon. With a sigh, I skirted the crowd and headed towards quad four to stake out a place near the club. Everyone else would hover around the sports bar, and I didn't want company.

Not for this.

Finding a place on the corner, a street lamp illuminating my willowy figure, I waited until a pair of drunk humans stumbled their way towards me. I hated myself with every footfall in my direction, silently begging the men to turn down a side street, to know better than to approach. A heavy bass drifted from the direction of the club they'd come from. They were too busy to notice me, caught up in conversation. One man nearly tripped on a discarded coffee cup. Maybe they'd walk on by. Maybe they wouldn't see me.

No.

Sadly, I knew that like so many before them, they were bound to take the bait. The thought set my teeth tingling as my fangs emerged to their full length, eager to pierce flesh. I could already taste the alcohol in their blood.

The blonde with dark eyes who had tripped on the coffee cup elbowed his friend in the ribs and gestured my way.

"Hey, are you waiting for someone?" His words came out in a barely intelligible slur, and I cursed myself when my empty stomach moaned its approval.

This would be easy.

"My name's Jake. Maybe I could, uh, escort you home?" His smile was sweet. Genuine even. Inwardly, I cringed while outwardly I smiled back at him, coyly tucking a crimson curl behind my ear.

"I'm a little lost, actually. Do you think you could show me the way?"

Jake beamed at his good fortune.

"Hey man, I'll see you at Wimpy's later, okay?" he told the other man, unable to tear his eyes from me.

"Sure dude, don't you get lost, too!" His friend ducked his head, his shaggy brown hair shaking and face turning red as he laughed with the abandon of one whose inhibitions were unnaturally low. With a hard clap on Jake's back, he stumbled off on his own to cross the empty street without checking for cars. I watched his progress with trepidation. If he kept going that way, he'd end up in the Bones' territory, and they certainly wouldn't pass up the opportunity to take a drunken human wandering alone. They were unlikely to kill him and risk a murder investigation.

They liked to play.

I spared a thought for the man's terrible fate, but there was no way to warn him without revealing the threat.

Smiling shyly at Jake, and hating myself the whole time for what I knew I was about to do, I peered up through my long lashes and into his concerned eyes. Cautiously, I moved closer to him, taking in the crisp scent of his soap and letting loose a small pathetic sounding sniffle.

It was an act.

I was an act, and I let the guilt lend emotion to my performance. Jake fell for it, his arms hesitantly wrapped around my back as he patted me soothingly on my trembling shoulder.

"Hey, it's okay. I'll help you get home safely."

Shuddering at the kindness of his words, I nuzzled into his neck, seeking the heat of his skin. His pulse throbbed against my lips—so close.

Starved, and being this close to sating my hunger, my fangs emerged on their own. Before the images of my past could swarm me, I sank my teeth deep into his jugular, moaning at the spurt of blood against my parched throat. Jake stiffened against me and shivered at the invasion, his fingers clawing uselessly at my back as I held on with my superior strength—a cat holding its squirming prey. Part of me was thrilled at how he tried to escape but couldn't. I sank in deeper, clutching him like the lifeline he was.

Blood rushed into my mouth, and I gulped it down greedily. His fear and panic set in as he struggled to get away, but I couldn't stop. The sounds of his gasps and my contented eating filled the night as I pulled ever deeper. Then he relaxed, his body slumping into me and his struggles ceasing. Instead of pulling away, he pressed his neck further into my mouth, moaning in pleasure as the feeding frenzy took over, duping him into believing I was doing something with my mouth he enjoyed.

He squirmed. This time, eager for more. I pulled harder, taking gulp after gulp of life-giving liquid. Hunger abating ever so slightly, my mind and my actions became clearer.

No

My memories flared to life until I could almost see a woman huddled in the corner still wearing a white frock, her throat torn open and practically ripped out. The fear in her eyes cut my heart like a dagger. She whimpered pitifully, as if that would stop the monster.

It wouldn't.

No

Another flash, a boy this time. I begged him not to leave the safety of my room, but he resisted, ripping his arm out of my hands and leaving to seek his already-dead family. A flash and he was on the floor.

My father stood over him. The boy clutched a wound at his neck, sitting in a pool of his own blood, his legs fighting for purchase on the gore-slick floor as he fought to get away.

He moved in for the kill, pausing a moment to turn my way and smile. His face still dripping with the boy's blood and looking every bit the monster I knew him to be.

"This is what we are, Sarah, what you are, and it's okay. We're vampires, and they're our food."

No!

I tore myself away from Jake, shoving him against the wall to force myself backwards. Jake was a person. I refused to think of him as anything else. Now that the hunger had lessened, I was thinking more clearly, and with that clarity came the memories. Breathing hard, I gathered myself from the horrors playing out in my head.

I wasn't him; he didn't control me. I'd run away. I was safe now.

Jake's eyes glazed over, and he smiled at me dreamily.

"Hey, don't stop now, baby!" He took my numb hand and gently tugged me in, chuckling. My bloodlust left him drunk on sensation.

"I think I'm okay, actually. You can go," I whispered, giving him a shaky smile I hoped was enough of a dismissal.

"What? I thought we—I mean."

"No, please leave now." Pulling my hand from his and balling it into a fist, I fought to resist the temptation of his beckoning arms. It would be so easy to nestle back in. The paltry amount I'd taken was barely enough to take the edge off, but no, I wouldn't.

I couldn't let my father win.

Not tonight.

Not ever.

"Come on. Maybe you want to come back with me to my place."

Go back to his place. Where we would be alone, and I could drink and drink until he was an empty husk, just as that boy had been so many years ago.

Do it, the boy wants this. Look how eager he is to place himself under your fangs.

"Just go!" I shouted. Jake's eyebrows shot up until they were lost in his feathery hair, and his eyes cleared.

"Okay, okay." He held his hands up, backing away. As he turned to continue down the street, he muttered, "bitch." Of course, he wouldn't realize my senses were sharper than his, hadn't expected me to hear him. Let him think I was a bitch if it helped him keep his distance. I'd be the biggest bitch he'd ever seen.

It was hard watching him walk away. My muscles clenched, and my hands curled so tight into fists my nails left marks. But the further he walked, the easier it became to resist the urge to chase and tackle him to the ground where I could take him at my pleasure.

Thankfully, he took a different route from his friend. He hadn't been safe from me, but at least he would be safe from The Bones. Exhausted, I stepped into the alley and leaned back against the wall, letting the cool bricks soothe my fevered skin through the thin fabric of my leotard.

I'd harmed him, taken his blood, proved I was just as much a monster as my father always assured me I was, and the guilt of it ravaged my mind.

The world spun, and I sank to my knees, putting my face into my shaking hands. Jake would go home thinking he'd had an amorous encounter with a woman he came across on the street. He would be okay. Maybe weak in the morning, but then, I hadn't taken much blood to be certain. He would be fine, and I would die without human blood, yet that prick of fear and panic I'd felt in his mind still haunted me.

Monster. That's what I was, and the reminder would be enough to keep me off the streets until I was starving once more and unable to resist the night's call.

Too cursed to live with any semblance of morality, too weak to die. I stumbled my way home, feeling my failure with every step and hating how good the warmth of Jake's blood felt in my stomach.

Nina was home and in bed already, a rarity and one I was thankful for as I quietly shut the door to our apartment behind me, turning the handle so it didn't click. The bar must've given her a much-needed night off, and as much as my roommate's eternal cheerfulness was a welcome break in my dismal existence, I was pleased to find her asleep. I couldn't stand the thought of company.

Not tonight.

Not after Jake.

I paused to pick up the paper towel roll from where it had tipped over on the counter—Nina hated seeing things out of place. Savouring the quiet darkness, I moved through our sparse apartment and headed down the short hallway to my room.

Tonight had taken an emotional toll, and I fell into bed, barely remembering to remove my boots before crawling under the covers and losing myself to the blissful nothingness of sleep.

Chapter 2

DAVID

The flight attendant was conventionally pretty, with doe eyes and a small chin that came to a delicate point, but I barely noticed until she ducked behind the podium, knocking her triangular hat askew to reveal a flash of bright red hair.

Red hair. Instantly alert, I stood up straight, scanning her features, searching for any hint of familiarity. She stood up gracefully, a crimson stain on her cheeks when she noticed my scrutiny. I cursed myself for the automatic reaction, but that didn't stop me from continuing my study of her face, from making absolutely certain she wasn't *her*.

No. Her face was all wrong, the lips too thin. *Hers* had been pouty, the bottom slightly more rounded. I could still see her laughing in my mind, red curls dancing around her face, and trailing out behind her as she raced on ahead to our special spot.

Damn. That familiar pang of disappointment struck me in the heart, but after five years of searching, I was familiar with the twist of a knife in my chest at every woman I met who was never her. And that was the point. It was too much, had gone on too long.

It had to stop.

I had to stop before the obsession consumed me completely.

"Something wrong, sir?" The flight attendant blinked prettily at me, and I cleared my throat to hide the momentary absence. Subtly, I checked the gold badge across her chest to learn her name and compensate for my rudeness.

"Not at all, Mary." With a polite smile, I handed her my ticket, doing my best to wait patiently while she checked my details against the passenger list.

Boston was the first place I'd be traveling to purely for myself since I'd first come to these lands. How fitting it was the first place I'd searched, and now, after five years, I'd return, not to scour the streets for the girl I'd once known, but to educate myself, to seek a life outside of this nightmare. Because the truth was, the girl I'd known was dead or hidden so completely in the teeming masses of humans that I would never find her.

Maybe someday I'd forgive myself for giving up. It certainly wasn't today, and it wouldn't be tomorrow. But one day, I'd look back on this and know I'd made the right decision.

Sighing, I turned to study the passengers still seated in the waiting area. Families, kids, a tall couple holding hands and laughing as the tall blonde leaned in to listen in on the man's headphones. Everyone here had a life, family, *friends*, and here I was wandering the earth searching for a ghost.

I'd forced myself to complete a high school equivalency, and discovered a love of chemistry that had given me hope for my future. Now I had a goal, something to truly look forward to. I'd finish my degree in Boston, attending lectures in person for the first time, and then I'd get into research, answering the unanswered questions still plaguing the pharmaceutical world.

It was a beautiful dream, and I could see myself living it. Starting small as a low-level research assistant until they trusted me enough to run my own projects. I was so close I could taste it, and that girl, the one I'd failed, didn't—couldn't—factor in.

I'm sorry. I tried. How I wished I could tell her those words, apologize to her for my selfishness, but I couldn't. She was lost, and it was time for me to move on. To think of something other than the way her face had crumpled when they'd ripped her from my arms.

"Sir? Sir?"

With an apologetic grin, I turned my attention back to the flight attendant and stretched out a hand to accept my now torn ticket.

"Thank you, miss."

The woman giggled, her white teeth flashing as she leaned on the podium in a way that jutted one hip suggestively outward. She was pretty, about my age. I *should* be interested, but I didn't think I could date someone with red hair. The constant reminder would leave me on edge.

"So, what's in Boston?" She quirked an eyebrow at me, and I grinned, feeling freer than I'd felt in years. What was in Boston? A future? A change? I didn't know or care. How many people had asked me that question? It was the standard fare for the frequent traveler.

Where are you going? Why are you traveling today?

I'd always give the same answer—the same lie—"I'm traveling for work." Because finding her had been my work, my mission. I would save her as a man the way I'd failed to save her as a boy. Only now, I was putting that foolish notion behind me.

The stewardess—Mary—cleared her throat, and I realized I'd been quiet for too long, that there was a line of people behind me.

"Everything." With a grin and a wink that brought a pretty flush to her checks, I stepped into the tunnel, whistling an old song, an ancient song, as I headed down the loading bridge and towards my new life.

SARAH

Between the dream robbing me of sleep, and the hunt ripping apart my soul, I'd nearly forgotten about the role of spy I was to play on Friday. Until Nina greeted me at the door with an oversized grin, a bundle of lacy fabric in her arms. Exhausted from an early morning lecture on particle physics and a day of dealing with a particularly bad batch of customers, I could only stare at her in surprise.

"This will be perfect for tonight."

Frowning down at the black lace, I beelined for my favourite spot on our squashy loveseat.

"Tonight?"

Seeing my confusion, Nina rolled her eyes, shaking her head and making the curlers in her short hairdance. She was in prep mode, with white cream caked on her face to 'open the pores' and one of my old band T-shirts fitting loosely on her smaller frame and hanging down past her waist to the edge of her low-cut jean shorts.

"Yeah, tonight. We're going out with Adam's roommate, remember? The guy you're supposed to check out for us?" I didn't like the way Nina's eyes flashed when she said check out. It was too much like she expected this to be a real date, and not some clan business I wanted to take care of quickly so I could get back to my life—pathetic as it was. Begrudgingly, I held up the dress, my mouth going dry when I realized just how impossibly short it was. The hem would fall to the middle of my thigh if I was lucky.

"Nina, what is this?"

"*This* is a dress that will suit your figure perfectly. To use your ability, the guy needs to let his guard down, right?" Feeling nauseous, I nodded. "Well, this will have his guard down in no time." She grinned, and I tipped my head in acknowledgement, loosing a breath as I took the dress to the bathroom to try on in front of the mirror.

The fringe on the skirt fell mid-thigh, and the open back left an exceptional amount of my skin exposed while the front ended in a v low enough you could see the swell of my small breasts. I had to admit the dress suited my willowy frame, even if it was uncomfortable to move around in. My lip curled in appreciation as I twisted in the mirror, getting used to the tug of fabric across my waist.

The sight of myself on display forced my thoughts down a different path. How long had it been since I'd taken a man to my bed? I couldn't recall. Lost in the dream and self-loathing, it'd been far too long. Maybe Nina was right. If sex was a way to accomplish my task tonight faster, maybe this was a good approach. I might as well put on some makeup.

Soft brown eyes set in an oval face framed with long curly red hair stared back at me from the confines of my eveningwear. Nina had told me I had an 'oval face' along with specific instructions on how to properly showcase my high cheekbones with the right blend of blush. The bathroom was fully stocked with Nina's cast-off makeup, and opening a drawer revealed an assortment from which to choose. With an unpracticed hand, I applied a streak of blush to my cheeks on what I hoped was the cheek line Nina had shown me and added a dash of wine-red lipstick to match the deep colour of my hair.

But no matter how I tried to smile or how much makeup I applied, my eyes always had a haunted look to them, and I hated the ever-present dark circles under them. Even Nina hadn't been able to cover those.

Satisfied that my appearance was as good as I could make it, I headed to Nina's room and sat down heavily on her bed, sinking further than I should have in the overly soft mattress she preferred. I could never understand how Nina could sleep on the monstrosity threatening to grab hold of me and never let go.

Dinner reservations were at six, which gave us half an hour to get ready, but she acted as though Adam would come bursting in any minute, moving in a flurry at the ornate white vanity she'd taken from the apartment garbage and refinished. She covered her forearm in several eyeshadow swatches, debating between them. You'd think she was going for a special outing and not a regular date with her long-term boyfriend, but that was Nina. I smiled as I watched her, wishing I had a fraction of her enthusiasm for life.

"The azure or the cyan?" she muttered, holding up an arm covered in swatches for me to review. She looked up in annoyance when I didn't have an answer ready for her. I squinted down at the shades of blue, having difficulty telling them apart.

"Um, the cyan." My tongue tripped on the unfamiliar word, and I hoped I'd just told her I preferred the lighter shade.

With a nod, Nina resumed her work, hovering around her makeup station like a witch at a cauldron, adding a pinch of this and a dash of that to her masterpiece, squinting worriedly at her reflection as if her high cheekbones and elven face could be anything short of beautiful.

"Are you even a little bit excited?" she asked, meeting my eyes in the mirror of her vanity and startling me out of the trance I'd fallen into.

I shrugged, not sure how to answer. No part of me was looking forward to the required socializing of the upcoming evening.

"I mean, what if he's hot?"

Chuckling into my hand, I entertained the idea. It would make it easier to play up the sexy angle if he was attractive. But it didn't matter. So long as I could assure Adam he wasn't a threat by the end of the night, I'd be happy, and if he wanted to come home with me, well, that would be a bonus.

A single knock sounded at the door, rattling through our small apartment, and I knew it had to be Adam. Only he knew how flustered Nina became when she was being rushed, and he kindly only knocked once, knowing any further interruptions would only send her into a panic. Even so, Nina turned to me with wide eyes before frantically searching through her makeup.

Knowing better than to disturb her, I quietly waited on the bed for her to finish. Talking was never my strong suit, and getting to know a stranger required a certain level of banter that left a bitter taste in my mouth. While the physical angle would help, we were going to a sit-down dinner at which there would absolutely be small talk.

Sighing, I stared around me at the memorabilia strewn about Nina's room. A high school trophy in volleyball on which she'd painted the fingernails a garish shade of pink. A photo of her and her family propped up on the top of her dresser, an edge curling. She was so normal and uncomplicated. Of course, she could easily talk about her past. The photo mocked me. In it, Nina was squashed between a younger sister, her mom, and her dad. She looked like her mom, and the matching purple T-shirts they wore added to the image of a happy family.

Family. With a shake of the head, I banished my father's hated face from my mind.

No. Not tonight. I wouldn't let him ruin this night like he had ruined so many others.

Instead, I focused on the man I was to meet. Adam had begrudgingly given me a few details. His name was David, and he was a student at the university where I attended. Maybe I'd even seen him around campus, though it was unlikely I'd noticed. As a mature student, I spent my time on campus hurrying to lectures and squeezing in lab sessions. I just wanted to get my degree and get out so I could start my career. I wondered which one of the fresh-faced youths so excited about their bright future my date would be.

I hissed a breath, hoping Nina didn't hear, and fought to work myself up. It was one thing to say I'd go on the date and another knowing some stranger waited on the other side of the door. It was torture knowing Adam was out there with him while I was stuck waiting for Nina to deem herself ready for the night. Why couldn't the date have been in a crowded bar with the music blaring too loud for us to have a proper conversation?

At last, she slammed the lid decisively on her makeup palette and stood, her heavy wooden chair protesting the sudden movement. She lovingly tucked it back into her vanity with a much quieter squeak before turning to me.

"Ready?" She bounced over and pulled me to my feet, looping an arm with mine. I tried to let some of her cheerfulness rub off on me, but my watery smile wasn't convincing, and she took my hand.

"Come on, Sarah. This could be fun, right?" Her lips twitched up into a smile and her expression brooked no argument. She waited patiently until I relented.

"Right," I muttered dejectedly. With a nod, Nina spun on her heel and headed straight for the door, and I hurried after her. She gestured for me to stand beside her at the door as she fixed her hair and shimmied her taupe velvet dress down the few inches it had managed to ride up. With a quick wink at me and a final wriggle, she pulled the door open with a flourish to reveal the two men.

Caught by surprise, Adam and his roommate were in mid-conversation, allowing me the briefest of moments to size up my date before he turned to face me. He was tall, and I had to tilt my head up slightly to stare up into his face.

I'd been wrong to dismiss his appearance as inconsequential. The tall, lanky man who stood in front of me could easily have walked out of a high-end fashion magazine. He leaned casually against the doorframe with the grace of a cat, laughing at something Adam had said. Possessing a lithe, compact frame, he was well dressed, wearing dark khakis, a button up white shirt and a soft brown coat that made me think he cared about his appearance. Oh yeah, definitely one of those bright-eyed idiots I'd seen on campus, but I was pleased to see he was in his early twenties, like me.

Spikey dirty blonde hair emphasized a long face while a strong jawline and strong nose gave his face an attractive profile. If I could clear him as a threat early enough in the night, maybe I could convince him to come back to my place later. I took in his long legs and broad shoulders appreciatively, but then he turned to me and all thoughts of appreciation for his body were stricken from my mind.

Pale blue eyes met mine and my focus narrowed on them to the exclusion of all else. The colour was indescribable, though my mind floundered for the words. Ocean blue? Cyan? Azure? I tried to think of the shades Nina had displayed on her arm, but none of them were quite right. They were all those shades and none at once, in a stunning blend that I couldn't stop staring at.

He kicked off from the door, to stand up straight. Confusion clouded his expression, but it was gone before I could say for sure I'd seen it. His gaze roved over my face hungrily, and the predatory look of it, the sheer force, was enough that I had to fight off the urge to take a step back. The strangeness of the moment and its intensity was overwhelming, and

I tore my gaze from his to fix my eyes on the front of his button-up shirt, nervously tucking a long tendril of hair behind my ear

The way he looked at me. It was too much. Too powerful. Strangely so. Cautiously peeking up, I found him still watching me, but now a playful smile curved his lips. Gone was the strangely intense look from a moment ago, and in its place, a warmth that made me feel oddly at ease.

At ease. The idea was novel.

At best, I was constantly on edge.

I surprised myself by returning the smile. Adam cleared his voice pointedly. "Sarah, this is my roommate, David. Shall we get going then?" His tone was brusque, and I knew why. He always gave Nina a wide berth whenever he made dinner reservations, but he hadn't accounted for any further delays. Like his normally stoic clan member simpering like a schoolgirl.

Smiling nervously at David, I tried to look away, to turn away from him, but I found it unusually difficult to do so. My eyes were drawn to his. So strange this feeling, like I should know what it means. He watched me expectantly, and I realized I'd been standing in place, watching him for an embarrassingly long time.

The doorframe was narrow enough I'd have to squeeze my way past, and I paused as I studied the gap. Chuckling, those beautiful blue eyes alight with amusement, David took a step back to leave me enough space to pass. Even so, I came close enough to catch his scent, and the hairs on my arms rose. Oddly sweet with a hint of wildness, I found it intoxicating. Working to calm my rising heart rate, I tried not to stumble as I walked a few feet ahead of him.

His eyes were on me the whole way out the door, and I swear I could feel them burning into my exposed back. Damn Nina for making me wear this dress. Overly warm and flustered, I crashed into the door, sucking in greedy gulps of the cool night air and welcoming the open space of the street. Nina happily bounced over to Adam, who begrudgingly bent at the waist to plant a kiss on her lips. Her lipstick left a smudge of crimson like a claim across his lips.

The restaurant was a quick taxi ride away, and I eased into the faux leather bench seat beside the driver. I caught Adam's look of surprise at my choice, but I needed the space to understand what was happening.

I could still feel David's eyes on me in a strange sort of awareness that left my senses tingling and sent prickles across my skin. It was like I'd been asleep, and he had woken me up. I shivered as I tried to organize my thoughts. A strange familiarity, peace, excitement. All of it warred within me, and the heady combination left me quickly soaking through my panties.

While Nina filled the silence with an animated story about a recent makeup gig she'd had preparing a rock star for his concert, I tried to clear my mind and focus on my goal here tonight. But even in the cramped taxi with a human directly beside me, cigarette smell permeating the air, David's intoxicating scent stood out.

I fumbled for his mind and came up against a barrier stronger than any I'd ever known. Frowning, I struggled to understand why someone as friendly as him would be so closed off. The only conclusion I could come to was that the taxi made him nervous. I just needed him to relax so I could finish my assigned task and slip off into the quiet night where everything made sense, and I could be alone.

Because this didn't happen to me. To other people, sure. But to me? I was uncomfortably warm just thinking about spending a night around the man in the backseat. My need for solitude, to escape him, was a physical thing riding along beside me.

The car shuddered to a stop, and David hurried out ahead of Adam and Nina to open the cab door for me in a gesture that, while gallant, was unwelcome. I clambered out awkwardly, sidling around to avoid coming too close to him. And then we were standing awkwardly opposite each other on the sidewalk.

The cold night didn't reach me, and I was about to say something—anything—to break the silence when Nina stepped up onto the curb beside me and continued her discussion of the lead singer's complicated skin tone. Relieved, I followed her and Adam inside.

The sign out front of the restaurant hadn't looked like much, a white rectangle with neat black script set back from the main street. But the inside was cozy and refined, though the low light made me wonder if our white tablecloths were as clean as they looked, and I squinted at a stain as our server led us to a table near the center of the space.

Colourful abstract art hung proudly on the walls and the servers wore tucked in white dress shirts and ties. A glance through the menu revealed nothing but three course meals. Our server appeared to take our orders.

"What can I get for you this evening?"

"Oh, chicken parmesan for me, and I'll have the house salad to start," I muttered hurriedly, remembering to smile in thanks.

Nina ordered a steak for Adam and a burger for herself, but David frowned at the menu, his brow pinched.

"Do you have a vegetarian option?" he asked. Adam and I shared a look of surprise. It went against the predatory nature of vampires and werewolves to be vegetarian. Werewolves, in particular, were known to eat an excess of meat, and David. Something about him *felt* predatory. Yet he was a vegetarian. It didn't make sense.

"Yes, we can do the Caesar salad with no bacon and gnocchi with a cream sauce for your main."

David smiled in thanks, and the server left with a bow and a promise to bring out the first course promptly.

A silence fell over the group, and panic nearly overtook me when I realized we were in for a long sitting, but Nina's cheerful voice soon filled the gap, and I relaxed back into my chair. Thankfully, she had no shortage of stories.

But I quickly grew flustered at the way David watched me like he missed nothing. Like he was biding his time. A shudder wended its way down my spine, and I shifted my legs, the backs of my thighs sticking to the wooden chair.

"And after all that, what a bullshit tip, right? I mean, buddy's making thousands for this concert gig, and he gives me five bucks. Oh, and my friend Cissy, who had the bassist, you would not believe—"

Adam cut her off, interjecting smoothly with the ease of someone used to Nina's constant chatter. "David is going to the university, too. Biochem, was it? Sarah, isn't that your program?"

Surprised to be called on, I choked on my lemon-infused water, coughing to clear the burning in my chest. My eyes watered, and I did my best to swallow down the treacherous fluid, but then Adam's words sunk in, and I looked up in surprise at the man across from me. The same program? David's eyes brightened.

"I'm sure I haven't seen you in any of my lectures," I replied, ducking my head to stare hard at my chicken parmesan. What I'd said was far too close to admitting my attraction, but it was also true. I would have noticed someone like him. I didn't notice much, but I had no doubt that if David had attended a lecture with me, I'd have known it.

"Oh no, you wouldn't. I just started. I know it's unusual to be joining partway into the semester, but I travel a lot..." His voice was deep and smooth as honey, and it danced across my frazzled nerve endings.

"Oh, so you've moved around a lot?" I asked, my voice coming out high and squeaky; an embarrassing contrast to his confident explanation. At least I could meet his eyes now, having grown more used to the intensity of his gaze.

He smiled down ruefully at his plate for a moment before looking back up to meet my eyes.

"Yes, actually. To be honest, I've mostly done correspondence school. I've never really settled down." He studied me with an unreadable expression. That would explain why he was an older student, like me. It'd taken me a while to finish high school after I'd come to Boston as a runaway, but I'd been damned proud to do it, and even more proud when I'd gotten into university.

So, what if I was older than the other students in my program? I had no desire to speak to any of them, anyway. But I wondered why David's education had been so delayed. There was a story there. I had my reasons, but what were his? He studied my face, and I struggled to think of something to say with his eyes pinning me in place.

"Do you like Boston so far?" I squeezed the words out past the blockage in my throat. He hummed in agreement, and I swear I felt the deep sound vibrate through me and go straight to my core. My breath quickened, and I squirmed in my seat. The strange power this man had over me was unnerving.

I was uncomfortable.

I wanted to leave.

I wanted more.

Adam nudged me under the table, reminding me that I was here with a purpose, and I looked over to find him irritated, his thin lips pressed into a line. Right.

It was hard to remember I was here to assess whether David was a threat to the clan. But that was the whole reason for this charade of a date—a thought that left me oddly deflated. David smiled at me, even as he studied my face, not missing a single microexpression, and I should be frightened, should find it disconcerting, but there was a warmth to his expression, and I couldn't help the answering smile tugging at my lips.

He didn't feel like a threat to the clan.

To me, maybe, but not to them.

If I could just see inside his mind, I'd be able to reassure Adam of what I felt to be true. But he was still closed off to me, his wall firmly in place. The more open and friendly someone was, the easier it was to read them, but David, I couldn't detect a hint of tension in his shoulders. Yet still, his mind was a mystery.

I was almost relieved when Nina resumed her tirade against the lead singer. David stayed focused on me, and I cleared my throat nervously at his rapt attention, struggling to hear any part of Nina's story. She'd told me all about the gig days ago, and I was sure she'd told Adam, too, but David was new, and she was bouncing in her seat, gesturing wildly as she reached the pinnacle of her tale. She looked more than a little put out when he didn't give her the entirety of his focus, glancing her way just often enough not to be rude.

Dinner ended with dainty round cakes covered in a drizzle of raspberry sauce that looked too much like blood for me to eat more than a small bite, and I was eager to leave the moment the last fork hit the plate. David held the door for me as we stepped outside into the cold, dreary night. It had rained while we were inside, the kind of rain on the edge of freezing, and I shivered at the bite of it against my bare skin. Before my teeth could start chattering, David draped an impossibly plush brown jacket lightly across my shoulders. His hand brushed my neck as he settled it in place.

But as gentle as he'd been, his touch tore across my nerve endings, leaving my skin tingling and hypersensitive, and I forced myself not to jump away in surprise. Worse still, his scent on the jacket surrounded me, as intriguing as the man himself, muddling my senses and clouding my thoughts. I managed to cast him a smile as I pulled the soft fabric close and cinched at my neck, enjoying the sweet scent with a touch of wildness.

Vanilla. That was it. The sweetness reminded me of vanilla, but that spice. His scent was sweet, but then there was the wickedly unexpected spice, and I gave a delicate sniff, eager for more, like if I could just soak it in, saturate myself in it, I could figure out what it reminded me of, figure *him* out.

"Can I walk you home?" His voice interrupted my thoughts, and I looked up at him guiltily, worrying that he'd caught me sniffing at his jacket. But nothing about his expression suggested he had. Instead, his eyes were fixed on mine as he awaited my answer.

Like I could say no.

Like I had a choice.

"Sure." I struggled to hide the thrill in my chest by clearing my throat and waving over to where Nina and Adam waited at the taxi stand to indicate they should go on without us. Adam flashed me an authoritative look before tilting his head, and I nodded solemnly in reply. I'd use this time to clear David as a threat so we could move beyond clan business, and then, well, I had no idea. I only knew that the lure of him was quickly outweighing my hesitation.

Though I had planned to find out as much as I could about David during the long walk back to my apartment, we both remained quiet, studying our feet and looking up occasionally to meet each other's eyes before looking away. He jammed his hands firmly into his pockets from the cold, and I felt a twinge of guilt at having taken his jacket.

Unsure of how to start up a conversation, I settled for reaching out my senses and exploring him more thoroughly. I drew in a full breath of his scent, trying to think through the complex layers logically and ignore the uptick in my heart rate.

There was definitely something strange about his scent, and I understood why it worried Adam. There was no doubt that the wildness of it reminded me of the few werewolves I'd met, but it was somehow more primal than that. It was wild; he was wild, of that I had no doubt, but his scent also somehow put me at ease. The scant impression I had of him through his walls was in direct contrast to the wildness of his scent. That of a peaceful lake with a gentle, consistent current ebbing and flowing under the surface. Could he be part human and part something else? Maybe he was unaware of being a supernatural?

Witches could manipulate emotions. Was that what this was?

Only, to do so he'd need to make contact with my mind and if anything, he was at a distance behind his barrier. I couldn't see how he could be doing something to me.

Lost in thought, it took me a moment to realize he was speaking. "...lect ure at four p.m. with Dr. Harrington. On Tuesdays, I have a biotechnology lecture at eight a.m. with Dr. Weir."

"Oh!" I shouted excitedly, interrupting him. "I have Dr. Weir's lecture with you!" The morning time slot was unpopular with students, but it suited my work schedule best with the diner opening at eleven thirty on weekdays. "When do you start?" The growing excitement had me talking fast and gesturing with my hands.

"I start next week. I'd love to get your notes so I can try to catch up..."

I smiled, annoyed with myself for how pleased it made me to know he didn't want this to be our last encounter. "Sure."

The initial tension broken, I found him surprisingly easy to talk to. Somewhat of a quiet recluse, I surprised myself by telling him about some of my favourite spots at the university

"There's a path past Rutland that leads to the most beautiful fountain." I tensed, ready for him to find it lame, but his eyes shot to mine.

"A fountain." He nodded to himself. "It sounds nice. Maybe you could show it to me sometime." He smiled over at me, and I couldn't help but notice how when he did so his bottom lip jutted out ever so slightly. His sculpted face was beautiful, but when he smiled, his eyes brightened in a way that made his looks almost inconsequential, and it took me a minute before I could tear my eyes away to stare studiously down at my flats and try to think of a different topic of conversation.

"There are some great bars around here, but don't go to the Tipsy Sailor on Wednesdays. It's half priced drinks, and it brings out the crazies. One time, Nina had a guy try to pay for his drink with a shoe."

He laughed, and the sound of it sent a thrill through my chest. Not full out laughing, but more of a deep chuckle that reverberated in his chest as mirth lit up his eyes like glittering sapphires. There was something so genuine about him, and I found it refreshing, like he was one of the few people I'd met who I hadn't been able to classify and dismiss.

"So, what'd she do?" he asked, and I struggled to remember what part of the story I was at.

"She calmly took the shoe so as not to upset him, poured him a drink, and called the bouncer. The poor guy was probably surprised when he woke up the next morning wearing only one shoe, but he never came back for it. Probably too embarrassed." I grinned fondly at the memory.

David chuckled again, and I caught a flash of blue when he glanced over at me.

"Of course, she still has the shoe. She put it up on the bar next to the high-end liquor. Don't tell her I told you the story, though. She loves to tell that one. Promise you'll act surprised?"

"Definitely," he agreed, his voice still touched by laughter.

A smile remained fixed on my face for the rest of the walk. David's laughter was infectious. There was an easiness to it I lacked, like laughing and being carefree came naturally to him, and I was shocked when I realized we'd had circled back to my apartment. The grey building with its large stone steps loomed overhead signaling an end to the night.

Despite the time we'd spent wandering the streets together, I had learned little about David, and I found myself scrambling for a glimpse into his mind that would clear him to the clan, but I found it just as inaccessible as it had been at the start of the night. Which meant I had nothing concrete to tell Adam. Just a feeling of safety he would certainly disregard.

The mental walls troubled me. Normally, even the most guarded person let themselves be seen when they became more comfortable, but then, what had I learned about David during this conversation?

Practically nothing. I'd been the one to lead the conversation, and while David had participated fully, he hadn't volunteered a lot of information. Lost in thought, I started up the steps, hand absentmindedly running along the damp stone of the railing as I ascended. I didn't notice how closely he followed until I turned to bid him goodnight and gasped at his closeness. He stood a stair down from me, putting us at eye level.

Our breath fogged together in a beautiful mist that engulfed our faces. I helplessly drifted closer to him until, but just when I thought he would lean in, he spoke.

"Can I take you out for ice cream tomorrow night?" he whispered, his lips so close they almost brushed mine. I barely processed his words. My body was humming. He wanted to see me again, to take me out. My heart hammered against my chest. I could barely breathe when he looked at me like that.

"I'd like that," I stammered. His eyes were lidded, and I was sure he would close the gap between us. Tension and arousal warred within me, and blood pounded in my head like a drum. Giving into the draw between us, I leaned forward eagerly. He was painfully close, and his strange scent overwhelmed me, the vanilla fading away in favour of the wildness. I wanted more of it. Wanted to know if he tasted of that spice. My lips trembled, and my body bowed to his in anticipation.

But David's lips brushed against my cheekbone, lingering in the lightest of kisses. My skin prickled as his hot breath withdrew. I shuddered and tried to clamp down on my body's response to him, barely catching myself from loosing a moan of disappointment as he pulled away.

"Goodnight, Sarah."

It was the first time he'd said my name. His voice was hushed, and his tone filled with a heartbreaking tenderness. His tongue seemed stuck on the word, dragging out the final syllable. A shiver traveled down the spine. I liked the way he said it, and all I could think about was somehow getting him to say it again, to scream it, to cry it, for my name to be imprinted on his lips.

But now that he was pulling back to create some distance between us, I could think more clearly, and I managed to mutter an almost unintelligible goodnight, before shoving his coat into his hands and hurrying into the building. I couldn't help but glance back one final time to see him still standing on the steps, wearing the same small smile.

I fumbled with my keys before gratefully collapsing and leaning my back against the sturdy wooden door. I tipped my head back and worked to control my breathing. My pulse pounded, and David's eyes danced in my mind.

The things he was doing to me were unexpected, and the thought of losing control terrified me. I was supposed to meet with him, do my job, and get out. But something about him had ensnared me, and I found the idea impossible. I didn't know if it would lead to anything good, and I was no closer to knowing his intentions towards the clan. I'd need to see him again. To put myself in his power.

And that both filled me with terror and brought me to life in a way I had long thought myself incapable of.

Chapter 3

DAVID

Fate was a cruel beast, and I was the helpless fool at the end of its leash.

Sarah. It was her. Somehow, it was her. But to find her now when I'd come to Boston to forget, to move on? Of all the women in this world, I was matched with her on the first real date I'd been on since deciding to shrug off her suffocating grip on my heart. The shock at finding her, of staring into those deep brown eyes I'd never been able to forget, had nearly leveled me.

How many times had I wondered if I'd even know her now? If the memory I had of the girl she'd been would allow me to recognize her as an adult?

But I *had* known her. Against all odds, I'd known her from the second I saw her. The past and present collided, leaving me reeling. Every feature I remembered from the girl in my memory had been refined into sheer perfection. To say she'd matured into a beautiful woman wasn't enough to describe my shock and awe at the sight of her.

The roundness of youth had given way to high cheekbones and pouty lips just begging to be claimed. It'd taken everything in me not to scoop her up and take her straight back home to the island. Only the lack of recognition in her eyes had given me pause.

I'd known if I found her she wouldn't remember the part of her life I'd shared with her, but the confusion in her eyes, the *uncertainty*, had still cut deep.

Had tonight really happened? Everything inside of me screamed that it was true. That I'd somehow done the impossible.

I'd found her.

With a shudder, I leaned back into the stone railing, locking my muscles to keep from springing up the stairs and knocking on her door just to see her face again and confirm her identity.

But I didn't need to. It was her. I could still taste her familiar scent at the back of my throat—honeysuckle and lavender. Only this Sarah had been through something the laughing girl in my memory couldn't begin to fathom. She was too thin, the bruises under her eyes apparent even under a thick layer of makeup. Pain came off her in waves though she hid it behind a brave smile. Whatever had happened when she'd been taken had been bad, and it had left her with a core of strength it was impossible not to admire.

And then there was that damned dress. So much of her pale skin had been on display for my hungry eyes. Round breasts and the most delightfully subtle curves captured me from the start, and I hadn't been able to pry my eyes from her. I'd spent most of the night worrying that I'd scared her off. Only, every time I'd worried I was staring too much, she'd been right there with me, watching me back.

I could still see her in my mind's eye, hear the way her breath had hitched when I'd brushed my lips across the delicate curve of her cheek. My attention had fixed on that one solitary sound until I had to force myself to step away. Even now, I was painfully hard, lost in a fantasy where I'd taken her into my arms and claimed her mouth.

What sounds would she make if I had?

Damn. I couldn't think like that. She didn't know me, and to meet her like this, on a date where romantic intentions were expected? It was too much. My head fell back, and I stared up at the cloudy sky, tracking the progress of the shifting grey clouds.

The elders had warned me, told me to stay away from her until her memories could be restored, but even the scant contact with her had left me nearly undone. How the hell was I supposed to do this?

Energy buzzed in my limbs, and I stood up with a jerk, feeling the need to run off the excess.

There was only one way forward, and I fought to clear my head as I settled into a light jog entirely impractical in the khaki chinos.

So, what if we dated? I could hold myself back. Show restraint. For her. I could do this. Even if I did see the entirety of my past and future in her soft brown eyes.

Because I refused to fail her again. That steel in her core, the haunted way she looked, all of it made me want to hold her and comfort her, to hold her to my chest and keep her safe. But instead, I had to add to her suffering, to share what had happened–what she'd forgotten–who she really was, what she really was. That wasn't what I wanted, and I struggled with the impossibility of pulling her aside and explaining the truth, of seeing her already stricken face fall just a little further until that last bit of light winked out.

Unfortunately, there was no choice.

SARAH

The hours faded into a blur of activity as I doled out greasy plates of food at the diner and squeezed in my course readings on break. Everything was so normal, and yet, it wasn't. Couldn't be. David haunted my mind as surely as the dream ever had, and I watched the big clock above the kitchen, some part of my brain counting down the hours before I was supposed to see him.

Everything about the situation made me feel angry with myself. Opening up to some stranger I'd just met, the way I'd craved him? Been ready to surrender?

What in the hell was wrong with me? He'd gotten under my skin the previous night, and while the strange connection between us couldn't be denied, being back in my normal routine brought some much-needed clarity.

Being so helplessly *infatuated* wasn't me, and by the time I was back home getting ready to go out with him, I'd convinced myself he'd somehow manipulated my mind.

This time, I wore my regular clothes: a pair of dark blue jeans with a stretchy black top and a brown knit sweater on top.

He'd caught me off guard. I'd been ready to use my body to gain access to his mind, of getting behind his defenses, and instead, it'd become a weapon pointed right back at me.

Now I'd be ready for the way his presence affected me, for his scent, and the way he stared.

I wouldn't be unprepared this time.

But I still jumped when he knocked firmly on the door. Taking one last look in the mirror, I smoothed out my hair in the front, twisting the curls down across my shoulders.

This was going to go great, I promised myself, before heading to the door and opening it with an easy smile plastered to my face.

But the grin slipped when I drank him in. He leaned against the door frame with one of his long legs crossed in front. The button-up blue shirt he wore strained across his chest from the posture, alluding to muscle beneath. The colour of his shirt emphasized the striking colour of his eyes, and when his lips curled up into a smile, I was reminded of the gentle way they'd brushed across my cheek, and how I'd wanted that mouth all over me.

The confidence I'd felt a few minutes ago vanished. My traitorous heart picked up its pace, and I choked on a greeting. My planned speech devolved into a coughing fit hard enough to water my eyes and double me over.

"You okay?"

I looked up to see his brows pinched with concern, a long-fingered hand reaching out to steady me, but I straightened before he could touch me. I forced a tight smile, my cheeks burning. He licked his lips, like he had something to say, but his mind was as closed off as ever, giving no clue what it could be.

"Yes, fine. Everything okay with you?"

"Of course." He smiled, and I was lost. The plans I'd made to keep myself cool and collected on this outing were gone as I threw on a long fitted black coat, and rushed David out the door, hurrying to leave before Adam or Nina interrupted.

I'd pour everything I had into trying to read him, so I could be done with the man and able to retreat into the comforting shadows where I belonged.

We stepped out onto the sidewalk and started walking up the street. Downtown was a busy place to live no matter the hour, and we skirted around pedestrians. David's shoulders were tense, his steps stilted as he awkwardly maneuvered around a larger crowd.

"So, you've traveled around, you said? Lots of big cities?" My question caught him off guard, and he stared straight ahead, his brows furrowing.

"Some, but I've been to many places. Never cared for downtown much."

"Why not?"

"Oh, it's just a lot of people. Where I'm from, things are quieter."

Well, that was interesting. Humming my understanding, we lapsed into silence.

The night was cold, and after a bit of brief inner turmoil, I twined my arm with his telling myself it would hurry things up, that this was what I was *supposed* to be doing—getting close so I could learn his secrets and getting out. But I was shocked at how good it felt to feel the warmth of his arm through the coat. Our height difference put my head perfectly in line with his upper arm, and I fought the urge to rest my head on the welcoming spot as we walked. To feel his deep voice vibrating through the fabric as he talked.

"What was correspondence school like?"

"Eh, it was fine. You get used to it." He huffed a laugh. "It's strange to be in a lecture with actual people after so many years of taking classes remotely." He chuckled, and I barked a laugh, quickly raising a hand to stifle it. To go from quietly learning on your own to a crowded hall would be quite an adjustment, and it was one I knew well.

"Yeah, tell me about it. I was homeschooled as a kid, and it was definitely a challenge at first."

"Oh, you homeschooled straight through high school?" His question threw me. I'd started high school being homeschooled, but finished it here after I'd run away. The complicated nature of my education no longer seemed a safe subject, and I tensed up as the horrors of that time replayed in my head. My heart pounded, and I licked dry lips, but David gently squeezed my numb hand before quickly filling the silence with his honeyed voice.

"Well, I did high school by correspondence, and it was not my favourite. Luckily, you can get through it faster that way and it only took me a few years to earn my equivalency."

Smiling, I nodded.

I was grateful when he didn't press me for details about my home life. After a while, I let myself lean into his arm, pressing my cheek against the rough wool and falling into the rhythm of our steps. He seemed to know where we were going, even if I didn't.

I wasn't surrendering to his hold on me. I was *supposed* to do this, to act infatuated with him so he'd let me clear him to the clan. So what if I drew some measure of comfort from laying my head against his arm?

We continued in silence, with David leading the way. Funny how this was my city, my *home*, but it was David who knew where the ice cream parlour was. Truthfully, I couldn't remember the last time I'd had the stuff, not because I hadn't tried it, but because I hadn't paid attention when I had. Seeking human foods for pleasure wasn't something I cared much about.

David shared how he'd traveled all over the country in the years since leaving home. Correspondence school had been the only option, and he'd gotten a late start on it, which explained why he was a mature student, like me.

"Where are you from originally?" I asked, peering over at him.

"Oh, I'm from a small island off the coast," he answered without meeting my eyes, and I sensed there was more to the story. But his arm tensed up, and it became clear he wasn't going to elaborate.

"So, Nina, huh? What's her major?"

I should be trying to steer the conversation back to him and his family to gain access to his mind, but he hadn't pushed me about my own troubled past, and I wanted to afford him the same courtesy.

I understood being uncomfortable talking about the past.

"Oh, she's not a student. Nina has great designs to be a celebrity makeup artist." I smiled fondly, fingering the cuff of David's jacket.

We reached a hole-in-the-wall ice cream shop with a narrow entrance leading into a small room consumed nearly entirely by large freezers. Two enormous bulletin boards consumed most of the walls, one for flavours and the others for toppings. David chose a simple vanilla cone—eschewing all the toppings, and couldn't help but smile, when I knew vanilla to be at the core of his scent.

"What?" His twinkling eyes begged to be let in on the joke, but I waved him away.

Rather than trying something complicated, I chose the first item listed, a praline. I watched David take a lick, following the gentle swipe of his tongue with fascination and the clear enjoyment he had in the treat. Looking down at my own ice cream, I wondered how I'd never bothered with it before, never paid attention.

I tentatively tasted it, hyperaware of how David's eyes followed the progress of my tongue. The ice cream was rippled with a sweet and salty caramel that tingled in my mouth, setting the taste buds aflame.

Ice cream was good.

Delicious.

David grinned, rushing to hold the door for me as we exited to step out into the chill of the night and continue walking the streets. Ice cream proved to be a great handheld treat, and I couldn't help but think it was an excellent choice. I took a swipe at a rebellious drip careening its way towards the cone, and almost moaned at how good it was.

Damnit, why hadn't I had this before? What had I been doing every other night of my life walking around without an ice cream clutched in my fist? David's eyes were soft as he watched me, his lips tilted up ever so slightly, and I grinned nervously back.

With a laugh, he stopped walking, chucking my chin and coming back with a blob of ice cream. He licked it off his long finger, and I found myself enraptured by the sight of his pink tongue caressing the digit.

We finished the treat, eating mostly in silence, and I twined my arm with his, leaning into him and pressing my cheek to the wool of his coat. His warmth leached through to drive away the chill of the night, and I thought it was something I could get used to.

The vibrations of David's voice soothed me even if the closeness of his scent was arousing. I felt safe with him, relaxed even, but that feeling was at odds with the tension between us, the craving that was building to touch more of him, get closer.

He walked me home, taking us on a meandering path down the near empty streets, and for once I didn't think about whose territory I was in. No one would attack us with so many pedestrians around, and most of us were pretty okay with vampires passing through, so long as it was obvious the other clan member wasn't hunting.

"So, why biochem?" It took me a moment to realize he was asking me a question, and I sheepishly looked up to meet his eyes. *Why biochem?* The answer was complicated, and I chewed my lip. In a life I'd had little control over, the lab was all precision and patience. I loved the stark difference between right and wrong, the tempestuous nature of chemical reactions, but it was more than that. I frowned to myself as I tried to think of how to articulate my need to know, to seek, to hunt.

There was a reason I was killing myself to finish the degree.

"Questions."

"Questions?"

"Yeah, there are so many unanswered questions, and I like the challenge of it, to think I might be the one to answer some of them." Surprised at how much I'd shared, I pressed myself more firmly into his arm, fixing my gaze straight ahead.

"I understand. Research is like a whole new world where you can be the explorer. Be the one to make the discoveries."

I'd never heard it put like that, and he was right.

We were explorers. A smile tugged at my lips, and one word came to mind.

Kindred.

David got it. He'd coaxed a true answer from me where I would normally mutter something about career prospects, and the way he'd described his own passion for the sciences connected with something in me, and the images of us not just working in a lab but out discovering new lands was exciting. It was a new way of thinking about it, a *perspective change,* and I liked it.

It was late when we arrived back at my apartment, but I'd barely noticed the time passing. We'd been walking and talking for hours, but it had felt like minutes, and now the night was over. I cursed myself for the wasted minutes I hadn't savoured, for the actions I hadn't taken, turning to David in alarm and realizing just how badly I wanted to prolong the night.

What's worse, David's mind remained closed to me, and while I was increasingly certain he harboured no ill intentions towards The Shades, I still had no definitive answer for Adam. I'd allowed myself to be lost in conversation instead of focusing on what I was here to do.

But was that why I was really here? I wasn't sure anymore, and I frowned down at my boots. I took a step up the stone steps and turned to find David's face level with mine once more. Confusion warred in my mind, clouded by the way his scent overwhelmed my senses and left the world a spinning mess.

A kiss. Maybe I'd be able to understand this if I could kiss him properly, but David kissed me on the cheek again, his hot breath feeling devilishly good against my cold skin, and I shuddered as the warring sensations shot right to my core. My hands reached up to pull him closer to keep him there, but he caught them with his and trapped them between us.

He pulled back to stare at me intently, the stunning blue of his eyes drawing me closer until I was leaning forward, my lips an inch from his. But there was a hesitancy in his expression that I couldn't understand, and he pulled himself back reluctantly, squeezing my arms gently as he did so.

The gesture felt like an apology I couldn't hope to understand.

"Goodnight, Sarah. I'll see you tomorrow."

"Tomorrow?" I stuttered, and David smiled.

"Yeah, class, remember?" He winked, but I couldn't help feeling dejected when I turned to head inside.

I shook my head as I unlocked the apartment and stepped inside, leaning back against the door and sliding down to sit against it. I pressed my head back into the thick wood. Coming back from an outing with David was like coming home from a battle. My heart pounded and my arms were shaky.

I didn't appear to be winning.

"Sarah, is that you?" Adam emerged from Nina's bedroom with ruffled hair and a pair of loose grey sweats slung across his hips. He slept naked, and it wasn't anything new to see so much of his body, but with him and Nina together, it felt impolite. I scrambled to my feet, smoothing my jacket to make myself presentable. "You were out with David, right?" There was a question in his voice I couldn't ignore, and I met his deadpan stare head-on.

"Yes, but I'm sorry. I don't have an answer for you. I've never met someone whose mind is so blocked off to me. I need more time with him to figure it out."

Adam frowned, his eyes as hard as steel.

"Sarah, you know how important this is." He blew out a breath, looking skyward like our pockmarked ceiling had an answer for him. "You have one week. If you haven't figured it out by then, I'll be taking over."

Swallowing hard, I reluctantly nodded. I didn't know what Adam would do, but whatever it was, David didn't deserve it.

Which meant I needed to find out in a week—a daunting task when I barely understood myself when I was around him.

Adam gave me a stern nod before heading back to Nina's room, and I sighed, leaning back into the door and thinking how true those words were. I needed more time with David to figure it out, but it wasn't just his intentions with the clan. It was this thing between us, and if the urgency in my voice, born more from my own selfish needs, was enough to keep Adam at bay for now, I'd use it.

Chapter 4

Breathing hard, I pulled myself from the tangled mess of my bed and sat up. My sweat soaked nightgown was glued to my chest, and I tugged it over my head, throwing it to the floor in a soggy heap.

The dream had been more intense than usual. So vivid that my muscles still ached, and I could taste saltwater at the back of my throat. I peered into the dark recesses of my bedroom, sure that the creature from the path must be hidden in a dark corner, preparing itself to spring for me once more. A pang of sadness nearly floored me when I realized I was also searching for the glowing figure on the beach—my salvation.

I wished the peace I'd found in its arms could stay with me, but the fear from the chase clung to me like a second skin. After switching on the light, I examined the skin on the pads of my feet. They still stung from my race down the path, but the surface was unblemished with no hint of the red my nerve endings were screaming should be there. I sighed and stood, wincing at the contact with the hardwood floor. I stealthily headed to the bathroom for a shower, determined to let Nina sleep, even if I couldn't. I turned the heat as high as I could before stepping under the water and letting it scald me clean.

Taking a few deep breaths, I worked to steady my breathing. This was now my fifth dream in a month. I couldn't remember the last time they'd come so frequently. Maybe when I'd first run away, but even then, they were more spaced out. What if they started happening every night? I didn't think I could take it.

My head muddled from lack of sleep, I massaged shampoo into my long hair as much to calm myself as to clean it. David and I had a lecture together this morning, and a smile danced across my lips at the thought.

Being up so early gave me ample time to get to the class early, and I threw my scarf on the seat next to me to save it for him. David arrived as the professor was preparing his notes, flashing me a heart stuttering grin and sliding into the seat beside me just as the class began.

"Hey, Sarah." His words reached me in a whisper barely loud enough for me to hear, and I smiled back at him, trying and failing to feign indifference. There'd been so few people I'd ever felt close to, and for him to know how affected I was, well, it was terrifying.

The dream faded into background noise as I drank in the sight of him in that soft brown coat I could still feel across my shoulders, folded into a seat that failed to accommodate his height, and left his long legs sticking out to the sides. He wore a polo that fitted to his broad shoulders with a bit of a stretch in the chest. I tried to turn my attention to taking notes, but with David seated beside me, the lecture was lost. I couldn't hear the professor over the pounding of my infatuated heart, let alone take notes, and I had to stop myself from reaching over to take his hand just so there would be some contact between us.

By the time the lecture was wrapping up, I was a sweaty mess, rubbing my palms on my jeans and fighting to stay still. David was annoyingly unaffected, still wearing a small smile and occasionally casting me an amused look.

"Well, that was interesting. Want to go grab something to eat?" His words were a purr that shot straight to my core, and I smiled tightly in reply.

"Sorry, David, I have to go. It's the lunch rush at the diner and I'm on prep."

He frowned.

"Oh, of course. Sorry. Don't let me keep you."

"Thanks." I turned to gather my things, but he caught my arm. Though I wore a thick sweater, the warmth of his touch seeped through to my bare skin, and I startled at the contact. I stilled in his grip, hoping he didn't pull away.

"Can I meet you after work?"

I hesitated, trying to think of what to say. The lunch rush would lead straight into dinner. It was a late shift, and I was lucky if I could grab a bite of burger, let alone a break.

"Even if I just walk you home?" His pleading tone pulled at my heart even as his hand on my arm muddled my thoughts.

Damn, did I want him to walk me home.

"Okay. It's late though." My words came out in a breathy whisper.

"I'll wait." David smiled and gave my arm a gentle squeeze.

"Are you sure? I get off at eleven."

"I'll wait." His smirking lips made me shiver, but I hid it with a shrug of my shoulders.

"Okay, the Sticky Spoon at eleven?"

He nodded his agreement and released me to collect my notebook and pencil. I bid him goodbye and was halfway towards the door when I heard him call out.

"See you later."

It was a threat and a promise, as everything with him was.

The diner was busy, but I knew the moment he stepped inside, because I *felt* him. Even across the room, and with a crowd of hungry customers all clamouring for my attention, his presence demanded I look up.

He met my gaze with a small smile from where he calmly waited in line to speak to the harried greeter at the podium. I could only see the greeter's back when David approached, but she stilled before putting a hand on her hip and leaning forward with a laugh that shook her small frame.

Irrational rage ravaged my mind when she turned with a cheek-splitting smile and led him over to an unoccupied booth in the corner of my section. She touched the sleeve of his coat as he sat down, and I wanted to rip her damned hand off. Jill, that was her name. A student like me, I'd seen her poring over a European history text in the back room.

Jill noticed me watching and cocked an eyebrow, smirking as she sauntered back over to the greeter's podium. I allowed myself a long moment to imagine what it would be like to rip out her throat before going over to speak to David.

"Heyyy, I thought we were meeting later?" I said, fiddling with my pen and pad. It was so strange to see him in my workplace, but I still felt a familiar thrill at seeing him.

"Hey!" he said, grinning at me. "I said I'd wait, and since I have some readings to catch up on, I thought maybe I could do that here." He sat up straight and cleared his throat, his eyes alight with hope. "If you don't mind, of course."

"That sounds nice," I stammered out before hurrying off to check on table six's chicken sandwich. By the time I circled back over to him, I was wiping my sweaty palms on my white apron.

"What's good here?" How strange to launch into this week's specials with David, but I did, the words rolling off my tongue with practiced ease.

"This week we're doing fish and chips. That comes with coleslaw and a side of tartar sauce." David didn't look interested, and I remembered how he was a vegetarian. Right. No meat or fish. Maybe something sweet. "Or, I'm told our apple pie is really good." His eyes darted to mine at that.

"You've never tried it?"

"Oh, no. Never." David tsked and handed me his menu.

"I'll take a slice of apple pie and a coffee, please." Then he leaned closer to me and said in a whisper, "and I'll get one to go for later so you can try it, too." Blushing furiously, I jotted down his order, and went to put it through to the kitchen only to be ambushed by Jill, who was very interested in hearing all about the man who had asked to be seated in my section. But she gave me a catty look when I stammered out that he was my boyfriend. He wasn't, not really, but she didn't need to know that.

"Hey, good for you," she cooed, and I was surprised to see an oddly proud glint in her eye. Sybil walked by.

"That's your boyfriend, huh?" She elbowed me affectionately, and for the first time, I felt like maybe the people I worked with could be friends. The ribbing and teasing continued when I made far too many rounds with the coffeepot to offer him refills.

David spent the next few hours poring over his textbooks while he waited for me. I caught him watching me a few times—his eyes sliding away quickly to refocus on his text. It was a strange sort of day with him there, and I struggled with the way his presence demanded my attention.

My shift ended, and I emerged from the white wooden shuttered doors to the kitchen in my plain clothes to tap David on the shoulder. He was so busy with his reading that he hadn't noticed me, but when he did, he appeared dazed, staring at my outfit a moment before packing up his things. We left to a wink and a giggle from a tall, thin waitress named Carole.

We stepped outside, and I sucked in a breath of the chill night air.

"Shall we?" David offered me his arm, and I took it, lightly placing my hand in the crook of his elbow. The city felt different with him at my side, less dark somehow. The bitter taste that had permanently lodged itself in my mouth lessened, if only a little, and I breathed in the crisp night air with wonder, staring up at the neon signs like I'd never seen them before.

He was relaxed at my side, taking easy strides, his long legs matching my pace perfectly. I studied him, dumbfounded at how closed off his mind was. It hurt every time I thought of it. The only other times I'd experienced such a closed off mind were when I dealt with rival clan members and some of the more standoffish witches from my old circle. But worrying about the reason he was so closed off to me wouldn't help. I needed to draw him out somehow.

If I could get a glimpse of his mind, I could clear him to Adam, but it had become more than that. I wanted to see inside his mind, to know him better.

I studied the easy way he navigated the other pedestrians, taking my hand to lead me in a line next to the building.

"Getting used to downtown?" I asked.

David chuckled, and I wished I hadn't said anything. It was such a beautiful, rich sound, and it always threw me off.

"Yeah, I think I could like it here." He winked at me before pressing his lips together and furrowing his brow in thought. "It's not that I don't like people, Sarah. I do. A lot, actually. It's just very different, but it's growing on me."

I raised my hand to hide my smile. He may have moved around a lot up to this point, but he didn't sound like someone who was planning to move anytime soon.

"Good." We reached my apartment stairs, and this time, he cupped my face, brushing my cheek with his thumb. I leaned into the delicious sensation before he lightly kissed my cheek.

"Goodnight, Sarah."

"Goodnight."

His mind remained closed to me no matter how I gently prodded it or how tender his expression. Oh well. There was always tomorrow, and the next day, and the next. David was a mystery I could spend my time unraveling, and Adam would just have to cope.

I'd stall him. With Adam and David sharing an apartment, and with me spending every minute I could in his presence, he was under near constant surveillance.

Returning home, I found neither Adam nor Nina. But I felt strange tonight. There was an energy in the air and an itch beneath my skin like the dream was waiting for me to go to sleep. Tired as I was, I had no choice. I headed to my bedroom, got ready for bed, and lay down, knowing it would take me.

DAVID

It was getting harder not to bury my face in her neck and let loose all the emotions threatening to consume me from the inside. The crush I'd had on her as a boy had been powerful, but I'd never thought those childish feelings would evolve into this. It wasn't just wanting to be with her; it was needing her touch, needing to join our minds, claim her mouth, her body. The desire to have every part of her warred with how little she knew. How *lost* she still was, and the need to explain her past without destroying who she was now. Then there was the warning from the elders, but I couldn't think of that right now, couldn't deal with another mine to sidestep.

It could wait a little longer. I needed some time to soak up her smiles and lilting voice like a sponge and store it somewhere safe for later. But there was never enough with her, and I was painfully aware of how easy it was to put off the task for one more day, another hour, a minute. I'd come to my hand every night since finding her, desperate for a release to the tension between us, and it was never enough.

What I wanted—needed—was us, and that was the one thing I couldn't have. Not now, and maybe not ever. There were rules I needed to follow, warnings I needed to heed. If only she hadn't been so heartbreakingly beautiful.

Letting out a breath, I ran through the streets on my way home from her apartment, hoping the exertion would help while knowing nothing but her could resolve the ache in my chest.

SARAH

The dream came to me every night. No matter how I exhausted myself, it was always there, waiting to pounce the moment I sought solace under the covers. The anxiety of the chase was creeping into my daily life, staying with me long after the dream had ended.

The only time I didn't feel its fist clenching my heart was when I was with David.

My manager had dismissed me early after the dinner rush had fizzled out to a few singletons, and David was set to meet me at my apartment after my shift. But for once, I didn't feel the urge to rush. Instead, I passed like a ghost through the crowds, peering into the face of each person, searching for something. What, I didn't know, but my eyes pricked with tears—the chase and the figure from the dream at the forefront of my mind.

David was already on the steps waiting for me. He leaned against the railing at the foot of the stairs and when my eyes alighted on his face, a sense of calm washed over me. The anxiety from the dream receded to the corners of my mind. His face brightened, and he tilted his head in greeting.

All the anxiety that had plagued me throughout the day melted as I drank him in. His eyes twinkled with delight at my approach, and he wore the small smile that seemed permanently and adorably fixed on his face. Relief drove me forward, and I all but fell into his chest. His arms wrapped around me, and he tentatively stroked my hair with a tenderness that made me feel as though he'd thought of doing it before.

"Hi," he mumbled, his chin resting against my head. The vibrations of his voice shuddered through me until I could feel his voice in my bones. I squeezed my eyes tight and let the moment wash over me. The sense of peace I'd always felt from him comforted my chaotic mind and stilled my racing thoughts.

At last, I pulled back to study his face. He stared back at me, all serious-ness.

"Are you okay?" he asked gently, eyes questing over my face. I must look like a wreck. He'd seen me after busy shifts before, covered in grime and stains, and he'd never mentioned my disheveled state.

"Yeah," I said, smiling back at him. "Fine." The world felt like a better place now that I was with him.

We walked for a long time that night, stopping to pick up some hot chocolate from a coffee shop. His hand in mine felt comfortable, as though it were an extension of my body.

I was quieter than usual, leaving David to carry the conversation. We lapsed into silence a few times and, for once, there was a tension to it. I peered over at him, taking him in; his long face with its crisp lines and his beautiful smile. The way he chuckled rather than laughed. The mirth lighting up his eyes with warmth. David. I had known him for such a short time and yet, I couldn't imagine not seeing him every day. The strangeness of it, the attachment I felt for him, didn't feel normal.

People talked about love at first sight, but this was different. There was more to it, and I was growing increasingly unsettled as the days wore on.

David. What was he? A werewolf? A vampire? Something else entirely? As much as I thought I understood him, it was alarming to not know what manner of creature he was. He'd quickly become someone important to me, and I had to know if I could trust him. Not for the clan anymore, but for myself. His mind was as closed off to me as ever, even as he smiled over at me, wrapped an arm around my shoulders, and pulled me tight against his side.

How could I be falling in love with someone whose very supernatural nature was in question? The thought of him out in the night stalking dance club patrons was at odds with the person I knew. Could he really be like that? We had spent as much time together as possible since we'd met, but there were times when we were apart. Was he bidding me goodnight and then heading off to lure some helpless woman into the shadows?

Would David do that?

The thoughts swirled in my head as we walked, and I listened to his voice. He was telling me about a first edition book he'd found at a bookstore across town. But maybe that wasn't the whole story. Could he be going to the bookstore to attract a fellow shopper and apply his charms? I felt a stab of disgust mixed with jealousy at the thought of him with his fangs sunk deep into the neck of some beautiful stranger.

Who was he?

By the time we reached my apartment, I couldn't put off confronting him any longer. I looked deep into his eyes, drinking in the brilliant shade of blue and searching for an answer. None came. He was about to lean in and kiss my cheek goodnight, as he had every night since we'd met, but I couldn't do it.

Not tonight. I stiffened in his hold, pulling back as he leaned in.

"Are you really okay? You've been so quiet tonight," he said gently, bringing a hand up to cup my face. I moved into it, craving his warmth and the fire it stirred in my blood. But the intensity of my need for him only strengthened my resolve.

"David. I need to know what type of supernatural you are."

He looked away, his whole demeanor closed off and his shoulders stiff with tension.

"I know you're not human...that much is obvious, but what are you? A werewolf, a vampire?"

He said nothing, keeping himself turned away from me. The outline of his taut jaw standing out against his cheek.

"You can tell me. Whatever you are. I just—I need to know if we're even compatible." I tried to capture his eye. He had to know this was important, and that whatever the answer, I was prepared to receive it.

He spun to face me, his brow furrowed and hurt flashing in his eyes before leaning forward to press his mouth to mine. His tongue darted out to lick the seam of my mouth in a silent request for admission. Hungrily, I opened to him, and the taste of him exploded across my senses. His scent had enticed me from the start, but this?

He tasted like heaven.

Our tongues slicked against each other, and I wrapped my arms around his neck, pulling him closer or preventing him from pulling away. Arousal spread through my body like fire until I wanted to mold myself to him, to press into him until we were one being. He kissed me until there was no time. No thought. Nothing but the feel of his lips moving against mine, The taste of him. And when he finally pulled back to nuzzle into my cheek and nibble at the skin, I was in a daze, drunk on him, my breaths coming in squeaky gulps.

He'd finally kissed me, and it had opened a gate I didn't think I would ever be able to close. Because how could I ever not want this?

"We're perfectly compatible, Sarah…" he whispered as he pressed himself closer, and I felt how hard he was. He gently ran his hands up my back in soothing circles that did nothing to soothe, but served only to rile me up until need consumed thought, and I was a wild thing in his hands. He leaned forward until his breath tickled the hair around my ear.

"I'm an *ancient*…" He spoke in a whisper before pulling back to give me a half smile as though his admission had been an answer instead of a riddle. He turned and walked away, leaving me reeling at his sudden departure—at the jarring absence of his warmth. He didn't look back once, though I stood watching him until he turned the corner.

An ancient. But just what was an ancient? Was it some clan name I was supposed to know? The way he'd said it made it seem he thought I'd know what he meant, but I had no clue. The name wasn't of any clan within Boston. I wracked my mind trying to conjure up maps and territory lines.

Ancient. Could it be the name of a witch's circle or a werewolf pack? I had no idea, and now I was wound up without a release to the tension building in my core. With no new information about what kind David was, I stumbled up the stone stairs, heading back to my apartment and the dream waiting within.

I'd just been to heaven, and now it was time for hell.

Chapter 5

Waking up drenched in sweat was becoming my new routine, and I headed to the bathroom immediately to shower off, my thoughts turning to David as I massaged a glob of shampoo into my hair. He'd called himself an ancient, but I'd pulled out my map of the territories in Boston and no such clan existed. He could be a witch. Ancient sounded like a name a coven would claim, more so than a werewolf, and unfortunately, I knew where I had to go to find the information.

The soap glided over my breasts and a shuddering breath tore from my throat as I slid it lower. The way he'd kissed me, that intoxicating taste I couldn't get enough of. Shuddering, I pushed the soap between my legs, wishing it was David's hand. I could see him in my mind. The intense way he stared at me warping into feral need as he slammed me against the bathroom wall hard enough the grooved tiles dug into the skin of my back.

Eagerly, I pressed myself back into it, lost in my fantasy. His mouth was at my throat, his hands exploring every curve. Pausing at each new discovery like he was fighting to memorize it, cherish it, worship it. Tension coiled in my core, and the bar of soap was dropped to the tub with a thud to be replaced by the pad of my finger.

He'd barely touched me when we'd kissed, just his hand on my cheek, but it had been the most erotic experience of my life. His mouth was on me now, his tongue thrusting into my mouth. Harder. Need built up within me until I whimpered against the wall, the friction of my hand not enough. I wanted it to be his hand, wanted it to be him between my legs.

Release found me, and I shuddered against my hands at the waves of pleasure. But the moment the bliss ebbed, the need rose up again. With a bite of my lip, I turned my face into the shower stream, attempting to dispel it.

It was always like that with me. My body craved more. I was used to taking lovers and needing to find my pleasure afterwards, even if I found release at their hands. I was insatiable.

I sighed and stepped out of the shower, grabbing a towel off the hanging rack. Drying off, I avoided lingering on my needy center. I didn't have time to spend a whole day in bed, and that's what it would take to be satisfied.

A quick change of clothes later, and I was rooting around the kitchen when the shrill ring of our phone caught me by surprise.

"Hey. Good morning."

Sleep clung to his words, and it was hot enough to remind me of just how unsatisfied I was. Squeezing my thighs shut, I gripped the receiver.

"I was wondering if you want to go walk by the pier this morning. You have the day off, right?"

Curse him for paying attention to my schedule.

"Yes, I have the day off, but I've—" I struggled to come up with an excuse even as a little voice inside was screaming at me to meet with him. "I have a lot of catching up to do." It wasn't a lie, but I also needed today to clear my mind. To understand and to approach those who might have the answers.

"Oh, no problem. Maybe tonight?"

Tonight, a moonlit walk. He looked so damned good under the stars. Taking a deep breath, I steeled myself.

"Sorry, but maybe tomorrow."

He quietly agreed with me, and I hated the disappointment in his voice, the way it tore at me and made me want to fix it. After a brief goodbye, I slammed the phone back into its receiver.

What was wrong with me? I could've just asked him and been done with it. But the way he'd said the word ancients was like he expected me to know what it was, and the desire to find out for myself was too strong. I could feel how deep I was getting with him already, and it was terrifying. How could I trust myself to someone with such a hold on me when I didn't even know what he was? What future we might have?

A *future*. Was I really considering that with him? I'd barely considered a future for myself beyond graduating and going into research. Now I was wondering how I could fit him into my plan. I was quickly realizing that I *needed* to fit him into my plans.

My fingers drifted to my lips. I had been waiting for him to kiss me, but I hadn't realized the depths of my affection until he had done so. Flushed, I remembered how we'd lost ourselves, how right it had felt. The way his passion had leaked into the desperate way he claimed my mouth.

Loosing a breath, I shrugged on my coat and grabbed my keys from their plastic tray. I wanted to understand what an ancient was without those piercing blue eyes studying my reaction. To process the information on my own and be ready with the knowledge when I saw him again.

The bus was already at the station when I arrived, waiting for me. I found the least scuffed up seat at the back by a window. A boy band poster was plastered to the back of the chair in front of me, curling at the edges. Thankfully, the bus wasn't overly crowded, and I sank gratefully into the chair, letting the hum of the motor at my back soothe me.

We started out, and I was fascinated with how quickly the bustling streets outside my window transformed into spaced out residential buildings with manicured lawns. It struck me as odd how such a different world was a short drive away. Some might have called this area more peaceful, but not to me.

The thought of the people I was coming to see left a bad taste in my mouth. My hands were sweating, and my face was flushed thinking about seeing them again. It'd been years since I'd broken from my old coven, leaving them when I realized how badly they'd abused my power. The Shades had taken me in, and I'd found my home, but not before The Witches of Stain had torn out a piece of my already tattered soul.

This beautiful neighbourhood had certainly impressed me when I was a sixteen-year-old runaway without a penny to my name. Then there were the promises they'd made me. How could I resist free room and board and the support I needed to get me through school?

Lost in my thoughts, I almost missed my stop, standing to pull the taut yellow cord at the last second. The busy driver screeched to a halt, glaring at me in his rearview mirror. I held up a hand in apology before getting off the bus, standing in front of the brown brick low-rise apartment where I'd once lived and where the witches conducted their business.

The building provided plenty of rooms to meet with clients who paid handsomely for their aid. From cheaters looking to make their spouses forget their infidelities, to criminals wanting to win over a jury, the Witches of Stain didn't discriminate. If there was money to be exchanged for their services, they would gladly assist even the most nefarious person. A chill overtook me, though I was dressed warmly in my thickest coat.

I remembered the shock of finding out the extent of what they'd been doing. How foolish and guilty I'd felt for being a party to it. I walked up the path lined with a short black wrought-iron fence to approach the seemingly innocent building that lay before me. Ringing the doorbell, I waited anxiously, my eyes taking in a bit of paint peeling on the beige door.

The door swung suddenly open to reveal a short, stern-faced woman with a pointy nose wearing a long floral dress. Her dark eyes narrowed when she saw me, and she made to close the door. Jamming my foot in the doorframe, I straightened my back and stared her down. She'd been all smiles when she'd first shown me my room.

That facade was gone.

"Hi there, Brenda. I'm here to use the coven's library. As an honourary member, I have that right." My anger flared, lending strength to my voice. How much money had my talents made the witches? Having access to their library was a pitifully small request after the things I'd done in their name.

Brenda sneered at me, but swung the door open. Hobbling off to the side to stand at the foot of a tall staircase, she watched me to ensure that I went to the library at the end of the hall.

Heading straight through the musty, old apartment building, I went to the unit they used as their library. Aisles of bookshelves filled the room, with a small reading area set up in the corner. The room was dimly lit, with only two cramped desks as a minor concession to the library's patrons. Knowing the arrangement, I'd brought a small flashlight with me. It was nearly impossible to read the titles without it.

I spent all afternoon poring over books about vampire history, werewolf history, witch history, desperate for any mention of Ancients. My heart hurt when I thought of how disappointed David had sounded on the phone. That and the unease which haunted my steps when I wasn't around him was getting stronger, the dream threatening to break into my daytime life.

"What are you looking for?" a voice said in my ear, startling me. The book of records on vampire clans in Florida slipped from my fingers and fell to the desk with a thud. The witch from the desk stood over me. She wasn't someone I had known when I'd lived here. A small plump woman who looked about fifty with a round, kindly face smiled down at me. I didn't know if maybe she had moved into the area or how she had come to be with the Witches of Stain, but I was suddenly pleased to have one of their members treat me with kindness.

"I'm trying to find out about some kind of werewolf pack or vampire clan. They call themselves ancients," I said, taking care to articulate the word. "Have you ever heard of them? It could also be a coven name."

The woman's eyebrows were nearly lost in her greying hair. "You mean *an* ancient? I haven't heard about them in a long time," she said, pressing her lips into a line. "No, not for a very long time."

My hand shot forward out of its own accord to grip her wrist.

"You've heard of them? What are they?"

"An ancient isn't any one thing, my dear, and you won't find them in any creature's history. You want to be looking in the human histories about demons. It's a terrible old beast that humans killed off eons ago." She smiled warmly and patted my hand before turning away like she hadn't just damned David, and my hopes with him. My hand fell limply to my side.

Shock washed over me, and I grew cold and numb. David's kind eyes flashed through my mind. I'd been prepared for him to belong to some obscure sect of vampires or werewolves.

The idea of him being something else entirely unnerved me. Had he been using a different kind of magic to make me feel the way I had? Something I was unfamiliar with? My mind recoiled from the idea even as I accepted the possibility.

My father had been popular. Oh, how his guests would laugh along with him, completely charmed and at ease before he'd struck.

But David? I steadied myself and approached the stack of books, making my way to the human histories section. Pulling a collection of the oldest books off the shelf and bringing them over to my desk, I took a deep breath and settled in.

The thick dust in the air tickled my nose. Human histories weren't a popular topic, and no one had touched these books in a long time. Hours passed and my stomach growled, reminding me I had other needs. But I couldn't stop. So, I ignored the rumbling, taking another book from the perilous stack beside me and resolutely opening it. My search was all-consuming. I needed to know what I was getting into. The word 'demon' still rang in my ears.

Finally, I came across a section that spoke of ancients. I gasped at the picture of a hideous half-man, half-animal creature with large wings and dripping fangs standing over a pile of human victims. Its enormous arms were little more than masses of corded muscle. The description wasn't much better.

Ancients were the original evil in the world. Before witches and vampires walked the earth, ancients terrorized the land. Beings of terrible age and power, a single ancient could decimate an entire village. The beasts took many forms and drained the blood of their victims, using magic to give them a false sense of security.

David's eyes flashed through my mind again. I wondered if the sense of peace I always felt from him was a part of his power. I steeled myself and read on. *A false sense of security.*

It fit. I hated it, but it fit.

Containing not a shred of humanity, these demons were particularly cruel, sometimes keeping humans in cages to act as livestock. The people lived in fear of their terrible power until they collectively gathered to drive them out and hunt them into extinction.

The book claimed ancients were gone but obviously they weren't. David had mentioned he was from an island. I closed the book with a thud and stood. I'd found my answers, and I felt confident I could at least confront him with what I'd learned. Heading out past the now vacant sentry post, I emerged onto the street. The cool air felt good on my face after so many hours in a cramped, dusty space, and I made the snap decision to walk home. It was a long way to walk, but I craved the solitude, the space, and the fresh air that the dark streets provided.

According to the book, ancients were the bane of humanity, but I couldn't imagine the man I knew as cruel or unkind. I couldn't believe it had all been an act. I'd always had such a powerful impression of goodness from him, but then there was the way his mind was blocked from me in a way that no other beings had ever been.

Had he kept his true nature hidden from me all this time? What did he have to hide? A shudder passed through me as the horrors of my past came unbidden to my mind; crying humans huddling in fear while my father approached without mercy, going in for the kill. He always allowed them to hide before seeking them out. It had been part of the hunt.

I felt my thoughts spiral out of control, the images coming faster now accompanied by cries of pain and terror. Reeling, I doubled over, trying in vain to slow my breathing. Usually, I could push it all down, but this business with David had me rattled. The thought of him hunting and hurting people like my father had terrified me, made even more so by how easy it had been to care for him, to trust him. I straightened, forcing myself to keep walking, using the cold biting air on my face to pull myself out of the memories.

I desperately needed to talk to him.

It couldn't be true.

He was supposed to be the light to my darkness. It was as bad as losing the figure at the end of my dream.

But instead of going to his apartment, I found my way home, changing and climbing into bed. My chest ached. The image from the book was seared into my mind; the unfeeling eyes of that monster crouched over the bodies of its innocent victims. Exhausted from the strain of the day, I drifted off to sleep, knowing the dream waited in the shadows. For the first time, I welcomed it as an escape from the horror of my reality.

I awoke in the dream. Not waiting for the wind to compel me forward, I started down the path at a light jog, my heart racing as I made my way forward. A crash in the bushes to my left spurred me to action, and I took off at a run. Faster, faster, faster. My feet beat into the ground.

They were coming for me. Coming to take me away. Who was? This was the first time the being from my dream had ever been a who.

The ancients. My mind whispered the answer, and I knew it to be true. I picked up speed, checking the foliage on either side of me as I ran. I'd always felt as though my feet knew where to step on the path, that it was familiar, and that sense was more powerful now. The forest didn't seem so foreign and strange. The trees didn't hold a sense of malice.

The ancients were coming, and they were gaining. I couldn't hear or see anyone, but I had the sense just as I'd had before. I pushed myself to go harder; the air searing my lungs. Muscles ripped, pushed past their limits, but still I pressed on. I couldn't let them get me. Let them *take me.*

Wait, take me? Take me where? I struggled to hold on to the thought even as a hand grabbed my foot. Shaking it off, I burst through the trees and onto the shore. A hand. I was sure of it. An ordinary being of some kind had reached out for me, not some dark, vicious creature of shadow.

I burst out from the tree cover and found myself on the beach, racing towards the figure standing at the shore. It turned towards me as it always had, and I saw for the first time that it was male. The sun shone behind him to create a halo, but its brightness obscured his face. It was only when I got closer that I saw who it was.

David stood at the shore. Smiling warmly, blue eyes sparkling, with his arms opened like he'd been expecting me. I raced into his embrace and sighed when his arms wrapped tightly around me. His voice whispered in my ear, "It's okay, Sarah, you're safe now. You're safe. It's okay." I felt the moment of peace that always came at the end of the dream as I relaxed into his arms.

David.

I woke up covered in sweat, head hammering to the rhythm of my racing heart.

A sense of calm and purpose came over me. *David*... It had been him. It had always been him. Something inside of me had known it from the moment I'd met him, and now the truth of it reverberated through me.

I showered off the sweat as anger flared to life in my chest. David had been keeping something from me, and my mind replayed all the times I'd caught him staring at me like he had something to say. He knew about the dream, or he was at least involved in some way.

But how was that possible?

It was three in the morning, but I couldn't make myself care. Adam's boots were crammed into the tray by the door which meant David would be alone at their apartment. Furious, I dressed quietly and headed out.

My eyes stung as I walked down the deserted streets. The image of an ancient from the book swam in my vision alongside all the details from the dream that had made themselves known.

A hand, I had seen a hand. Whoever had been after me, they'd been people. The ancients had been people. I thought about the peace I'd always found in David's arms at the end of the dream, the warmth of his embrace and how his eyes had shined with love as he'd opened his arms to receive me.

Reaching the grey high rise where he lived, I took the stairs instead of waiting for the elevator, leaping up them two at a time to emerge as breathless as I'd always been when I'd found him on the seashore. Pounding on his door, a powerful need to see him gripped me. To prove to myself that he was real, no longer a glowing figure on the beach, but a person I could touch and feel. Out of control, my hair flew around my face with the force of my strikes as I banged loud enough to shake the door in its settings. Each second it remained unanswered was agony.

Had I dreamed it, dreamed him?

Just when I was about to hammer the door down with my feet, it opened. David regarded me groggily for a moment, his hair disheveled, flannel pants and loose shirt crumpled with sleep. He looked as beautiful as ever, and relief pounded in my veins nearly as strong as the anger. David's expression turned serious and concern filled his eyes.

"Sarah, are you okay? What's going on?"

Damn him and the way he said my name. It pulled at my heartstrings and weakened my resolve. He ushered me into the apartment, poking his head out into the hallways and checking both ways worriedly, like he was worried I was being chased. He turned back to me, studying the tear streaks down my face and my disheveled appearance. It was hard not to seek the comfort I knew I would find in his arms.

But that's not why I was here. I needed answers, and I knew now that he had them.

"We need to talk," I said, my voice thick with emotion.

"Of course," he replied in a calm, reassuring tone, closing the door quietly behind him.

Turning to him, my hands clenched into fists, and I stared him down.

It was time to get some answers.

"I need you to tell me what the hell an ancient is because, according to the human histories, you're some kind of demon. I need to understand why you would appear in a nightmare of mine that I've had since I was a child. Why would that be? What are you really? What are you to me?"

It was out now. I expected him to refuse to give any credence to the dream, but when I mentioned that part, his eyes jumped to mine in alarm.

Sighing, he looked me over, meeting my furious glare head on.

"Okay, just please calm down. You're right, there are some things we should talk about, but everything is alright. I promise."

I hated the way his words and the hand he laid on my shoulder made me feel instantly better, threatening to diffuse the rage I'd felt so keenly upon my arrival. He gestured for me to have a seat on the ratty old couch at the far side of the room, and I moved to do so.

Sitting beside me, he studied my face, licking his lips as though buying time before starting.

"I'm an ancient, Sarah, but I don't think you know what that means. It's my fault. I guess I thought that the old stories would have been better known. I didn't expect you to find old human histories. Humans come up with all kinds of strange stories for creatures they don't understand. Vampires, witches, werewolves, are vilified by humans and are basically demons in their eyes. You know that's not true. They're just creatures different from humans."

I nodded numbly. I'd heard that story before, but I'd also known a few vampires who would qualify as demons.

He sucked in a deep breath. "Ancients were here long before vampires, werewolves, or witches. There were ancients and then there were humans. No one knows which came first." As he spoke, images played in my mind like a movie. Separate communities of humans and ancients had stayed away from each other, the mistrust apparent in their cautious eyes. The whole image was oddly clouded by a sense of him. Alarmed, my hands shot up to cover my ears to stop the invasion.

"What are you doing to me?" My voice came out in a squeak.

"I'm sorry, Sarah. I should've asked. I'm already messing things up." He sighed, scrubbing a hand across his face. "It's bad manners to project or probe too deeply without permission." His words were muffled behind his hand. "There's nothing to be afraid of, Sarah. Memories are handed down this way. It's our way of showing the histories. Is it okay if I show them to you?"

Numbly, I pulled my hands away from my ears and rested them on my lap, nodding my consent.

"The humans were terrified of the abilities the ancients possessed. Most often, ancients maintained a human form, but they could also transform into an animal at will. Surviving off the blood of animals and using magic to manipulate plant life, the humans found ancients terrifying."

I could see them in my mind. Not just wolves but different animals, every ancient unique. Some were birds, others were rabbits, still others were tremendous animals like bison or lions. There was a young human villager boy, watching an ancient transform into a cheetah and then running away. The villagers marched on the ancients, destroying their homes and driving them out. A woman wearing vines that snaked around her body to take the form of a dress sat on her knees, crying in front of a burnt-out hut. With a start, I recognized the same leafy fabric I'd worn in the dream.

"Ancients were peaceful and had no quarrel with humans. Most of them stayed far away from human society to reduce the conflict. Ancients can, and do, live for an exceptionally long time, but we don't reproduce easily. An ancient couple can have maybe one child over the course of two hundred years if they're lucky. Humans reproduce much more rapidly and as their numbers increased, it became harder and harder for ancients to stay away from humankind."

I saw groups of ancients moving away from their homes as new lands near them became occupied. Whole groups of ancients wept to leave their lands. I could feel their despair at being displaced again and again. It hurt my heart to watch them, as if their emotions seeped through and became mine. Tears leaked down my cheeks. I realized where this was going, and I pulled away from the sorrow.

"What happened then? The ancients fought back? Killing groups of humans as a warning for them to stay away?" I interrupted, my voice dripping with contempt. How could such powerful beings fight back against a group that was so much weaker than they were? It was cruel. No wonder human history had described them as demons.

David's eyes shone with hurt, and he straightened. Distracted by the swirling images in my mind, I hadn't realized how close he'd come to me while we'd been talking. I had been so engrossed in the story that the physical world had fallen away. Now his widening eyes consumed my vision.

"No, no, the ancients never sanctioned any retaliation, although there were some few ancients who took it upon themselves to attack the humans. Those were never condoned by the elders." He looked down at his hands a moment before meeting my eyes. "Sarah, you should know that doing no harm is the basic tenet of ancient society. We're peaceful to a fault in a lot of ways. Our most cardinal rule is to never take a life. Even animal life is sacred to us. Unlike humans, we don't need to kill to eat. Ancient communities keep animals for their blood but we care for them, and we'll often cycle a group of animals, capturing them from the wild and using them for a while as a food source before rehabilitating them and releasing them."

I saw the community in my mind. Pens of animals with ancients tending to them, feeding them, and using some kind of tubing to withdraw blood.

"Eventually, so many ancients were killed by humans that our numbers dwindled. A great meeting was called by the elders in Europe, where most of our kind remained. Some wanted to mix their blood with the humans and hide themselves in human society, allowing them to integrate among mankind—to take human mates and drink blood discreetly. Others wanted to preserve the ancient way of life. That group proposed the establishment of a safe place—a community set apart from humans. The choice was put to all who remained: To integrate with the humans or to move to an island under magical protection that allowed it to be hidden from human eyes. This group formed a large clan on an island and carried on in much the same way they had, unchanging, while the other group became a part of human society. The humans came to know it as the Bermuda Triangle due to the mystical protection the elders have cast over the island to hide it from outsiders.

"Over many generations, the blood from ancient parentage became diluted and the children of those who remained in human society came to possess only certain abilities. These are the vampires, witches, and werewolves you know. They are all descendants of the ancients who stayed in human society. Some are stronger than others or possess more abilities because they are closer to the ancient line."

I stared at him wide-eyed.

Not a witch, a vampire, or a werewolf. He'd never been any one thing. That's what had made him so hard to place.

"And you're one of these ancients? You can transform into any animal, you drink blood, and you do magic?" I asked, trying hard to wrap my mind around what he was telling me.

"Not any animal, Sarah." He pressed his lips into a thin line for a moment before continuing. "Each ancient is born with a human half to their soul and an animal half. We all have that animal inside of us. What type of animal an ancient transforms into is entirely dependent on the person. We can only change into the animal that is a part of us," he said, staring into my eyes as though there was more to say.

I interrupted him before he had the chance. "That's insane, David. The only type of animal that's ever been transformed into is a wolf by the werewolves."

It *was* insane, but I'd seen it in the strange images he'd shown me.

"Yes, werewolves are the only type of shapeshifter that seems to have survived in human society. I've often wondered about that. My theory is that the wolf is such a strong animal to share a soul with that it's easier for those with ancient blood to access."

My hands shook, and my face burned. None of this made any sense, and the images I'd seen in my mind had been impossibly strange. It was clear they'd come from David. They had a sense of him, but how had he done such a thing? It was too much, and a wave of exhaustion rose up to consume me even as tears pricked my eyes.

I needed to go home. To process this. The answers I had would have to do for now.

But as I turned to go, David grabbed my hand. "Sarah, there's more... A lot more. More you need to hear."

I froze. The way he said *more that I needed to hear* sounded personal. His hand on mine was gentle as he pulled me back down to sit on the couch.

"I'm an ancient. The history of which I've been describing to you but, here's the hard part." He drew in a shuddering breath and met my eyes with an apologetic look that sent fear racing down my spine. "So are you."

Chapter 6

David watched me steadily, and in his eyes, I found nothing but truth.

"I don't understand how that could be. My parents were vampires. They were sorry excuses for vampires, but they were vampires." I looked down as I spoke, staring at his hand with its long fingers and neatly trimmed nails.

"I know this is hard for you to accept, but it's the truth. You have no memory before the age of eleven, right?"

My eyes shot to his. I'd never mentioned that to him before. Thinking about my family was painful enough without bringing the accident and my lost childhood into it.

He nodded knowingly.

"When you were eleven—well, come here. Put your forehead against mine, and I'll show you."

I held myself back when he leaned forward.

"Why?" I squeaked. I wasn't sure I trusted something more powerful than the film-like images he'd shown me.

"It helps to emphasize our mental connection, so I can better show you what happened. Sort of like what I did when I explained to you about ancients. But this is something I think I need to properly show for you to understand." Tenderly, he took my hands in his, unclenching my fingers and twining them with his. "Please."

My forehead drifted forward to rest lightly against his. Whatever he had to show me, I needed to see it.

Our breath mixed, and I shivered. It was a reminder of how unsettling it could be when we were this close. The memory of his lips against mine and of the way he had tasted made it difficult to think. That fire was just under the surface for both of us, and all it would take would be for me to tilt my head and claim his lips. But before I could act, I became aware of that peaceful sense of warmth I'd always felt from him growing stronger, like it was coming closer. Closing my eyes, I tried reaching out to him and found his walls down.

Contact.

I'd never seen into his mind like this, and the ability to properly feel him and see him for the first time left me breathless. His thoughts skimmed under the surface like an unseen world hidden beneath cloudy water, and I could feel what he felt—love and protectiveness so powerful it left me reeling. His hand tightened on mine, urging me to stay in place, but I broke away, the depth of his emotion too jarring.

Gasping, I sat up straight, struggling to comprehend what I now knew to be true.

Since I'd met David, he'd had a hold on me. A grip so tight I'd felt helplessly drawn to him. It had never occurred to me that it'd been the same for him, that he was just as caught up in me as I was with him. But it was more, deeper. Affection, attraction, and a soul deep knowledge that we belonged together.

"You love me." I stared at him in shock until he dropped his gaze. The words hung between us. He turned away, and his hands clenched in his lap.

"You weren't supposed to see that part."

He would do anything for me. Would put me above everything. And the *need* he felt for me. As much as I'd craved him, wanted more of him, he'd nearly been ripped apart by it.

He loved me, and it wasn't passing or simple. The knowledge of it, his absolute commitment to protect me at all costs, was astounding.

"David." I didn't know what to say. I'd never known that from another person, and it was so powerful—cruelly so. Like a force of nature. He cleared his throat, and when he met my eyes again, I saw the longing there, the same need I harboured for him.

He tilted his forehead towards me in silent invitation. "We need to continue."

My heart clenched. I wanted to reach out, to hold him and reassure him, but I didn't know how. Did I love him, too?

Yes. My soul screamed it, but that was insane. I'd known him for just over a week. That wasn't long enough to care so deeply.

But it was, and while I couldn't speak the words, I took his hands in mine and rubbed soothing circles over his thumbs as I leaned my forehead against his and reached out for his mind. I swallowed hard against the lump of emotion lodged in my throat.

He spoke out loud as though needing to create a distance between us, but I saw the images through his mind as he explained. "We were children together, Sarah. It's rare for ancients to have children, and you and I were born only six months apart."

I saw a little redheaded girl in his memory. Me? She smiled and raced him around the winding jungle paths, smiling and giggling. I felt the unbridled joy he had experienced, roaming the jungles with her at his side, playing, laughing, wrestling. Always together.

"Then when you were eleven, the elders hosted their great seasonal party. It was the first time either of us were allowed to have the special blood with herbs. It's intoxicating, like the alcohol humans here drink. Not harmful, though it can affect memory afterwards."

It had burned in his throat with a strange spiciness, but the party had been fun, and I saw him dancing around a great bonfire with the redheaded girl, careening back and forth with her as adults sat around us in a circle clapping. Only, at some point, he lost track of me. He'd searched the area, and I felt his worry within the memory, and how he'd gone back to dancing with a dark-skinned woman—*teacher*. A tear escaped my eye as his sadness and regret washed over me. He'd hated himself for not searching for me harder, for staying at the party.

"The next morning, you were found on the beach with no memory of what had happened the night before. Just up the shore from where you were found, a fisherman had somehow navigated through the magical protection that encircles the island. It happens every once in a while, and it happened that night. The man was brutally murdered in an animal attack. As you were found so close to the killing and your animal half matched the wounds, you were blamed."

He shuddered, and sorrow reverberated through his mind. He let out a breath, as though steeling himself, before continuing.

"Killing any animal is our one absolute rule and to kill a human was... Well, it was an atrocity, Sarah. Something not to be tolerated. The elders didn't know what to do. Children are precious in ancient society, but they couldn't overlook a murder. They chose to send you away to the human world to live. They said that it would be"—his lips twisted—"kinder for you to forget about the island as part of your exile." He pulled away, disrupting the bond and creating distance, but not before I was hit by the shock and horror accompanying his memory of the event.

How deeply it had hurt him. How painful it still was.

It was hard for him to share, and he instinctively pulled away to protect himself. I caught his arm to keep contact between us.

"Then what happened?" There was such pain in his mind, but this was about what had happened to me, and I needed to know.

"They sent you away and placed you with a vampire family, but I knew." His eyes blazed. "I knew there was no way you could do something like that. I refused to believe it. Your parents and I spent days combing the area and sleeping outside in the brush until we found evidence of a juvenile panther nearby. We were able to capture it and bring it before the elders, who looked into its mind and saw the memory of its attack." He sighed and stared over my shoulder. "But we were too late. By the time the panther was caught and your innocence determined, you'd already been placed with a vampire family, and the elders had altered their own memory to safeguard your location."

My stomach twisted. "And my memory?"

David's brow furrowed, and he rubbed at my knuckles.

I barely felt it when he traced the length of the digit with his thumb.

"They erased your memory in the hope that it would give you the best possible chance of a fresh start in the human world." His voice was strained. "But your parents refused to accept your banishment, and they left to search for you."

I saw an image of a redheaded woman with an elegance to her movements and a tall brown-haired man with a straight nose. My parents. I was looking at my parents. Those faces must've been precious to me once, but now they were strangers. I searched my mind, hoping something about them was familiar, some piece of their love shining through the dark veil over those years, but I had no memory of them.

"They left to search for me, but what happened to them?"

A parent's love. It was something I'd never known, never expected to know. My father had cared for me in his own twisted way, had set certain *expectations*, but love? No, I couldn't believe he'd ever loved me. Those people in David's memory, though, it was obvious they'd cared when I'd been taken. They'd left their home and everything they knew to search for me. A warmth kindled in my chest.

"And where are they now?" If I could find them, meet them, maybe I'd be able to understand myself better, to experience what it meant to truly have a family.

My heart broke when David's face fell.

"I'm sorry, Sarah, but I don't know where they are. They never returned. It's a requirement of ancients traveling in human lands for them to check back at least once a year. Otherwise, they are declared dead. Your parents never did check in, and it's been twelve years now. We assumed that something terrible happened to them. There was a funeral." He trailed off, and I was thankful for it. The last thing I wanted was to hear the details of how they were mourned.

I blinked back tears at the wave of emotion, of sorrow, that squeezed my heart. How strange it was to grieve for something I hadn't known until a few short minutes ago.

But there was more to it than the family I'd lost. If what David said was true, it meant I wasn't related to the man I thought was my father. The realization hit me, and I felt instantly lighter. How long had his 'teachings' haunted me, his voice echoing in my ears?

I was his only daughter, a part of him.

Only I wasn't. It had all been a lie.

Which meant.

That voice. It held no power over me anymore.

David let out a shaky breath and squeezed my hand. "The ancients allow whoever wishes it to act as scouts in the human world in order to gain knowledge about human customs and inventions. I offered myself for the role as soon as I was of age to do so. I've been searching for you ever since. To—to bring you home," he said, closing his eyes and touching his forehead to mine once more. The outpouring of love and protectiveness as his mind brushed against mine in a delicate, intimate caress.

As shocking as it seemed, I could feel the truth of it. He looked down at me, cupping my face in his hands. "I love you. I know how crazy that sounds because it probably feels to you like we've only known each other for such a short while, but I've loved you all my life. I can't remember ever not loving you. I know that if I met you for the first time today, I would love you in an instant. Since you were taken from the island, I've felt as though my heart was ripped out, like a piece of myself was missing. I was restless, stuck, waiting until I was allowed to search for you."

In shock, I placed my hand in his, twining our fingers together as tightly as I could in a silent promise to never let go.

Something missing.

A piece of myself.

The figure from my dreams.

His words could have been mine.

"David." His name escaped my lips in a breath that carried me towards him until my lips pressed gently against his, and my tongue traced the seam of his mouth in a silent request for admittance. He shuddered against me, a hand reaching up to stroke my cheek tenderly before he pulled back to stare into my eyes, rubbing a thumb across my cheekbone. His pupils were blown, the blue nearly consumed by black, and the realization of how I affected him was so tantalizing, so perfect, that I couldn't help but moan my approval.

His control snapped, and he fell into me, nuzzling and kissing my neck. His touch sent my pulse thundering until I was lightheaded and giddy. I tangled my hands in his hair and pulled him back so I could explore him, trailing kisses along his strong jawline. He groaned in response, and the sound set my core to a low thrum. Attuned to him. Every sound he made, every movement, echoed in my core. The tension wound tighter. I climbed across the space between us, sinking down into his lap to feel his hardness and claim his mouth.

I was lost to him, to the feel of his lips, his tongue eagerly tangling hot and eager with mine. The taste of him, that intoxicating scent.

This was home.

My mind opened to him, connecting us on a new level, deeper, because now I was as open to him as he was to me. I should have felt nervous to know he could feel my emotions and have a sense for my very soul, but I didn't. He'd bared himself to me first, and I wanted him to see me just as clearly. He gasped against my mouth at the deepening connection, and I quickly swallowed it.

This was how we were meant to be, connected in body and mind. My breath was ragged as his hands began moving lower. He shifted back to my neck, nibbling the skin under my ear as love and contentment poured from him in waves.

My sense of him heightened. I'd been wrong. His mind wasn't a stream, it was a crystal; shining pure and clear. He had such a strong sense of right and wrong combined with a deep, burning desire to be good. To protect those he loved and, most of all, to help.

He was good, like I'd always known, if naïve. A surge of protectiveness nearly overwhelmed me. There was a danger in believing the people of the world were filled with good intentions. The focus and passion in his heart struck a chord deep down in my soul, and I soaked him in like the desert soil, parched for rain. A small moan escaped my lips at the beauty of it.

As I explored his mind, I found an image of myself as he saw me. The image was shocking. A woman he admired deeply, with a brave soul and a deep capacity for caring.

A beautiful woman, inside and out.

No.

I couldn't stop myself from flinching away, pulling myself back. Physically and mentally. I stared into his beautiful eyes, still glazed from the peace we'd been slipping into. The few inches of separation between us were so sudden and jarring that I snatched his hand and twined our fingers together.

I wanted this, wanted him, wanted to believe every bit of what he'd told me. What he thought of me. But that woman I'd seen in his mind.

That wasn't me.

The image he had of me, the girl on the island. None of it added up. I stared at him, not sure how to explain I wasn't the person he thought I was.

I couldn't be. I was my father's daughter, and he'd made a mistake. There was no way I could be anyone, anything else, but a monster.

"I'm sorry, David, but...you don't understand. I knew my parents. There's just—there's no way I can be the person you say I am. That person you have in your mind, that's not me." Which also meant he couldn't love me, a fact that nearly broke me as I struggled to breathe through the pain and fight the tears pricking at my eyes. The thought of him feeling that way for another person was physically painful, but it had to be true. There was no way I could do the things he'd said, be the things he felt sure I was.

He studied my face, his expression filled with a tenderness that I no longer deserved.

A tenderness meant for someone else.

"I'm sure, Sarah. I was sure the second I saw you." His eyes burned into mine at the last, threatening to pull me back down into him. Back into the world where there were only the two of us.

When he'd first seen me. On our date. The look of confusion and how intensely he'd stared until I'd had to look away. I'd always wondered why he'd reacted so strongly.

Now I knew it was because he'd *recognized* me. Or so he thought.

Then there was the dream. The things he said fit perfectly with it. The beach, my clothes, the chase down the path, and him being my safety.

My eyes shifted down again. "I'm sorry, but I just—I don't know. This is all so confusing," I muttered, looking anywhere but at his beautiful face.

He was the only thing I was sure about, but I couldn't let him continue to believe I was the woman he'd been searching for. Not when I knew it couldn't be true.

"I was in a car accident when I was eleven. I suffered a significant concussion. They admitted me to the hospital for four days. My parents sneaked blood in by mixing it with the soup." A tear escaped, and I brushed it away. But I continued to go over the facts as I knew them, listing them off on my fingers and taking comfort in the familiarity.

David shook his head, his eyes soft.

"No, Sarah. You weren't in an accident. They told you that because it's what the elders made them believe, just like they made them believe you were their daughter, but none of it was true."

Tears streamed down my face, and I angrily wiped them away, squeezing my eyes shut like doing so could stop his words.

I felt so lost. Adrift. What was true and what wasn't? Who even was I?

"Hey, look at me." The concern in his voice forced me out of my thoughts. He took my hand and gently pressed it to his cheek, waiting patiently until I found the courage to meet his eyes. Those feelings he had must be for someone else.

I couldn't look at him. Not now. Only he waited until I lifted my eyes to his and when I did, I saw nothing but love and certainty. Gently, he turned my hand and pressed a tender kiss to the palm in a gesture of affection that nearly split my heart in two.

"I'm sure, and I know who you are. I'll be sure for both of us," he whispered, and I nodded mutely, unable to do anything else.

"There's also... Well, I can prove that everything I've said is true. If you'll let me." He was so sure about me, and who he thought I was, and I was terrified of disappointing him. Words weren't possible, but I tipped my head forward, squeezing out a new wave of tears.

He stood up, filled with purpose, and gently tugged me to stand beside him before leading us further into the apartment.

"You don't believe me because you don't think it's possible for you to be an ancient, but we both know you drink blood and can use magic, so all that's left is the animal part."

He walked with me down the short hallway as he spoke in a low, soothing voice. "Your animal is a tiger, Sarah," he said as we stopped at his closed bedroom door, and I stared at him wide eyed.

A tiger? It was ludicrous. Impossible. By the seriousness of David's expression, I could tell he wasn't joking. My heart sank further as the impossibility of being *his* Sarah seemed more certain. "I'll explain how to make the shift, and if it works, you'll have your proof." Ever the scientist, he'd found the most logical conclusion, even if it was one that chilled my bones and left me weak. I nodded shakily.

He meant me no harm. I knew that, knew he was trying to help, but what if it worked? And what if it didn't? If I wasn't the woman he was looking for, he'd leave, and if I was.

It would mean my life as I knew it was based on a fabrication.

My mind was in a state of pure chaos as David turned the cheap gold knob to his room and gestured for me to enter. "I'll be on the other side of the door. Take off your clothes, and I'll walk you through it."

Beyond fighting, I crossed the threshold, dimly noting that this was the first time I'd been in his room. There were clothes thrown across the floor, but what struck me was the sheer number of books.

Novels of every genre next to books on quantum physics, all of them opened partway and on nearly every surface, like he'd been in the middle of learning when something new had caught his attention. His scent was everywhere, and I struggled to ignore its effects on me as I breathed through it. Gingerly, I removed my jeans and sweater.

Should I sit for this? Stand? I finally decided since I couldn't bring myself to sit naked on his bed, I'd stand at the foot of his bed.

"What do I do next?" My bare skin tingled with a mix of the chill air and anticipation.

"Close your eyes and turn inward. Quiet your mind. You need to find the part of your soul that is the animal and embrace it. The act of embracing that part of yourself will start the change."

I closed my eyes and could think of nothing but how ludicrous the idea of turning into a tiger seemed. Still, I would do this, and in doing so, learn the truth. I slowed my breathing and turned inward as he had instructed.

"You may have to dig deep, Sarah, really search for the animal. It's there. You just haven't embraced it for so many years now that it may be hard for you to find."

I dug deep as he had said, turning inward and quieting the thoughts of him and the sensation of the cool air pricking my skin. David's scent in the room distracted me; the wild spicy aroma tinged with sweetness triggering a deep ache in my core as I tried to concentrate. But I pushed it aside, hunting around the corners of my mind.

"David, I don't feel anything like an animal!" I said with a measure of sadness as I imagined how disappointed he would be. He would leave me then to find his lost love. Already, I could feel my heart hardening towards him in an effort at self-preservation.

"Deeper, Sarah. Go to the deepest part of yourself." Was his muffled answer from the other side of the door.

With a sigh, I tried again, concentrating until my surroundings faded away.

An animal. I was searching for an animal, but I had no idea what I was looking for, and turning inward only led my thoughts into a spiral I had no escape from.

I couldn't do this.

It wasn't me.

Frustrated, I groaned loudly enough that David must've heard it from the doorway.

"Try again, Sarah, please. It's there. I promise."

I closed my eyes and found it easier, more natural, to let the room fall away until I felt as though I floated comfortably on a cloud. Nothing could reach me here. Not the feel of the hardwood floor on my bare feet, the shiver of my bare skin in the empty room, or David's maddening scent.

David had said I was looking for an animal, a tiger, but had I ever felt it before? What would it even feel like if I had?

Like hunting. With clarity, I thought of how I'd always had to suppress that need to give chase when my victims left.

An animal.

A tiger.

My father threatened to resurface, to damn me, label me his kin, but I dismissed it. If David was right, I wasn't his kin, had no connection to him. So, I searched and found *something*. Maybe. Waiting in the dark. A wildness. It rose, eager to greet me, and I embraced it. Doing so pulled me out of the floating state I'd been in.

I opened my eyes to find the room looked the same as it had before. Disappointment warring with sorrow, I went to shout out to David to let him know I'd failed, but the sound I made wasn't human. Incredulous, I looked down to see paws and burnished orange fur. An animal growl escaped me, and I propelled myself backwards, ending up half on the bed before tumbling sideways. I didn't have arms to catch myself anymore, but my body knew how to fall, and I twisted at the torso to land on my feet.

No, not feet, paws.

Terrified little panting animal sounds escaped me as I lifted my paws and dropped them again. Long claws emerged and retracted. Panic gripped me, and the sound I loosed out was more of a yowl as I backed myself into the corner of the room and pressed my body tightly against the wall. The wall was stable. The wall was the same.

It was me who was different.

I stared around in terror, struggling to comprehend that I was no longer in the body I knew as my own. Panic rose as a scream in my throat, but the sound that escaped was far from human and only served to further frighten me. But David was there a moment later, his concerned face consuming my vision.

"Calm down, Sarah, it's okay. This is okay. This was what we were trying to do, remember?" He was right. The goal had been for me to shift into a tiger, and damn if I hadn't done just that. "I knew you could do it." He smiled at me, and I tried to focus on him. The way his lower lip jutted out slightly when he smiled. The twinkle of his eyes. Slowly, I breathed normally. "Now, just calm your mind and close your eyes. Try not to think of the form you've taken. Just stay calm and turn inward like you did before. Find yourself again and embrace it. That's it." At his words of encouragement, I closed my eyes and awkwardly perched back on my haunches, trying, and failing, to ignore my twitching tail.

My tail. Panic threatened to consume me, but David continued to insist that all was well, and focusing on his voice helped.

I turned inward and felt myself fall and float as I had done before. Now I had to find the opposite, the human part of myself. But what was the opposite of wildness? I didn't know, but I tried to think of myself. My normal shape doing an activity I associated with humans—quietly reading a textbook. There she was. I could see myself squeezing in a bit of reading in the back room next to the lockers, perched on the uncomfortable bench.

Embracing her, I abandoned the wildness.

I was Sarah. *Please, please, please,* I begged as I opened my eyes, and trembling hands swam in my vision. Relieved, I reached up to feel my face. Yes, that was a nose. Breathing deeply, I ran my hands over my arms, my thighs, my torso. I didn't dare look down until I was sure I was myself.

Breathing a sigh of relief, I rubbed my arms, needing to confirm I had skin again.

Yes, skin.

Not fur.

At some point, David had stealthily left the room and had closed the door behind him to give me some privacy.

Eventually, my breathing normalized, and I stood to dress. I did so in a haze, barely aware of what I was doing.

My mind was reeling. Was I really the girl from his story? Had my community really exiled me for a crime I hadn't committed? The cruelty of exiling a child made me gag, and I put my throbbing head in my hands.

It was so much to take. Too much. I threw on my clothes and came out of the room to find David seated on the couch. He looked up with concern in his deep blue eyes.

I barely managed to walk over to him before I crumbled and launched myself into his arms, sobbing with helpless, wild abandon. He'd told me the truth, and what it meant was staggering.

Those things, those *elders* on the island, had sent me to live with the monsters who still haunted my every step. They'd forsaken me; exiled me from those I knew and loved. I sobbed into David's chest as the betrayal of it all consumed my mind, and he held me through it, whispering words of comfort in my ear that I couldn't make out over the sounds of my own violent cries.

It didn't matter. The warmth of his body and the vibrations of his chest were what I craved—not words. I cried so long and so hard that I was sure he would pull away, that he would reach his breaking point, and leave me to deal with it alone. Always alone.

Only he didn't.

Instead, he shifted us so we leaned sideways on the couch together, my head pillowed on his chest. I cried until there was no moisture left for tears, and I drifted to sleep, feeling loved, and safe, and protected. The way I always had when I found the figure on the shore in my dream. Peace came over me like a warm, featherlight blanket, and I knew without question that I would never have the dream again. I had found the answer to the questions my mind had been desperately seeking, and this time, the figure would be there when I woke.

Chapter 7

I regained consciousness to the rhythm of David's breathing, the rise and fall of his chest pulling me from a deep and blissfully dreamless sleep. Blinking into the sunlight, I instinctively covered my eyes, wincing at the blinding pain of the light. When was the last time I'd woken after sunrise? I couldn't recall. My sleep had been disturbed for so long that I was used to going to bed at night and waking up at night. To calculating how many hours I'd managed and trying to determine whether it was enough to leave me somewhat functional in the day. And with the dream visiting me nightly since I'd first met David, this was the first proper rest I'd had in over a week.

I should've figured out the connection sooner. Smiling to myself, I propped my face up and stared down at David. He was beautiful in sleep, and I marvelled at the pure relaxation on his face—the smooth forehead, and parted lips. A few strands of hair hung over one eye, and I longed to brush them away if only it wouldn't risk waking him and disturbing the moment. His face may have given the appearance of pure relaxation, but he couldn't have been comfortable. Not with his long legs twisted half off the short couch, and with nothing but a threadbare pillow to prop his head up.

Yet he hadn't moved me, hadn't disturbed me. I frowned down at him, struggling with the stab of guilt and rush of gratitude until I had to act, had to touch. Laying my hands on his chest for balance, I leaned forward to press my lips to his.

He stirred beneath me, cracking an eye, a slow smile spreading across his face.

"Good morning," he murmured, his voice still laced with sleep. His hands came up to rest on the small of my back.

"Thank you for last night," I spoke earnestly, willing him to understand the depth of my gratitude for what he had done. Not just for the sleep, but for gently explaining our shared history. For being patient, but most of all, for being someone I could trust.

He turned serious. The smile dropping from his lips as he reached out to cup my cheek. I leaned into it, wanting more. Always wanting more.

"You don't need to thank me for that."

He'd really left the island to come here and find me for me. A lost child. And then there was his love. Furious. Vibrant. Powerful. How certain he'd been of it, of me.

What I'd felt in his mind had been life changing. I'd never expected to fall so completely in love with someone I barely knew, but he was right. I did know him. I knew him on a deep and intimate level in a way I hadn't known anybody. Maybe it was because we had had such a close bond as children or that we'd glimpsed each other's minds. Our thoughts and feelings laid bare for the other to see. It had been the most vulnerable experience of my life.

His thumb glided over my bottom lip, and it was too much for me. I sank down to kiss along the seam of his mouth, my tongue darting out to taste him and find the heaven I knew waited within. He kissed me back. All that passion I knew swam in his mind, apparent in every slick of his tongue. Groaning at how good it felt, I brought my hands up to frame his face, and he responded by claiming my mouth, his taste exploding across my taste buds and leading me to the place where it was just us, just this. I wanted to live here forever.

Heat pooled in my core as he grew hard beneath me, and I eagerly slid up against his length, cursing the material between us. His kiss became more forceful, the thrust of his tongue more urgent. He pulled us up into a seated position, hooking my legs tight to his hips as he took control. Whimpering at how good it felt to have him between my legs, I tangled my fingers in his hair, the glorious taste of him making my heart rate pick up until it pounded in my ears. Gasping, I broke from the kiss to press his face into my neck. He found the sensitive spot behind my ear. Mercilessly, he explored it with his mouth, sucking and nipping. Whining, I bucked my hips helplessly against his erection, knowing that I was soaked beneath my jeans.

But without warning, he reined himself in and pulled back. He still kissed me, but lighter and more tender, his palms relaxed against my back. Gone was the intensity, the urgency from before. I fought to slow my erratic breathing, even as I forced his face back to my neck in a silent plea for more. I'd always been embarrassed at how helplessly attracted I was to him, but now that I knew he felt the same way, it was liberating.

So, why stop?

Releasing his head, I searched his eyes and found a mix of the feral need I felt between us and confusion. Cupping his cheek, I gently kissed his lips. Whatever was bothering him, I wanted to meet it head on.

"I have to get to lecture," he whispered, the movement against my lips sending a shiver across my skin. He acted as though he hadn't wanted me just as badly as I wanted him a moment ago, but the panic I saw in the pinch of his brows convinced me he truly meant to stop.

Shifting to the side, I watched with disappointment as he extracted him-self from our embrace. He headed into the other room to change, smiling back at me reassuringly. The warmth lighting his eyes calmed my nerves. There would be time for the physical stuff later, even if I felt like I needed to go home and relive every moment of what had just happened with a very different ending. Running my hands along my peaked nipples and willing my body to settle, I perched on the edge of the couch, realizing that I was alone with my thoughts for the first time since David had explained to me the truth of my past.

It was a lot to process. Had I really transformed into a tiger? I looked down at my dainty fingers with their chewed-up nail beds. My hands hadn't been hands, but paws with sharp, retractable claws. I shuddered at the memory of how the claws had slid in and out of their casings without my intent.

Closing my eyes, I searched my mind for the tiger as I had done the night before.

Wildness, that need to hunt, to give chase.

And there it was. Much closer and easier to find than it had been the night before. Startled at how easy it would be to embrace it and take that form again, I flinched away, taking a few gasping breaths. I didn't want a repeat of last night. It had been terrifying to be thrust into such a novel form. After I'd steadied my breathing, I searched for it again and found it waiting patiently. Tears stung my puffy eyes. The tiger was there. Waiting for me to take control of it. There was no separate entity, but a part of myself I'd lost along with my memories. And I understood. It wasn't something to be feared, but another piece that made me who I was.

Those people on the island. They'd done this to me—ruined my life and put me at odds with myself. Had been the source of all my nightmares for years, and for a good reason. My stomach churned.

I'd had parents who loved me. I'd had David. It was all I'd known, and they'd forced me to leave, taking from me even the memory of the place in a cruelly designed punishment for a crime of which I was innocent.

Then they'd sent me there to *them* in their compound of horrors. Shuddering, I hugged myself, rubbing my arms to dispel the chill. I hated the people on the island in a way I'd never hated anyone before. Even the monsters who I'd thought were my parents didn't compare to this. They'd been true to who they were, and while I hated them for what they'd done to me, the people of the island had placed me with them, taken me from my idyllic home and left me to the beasts.

David came back into the room fully dressed in a pair of casual brown pants and a loose white shirt. He somehow made whatever clothes he wore look good. I hated how the looseness of his shirt hid his lithe figure from my eyes, but it contrasted the way his brown pants hugged his tight ass perfectly. My eyes trailed him to the kitchen, where he prepared two bowls of blood.

He brought them over to me, and I gratefully accepted the thick earthenware bowl he offered. It was sturdy in my hands in a way that my thoughts were not, and I held it tight, allowing its warmth to seep into me.

We sat in a comfortable silence for a few minutes, enjoying our meals. I got the impression by the way he occasionally looked up to study my face that he wanted me to be the one to bring up the revelations from the night before. But I didn't want to talk about it, not yet, and I was overwhelmed with how much there was to know about him, about the people we'd both come from. That, at least, I could discuss.

"So, if my spirit animal is a tiger and every ancient has a different spirit animal, what's yours?" I asked, genuinely curious.

David smiled, and his brilliant blue eyes crinkled with mirth.

"I'm a tiger, too. It was pretty strange for two ancients born so close together to both be tigers, but that was the case with us."

"There are other kinds of soul animals, though, right? You said not everyone is the same?" I'd seen it in the histories he'd shown me, but I needed him to explain it better, to understand how all those people with their differing animals somehow lived in harmony.

"Oh no, we have a few birds. One rabbit even." He trailed off, his eyes fixed on the kitchen cabinets. "You'll learn all about ancients when we go back, and they restore your memories." He let out a low chuckle, but my blood ran cold. "They're going to throw you such an incredible welcome home party." He grinned at me as though he hadn't just suggested we go face my nightmare, but the grin dropped when he saw my expression.

Go back.

Like it was nothing.

Just accept they'd made a mistake and return so they could play with my mind some more? As if they hadn't done that enough.

What would they do this time?

What—who—would they take? Panic stole my breath, and I gripped the bowl like a lifeline, thankful it was sturdy enough to resist the pressure without shattering.

"I can't go back, David. They cast me out and sent me to those monsters who raised me. I hate them...I hate the people who did that to me. I can't ever go back there. I won't. I can't." Words poured from me in a stilted stutter from the rising panic at facing the dark creatures from my dreams and what they'd done to me.

"I know it's been hard, Sarah, I do."

But he didn't.

"No, you don't. They ruined my *life*, David. I can't just go back so they can do it again."

His mouth snapped shut like I'd slapped him, and he stared down at his bowl with pinched brows.

"I'm sorry, Sarah, I wasn't thinking. It's just—well, I've wanted to bring you home and have your memories restored since the second you were taken away."

I put my hand gently on his and attempted to speak more softly. I'd seen into his mind, and I knew he was only thinking of me. He didn't mean any harm, and I forced myself to remember it wasn't him I was angry at.

It was them.

"I know that, David. I do. I know that bringing me back is important to you, but I can't do it. To put myself into their power again, knowing what they're capable of." I shuddered, fear and panic threatening to rise up even as my tears blurred my vision. They could do it again. Take me from the few connections I had and drop me somewhere even more horrifying. "Those people are the things from my nightmares. I never want to go there again. I never want to see those people again. As far as I'm concerned, I got the best part of that island when I got you back."

He squeezed my hand. "Well, maybe you'll change your mind. This is all still so fresh for you. It's not fair that your memories were taken from you. They're a part of you, Sarah. They're your history, and they can be restored."

Restored. Would they really give me those memories back? I didn't—couldn't trust them. They'd ruined my life once. What was to stop them from doing it again?

It was a risk I couldn't take.

Nodding, I looked away, swallowing the lump in my throat. "I know. I do, but I can't face them." And that was what it came down to.

We finished the rest of our meal in silence until he collected my empty bowl, and leaned over to kiss me gently on the lips, lingering for an extra moment that drove all thoughts of Ancients from my mind.

"I've got to go, but I'll call you tonight, okay? You're all right?"

Numbly, I nodded, meeting his eyes so he could see I was dealing with it.

"Just pull the door shut to lock it when you head out." He leaned forward to gently brush my curls aside and kiss my temple before heading to the door.

"I'll call you later," he promised from the doorway, and I nodded again. With a parting smile, he slipped out the door, and I sighed, an ache growing in my chest immediately at his absence. But now that I was alone, I could allow myself the weakness I needed.

Dropping my face into my hands, and hating how pathetic I felt about the island and the people there, I allowed myself a few tears.

I couldn't imagine a time when I would have the strength to return.

David's face swam in my mind as I took plate after plate out to eager customers. He'd told me he loved me, and the memory filled me with joy and a tenderness I hadn't known I possessed. How many times had I felt broken by how unaffected I'd always been in relationships? Even the breakup with Adam hadn't meant much to me. I'd been happy to get out, to see him with Nina, and be done with the effort it had taken to engage with him so closely.

He seemed so sure I was this lost little girl from his past, but was I really? Even with the evidence I had, and the feeling of rightness, it all still felt like an illusion. Some part of me held back from truly believing it.

Perhaps it was the deep fear I felt at allowing myself this. To be happy. To let go of all the terrible things I'd done in my past and let myself love and be loved.

Maybe I *had* been that little girl David had known so many years ago, but I was a grown woman now. A grown woman who had seen and done enough terrible things that I was under no illusions of myself as a beacon of goodness. I could never measure up to the person I'd seen in his mind no matter how badly I wanted to, and the thought left me sick with worry.

My shift ended, and I returned home, my hair greasy from too much time spent lingering in the kitchen hunting down delayed plates. My eyes sought the answering machine even before I dropped my bag, but I was disappointed to see it wasn't flashing with a new message.

No messages, and David had finished his lecture about three hours ago. Not once in my life had I been the one to chase someone, and I'd grown used to the power that comes with being the one chased; never really caring what the outcome of the relationship would be, just along for the ride.

Now I was terribly invested, and the only consolation I could find was that I knew from touching his mind that he was invested, too.

There was no answer when I phoned him. Frowning to myself, I set about retrieving my chemistry textbook, and opening it to the page I'd marked with a napkin. Settling into the lumpy couch, I tried not to think about David. Working full time at the diner had left me permanently behind on readings, and this was a great opportunity to catch up. But as much as I tried to concentrate, I could feel my gaze slide off of the page and over to the phone, willing it to ring.

I could see no reason why he wouldn't call as he'd said he would. He had always been completely consistent and reliable. Then there was his smile and parting kiss from this morning, how the warmth of his lips had lingered on mine.

My mind was in turmoil, my stomach churning so violently that the dinner I had planned to eat was forgotten. Had David somehow discovered that I wasn't the Sarah he was looking for? Maybe he'd come across the real Sarah and was sitting down with her right now, holding her hand and explaining things as patiently as he had done for me.

The thought of his honeyed voice, of him being close to someone else, of caring for them, stuck like a blade between my ribs, hurting with every breath.

He had come to the human world with one goal: to find his exiled friend and bring her home. If he'd somehow found the real Sarah elsewhere, he'd go to her. Or maybe I'd offended him by refusing to go back to the island. He'd seemed to understand, but I knew it had been deeply important to him, and it must have crushed him when I refused.

By midnight, I was convinced he had left. He had told me all about his nomadic life of traveling from place to place, and now I knew why. He'd been searching for that lost little girl from his past. Maybe he'd felt she was still out there, and he needed to save her.

Deep down, I'd known this wasn't for me, that I didn't deserve to have this. My heart hardened until it was a heavy stone in my chest.

I wasn't surprised. Not really. David had always seemed too good to be true, and I'd always known that the woman for him would have to be as good as he was.

I wasn't her, couldn't be her.

I was about to give up and force myself to sleep when the phone sprang to life, its shrill ring filling the air. I jumped on it, realizing at the same time how much hope I'd still held onto that this was a simple misunderstanding. I'd told myself that he was gone, but my heart hadn't believed it. I held the receiver to my ear eagerly, but a chill raced up my spine when I heard Adam's voice on the other end.

He hated using the phone.

"Sarah, you need to get down here right away."

"Why? What's wrong?" I asked, a pit opening in my stomach.

"I'm at headquarters. It's David. Come quickly."

The phone went dead.

CHAPTER 8

DAVID

Earlier that day

It could've gone worse. At least that's what I told myself, but no matter how I tried to convince myself, Sarah's haggard face stayed at the forefront of my mind. Seeing her cry had been nearly unbearable, just as I'd known it would be.

At least now she knew.

I'd had to do it, but doing so had left a bitter taste in my mouth. The only thing that helped was thinking about seeing her after work tonight, of showing her how special she was. How beautiful. How brave.

The doubt in her mind had jarred me. She thought my impression of her was based on the little girl I'd known on the island, but the remarkable person she was now had left me stunned. There was so much to admire, and it killed me she didn't see it.

It was the thought of loving her so well and deeply that she couldn't help but see it in herself that finally dispelled the image of her sobbing face and quelled the panic threatening to drive me straight back to the apartment.

We had plenty of time.

When the lecture finished, I forced myself not to rush back. I wasn't surprised she'd headed to work, but I couldn't help the swell of disappointment at not seeing her still on the couch.

Sighing, I leaned against the door, tipping my head back to stare at the pockmarked ceiling.

Of course, she was at work. I'd known that coming back, but my heart insisted she'd be here somehow.

With nothing to do until she finished her shift, I headed back out.

The antique book dealer across town had left a message that my book was in, and I'd been meaning to pick it up. It was a first edition of *Moby Dick*, and I couldn't wait to feel the textured pages and the thick paper they used.

I needed the distraction.

Crowded buses weren't new to me, but I still got a thrill at the press of so many bodies. The experience was unlike the island with its wide-open spaces, and the sheer number of strangers was at once alarming and exciting.

Automatically, I scanned the faces of the passengers—too old, not a redhead. She wouldn't need glasses.

What was wrong with me?

Shaking my head, I tried to remember that I'd found her. I didn't need to search anymore. I knew where Sarah was and would see her in a few hours.

She was worth every agonizing moment I'd spent searching through the crowds.

Grinning, I replayed every touch, every word. It'd been hard to explain things, but worth it. Sarah needed some time to accept the truths I'd forced on her, which is why I was heading out to the bookstore instead of going to wait at the diner. Sighing, I reached through the throng to pull the resistant yellow string. Then I was stepping off the bus and onto a quieter street than I was used to—wide with small shops lining either side.

The bookstore was here somewhere, and I pulled the slip of paper out of my pocket to confirm the name.

Inkwell Stone should be along Howard Street. Cursing myself for not bringing a map, I continued straight, hoping I was heading the right direction and would come across the street. Howard street appeared after another block of walking and I turned down it, relieved when I spotted the shop.

The interior was dim and there was an off putting musty scent in the air that made me glad my book hadn't spent long at this location, but the man wearing thick glasses behind the counter was kind and clearly excited to show off the leatherbound volume he'd located for me.

It was expensive, and my palms were sweaty as I handed over the cash and accepted the brown paper bag with my treasure inside. This money could've gone to help Sarah with her expenses, but she'd been so angry with the elders and what they'd done to her that I didn't know if she'd accept money from them. I'd have to ask her about that, and try to find some way to help. She shouldn't have to work so much.

Lost to my thoughts, I headed back in the direction I'd come, but my surroundings quickly grew less familiar. The shops on either side of the street had started out vibrant, with clean windows and colourful store-fronts, but as I walked, they faded until the brown brick blended into each other. I stepped to avoid a puddle of spilled liquid, but jumped back into it when my path put me directly under a neon sign that was held up by a dangerously thin wire on one side.

Mourning the filth now saturating my shoes, I kicked to shake off the excess liquid.

A heavy hand fell to my shoulder, and two men stepped up on either side of me.

"Hey, man. So, like, what the fuck are you doing in our territory?"

SARAH

The pit of anxiety in my stomach quickly became a yawning chasm, and I grabbed my coat off the hook before running out the door. Stepping into the street, I managed to flag a taxi when it swerved to avoid hitting me. The driver glared and cursed, but he unlocked his back door anyway, and I hurriedly climbed in.

"Where to?" The cabbie's voice was rough and edged with irritability.

Numb, I moved in a haze, barely feeling my body. My mouth worked, and I was surprised to hear it come out calm and even as I told the cabbie the address.

I was anything but calm and even.

The short drive was too long, and horrifying scenarios swam in my mind.

The urgency in Adam's voice hadn't been normal. What could have happened? Adam wanted to see me because of David? It had been just over a week since he'd said he would get involved. Maybe he'd made good on his promise. Now something had happened to David, and I'd been too preoccupied assuming he'd skipped town to consider any other possibility. My mind was spinning as we pulled up to the familiar brown brick house.

I sprinted up the two stone stairs and swung open the door to find Adam waiting inside. He tapped his foot impatiently as if I'd taken my time getting here.

"Adam, what's happened?" I demanded in a shrill, panicked voice I barely recognized.

"First, you need to fess up. I gave you a job to do, and you blew me the fuck off. Now I find out David can change into a fucking tiger? You either did a shit fucking job or you've been lying to me." Adam was livid as he gestured around. What the hell had gotten him so worked up, and how the hell did he know David could change into a tiger?

Rage swam in my vision, and I glared up into Adam's face.

David would've only changed form if he'd been threatened in some way.

DAVID

Searing pain blossomed across my ribs, and I reeled back from the violent kick, slamming into the brick of the alley.

"So, you're with The Shades?"

The Shades? I had no idea what he was talking about, but when I tried to speak, the smaller man wearing an open leather jacket struck, his fist crunching my nose in a spray of blood that left my vision blurred.

"Fuckin' speak up." The sound of laughter reached me through the ringing in my ears, but before I could process what they were saying or try to get a word past my mangled lips, someone grabbed me and roughly threw me to the ground. My shoulder screamed as I collided with the concrete, but there was no moment to collect myself, no respite.

They were both on me, and it was all I could do to curl into a tight ball to protect myself. Metal. There was metal in their boots. Right at the tip. Stinging and splitting skin across my forearms until an involuntary spasm twitched me out of my position, and they laid into my ribs. One circled around back, lifting me and throwing me to the ground again before slamming that metal into my already screaming shoulder blade.

Pain took over, the sensation overwhelming everything until I detached from myself and floated away from the man lying in the alley, not able to get enough air or time between the blows to scream. The pain was still there, but now a rage grew and in the darkness of my mind, the animal part of me waited eagerly, a growl already in its throat.

Claws, fangs, more people coming, surrounding me, hurting me.

Roaring a challenge, fighting back.

My claws sinking deep into flesh and tearing.

A pitiful scream that filled me with satisfaction.

I drew away, but they kept coming.

They'd kill me. Growling, I fought my way back to my feet, adrenaline giving me the strength to force my battered limbs to obey.

They could try.

Someone came behind, a sharp pain in my head.

Then, nothing.

The cage I woke up in seemed to be part of a house, with a metal covered window and muffled voices through the hardwood floor, but it was too painful to look around properly. At least the cold floor soothed the pain in my back, and while I should've been ashamed to find myself naked and stretched out on a floor, the press of coldness directly against my injuries felt good.

A door opened somewhere behind me, and the noise was jarring enough that I pulled myself to sitting, biting back the accompanying groan.

You didn't show weakness in this situation.

The only card I had left to play was strength. Whoever these people were, I would face them down with a semblance of pride. A tall man entered the room, shutting the door behind him and turning, casting his face into the light.

"Hello, David."

Incredulous, I stared into the face of my roommate. He looked perfectly composed, flipping his beige coat over the chair opposite my cage.

The rising panic subsided when he took a seat, the animal part of me recognizing the vulnerability in his posture. Who was he really? More importantly, what did I even know about the man whose apartment I shared? He'd always seemed aloof. Quiet, kept to himself, and I'd been too preoccupied with Sarah to care much about seeking him out.

Apparently, that had been a mistake.

"So, you're some kind of tiger shifter?" he said matter-of-factly, but there was a question in his eyes that soothed the tension in my aching shoulders.

He might know something, but he didn't know everything.

The island was safe.

For now.

"Something like that." My voice came out unexpectedly gravelly, and I tried to clear it, only to wince at the biting pain in my jaw.

"Hm, interesting." He smiled and tilted his head, studying me like a specimen trapped in a test tube. But I refused to acknowledge my position or my nakedness before him. "It's a pity Sarah couldn't find out more."

Sarah. Alarmed, I struggled to process what he was saying. What could she have to do with any of this?

"Maybe if she'd had a little more time to get closer to you, but I guess you couldn't help showing your true colours." Adam's lip curled, but I barely processed the disgust dripping from his tone. "I thought she'd have you figured out after one date."

Sarah had been watching me? Trying to find out about me? *Spying* on me?

A pain deeper than anything that had been inflicted on me physically burned in my chest.

She'd been working for Adam the whole time. The sheer betrayal of it. She'd never been with me, never been mine.

She'd always been his.

As if knowing the blow he'd dealt, Adam smiled smugly and stood to exit the room.

I barely heard the click of the door when he shut it behind him.

SARAH

"Damnit, Adam, you tell me what happened. Is David all right? Where is he?" I demanded. The need to see David and confirm he was okay consumed me, and I clutched Adam's arm.

"You think you get to make demands? After you kept giving me the brush off about this guy?"

Anger unlike anything I'd ever known tinged my vision red, and I snarled into his face, realizing for the first time just how much stronger I was than my clan leader. My grip on his arm tightened. He tried to shrug me off, but failed.

"Let me the fuck go, Sarah."

"Not until you tell me what the hell happened." My words were barely audible through the clench of my teeth, but I knew Adam had heard me because he glared down at my insubordination. I'd never stood up to Adam in this way, but the thought of something terrible having happened to David made me desperate. I'd only just found him. I couldn't lose him again. The shock and possibility penetrated through the haze I'd been in, and tears clouded my eyes. I expected Adam to shout, to put me in my place, but his features softened, and he put a hand over mine.

"He's fine, Sarah. He's upstairs. He was wandering in The Bones' neighbourhood and he got jumped. I guess they didn't know what the hell he was either and thought someone was trying to horn in on their turf. They started wailing on him, and he changed into a *fucking tiger*. You know, you could've given us a warning, at least." When my only response was a glare, he continued, "Luckily, I had Tom trailing him. He saw the whole thing, but when he tried to step in to help—well, he got clawed up pretty badly. I don't know what he is, Sarah, but I do know he's dangerous. Damn dangerous. Tom needed twelve stitches in his arm. He's just lucky he managed to find a payphone and call for help, so we could knock that thing unconscious and bring it here."

That *thing*. I was livid imagining David cornered and fighting for his life. How *dare* Adam blame him for fighting back, for defending himself?

"So, Tom, a total stranger, jumped into a fight with a wounded tiger, and you expected David to, what? Somehow know he was there to help?" A knot of rage pounded in my chest until everything was red again, and Adam wasn't my friend anymore, wasn't on my side as he'd always been.

David would never intentionally hurt somebody.

"Take me to him," I said, my face going slack. I let the anger wash over and pass through me, leaving me cold and bitter. It wouldn't help the situation, and no matter what had happened, Adam had assured me that David was okay.

It was all that mattered.

He led me upstairs, the rickety old stairs creaking on each step. A gaggle of teens were lounging in the main room, laughing and chatting as we entered. But they quieted down when they saw us, whispering among themselves and peeking up at us curiously as we passed. I had no patience for them tonight, and I glared daggers in their direction, daring them to say anything. They blanched, busying themselves with the tabletop game. A girl with bleach blonde hair rolled a set of dice.

My heart clenched when I realized where we were going.

Adam led me to the furthest bedroom where we kept the cage.

The cage.

It was necessary to have a cage large enough to hold a person in case someone in the clan went berserk or if we needed to house a prisoner from a rival clan. We hadn't used it in the many years I'd been with the clan.

Metal bars sectioned off a bedroom, leaving a walking path and a hard-backed chair while a tight metal grating spanned the only window. A single floor lamp on the outside of the bars cast a dim light across the room, illuminating the cell's occupant.

David. There he was. Dark purple bruises stood out on every inch of skin I could see in the low light. That I could see as much as I could in the dim light was a testament to how bad it was. David wore no top but had on some old grey sweatpants I recognized as some of the donated clothing we kept on hand at headquarters.

He was turned away from me, hunched over at the far end of the cage, and it broke my heart anew. I couldn't tell if he was hunching over due to what must have been immense pain or if he was trying to avoid whoever was there to visit him.

Had they been interrogating him? My stomach turned. I'd been home like an idiot, assuming he'd left, not trusting he'd talk to me first, and he'd been here in hell with my own clan.

He'd needed me, and I hadn't been there for him the way I should've been.

The way he'd been there for me.

My eyes didn't leave David's huddled form as I spoke to Adam. "I need a few minutes alone with him." I was expecting David to turn at the sound of my voice, to know I was in the room and acknowledge my presence, but he only curled further into himself in a protective gesture that broke my heart.

"Sarah, I really don't think it's a good idea for you to go in there with him. What if he freaks out again? He's dangerous."

David stiffened, and my heart twisted painfully. My hand shot out to grip the iron bar the way I wanted to grip his hand.

"He's not dangerous to *me*, Adam, now give me the goddamn key," I hissed.

Adam sighed and dug out a rusty gold key from his pocket.

"Just be careful and keep your distance. Don't forget to close the door behind you." He glanced pointedly at David before taking his leave.

"David...?" I called out, keeping my voice low so as not to startle him. I didn't know what he'd been through, and while I liked to believe my clan mates had treated him decently since bringing him back here, I shuddered to think how many of the hideous bruises covering his body had been inflicted by them. Then there was the way Adam had alluded to an interrogation of some sort. Bile threatened to rise in my throat, and I fumbled to get the key in the lock, my shaking hands finally clicking it open after a few clumsy attempts.

"Are you okay?" I asked, gently pulling the squealing cage door open enough to admit me before begrudgingly closing it. Fuck Adam and his orders, but I had to do what he wanted for now if I had any hope of seeing David released. My instinct was to rush over to him, but something about the way he sat stiffly turned away had me cautiously approaching, stepping softly on the hardwood.

"Stay away from me," he growled, keeping his back turned. I had never heard him take an angry tone, and it worried me all the more.

"David, please, are you all right?" The fear and anxiety leaked into my voice. Bruises riddled his back. They wrapped around his torso, concentrated at his sides like he'd been kicked while on the ground. There were lacerations across his shoulder blades where the force had been strong enough to split the skin.

My breath hitched. He needed ice packs and bandages. Disappointment burned in my chest. My clan hadn't provided him with the most basic of medical care. But then it made sense when I thought of Adam's face and the way he'd told me to stay away from David.

They were scared. It didn't excuse their behaviour, but Adam wasn't a cruel man. David's silence stretched until I couldn't stand it anymore.

"Please, will you talk to me?" I sat cross-legged on the hard floor beside him and placed my hand gently on his shoulder. I was afraid that even my hand placed lightly there would be painful, but I needed to touch him—to connect to him.

His silence cut like a knife, crueller than any words.

"I said to stay away from me," he growled and I saw the slit of an eye peek out at me over his shoulder before he shrugged away my hand. "I'm an animal, remember?" His voice was harsh, and he turned himself further away from me.

"You're not an animal. Adam just—well, he doesn't understand."

David stayed quiet.

"I'm not scared of you. I'll never be scared of you," I whispered softly, reaching out a hand to hover over his shoulder. My eyes burned, and a lump formed in my throat.

"Was I a joke to you?" His voice was deadly cold, tension emanating from the stiffness of his figure.

"What are you talking about?" Frowning, I fumbled for his mind, but came up against the same walls that had baffled me when we first met.

"Adam told me everything. How he asked you to spy on me. How he set us up on a date so you could 'figure me out.'"

Pain and betrayal laced his words, and it felt like a knife twisted into my gut. I was so taken aback that I didn't know what to say. The air between us was thick with anticipation.

"A joke? Doing Adam's bidding. Is that really what you think?" My mind struggled to process what he'd said, and I couldn't keep the strain from my voice. And then I was crying, the tears pouring from me, releasing all the emotion that had been churning inside for the past few days. It was all too much. The dream, my past, and now the way David looked at me. He peered over his shoulder before turning away, and I fought to bring myself under control.

I hadn't meant to cry like this. To break. He had a right to ask questions, because I *had* met him in service to the clan. Everything Adam had told him was true, but he'd left out so much, and the words burned in my throat.

"David," I began quietly, cautiously resting my palm on his battered back. He allowed the touch, and I relaxed into it. The contact with his skin, providing some connection between us, helped.

"Adam asked me to go on a date with his new roommate because he was worried you could be a threat to us. I didn't know you then. He's my clan leader, so yes, I agreed. Then I met you, and none of that mattered." I gently stroked his back with my thumb, keeping my touch light. "Are you okay? Really? You look awful. Those bruises look so nasty. Is anything broken? I know Adam wouldn't take you to a hospital." I was rambling, but I couldn't stop. That energy, the fear and worry, was overwhelming me with a need to do anything, say anything, to make things better.

The muscles beneath my hand softened, and he turned to look at me, his eyes questing across my tear-stained face. I gently took his large hand in mine, unfolding his long fingers and pressing his hand to my cheek. I turned to tenderly kiss his palm the way he had done the night before. He studied me, his expression cautious.

"You're not here for Adam. He didn't ask you to question me?"

I laughed, a tear breaking loose and sliding down my cheek. "Of course not."

He turned more to look at me, stiffening as he did so—his face a mask of pain. He studied me with those heartbreakingly beautiful blue eyes of his, and I welcomed it.

"But when we first met, you were watching me? For them? For *him*?"

Flinching at his words, I stared down at my folded hands.

"I was, and I'm sorry. Adam is protective of the clan, and he asked me to help. To try to feel what type of creature you were and whether you might be a threat."

"And did you tell him what I am?" There was a tightness in his voice.

I swallowed around the ball of emotions lodged in my throat. "No. I'd never tell him. It's your secret to share. This wasn't—the clan wasn't"—his eyes shot to mine, and I quickly amended my speech—"isn't why I continued to see you." Letting out a shuddering breath, I faced him head on. "You told me you loved me last night. Well, I-I love you, too."

His eyes dropped, but not before I'd seen the shock in them.

The hope.

"Are you okay? Will you please talk to me?"

"I'll be alright," he said, studying my face for an answer to the unspoken question.

"Thank god," I said with relief.

"You're not here for them. You're sure?"

I wanted to scream, but I deserved this, because he'd had to learn I was Adam's spy from Adam and not from me. It should've been from me. I could've reassured him and explained about the clans of Boston and how they were in a delicate balance. If I'd done that and he'd known, maybe he would've been more cautious wandering around. Maybe this wouldn't have happened. I opened my mind to him and felt him reach out to brush against it. It was only a heartbeat, but I put every ounce of love and worry into the contact.

"I'm sure. I was sure the moment I met you," I echoed his words from last night, my watery eyes meeting his. He'd been the one so certain of me, of us before, and now it was my turn. David seemed to have found his answer, and I saw the trace of his usual smile tug at the corners of his mouth, though his swollen bottom lip marred the image.

"Can I get you some clothes, or what can I do for you?" I said in a rush. Nervous energy filled me with the need to be helpful.

He smiled and looked down before meeting my gaze with a twinkle of amusement in his sapphire eyes. "I'm feeling much better all of a sudden."

I smiled shyly, moving cautiously closer to him, relieved when he didn't pull away. I touched my lips lightly to his, as light as a feather, though I so badly wanted to press myself against him. The warmth of his lips was a balm after the events of tonight, and I touched my forehead to his, feeling the comfort of his mind relaxing into mine. No longer closed off and cold, opening to me. He was okay, and we were together.

"I thought maybe you'd left," I whispered, needing to speak the words aloud. I opened my eyes to stare at him, our faces inches apart.

He frowned. "Why would you think that?" He reached up to cup my cheek, his thumb skating across my cheekbone.

I shrugged, looking away. "I don't know. Last night was pretty intense. I thought maybe you'd changed your mind."

He leaned in to kiss me more deeply than I had dared, pressing the swell of his injured lip against mine.

"I would never leave you and no, I did not 'change my mind,'" he said, his lips brushing against mine with every word. He was topless, and now that I knew he was okay, I was aware of just how much of his skin was exposed. The need to taste him, to drink him in and bask in our togetherness, was overwhelming, and we turned towards each other at the same time.

His mouth was hot against mine, his kisses growing ever more insistent. I welcomed it, but he pulled away, gasping in pain with a hand pressed to his ribs. Shock slackened my jaw.

"David? Oh shit, are you okay?"

Eyes squeezed shut, he didn't answer me right away. All I could do was watch helplessly as he worked through the pain, his eyes squeezed shut and his mind barred to me as he dealt with it.

"Yeah, sorry. I think so. Everything's just a bit painful right now." His voice was a raspy gasp, and I watched him with worry as he failed to take a full breath.

"I'm so sorry this happened. Is there something I can do for you? Anything?" And I would do anything. If I could take the pain from him and suffer it myself, I would.

"Yes, actually, there is something you can do. It's something ancients can do for themselves and each other. I would do it for myself, but I'm too weak."

"Okay. What is it?"

"Well, ancients can heal each other." I balked, sitting back on my tailbone. "It's not as complicated as it sounds. It's more like a transfer of energy where you speed up the person's own healing process."

"What do I do?" I held my hands out to him. Being able to heal someone seemed beyond anything I had imagined myself capable of, but I hadn't thought I could turn into a tiger either. It had been David who had shown me it was possible, and now he watched me with the same steady gaze. I let his confidence sink into me and banish the tension collecting between my shoulder blades.

If he said I could do this, I believed him.

"First, you need to touch the injury and feel it with your mind." He took my hand and placed it against the left side of his ribs. The muscles beneath my hand knotted with tension at each shallow breath, but I couldn't help shivering at the heat of his body, his closeness. Even now, when I could barely think straight for worrying, I wanted him.

"It helps to close your eyes." My eyes drifted shut, and he was right. With them closed, my mind was easier to focus. "Can you feel it?"

Using the touch of my hand to guide where to focus, I reached out with my mind, like I was trying to connect with another mind.

Reaching out was easier than it had been, the muscle of my mind strengthening as I used it more. I turned my attention to the injury, applying some pressure through my palm as I tried to feel it through my mind. David winced, and I froze, but his hand covered mine.

"No, don't pull away. You're doing great. Don't move your hand from the spot. Use it to focus your mind until you can sense something wrong there." Swallowing hard, I tried again, feeling with my mind and making an effort to keep my hand still where David had caged it against his ribs.

"Something doesn't feel right there? Feel that with your mind, how wrong it is."

Frowning, I reached back out.

A wrongness. I could feel it, and as soon as I did, I was shocked that I hadn't been able to before. David's ribs pulsed with pain beneath my palm. They were damaged, and I could tell they weren't as they should be.

I opened my eyes to find him watching my face. He nodded.

"Yes, you can feel it. Next, pour your energy into it."

Reaching out with my mind, I gently prodded, this time mentally, but I didn't know how to pour my energy into the site like David had said. All I knew was that I wanted to help, and I poured that feeling, that need to fix the wrongness, into the place where I could sense it. Something moved from my hand to his ribs, and I pushed harder, feeling the flow more clearly now.

David let out a sharp gasp of pain, and I startled, breaking the connection in an instant and snatching my hand away from his heaving ribs. His eyes were screwed shut again, and my hands hovered over him, not sure where I could safely touch or what I should do.

Shit.

"Are you okay? Did I do something wrong?" What a fool I'd been to think I could do this—I'd injured him further.

"I'm fine, Sarah. Sorry, I forgot to tell you. Healing isn't—well, it isn't pretty. You speed up someone's healing at the site, and all the little tiny things that happen while we're slowly healing happen all at once. It's an extremely painful experience. It's worse than the injury, and this one's pretty bad. I wasn't prepared for how painful it would be, is all. You did nothing wrong." He closed his eyes tightly and braced himself, white knuckling his knee with one hand and placing his other over mine to hold it to his ribs. "I'm ready now."

I struggled to believe him. But the sight of him ready for a shock of pain broke my heart, and I called his name gently, leaning forward to press a kiss to the tight line of his lips. As I did so, I could feel his swollen lip. The wrongness of it, and I slowly transferred my energy there as we kissed, pulling back to survey my efforts once the feeling faded.

Much better. His lip looked much better. Surprise registered in his eyes. It was my turn to comfort him, to help him. I laid my hand on his cheek and whispered, "It's okay."

I'd healed him, and he hadn't reacted as violently as he had when I'd worked on his ribs. His eyes were hooded as he looked into mine. I went up on my knees to his cheekbone, sure I'd seen a bruise there. Kissing the spot, I sent my energy there before moving across his face, kissing and healing as I moved.

"Sarah." His name reached me on a whimper even as his arms came up to wrap around me gently. I stiffened, but I could detect no pain in his tone, only a longing that set my heart racing.

"Lay back," I breathed against his neck. He pulled back to look at me questioningly, but obeyed, wincing as he did. I offered my hand and helped ease him down until he lay flat. Laying down beside him, I kissed his shoulder, transferring more energy to the joint before moving down his body and trailing kisses and transferring energy with each one.

He shivered as I went, though from pleasure or pain, I wasn't sure. I only hoped it was from pleasure. There were so many painfully wrong places across his body, and I could hardly stand how much there was to do. How hurt he was. I moved my mouth to his ribs. They really did look awful, with blue-black bruising throughout. At least one rib was cracked. No, two. It was two ribs that were cracked.

I gently took his hand in mine, feeling him brace himself as I did so. I kissed the area, gently transferring a small amount of energy to see how he would react. I didn't pour it into him the way I'd done before, and his reaction was much better this time. A bit of a sharp breath, but nothing like the terrible gasp of pain from earlier. I continued, gently kissing and transferring more energy. After a few more kisses, I moved back to his face, claiming his lips. His hand came up to cup my face.

My hand snaked down to find the place at his ribs where the wrongness was worse. This time I stayed with my lips pressed against his, letting my tongue slip into his mouth to taste him, and when he moaned against me, I focused on his ribs again. I transferred much less than I had done the first time. Still, he grunted with pain, and I winced at the sound, pressing my lips more insistently against his, parting my mouth so that our hot breath could mingle.

The goal had been to distract him, but the more I tasted him, the harder it was to concentrate. Forgetting myself, I accidentally pushed my palm against the spot where I was working, and he lurched forward in pain. He was back in a sitting position, hunched over, clutching his sides.

"Oh David, I'm so sorry. I just—I'm sorry. I got carried away."

"It's fine." His voice was filled with pain, but he looked up to give me a slow smile that melted my heart, his eyes twinkling with amusement.

"I've never been healed quite like that."

"Well, I thought it might be a good distraction for you." I looked away shyly, hoping I hadn't offended him by taking the healing process and changing the way it was done.

"A distraction?" He chuckled before gasping and leaning forward, a hand clamped to his left side.

I was there in an instant, my hand lightly on top of his as he worked through the pain.

"I really will be okay, Sarah. Last night shouldn't have happened. I lost control. Adam was right, I am dangerous. I lashed out. This is my fault as much as it's anyone's, and I deserve to be punished." He turned his face away from mine as he spoke, as if lost in his thoughts. I could feel how troubled his mind was, and I rested my other hand gently on his back to provide some comfort.

"David, you were attacked. You were just defending yourself."

"Maybe at first Sarah, but"—he looked at me with hollow eyes—"the animal instincts can take control sometimes. I panicked when they had me down on the ground. I was so crazed and wild that I think I would've attacked anyone. Maybe even you." His voice was harsh. Unforgiving.

"No, you wouldn't have."

"Yes, I would have, and I did hurt someone badly. I remember that." He shuddered, and I knew without connecting to his mind that he was remembering the flare of satisfaction he'd felt when he'd torn into the person reaching for him.

"You hurt someone, David. You didn't kill anyone, and maybe you couldn't tell friend from foe in that moment, but I know you and I know that you wouldn't mean to hurt anyone." I took his hand in mine and held it to my cheek. He watched me the whole time. I went on my knees and gently touched my forehead to his, closing my eyes and reaching out with my mind towards him.

The deep shame he carried for what he'd done nearly rendered my heart in two. Hurting another person was so against who he was at his core. He was a protector, someone who felt he was meant to help others, never harm them. Especially those weaker than him. Tears slid down my cheek as the sorrow in his heart overwhelmed me. His fingers followed the path of a stray crimson curl, and I marvelled at the comfort it brought him, the way it calmed the chaos of his mind. Closing my eyes, I silently urged him to continue.

He had concluded his memory of the attack, and of what Adam had said about me. He'd been devastated. He shuddered against me, his body trembling in my grip.

"It's okay. You know what he said wasn't true. You know that," I insisted gently. He must know that. It hurt to think of him here in such terrible pain, thinking he was some kind of clan obligation to me. "You know I love you." I leaned forward to press a kiss to his lips.

Nodding, he breathed in a shaky breath and worked to calm himself, his fingers tangling in my hair. He looked up at me, and I took his hand, holding it to my cheek and opening my mind to remind him of how I felt for him. How deeply he affected me. How I always wanted to be near him. How happy he made me feel when we were together. I could feel my emotions wash over him like a balm to the mental anguish he'd felt on hearing I was a spy.

"Okay?" I asked him gently, searching his face.

He nodded, looking up at me cautiously. I wrapped my arms around his neck, going up on my knees in front of him.

"What happened wasn't your fault." He let out a sharp breath and looked away. "No, David. Listen to me." I took his hands in mine. "You were hurt, trapped, and alone. No one should have approached you in that state. They could have kept their distance, but they chose to try to take you back with them. You didn't mean to hurt anyone." I implored him to believe me, taking both his hands and squeezing them.

"But I did hurt someone, Sarah. Badly." He looked away, and he hadn't said it, but I could feel he was thinking about his danger to me.

"Hey," I said, twisting to meet his averted gaze. "You could never hurt me. Never." I was sure of it. He'd die before hurting me.

We stared at each other, and I shared my conviction with him mentally. Steadying himself, he blew out a breath and nodded, his eyes clearer.

The door swung open with a bang, startling us both, and we jumped apart as Adam stepped in, clearly agitated.

"Sarah, I need to talk to you. Alone," he said, giving me a meaningful look.

David stiffened beside me, and I squeezed his hand reassuringly.

"I'll be right back," I whispered, kissing him quickly on the cheek before standing and moving to follow Adam. Scowling, he held the cage door open for me before slamming it closed the moment I was through and locking it with one quick movement. He glared at David.

Adam led me to another room furnished with some couches and chairs. He had to shoo away a couple who was using it to make out.

"What'd you find out?" he demanded, staring hard at me.

"I'm not your spy, Adam. I didn't 'find out' anything, except how terribly you treat your prisoners."

"Treat *him* terribly? *Him*? Like he's the victim? He almost tore Tom's arm off, and I'm supposed to, what? Put him up here so he can have a rest until he feels well enough to try again? That guy is a killer. I saw it in him."

Spittle flew as he shouted. A few droplets landed on my cheek, but I didn't step back. Not this time.

"He was hurt and scared, and you sent people out to capture him? Do you get how incredibly careless and stupid that was? He would never hurt anyone who he didn't think was trying to hurt him. How the hell was he supposed to know you were there to help?" I shouted back.

"Bah!" Adam threw up his hands and took two paces across the room to stare out the window at the street below. All those humans, all this territory to protect. There were so many people depending on him. It was a reminder of the burden he shouldered. Not just to protect the clan, but to ensure the humans in our territory were kept safe from us. It was Adam who went out on every hunt to supervise as much to assist.

"I have to think about what to do," he muttered, more to himself than me as he leaned against the window frame thoughtfully. He left without slamming the door, and I hurried back to the room where they kept David.

His eyes lifted to mine as I entered.

"Hey," I said as I quietly closed the door behind me. Adam had left the key hanging on a small brass hook by the door, and I quickly unlocked the cage to go inside, not wanting David to think I feared him again.

"What happens now?" he asked wearily as I sat cross-legged in front of him. I looked off into the room, my brows furrowed in thought. "I'm not sure even Adam knows. He asked me to tell him what you are. I want you to know that I refused. It's your story to tell, not mine."

"But it is yours, too, Sarah. It's our story and our history."

I shook my head, meeting his eyes. "It's your story to tell him if and when you are ready. Will telling Adam help him trust you and release you? I don't know. What I do know is that Adam is a good person. I came to this city as a runaway, and he took me in—saved me from a bad situation. The clan took care of me. I owe them my life. They aren't aggressive, and they don't go looking for a fight. They keep to their territory and defend it from other clans. Adam set me up on that date with you because he was worried about the clan. He didn't do it to be malicious. He was worried you could be a threat to them. He's not bad, David, he's just protective." I smirked. "You're alike in that way. Unfortunately, you've just proved to him you *are* a danger to the clan. I'm not sure what his next move is, but I know you make him nervous."

David turned to look at the door, but when he did so, his hand shot to his side, and he winced.

"Are you feeling up to a bit more healing?" I asked him gently.

He nodded. "Yes, please." He pulled me in closer and touched our foreheads together lightly, elevating our connection.

I kissed the tip of his nose and moved my hand back to his ribs. Despite all my efforts earlier, his ribs still throbbed with wrongness. I sent a little pulse of energy into the area while tipping my chin to kiss him as I had done before. He seemed to be much less stiff than earlier. He must be worried about what would happen next, but I wanted him to know that I was there with him no matter what it was.

Adam came into the room, and we didn't spring apart this time. Let him see us together as a unit, I reasoned, scooting over to position myself at David's side. I looked questioningly at David, who nodded. Standing, I offered David my arm, but he denied it. Although I could feel the pain in his mind, he struggled to his feet before laying an arm across my shoulder and leaning heavily into me.

Adam sized him up, and David stared back, unblinking. Adam sighed before looking away.

"All right," he began. "Here's the deal. I need to know what the hell kind of creature you are. I don't know anything that can change into a tiger, and I need to know what we're dealing with. That's step one."

David stared at him a moment before looking at me. His blue eyes studied me carefully before he responded. "Okay," he said, his gaze fixed on me. He turned back to Adam. "It's a long story, and I need to know that it stays with you."

"Agreed." Adam uncrossed his arms to let them hang at his sides in a more relaxed posture, but I didn't miss the way his critical gaze flicked over to me, taking in the way I held David's arm draped across my shoulder.

David explained the history of the ancients much the same way he had explained it to me. Adam wouldn't be able to see the images I had seen in my head, but David told the story well, and Adam didn't interrupt him once to ask questions. He stared at David stone-faced the entire time he spoke, giving nothing away.

"And you? You're one of these ancients?" he asked when David had finished.

"Yes," he answered. I was getting worried that he wouldn't have the strength to stand much longer. He had been upright for over a minute and the longer he spoke, the more I could feel a deep-seated fatigue in his mind.

"You're a vampire, a shapeshifter, and a witch?" Adam exclaimed, his bright eyes betraying a glint of eagerness as he looked David over.

David nodded.

Adam paced the space outside of the cage, ignoring us before turning sharply to address David.

"Okay, here's what's going to happen. You're going to join our clan." Adam grinned, and I swear I'd never seen him so happy. The sight made me sick. "Once you've joined, then we'll know you're with us and not against us. We'll feel comfortable letting you loose because you'll be one of ours." He spoke quickly, with a hint of excitement.

But David watched him coldly.

"I won't fight for you, Adam, and I won't join your clan. It goes against who I am. My people are peaceful. We do not condone violence, despite what you may think of me after last night. I've told you what I am, as you asked. The agreement was that once you knew, I would be free to go."

Adam smiled without an ounce of warmth. "I said that was step one. Step two is joining the clan. If you agree to that, I'll let you go. If not, you can stay here and rot. We're perfectly willing to keep you contained and off the streets for as long as necessary."

As long as necessary. Adam's words sent a shiver down my spine.

David returned the mirthless smile, and I saw a dangerous glint in his eye as he replied. "Knowing what I am, Adam, do you really think you'll be able to keep me locked up?"

Adam laughed, and this time there was genuine amusement in it.

"That's fair, David. Maybe I can't keep you here, and maybe I can't control you, but I know what you want..." He looked pointedly at me.

David's face blanched.

"You want to get involved with a member of my clan, and that is forbidden. No member of my clan is allowed to 'date' any member of another clan, and you, my friend, are an outsider."

I looked at Adam in horror. How could he invoke that rule for David when he was clearly *not* the member of a rival clan? He was intentionally unattached. It was a cruel thing to use me against him in this way, and I glared into Adam's smirking face.

Bastard.

David studied my reaction, looking at me for an answer. I shook my head.

"No, David, you don't have to do this. He's just trying to twist your arm. He can't decide that."

"All right, all right." Adam held up his hands with the palms out.

"Join the clan, David, and I swear to you right here, right now, that I won't ask you to fight for us. I won't ask you to take territory, or fight in some random bar fight. You won't have to do any of that. What I will ask is that you protect us, protect *your* clan, if we're attacked. If we are protecting ourselves, you will help defend us."

David watched Adam closely. He was considering it, mulling over the deal in his mind.

Adam sighed, holding up a hand. "Look, Sarah is a member of our clan. She'll always be a member of our clan, and if we were attacked, she'd be with us. She'd be in just as much danger as any of us. If we were under attack, could you really stand aside and not help? Wouldn't you want to defend her? That's all I'm asking you to do. The rival clans already know you're a tiger shifter. No one would dare fuck with us."

David glanced at me, and I frowned at what I saw in his expression. He would fight for me if I was in trouble, but to commit himself to the clan? I shook my head, but couldn't dispute what Adam had said.

If the clan were attacked, I'd be called in to protect us and be put in danger. But David. Violence was something he wanted to avoid at all costs, and the thought of him being used as a weapon was sickening. Still, I knew Adam, and I knew that he truly wanted to protect the clan. If he gave David his word, maybe he would only use him defensively.

It still left a bitterness in my mouth when David muttered his agreement. A friendly smile spread across Adam's face.

"Excellent. Good decision, buddy." The last word didn't reach Adam's eyes, and I felt the threat in it. He was a friend, or he was an enemy. There was no in between.

There never had been.

"In that case, you're free to go. We'll wait until you're well enough before we perform the initiation ritual. I'll call a cab to meet you out front." Grinning, Adam gestured towards the door as though we were great friends, and he hadn't threatened to keep David prisoner indefinitely a few minutes ago.

It was slow going as I helped David to take painful, shuffling steps down the hallway. He leaned on me, but he made an effort to walk as independently as possible. I could sense his desire to appear dignified in front of anyone we passed.

We passed a group of clan members in the common room. They all grew quiet, watching as we made our way across the room. We were just passing a spare bedroom when David stopped short and turned towards the door.

"What's wrong?" I asked, filled with confusion at his sudden pause and the strange way he cocked his head at the door as though listening.

"I need to do something," he said, staring at the peeling white wood of the door.

"It won't take long," he promised, giving me a reassuring look, but all I could see was how haggard his face was from the brief amount of walking we'd done.

He quietly turned the knob and pulled open the creaking door. Inside, a dark-skinned teen with a bandaged arm was lounging on a second-hand loveseat talking with one of his buddies. I hadn't met the kid, but by the injury to his arm, he must be Tom.

I understood in an instant and reached out to grab David's arm.

"No, David. You don't have to do this now." But I wasn't willing to hold David's arm properly lest I cause him more pain, and he slipped out of my grip to approach Tom on his own.

"I'm truly sorry for what I did to you." Regret filled David's voice. Tom was on his feet in an instant. A look of fear fixed on his face as he glanced between David, his friend, and me, his body riddled with tension. Maybe he would've bolted, but David blocked the narrow doorway.

"Please," he said, gesturing to Tom's arm. "I can help."

Tom considered David for a long moment before realizing there was no way past, and it was easier to give in to his request. He cautiously approached, extending his ebony arm into David's waiting hands. Gratefully, David took the bandaged limb in both hands.

"This will be painful," he warned, and Tom nodded, understanding passing between them.

Then David began to heal him. Tom was a big kid with a sleeve of tats on his opposite arm. I prayed he could tolerate the pain well enough to allow David to complete the healing process.

Tom grunted in pain as David worked, but I was relieved when he didn't pull away. The process lasted maybe a minute before David withdrew his hands, swaying on his feet. I almost moved forward to help him, but he held up a hand for me to stay where I was.

"I'm deeply sorry, Tom. I know now that you were just trying to help me. Please forgive me for what I did. I'm too weak to heal you anymore right now, but it shouldn't hurt as much. Come see me in a day or so, after I've rested, and I can finish."

Tom nodded, pulling his arm towards his body protectively and tentatively flexed his hand. Something passed unspoken between them. David nodded and headed back towards the door. He walked on his own until we closed the door behind us, and he all but fell into my side, breathing heavily.

"David!" Alarmed, I stumbled, struggling to take on his weight.

"I'm okay, Sarah. It just took a lot out of me to do that right now."

"Well then, maybe you should have waited! You're injured too, you know!" I hissed as I secured his arm across my shoulder and gained the leverage I needed to better support him.

"That man was suffering. It wasn't fair to leave him in that agony. I needed to help."

Sighing at the impossibility of protecting David from himself, I focused on getting us out of the building, of helping David down the hallway. The stairs were tricky, and I was sure that the cab driver might refuse us entry given David's lack of shoes, but he either didn't notice or didn't care. I suspected that David's bloodied appearance may have shocked him into silence. I passed him an extra five dollars in thanks as we climbed our way out of the vehicle.

Getting David into his apartment was harder, his energy flagging as we went up the stone steps, but after several stops to rest, I got him inside.

Once I lowered him into the bed, I headed to the kitchen, locating a bag of blood with no label and emptying it into a bowl before hurrying back and shoving it into his hands.

"You need to keep your strength up," I insisted, sitting at the edge of the bed to make sure he ate.

He ate, and I waited to take the bowl so he could settle down and sleep. I knew I could go home now and he would be okay, but I hadn't really considered how hard it would be to be apart from him after everything that had happened. Standing over his bed, not sure what to do, a wave of exhaustion struck me and my legs gave way. I caught myself on his small nightstand, nearly tipping the small lamp over.

"Whoa, Sarah, watch out!" David said, pulling himself to a sitting position. He paid for it, squeezing his eyes shut.

"Sorry, I just felt so tired all of a sudden." Even my voice sounded weak. The sensation of it was so strange. I'd felt fine a moment ago, but now I could barely hold myself upright.

"It's the healing. You pushed yourself too hard. You gave me a lot of your energy and it's catching up to you," he explained tiredly. "Come lie down." He patted the bed beside him.

Using the edge of the bed to support myself, I slowly made my way over to him. My limbs were like jelly, and it took me a while, but at last I crawled in bed beside him, beyond caring that I was fully dressed. Curling into his shoulder, I basked in the peace I found in his mind. His hand came up to rest on mine.

His scent was home to me. Exhausted emotionally and physically from the night's events, a part of me struggled to be awake a little longer, to enjoy our closeness for as long as possible before sleep took me. But I never slept so well as I did when I was near him, and eventually the sound of his deep breathing lulled me to sleep.

CHAPTER 9

I awoke the next morning to the delicious sensation of David tracing comforting circles on my back, his fingers gliding over the thin fabric of my old T-shirt. Eager for his warmth, I curled groggily into his broad chest. He gasped in pain, and I withdrew hurriedly. It was all I could do to run a comforting hand lightly across the spot I had intended to occupy.

"Sorry," I murmured, my voice thick with sleep. Yawning, I pulled back to prop myself up on an elbow. He watched me, his beautiful eyes roving my face hungrily. I liked how he studied me, like the time spent asleep had made him eager for the sight of me. To be loved, so cared for, was new and a flush crept up on my neck.

Our minds joined, and the tenderness I found within our connection filled me with warmth. He reached out to cup my cheek, and I nestled into his palm, savouring the extra layer of contact before reaching forward to lightly press my mouth to his, careful to avoid applying too much pressure on his lip.

The swelling was down, but not by much. I'd get to healing it later, but for now, I lost myself in the taste of him, and the sweet glide of his tongue against mine. Breath stolen, I shuddered at the need he so effortlessly drew out of me.

"Good morning." My voice came out in a whisper.

"Good morning," he replied groggily before closing his eyes and laying his head back into the pillow. "How are you doing with everything? It's been quite a few days."

"Yeah, that's one way to put it." Only two days ago I'd thought myself a vampire, the product of a family who hunted and killed humans for sport. I'd been in love with a man who I didn't know a thing about, and now.

I rested my head lightly on his arm, feeling for any tension in his body that would suggest I was hurting him. I wanted more closeness, to lie across him until every inch of me was touching him, but I settled for letting my hand drift across his chest. The knit blanket he used had been dislodged in the night, leaving him exposed for me to see, and I studied the dark bruises snaking across his torso. It was physically painful to look at them, but while there were enough purple-black blotches to make me wince, the area was less angry and swollen.

Done with my assessment of his health, my mind turned to other thoughts and my hand ventured lower to skate across the subtle definition of his abs. His body laid out before me was perfectly sculpted. Not heavily muscled, but lean and lithe. My breath caught as the beauty of him overwhelmed me. The night before, I had been so worried that I'd barely processed his nakedness. Making sure he was all right had been all I'd cared about.

But now.

I couldn't stop staring, and while I knew David wasn't well enough for the way I wanted to climb on top of him and ride him until we were both writhing with pleasure, my hand drifted lower of its own accord. His breathing stuttered when I reached the blanket, and the sound was so pathetically shallow that I yanked my hand away, curling my fingers into his chest.

Not now.

Not like this.

There would be time for that later when he was well. What he needed now was rest and care. I beat back that part of me that tried to resist, that wanted to kiss him until all thought was gone.

I needed a distraction before I gave in to those urges, and demanded something he was in no shape to give.

"David?"

"Hm?" That voice. A shudder tore through me and goose bumps bloomed across my bare arms. I needed him to talk to me, to tell me more about the mystery island I'd dreamed of for so many years, but mostly I needed to distract myself from how badly I wanted to strip his blanket away and trail my tongue across his broad chest, to explore every delicious inch of him.

The taste of his skin would be divine. There was no question. I hooked a leg over his, needing the pressure of his thigh against my aching cunt. I had to stop thinking about David's body and all the things I wanted to do with him physically.

Luckily, there was a lot to talk about.

The island. That mysterious land where I'd been born and raised. I wanted to know about it, about him, and I frowned as I realized how much of our conversation had centered on my life and what I'd been like. He'd grown up there, too, and the need to know every detail of his past consumed me.

What had his family been like? What kind of school had there been in a place where they wore plants for clothing? Then there was us and how close he said we'd been as kids. David had told me children weren't common, but in a large enough community, surely there were others. The questions burst out of me in a flood I had no hope of stemming.

"What was it like growing up on the island? Were there any other kids there?"

"Yes, there were two others. Both younger than us and more like little siblings. It was often just you and I, but we played with them, too." He sighed, and I tried to follow the movement so as not to put pressure on his arm. "You wouldn't remember them, but their names were Stewart and Susanna." He quirked an eyebrow at me, and I flinched at the hopeful look in his brilliant blue eyes. "Anything?"

Stewart and Susanna. If they were like little siblings to the two of us, you'd think I'd remember them. Then again, I couldn't remember my own parents. There was nothing but a black cloud in my mind where those memories should be, and the names did nothing to clear it.

"No, sorry."

He patted my hand comfortingly.

"It's okay. Not your fault."

Maybe it wasn't my fault, but it was hard knowing we had so many shared memories that were lost to me. Sighing, I pressed a kiss to his shoulder, letting my lips linger against his skin. At least knowing about Stewart and Susanna helped me to imagine what life on the island had been like. Had they tagged along with us when we went running through the trails?

"What were your parents like?" A prick of pain pierced through his mind, and he pulled away, but not before I sensed a well of deep hurt. Alarmed, I propped myself up to lay a gentle hand on his arm, studying his face and the clench of his jaw.

Without the ability to see into his mind, it was all I could do to wait for him to speak. His eyes remained fixed on the ceiling, his face giving no indication as to what he was thinking, though I could feel the waves of pain barely hidden behind his barriers. At last, he spoke in a hushed tone laced with misery.

"My parents died when I was five."

My hand froze on his arm. They'd died on the island where people lived for thousands of years? Frowning, I studied his face. I'd been able to heal his injuries, terrible as they'd been. What had happened that both of his parents had been beyond saving? I'd been lamenting the loss of my childhood memories, but at least I'd had parents through my early years.

"What happened? I understand if it's too painful, but—" I twined my fingers with his. His fingers settled against mine gratefully. "I'm here if you want to talk about it."

He swallowed hard, his eyes still fixed on the ceiling for so long I thought he wasn't ready to share, but then he spoke.

"We're not immortal. I know you just learned about the way we can heal, but it's not—We're not..." He sighed and winced at the motion of his chest, pausing to wheeze in a few breaths before continuing, "We can heal many terrible wounds, but not head wounds." He frowned, his eyebrows knitting together. "The brain doesn't. Well, it needs to heal on its own. It's forbidden to heal a head injury. My father had an accident. He fell scaling a cliff and hit his head on the stones below." He paused a long moment before whispering, "It was two days before he died."

Two days of waiting and hoping only for his father to die.

Two days of watching him fade. I stared at him in horror. But he'd had two parents, and if his father had died so tragically, that didn't explain how he was orphaned.

"And your mother?" My voice came out in a squeak, and I cleared my throat to settle it.

He tilted his head towards me, and the pain I saw in his eyes was heartbreaking. It made me want to reach across time.

"If an ancient dies…Well, we have a way to bring them back from the dead. There have only been a few times in our history when it's worked. They tried to bring my father back and when they failed—my mother couldn't take it. She took her own life." There was a bitterness in his tone that squeezed my heart.

She'd left him.

His unspoken words hung in the air between us, and the desire to banish those old feelings of abandonment still plaguing him was overwhelming. Nuzzling into his neck, I held him tight, wanting so badly for him to know I would never leave him the way his mother had.

My mind reached out to him, eager to provide whatever comfort I could, and he opened to admit me. Turmoil swirled within the brilliant diamond of his mind—the shock and horror of his father's accident followed by his mother's suicide. How it had forever changed him. How alone in the world he'd been.

My fingers curled against him in shock when I saw the image of her in a pool of blood on the floor. He'd been the one to find her. Still reeling from his father's death, he hadn't been able to understand, to process why his mother was also gone.

"I'm so sorry," I whispered as tears slid down my cheeks. The pain of loss and abandonment haunted his mind. How badly I wanted to reach across time and do something, anything, to make him feel better. I sat up to rest my forehead against his temple, drawing him into my mind where I could envelop him in the warmth he'd needed back then.

He wasn't alone anymore. I'd never let him be alone like that again, and I shared the thought with him, watching him accept it and hold it close.

The promise helped, but I wished there was some way to comfort the child he'd been. The horrors he'd seen and at such a young age. A shudder tore through me at the cruelty of it, and I fought the sting of tears. David's arm snaked up to rest across my shoulder, and he turned to smile at me, a glimmer of amusement replacing the pain in his eyes, like a rainbow after a downpour.

"It's okay, Sarah. It happened a long time ago." He pressed a kiss to my forehead, his words rumbling against my skin. "I know you don't remember this, but—well, let me show you." He wiped away the tears helplessly streaming down my numb face and pressed his palm against my cheek. I returned to the boy in his mind, watching as he sat, scared and lost on a bench by himself, when a little redheaded girl ran up beside him.

She'd stared at him a moment, and he tensed, expecting her to want to play like they usually did. Something he had no interest in doing. But she'd only leaned forward to hug him tight, her hair tickling against his face. He'd waited for her to let go, to get bored, to beg for him to go running down the paths like they always did, but she just held on until he'd released his grief into her embrace. She'd stayed there while he'd cried over the loss of his parents. The shock and realness of what had happened bubbling to the surface now that he was in his safe space. Because she was his safe space.

I was his safe space. Shocked, I tilted my head up to stare at him.

"So you see. You saved me," he said, eyes shining.

I gave a breathless, tear-filled laugh as I lightly pressed my lips to his and settled myself back into his neck. I'd been there for him, and now I understood his amusement. Here I was weeping for the child he'd been, wishing I could somehow help. But I'd already done that. As a girl, I'd wept with him. Comforted him.

"What happened to you after that? Did you have some other family on the island?"

He stiffened beneath me, pausing before answering. "No, I didn't. I had no family on the island, and they didn't know what to do with me. I told you before about how rare ancient children were. So many couples on the island had been trying for hundreds of years to have a child, and to suddenly have an orphan within the community? Well, the elders determined that the only way it would be fair to the childless couples was if I would be a child for all of them."

I noted the raw bitterness in his tone at the last, his mouth curling as he spoke the distasteful words.

"I don't understand. A child for all of them?" What would that have meant for David? There would've been no way for him to belong to so many.

"The council determined that there would have been too much fighting and jealousy if one couple had taken me in, so they decreed that I move from home to home. That way, all the childless couples could have a part in raising me. I would spend two weeks with one couple, and then move to the next."

He had never truly had a mother and father again after his parents had died. From the age of five, he'd been a drifter; passed from family to family as though he were a valuable commodity of the island and not a person. My heart squeezed, and I cuddled into his neck all the tighter, wrapping my arms around his arm.

"That sounds terrible," I said once I was finally in a position tight enough that nothing would dislodge me.

The elders had done that to him, taken an orphaned boy and denied him the stability he'd needed. Anger brewed in my breast until it was like a living thing, eager to lash out. The elders had ruined my life, but to learn they'd done something like this to David.

The fire of my hatred burned brighter than ever.

"It was difficult, but one of the elders, the oldest amongst them, was really the one who raised me. I spent most of my days with him, no matter who I was currently staying with. He was always there and always happy to see me. It was him who I went to for guidance. He became my father in a way that none of the ancient men I stayed with ever was."

I could see the elder in his mind, a loving man who looked old despite the agelessness of his appearance. It was in the wisdom of his honey-brown eyes and the subtlety of his smile, like nothing could surprise him after a life filled with every possible experience. The elder had quietly kept himself apart from the rest of the community, and it was there that David had often joined him.

He liked to quietly work alongside him, shaping trees, and spending time in nature. The elder didn't force him to speak or riddle him with questions the way the couples he stayed with always did. He provided a stable sense of love and support without any pressure to respond. But in all the fond memories David had of the man, there was no name associated with him. Frowning, I tucked my chin in tight and pressed my lips to his shoulder.

"What was the elder's name?"

"The elders who govern our community are the oldest among us. In the time when they grew up, ancients didn't really use names. It's like—" He pressed his lips together thoughtfully. "When you think of me, you have a sense of me in your mind. I'm more than just my name, just like anyone is more than just their name. Back then, names weren't necessary. Ancient communication was largely mental and everyone knew who you were thinking about by the sense of them in your mind. As we adopted human language and began speaking to each other more, we started to use names. Some elders refused to adopt the custom, but most other ancients did take on a single name to help differentiate them from others in speech."

My thoughts turned to David and his childhood. He had a name, but he also had a last name. Frowning, I curled my fingers, instantly worried I'd been calling David by the wrong name.

"A single name. No last names? I know yours is Giert, so was that what you were called on the island?"

"No." His chest vibrated against me in a deep chuckle. "My name has always been just David, actually. We don't have last names on the island, and I needed a last name when I became a scout in the human world." He looked away, smiling, and a trickle of amusement vibrated from him in ticklish waves.

"What?" I asked, eager to be let in on the joke.

"Well, I'm a tiger, Sarah...my soul is part tiger. Giert is..." He gave a small chuckle, and his lips curled up into a self-mocking smile. "I probably should have thought of something better, but Giert is an anagram for tiger, and seemed like the most appropriate second name for me to give myself."

So his name was based on the animal part of himself. It made sense, and I gently tucked myself back into the place at his neck that I had claimed as my own. My lips rested there a moment before he began to speak. His honeyed voice vibrated through his arm, and relief flooded me at how quickly the grief had been driven away.

"How about your last name? Bloodcharm. Is it your vampire family name?"

"Sarah Bloodcharm. It sounds strange, doesn't it? No, it's not a family name. I left that behind when I ran away." I paused for a moment, thinking about how freeing it had been to be done with those people and anything associated with them.

"Adam gave me the name when I came here to Boston and joined his clan. It was a nickname he gave me for my red hair and ability to use magic." I smiled against the tender skin of his neck, momentarily preoccupied with imagining how his blood would taste. "It just seemed to fit."

"Bloodcharm. I can see that," he said, affectionately moving to rub his cheek against my forehead in an almost feline gesture. I allowed myself to sink into contentment, the terrible truths of the moment temporarily forgotten with the gentle hum of David's mind beside me. Our minds weren't joined, but I had a sense of him and his emotions, and it was pure bliss to lie there together in our own little worlds, drinking the feeling of each other without that extra layer of intimacy.

My mental ability had always been present, but before I'd met David, I'd wielded it like a child fumbling her way through the dark. Even the blood lust I'd instilled in my victims wasn't real, but my enjoyment naturally projected into their minds to ease the feed. Since I'd joined my mind with David, I had a better understanding of how to reach out and pull away, how to use my gifts like a muscle to explore and communicate. The way barriers were formed and held was becoming more clear to me—more intentional.

The strange part was how familiar it all felt. I'd grown up knowing how to do this, and while it was strange to think of the life I'd forgotten, I was pleased to learn more about my abilities. David's voice startled me out of my thoughts.

"Why did you run away?" he asked in a hushed tone.

It was a simple question.

We were sharing. But the moment he asked, blood-infused memories began to swirl in my mind, and the familiar anxiety rose up, threatening to consume me. It was too much, and I untangled myself from his embrace, sitting up hurriedly.

David tried to sit up with me but fell back, his face ashen and a hand pressed to his side. He rested his hand on my arm as the remembered horrors tore through my mind.

"I'm sorry, I—I can't talk about it." I barely managed to get the words out around my stuttered breath. Heart pounding in my ears, I rubbed my temples furiously in a frantic bid to dispel the dead faces swarming my vision. He rubbed my arm, and I fought to get myself under control, if only to take that worry from his eyes.

"No, I'm sorry. We don't have to talk about that. Come here," he whispered, tugging me back down. I went to him eagerly, curling up beside him and letting the comfort of his mind and body chase away the demons. His mind radiated warmth and love, and I focused on it, reminding myself that I was okay now, that I was far from those people.

Safe.

Loved. He stroked my hair until the panic faded.

Slowly, my heart returned to normal, and my breathing eased. I pulled his hand to my chest, kissing the knuckles.

I'd never let anyone close enough to comfort me like this. Squeezing my eyes shut, I rested a moment until the last of the tension in my muscles had eased.

But David. He'd come here to find me, and my mind reached out to him, eager for the flow of love and comfort.

The love he had for me, and the ease with which I could access it, was addictive. It was something I'd never had, and the way it softened the edges of my jagged pieces felt so damned good. David's mind enveloped mine, and I rested, allowing my love and appreciation for him to drown out the horrors of my past.

He had come here to find me, to rescue me, and he had in so many ways. He'd left his home for me, left everything he knew, and he hadn't given up. He was the only person in my life to have stayed the course, and I swiped angrily at a tear leaking from my eye at the wave of emotion.

David tensed beneath me, his mind pulling away, and I blinked up at him in confusion, desperately craving the return of our connection.

"Sarah, please don't."

Confused, I sat up to stare down at him. "Don't what?"

His eyes glistened, and he looked away. "Don't think about me like I'm some kind of perfect person."

Frowning, I put a hand lightly on his shoulder. "David." I had no idea what he was talking about, but I understood the way he recoiled from the image I had of him. I'd felt similarly when I'd first seen the pedestal he had me on.

"I didn't—" He gasped in a shaky breath. "I gave up, Sarah. I came to the human world to find you, and I spent years searching, moving from place to place, and none of it mattered because you were lost." He blew out a breath. "So I gave up. I came to Boston to finish up school in person instead of doing everything correspondence. I was done." He twisted his head to study my face. "And then my new roommate set me up with a woman named Sarah, and I thought it was some kind of sick joke. What are the chances that in this new life I had chosen for myself, the first woman I would go on a date with would be named Sarah? What a coincidence." He gave a bitter laugh and looked away. "When I realized I'd found you by chance." His lips twisted. "It's been killing me ever since."

He'd stopped searching for me.

Of course he had.

It made complete sense. He'd left his home and traveled around for years with nothing to show for it. Anything he might have done, all those hopes and dreams, he'd put on hold for me. How could he think I would resent him for it? There was nothing but gratitude in my heart for every day he'd sacrificed wandering aimlessly, hoping to somehow stumble across me. But of course, he wouldn't feel that way. Instead, he focused on the moment he'd decided to put the search for me aside. Placing a hand on his cheek, I tilted his head towards me, forcing his eyes to meet mine.

"David, you gave up years of your life for me. Years." He tried to interrupt, but I pressed my index finger to his lips. "You didn't owe me anything. What happened to me wasn't your fault." I reached out my mind to brush against his and show him my sincerity. "No, listen to me. It wasn't your fault, and for you to search for me at all." A smile tugged at my lips. He relaxed back into the pillow, and I gently pressed my lips to his in a featherlight kiss. "I don't blame you for stopping. I love you for trying."

He nodded but didn't reply, but his eyes were glistening when he reached out to cup my cheek.

And because I'd been in his mind and knew he needed to hear it, even though it was ludicrous, I trapped his hand against my cheek, and spoke the words he was silently begging for me to say.

"I forgive you."

"Sarah," he said my name in a whisper, and I drifted towards him until our lips connected. My mouth slanted against his, trying for a better angle as he opened for me, and our tongues connected. I groaned at the taste of him, but as much as I wanted to lose myself to the sensation, I caught sight of the clock on his nightstand.

I only had fifteen minutes before I needed to leave, and a pang of sadness struck me at the upcoming separation.

"Are you up for some more healing before I have to go?" I asked lightly, resting my palm against his chest.

"Only if you are." David studied my face. Sighing, I tried to take stock of myself and think about whether I had the energy to spare. I didn't. My shoulders were sore from helping him into the apartment, and while they would normally have healed already, their continued stiffness was a testament to my body's exhaustion. But David didn't need to know that, and there was no way I could get through a shift at the diner knowing he was here confined to bed writhing in pain.

"Yes, I'm okay." I started by pressing a kiss to the bruise above his eye, the one causing him to squint around the swelling, transferring my energy into the wrongness, until it began to feel more correct. David shuddered as I worked, and I put a hand on his opposite cheek, stroking it lightly to offer some comfort.

Satisfied with how it was improving, I let my hand drift down to his ribs on the left side, where the worst of his injuries were concentrated. Trailing kisses along his sharp jawline, I worked my way around to his mouth, letting my tongue slip inside to taste him, as I worked to focus on the energy transfer. But when he moaned against my lips, the vibration shot a bolt of arousal straight to my core, making it hard to think straight, let alone heal. I turned my face to the side, seeking relief from the sensation, but he gasped against my cheek, nuzzling in and nibbling in sharp flashes of pain that left me aching with need.

He went rigid against me, his arm snaking around and trying to pull my body flush with his, but I kept my place at his side, knowing it was unfair of me to demand more than he could give.

His hand caged mine against his ribs as he deepened the kiss, his tongue connecting with mine in little tastes of heaven that quickly blotted out everything else. This wasn't just a kiss. He thrust me with his tongue, each press of it into my mouth communicating all the urgency between us. All thoughts of healing and work were blown out of my mind, and I struggled to hold on to the energy transfer, because that's what we were supposed to be doing. I gave in and allowed myself to be drawn in tight, but the moment I pressed truly against him, he shuddered in pain. Reluctantly, I pulled back.

He loosened his grasp on my hand and groaned. I was eager to swallow the delectable sound down, to take all of his sounds, his words, but I didn't dare get close to him again. Not when both of us were barely finding the necessary reserve to see the healing through. I gently trailed my fingertips across the injury. There was such a tremendous amount of wrongness there that it made me nauseous, and I carefully poured a new trickle of energy into it as I cautiously dropped my mouth to his once more. He gasped, and I captured his lips, sucking his bottom lip and teasing the seam of his mouth with my tongue to distract him from the pain.

We carried on that way until a thin coat of sweat covered every inch of David's skin and his colour had paled. I stopped to rest my head against his heaving chest, waiting anxiously while he recovered, his breathing growing more even and deep. Sitting up, I found he'd drifted off to sleep. I relished the peaceful way he slept, and how it reminded me of the lost boy I'd seen in his mind.

Skeptical about his ability to move around the apartment, I hurriedly emptied a plastic bag of nondescript blood from the fridge into a bowl and placed it on his nightstand, tiptoeing into the room to keep from waking him. I wanted so badly to kiss him goodbye, but to do so would be to wake him and replace this vision of peace with one of him struggling to shift around without pain. So I kissed my index finger and touched it to the pillow next to him before quietly exiting the room. Even with the thin wooden door between us, the separation was almost too much, and I longed to turn back, to call the diner and tell them I was sick. But David was asleep now, and there was nothing more to do. My desire to stay back had nothing to do with him and everything to do with finding an excuse to stay near him. With a sigh, I turned and continued out the door, knowing I was leaving a part of myself behind.

Chapter 10

"What exactly do I have to do for the clan initiation?" Cracking my jaw, I settled into David's chest and trailed a hand across his abdomen to soothe the note of worry in his voice. I'd hurried back from the diner to find him awake, and with more colour in his cheeks. The tension I'd felt during the day apart had eased every minute in his presence, and the relief had left me languid and playful.

"Oh, it's just a little ritual to show that you are part of us and we are part of you." Another yawn stole my words. Healing was exhausting, and we'd only done a brief session since I'd come back. I wanted him able to sit up by the time I had to head off the next morning. But for now, I allowed myself this break in his arms, lulled by the soothing sound of his voice.

"Each clan member lines up and you drink from them as they drink from you then—"

He started chuckling, and I propped myself up on an elbow, quirking an eyebrow at him and waiting to be let in on the joke.

"What? That's what we do for our initiation. How is that funny?" My eyebrows knitted together in confusion at the twinkling amusement in his eyes.

"It's just—we have a ritual similar to what you described, and it's our equivalent of marriage." He chuckled. "We call it becoming lifemates, but the core of the ritual is that you drink from each other and share your blood. I guess what I'm saying is that this is going to be strange for me.

Almost like I'm getting married to everyone in the clan." He laughed again, his face transformed by mirth.

Now that I understood, I didn't find it funny. He'd feel as though he was sharing something special by doing the ritual initiation and with everyone in the clan, not just me. I didn't want that. David was the first good thing I could remember having, and I wanted him all to myself. He shifted painfully down to kiss me hard on the mouth, slipping his tongue inside to connect with mine, and cupping my cheek until all thought left me, replaced with a deep hollow feeling in my core.

"You know the only one I want is you." His breath tickled against my lips, and I swallowed hard. "Plus, the last time I checked, you're a member of the clan, too, so we'll also be a little bit married," he said, pulling my bottom lip into his mouth and sucking on it in a gesture of primal claim that left me shivering.

"Is the ceremony really so similar?"

"Yes and no, the sharing of blood is supposed to enhance your mental connection, and it's at the core of the ceremony. But it's not a taste like your initiation. The point is for both partners to drain as much blood from the other as they can. You leave completely weakened, having taken as much from the other as possible. Of course, there are words and a marriage bed, but blood-sharing is at the core of it."

I nodded. It really would be like marrying the entire clan. I shook my head to dispel the thought and found him studying my face, a dimple creasing his brow. It was my turn to laugh and pull his face down into a sinfully deep kiss that left me dizzy. I reached out with my mind and felt him eager to connect.

Feelings and thoughts flowed between us.

"I love you," I whispered. The words came easier now, and the truth of them sang in my heart.

"I love you, too," David said, smiling against my lips. Contentedness flowed between us, and I saw my lust reflected in his mind. He tried to hide it, to keep those thoughts contained, but the way he reacted to me, the way his body reacted. He wanted to pull me onto his lap as badly as I wanted him to. Unfortunately, I had healed him as much as my body would allow, and the exhaustion was marrow deep. Sighing with resignation, I pulled back to settle down. Our fingers twined, and everything felt peaceful and right with the world.

We settled into a routine with every waking moment spent together focused on healing and resting. David's improvements were remarkable, but I pushed myself to heal him as much as possible.

On the fourth day, I awoke to David standing on his own beside the bed.

"Are you okay?" He looked steady, but I thought I could detect a sway through his torso. Frowning, I processed what he was doing. Somehow, he'd managed to dress himself in a white button-up shirt and loose grey pants.

"Why are you dressed?" The sound of the door and the hum of voices drew my attention. David was unsurprised at the intrusion, securing the last button without meeting my eyes.

"What'd you do?"

David didn't meet my eyes.

"I'm better now, Sarah, and this can't be put off any longer."

Cursing under my breath, I extracted myself from the bed and threw a sweater over my shirt. He must've called Adam while I was out.

"What? Now? You really think you're up for this?" I glared daggers back at David, who was leaning against the wall, his face tight with pain. He wisely looked away as he spoke.

"I'm sorry, but Tom's in pain from his wound and the longer it sits unhealed..."

I rushed over to him, my hands clenched into fists at my side.

"Or I could've healed Tom." It would've been the smart and easy choice.

I was well, he wasn't. But instead, he was undoing the work I'd done to help him, and it made me furious.

He swallowed carefully before replying.

"I know you could, but I did this, Sarah, and it has to be me who undoes it."

Spinning on my heel, I turned away from him.

He was stupid.

An idiot.

"Sarah. Please? Help me?" The simple request pulled at me until I couldn't take it anymore. When I turned, I found he'd taken a shaky step towards me, eschewing the support of the wall. He looked vulnerable and weak.

A lump in my throat, I moved wordlessly closer to tuck myself under his free arm and take on some of his weight.

When we slowly emerged into the main room, Tom was already seated at the card table, his hands clasped tightly enough to leave his knuckles pale. His eyes darted around the room nervously, as if looking for signs of danger. The youth was dressed comfortably in a pair of loose joggers and an old 80s band T-shirt.

Adam stood protectively over him, and I glared at the tall clan leader standing so imposing in the room, like he had a right to be here. Like Tom needed his protection from us when it had been David who had sought him out and was eager to make amends.

This was my first time seeing him since he'd used me to bully David into joining the clan. Bitterness made it hard to stomach the sight of him. Particularly when he grinned and gave me a small wave in answer to my attentions.

Ignoring him, I turned to Tom.

"Hello, Tom," I said casually, hoping my light tone would put him at ease.

"Hi, Sarah. Hi, David." Tom's fear radiated off him in waves, and I gave him a friendly smile in an attempt at diffusing it. There was a tremor in his voice when he said David's name, and I felt David's arm across my shoulder tense at the obvious fear Tom was displaying.

Adam watched my interaction intently. I could feel his eyes on me, but I refused to meet them.

"Hello, Tom. I'm sorry I wasn't able to finish this the other night." David's apologetic expression was enough to make me grit my teeth. His gaze flickered over Adam, and I knew he was saying an apology to him, too.

An apology he didn't deserve after the shit he'd pulled.

"That's okay. I just want to hit the gym again. You said you could fix me up, right?" He spoke too quickly, looking down as soon as he finished.

"Yes, of course, and I promise you'll feel perfect afterwards" David braced himself as he began lowering gingerly into the chair beside Tom, breathing a sigh of relief once he was seated. He extended his hands towards him, and after a moment of hesitation, Tom placed his bandaged arm in David's hands.

He held the limb gently with one hand while he used the other to unwind the poorly wrapped wound, stripping the thin strips of gauze and apologizing when the last bit pulled against Tom's wound. At last, the gash was revealed, and it was ghastly.

David's first attempt at healing must've dislodged the stitches because there was no sign of them now. The sight of the cruelly torn flesh was enough to turn my stomach, as was the knowledge that the three bloody streaks snaking their way up Tom's arm had come from David. The pain and wrongness of the injury filled my mind the more I stared at it, and it was all I could do to keep myself from taking his arm myself and pouring energy into it.

"I'm so sorry, Tom," David said in a tight voice. His face was a mask of misery, and I could feel his renewed horror and shock at seeing the extent of the injury. Even when his walls were up, we weren't truly closed from each other anymore. It came from the way we connected, from anticipating how the other felt.

I touched his shoulder to offer physical comfort, though I knew the only way he would feel better was to heal the wound. Strong jaw set and a steely look in his eye, David adjusted his grip on the arm to hold it more securely. "I'm going to start healing you now. Remember that there is some pain to the process."

Tom gave a curt nod, pulling a frayed tennis ball from his pocket to fist in his free hand. After a deep breath, he straightened his shoulders and gave a nod.

"Okay, I'm ready."

It seemed like a private moment between the two men, and now that I knew David was seated and in no danger of collapsing, I retrieved my particle physics textbook from my overnight bag and settled down to read it on the couch. Reading in the bedroom or the bathroom, where I could keep my distance, was appealing, but I wanted to be nearby in case David needed me.

So I sat centrally on the couch, to make it clear I didn't desire Adam's company, but he ignored my social cue, cheerfully flopping down in the too-small space beside me. With an irritated huff, I moved over, angling my page to get more light.

The silence between us was filled with tension, but Adam didn't speak. I tried to concentrate on the text, not willing to give him a moment of my precious time.

The clan leader blew out a breath, leaning back into the seat, and disturbing the worn cushions.

"I know you're angry with me, Sarah. I know you don't understand why I did what I did, but it had to be done." There was a pleading edge to his words that irked me, and I flipped to the next page of my text more violently than was necessary, refusing to answer him.

"That kind of power loose in the city?" His voice trailed off. "You'd agree with me if he wasn't your boyfriend."

"But he is, and you don't know him," I bit out, still refusing to meet his eyes, though I could feel him studying me and gauging my reaction.

"For what it's worth, I'm sorry it went down like it did."

Bristling, I turned to him. "You're just trying to smooth things over with your two favourite weapons."

"Sarah, come on. I've known you since you were sixteen. Do you really believe you're just a weapon to me? That I want to use people? That I'd go looking for a fight?"

I didn't have an answer for him. My mind drifted back to those early days, and the way he'd invited me into the clan. Shown me how they functioned. Taken me in and given me a place to go when the witches had revealed their true selves.

"It's just that I know what he can do, and I needed to know he was on our side." He held up his hands in a placating gesture as I began to mount a defense. Stewing, I settled for glaring daggers in his direction.

"I know what you're going to say, and I do hope he's someone who won't go looking for a fight. I really hope that. I swear to you—not to him, to you—that I won't make him fight for us unless we need his help with our defense."

We'd been a couple once, and friends long before. I knew him, and how he prided himself on being true to his word. But could I trust him?

"Do you swear it?"

He had the audacity to look affronted before placing a hand over his heart.

"Absolutely. He'll be one of us, Sarah, and you know I look after my own."

I studied the steely resolve in his eyes—the firm set of his jaw.

I believed him. Maybe I shouldn't, but I did. At last, I nodded, feeling the tension between us ease. He smiled, turning to find the TV remote and lean back into the couch, throwing an arm across the back, his legs splaying out enough that I had to swat them away to maintain my space.

The way he'd treated David still made me want to punch him in the mouth, but I couldn't deny that he'd done a good thing by staying away these past few days while I was healing David. It had been decent of him to give us the space.

We sat in a comfortable silence for the next hour until David announced he was done in a voice so strained that I let my text close without marking the page and hurried over. He nearly toppled out of his chair, and my heart lurched. Adam got there before I did, steadying him with a hand braced on the shoulder. David accepted the aid, giving Adam a tight smile of thanks.

I walked Adam and Tom to the door, leaving David to sit and recover his strength. His colour looked terrible, his lips nearly white. On the way out, Tom showed off his unblemished arm to Adam. All the nervousness I'd sensed for him when he'd first entered the apartment was gone.

"There's not even a mark! This is incredible!"

I was happy that David may have made a friend out of the experience.

"Oh, I almost forgot." Adam reached under the table to pull a crumpled brown paper bag from his black knapsack. David reached out to accept it, sliding out an old leatherbound version of *Moby Dick* with yellowing pages. His gaze roved over the book excitedly, and he smiled up at Adam.

"Thank you."

Whether it was Adam who had returned to the alley where David was attacked to retrieve his book or a thoughtful clan member, I didn't know, but I nodded at Adam to express my gratitude for the kind gesture.

We said our goodnights, and I walked Adam and Tom out the door. When I turned, the mask David had been wearing in the presence of the others slipped to reveal the pain beneath.

"I had to," he said, his eyes pleading with me to understand.

Letting out a deep sigh, I nodded before heading over to David's side. He was back to gasping at every movement when I helped him to stand.

After three more days spent healing, I returned to David's apartment to find him walking around the kitchen with only a bit of stiffness lingering in his gait. Even in loungewear he was sexy as hell, and I stopped in the doorway for a moment to appreciate his broad shoulders and thick forearms before approaching where he stood at the stove with a spatula in hand. Wrapping my arms around his waist and clasping my wrists, I let his scent comfort me after our time apart and mumbled a greeting against his shirt.

"Shift go okay?"

I mumbled a yes, turning my face to press my cheek into his back before curiosity got the better of me, and I peered around to find he was frying some kind of blood mixture into patties. My mouth watered as I took in the heavenly scent.

"Food's almost ready. Have a seat." David gestured to the table, and I grumpily disentangled myself before dutifully pulling up a chair at the card table.

"It's usually a lot better," he said, sliding a plate over to me with barely concealed enthusiasm in his voice. "I like to put in some fresh rosemary and thyme, and fry it up in a pat of butter, but we're out of the fresh stuff right now. I'll have to make it for you again once I can get out and do some shopping." He leaned across the table to brush his lips across my cheek, and I shivered—the meal momentarily forgotten. He left to retrieve a plate for himself, giving me a moment to consider the dish.

Browned bits crusted the edges of what looked like hamburger patties, but gave too easily with a fork when I moved to spear it. I frowned, thinking about all the trouble David had gone through to prepare this. Had he limped around and favoured his left side? Worn himself out just to make me a meal when I was happy to drink down cold blood without complaint?

"I'm doing much better, Sarah. Really."

I looked up to find him studying my reaction, not missing a single micro expression. And he was right. The colour was back in his cheeks, and the easy way he smiled at me was much more like himself. I smiled back at him and took his hand, twining our fingers.

"Thank you for dinner, but you didn't have to do this."

"Well, there is something I wanted to talk to you about." He grinned shyly, and I stiffened. Whatever he'd buttered me up to talk about couldn't be good news, and I stared down at my meal without seeing it.

"Adam called while you were out."

Shit.

"The initiation is to take place tomorrow night. He said you'd know the spot."

"Yeah, I know the spot," I muttered, looking away so he wouldn't see the tears that pricked at my eyes. It had been easy these past few days to forget about the commitment David had made to join the clan, to forget that it had ever happened. The way Adam had forced this upon him, how he'd be joined to them for life because of me.

"Sarah," he said, twisting to catch my eye. He grimaced in pain at the movement, and I moved instinctively to support him, but he held up a hand to ward me off. The look in his eyes was pure determination. My hands dropped to my sides in defeat, knowing he wouldn't listen to any health concerns. He was improving, but it was hard to accept when the image of him injured on the cell floor was still fresh in my mind.

Then there was the initiation, and what it meant. Was he truly well enough to go through with it? To risk losing so much blood? Once David completed the initiation, there was no going back. Even if he moved away, he'd always be a part of this clan, and they'd be a part of them. The bond was unbreakable, and for him to be forced into it... My lips pressed together in a line.

"I want to do this. I know you hate it, but do you know what really convinced me?" He ducked his head, forcing me to meet his eyes. "When Adam said you are a member of the clan."

Fuck Adam for threatening David with our outdated clan relationship restrictions when they were never followed. The restriction had been more about keeping clan members from dating rival members than an outsider, which didn't apply to David. I went to explain, but he held up a finger.

"No, not that nonsense about not being allowed to date outside of the clan. The part about how you're a part of them, and you'd be obligated to fight for them if they were in trouble." He looked down, playing with my fingers before bringing my hand to cup his face. He turned to gently press his lips to my palm in the lightest of kisses, and my heart broke wide open, a helpless beating thing devoted completely to the man across from me. "So you see, I'm already invested in the clan. I want to join the clan because it's a part of who you are, and maybe it's greedy of me, but I want to be involved in every aspect of your life." His lips tickled the sensitive skin of my palm, and I shivered at the sensation, curling my fingers against his cheek.

He waited until I nodded shakily, fighting to hold back the tears that threatened. Adam had got him with that one; he wouldn't be able to stand by if I was being attacked any more than I would be able to if he was. From now on, we were together in all things.

His joining the clan made perfect sense.

"Okay," I said, nodding firmly. I couldn't manage much else beyond that one word, and he seemed to understand. He kissed my knuckles, and we turned back to our meals. The food he'd prepared was fantastic, the cow's blood greatly enhanced by whatever David had added to make it appear so much like a meat patty. I dug in, not realizing just how hungry I'd been, how hungry I always was. My stomach moaned its approval, and I rubbed at it absentmindedly.

"This is mostly just blood?" My words were muffled around a mouthful of food, but I couldn't help myself from shoveling more in the moment the words were out. He watched me with rapt attention, his own meal untouched.

"Mmm, yes, with some thickening agents and spices. The secret is using a cast iron pan." He winked, and I stifled a giggle, nearly choking on the excess blood patty I'd stuffed in my mouth.

I'd never given much thought to how to prepare blood and usually just grabbed a bag of it and headed out the door on my way somewhere. I couldn't remember the last time I'd had it warmed beyond the microwave, and then it was usually still in the plastic container it came in.

Bowls were too much of a bother. But now? This food was incredible. I wanted it every day for the rest of my life, and watching David dig in with gusto, I winced, thinking how I'd been serving him reheated blood over the past week.

There was no way microwaved blood could compare to this.

"With the initiation tomorrow, I was thinking maybe you should head back to your place tonight."

My eyes shot to his in surprise. The food I'd speared onto the end of my fork forgotten. We'd only been apart when I'd needed to attend a lecture or work. The time we had spent together, I'd been focused on healing him, and telling myself we could explore each other's bodies once he was feeling better.

David frowned, his eyes fixed on my hand. "Just to make sure we both get a good night's sleep, that's all." His gaze shifted to me, and I reached out automatically for his mind, only to find it shut. I turned back to the delicious food, the taste unable to reach me.

"But I'll see you tomorrow at the initiation, and then it will be behind us."

Nodding, I attempted to meet his eyes and smile.

He wanted me. I didn't just believe it, I'd felt it, and I had to trust there was a reason he was holding himself back. If he wanted to do the initiation first, to face that challenge before taking the next step between us physically, I had to respect his decision.

Even if it felt like there was more to it, like there was something he wasn't saying. Whatever it was, I just had to trust him and the truths I knew.

He loved me.

He wanted me.

For whatever reason, he needed more time.

"Okay. Let's get through this." I nodded.

David smiled before launching into an explanation of his favourite spice combinations, and how he was excited to try sage and sriracha at our next meal. Apparently, it paired well with pig's blood, and the butcher on Charleston had a fresh supply. I couldn't help but smile down at my dish at just how much thought he'd given this and wonder at how many meals he had planned out for us.

Chapter II

The sun had long since set and with it went the day's warmth. The thick, brown wool of my coat couldn't keep me warm enough and I shivered, shuffling my feet at my place in line.

The alley beside the clan house was crowded with clan members stretching from one end all the way up to the pile of pallets Adam used to address us. This wasn't a hunting night where a subset of the clan showed up. No, tonight every member was required to attend, and excuses were not tolerated. If you had to miss work, cancel a date, skip class, you did it. No obligations were more important than this. As far as the world was concerned, you were deathly ill.

The lineup stretched the length of the alley, with Adam standing at the end by a tall fence blocking the way. We were organized by rank with younger members at the start of the line. As one of the oldest and most powerful clan members, I was third in line to Adam, preceded only by Nina, who held the status of second purely through her relationship with Adam. She was his partner. Therefore, she shared his role—one I had once begrudgingly occupied.

Tucking a curl behind my ear, I nervously watched the back steps of our clan house for David. Nina rolled her eyes and leaned into Adam's side.

"You really have to take it easy. He's just another guy." When all I did was smirk, Nina tsked.

But David wasn't just another guy. Not to me. There were no words to explain the closeness of joining minds, or the way he had appeared in my dreams as a figure for as long as I could remember. How we'd been childhood friends, even if I didn't have any memory of it.

Nina was my closest friend, and she would've been my confidante, but explaining about him and how we were connected would mean yet another person knew about the ancients and their island, not to mention my own history. Would Nina offer me comfort if I explained how I'd been exiled from the island, set adrift in the human world?

How would she feel knowing she was sleeping ten feet away from a tiger? Would she look at me differently? Would the cheerfulness I'd come to rely on turn to fear if she knew what I was capable of? It wasn't something I wanted to find out, so I kept my mouth shut, smiling and nodding at her, my eyes still fixed on the back stairs.

The musical tones of laughter from a chummy group near the end interrupted my thoughts. I peered down the line to find a youth I didn't recognize nearly doubled over as his friend, a girl named Meril, turned an angry red. I had no idea what was going on with them. No clue if the pair of them were related, dating, nothing.

I'd been a member for over six years now, and not once had I felt the need to engage socially with any of my clan mates beyond what was necessary. The thought of striking up conversation, of joining in a cheerful conversation, had never appealed to me.

My constant avoidance of the hunts and choosing to separate from the others when I was forced to attend hadn't helped. Hunting had always felt too private, too personal to include anyone else. Especially since it inevitably dredged up my past and left me a quivering mess. It took me at least an hour to gather myself before I could safely stumble home, and I'd never wanted to bring anyone into the world where my weakness was so apparent.

David, though, I wanted to share it with him. Wanted him to know every bit of my past so he could tell me he still loved me in spite of it. The only problem was thinking about it made my throat close up and choked me into silence. Would he turn away from me if he knew the things I'd done? The things that haunted my waking hours as surely as the dream had haunted my slumber?

It didn't stop me from wishing for the kind of closeness that would heal my soul.

David appeared from the doorway at the back of the building near the start of the line. He looked beautiful in a black trench coat that hit below his knees with his blonde hair a spiky tousled mess, and I eagerly drank him in, starved for the sight of him after a day spent apart. His blue eyes flashed in the dim light from the only streetlight in the alley, and he wore a small smile as he stepped into view, his eyes roving over those assembled until he found me. We stared at each other across the distance until Nina nudged me with her elbow, and I became aware of Adam stepping forward and beginning the ceremony.

"Who approaches and asks to join our family?" Adam's voice boomed down the line, and the din of chatter cut off sharply.

"I, David Giert, humbly ask to join your family," David answered, lifting his arms, palms forward as the ritual required.

"Your request is granted. Let our blood be joined as one." Adam gestured to the first clan member, a dark-skinned woman with a permanent mischievous grin on her face. She was at the start of the line, the weakest among us though far from the youngest. She looked to be about my age, and I begrudgingly noted that she was pretty.

David approached her and spoke a few words before tugging her into a light embrace. He had to crouch for her to reach his neck, but then they were both drinking from another, and I was unprepared for the way it affected me.

I'd attended plenty of initiations, but to see David sharing that kind of closeness with somebody else was physically painful, and I fought to keep myself from bolting down the line and prying them apart.

He was doing this for me. I had to remember that. But it was hard when I knew that to David, this was a deeply intimate experience. I could barely watch, but couldn't look away as he moved down the line, speaking a few quiet words to each clan member before embracing them for the blood sharing component the initiation demanded.

My chest tightened with anticipation as David moved down the line, getting closer to my position. He paused to say something to Tom, and I breathed a sigh of relief when I didn't notice a hint of fear or tension in Tom's body language when he tilted his neck for David to drink. I knew what the trust of the gesture would mean to David, and it warmed my heart to think he might have made a friend out of the youth.

David was four people away.

Three.

Two.

One.

He was so close, I could hear the whispered words he spoke to the man beside me before they drank from each other. I stared at the dingy brickwork across the alley, my body alive with anticipation as I waited my turn. My limbs were trembling with nerves, and my chest was heavy with jealousy by the time he took his place before me. My eyes fixed on his boots and the tails of his trench coat.

David took my hands in his, squeezing them gently, and I drew in a shaky breath before forcing myself to meet his eyes.

The way he looked at me. There was no mistaking the devotion I saw in his eyes. If the initiation was a bit like marriage for everyone else, it was also that way between us, and I swallowed hard to tamp down the rising emotions.

"My blood, your blood, our family," he said, his blue eyes piercing straight into my soul.

My blood, your blood, our family. A simple phrase, but so much was contained in it that it took three tries before I could get the words out. I moved into the warmth of David's embrace, savouring the feeling of him, his scent, his touch. He felt so good, so right.

His hand stroked my back, and I felt it through the thick wool coat I wore, like the fabric wasn't enough to dampen his effect on me. He leaned down to my neck, and I remembered what we were supposed to be doing. My fangs emerged eagerly as David's hot breath tickled the shivering skin of my neck a moment before we drank from each other.

I'd had vampire blood during the initiation ceremony before, but David's blood was richer and fuller, like every other taste of blood had been watered down in comparison. It sang on my tongue, and I clung to him, pulling more deeply, wondering what it would be like to complete the life mate ceremony with him. Where I drank my fill of him even as he drained me until we were too exhausted to continue.

David withdrew his fangs, lightly kissing the bite at my neck and transferring energy to heal it with a sting of pain. I released him reluctantly, letting my tongue linger on the wounds my clan mates had left on his neck until the skin was unblemished.

His lips brushed against my cheek as he pulled back to stand at arm's length. The tension I'd been carrying since he'd stepped into view eased, and I smiled up at him. He held my hands an extra moment before moving on to Nina. To her credit, she was stiff in his arms. I was only able to bear watching them together knowing she was in an awkward position with David at her neck, and Adam looking on.

After he and Adam exchanged blood, Adam raised his arms and declared in a loud, booming voice, "David Giert, we welcome you to The Shades. You are a part of us, as we are a part of you."

With those words, a whoop rose up from somewhere towards the back, and David turned back to me with a grin, opening his arms to me. I hurried over, and he pulled me into his embrace, tucking me into his side when a swell of well-wishers began to crowd him.

There was a lot of slapping on the back and cheering. The clan was happy to have David join, and it warmed my heart. They didn't know what he was, but the idea of having someone in the clan who could shapeshift into a tiger must have been appealing. Relief was thick in the air, and I hated it. David didn't need this kind of pressure.

At least he took it all in stride, though he must have felt how heavy their expectations were. He appeared to be in a great mood, his blue eyes twinkling with amusement, and a quiet smile on his face.

At least it was over with. David was a member of the clan now, for better or for worse.

The after party involved moving through the streets, looking for drunken humans stumbling through the dark streets. Slowly, the others trickled away, heading off to begin their hunts.

When it was just David and I left, I cleared my throat and turned to him.

"Should we go?" I asked, gesturing to the street beyond the alley where we heard a beer bottle shatter somewhere in the distance.

"Am I allowed to say that I don't want to?" He stared unseeing towards the street ahead, his brows pinched.

I had a feeling he might not care for tonight's activity, and I licked my lips, stalling for time as I thought it through. David had mentioned how the ancients cared for the animals they drank blood from, but he had never said anything about drinking from humans. Most vampires believed it was necessary to drink from humans at least weekly. Now that I'd connected to another person's mind through David, the thought of feeling the terror in a human mind as I bit into them was nauseating.

"I don't think anyone would mind, so long as you're a member of the clan." I smiled up at him, looking up through my lashes, and he beamed in reply, offering his arm. We left the alley together, walking the streets as we always did. I pillowed my head on his arm, listening to the deep rumbling vibrations of his voice through the warmth of his shoulder. He was much better, and I couldn't detect a trace of pain as I leaned into him. I sighed contentedly as we wound our way towards the main street.

My stomach rumbled grumpily, and I lay a hand across my abdomen. I should have forced myself to join the clan on tonight's hunt.

Wait. I stopped short, tugging David to a halt beside me. When had I last gone on a hunt? David had occupied every minute I could spare since the moment we'd met. Which meant the only thing I'd eaten for the past two weeks was animal blood.

But it couldn't be. This was ludicrous.

"This may be a silly question but, vampires don't really need human blood, do they? They think they do, but they don't." I studied his reaction carefully. If David had never drunk from a human before, and I was the same as him, it meant that I had never needed human blood. All the pain I'd caused could have been avoided if I'd just been willing to try to live off animal blood. Shame filled me at the realization, and David's next words added fuel to the blaze.

"No, they don't," David answered, his voice tight.

"I was always taught to believe that we—vampires—required it to survive." I played with the sleeve of his coat to distract myself. My father had gone a step further, insisting we needed the hunt, the struggle, the death of humans. He claimed we were the predators, and they were our prey. But were we?

"They don't need it, but well, on the island, it's clear that the stronger predatory animals taste different from the weaker animals. They seem to give a sort of high when you drink their blood. It's like a rush of power and adrenaline. We don't drink the larger predator blood very often, as it's harder to capture those animals. We save it for special occasions. I've never tried human blood, but maybe it's similar. Maybe it gives vampires a rush of power. I'm not really sure. It's interesting to think about, but no. There's no way they need it to live," he finished, brow furrowed as we moved to skirt around an old woman.

I'd never needed it.

I'd never have to drink from a human again.

The thought was both freeing and damning, and I fought to deal with the euphoria tinged with guilt. The resulting bout of clipped laughter was so unexpected and piercing that David's eyes shot to my face in alarm.

"What is it?"

"Nothing," I murmured, curling myself around his arm and dragging him forward. My father's house and the memories of him threatened to pull me down into a place of panic.

They hadn't needed blood to live either, but somehow, I didn't think the discovery would stop them from drinking, from killing.

Breathing fast, I hurried my pace, pulling him along beside me as if I could outrun the faces of my past.

"Sarah, whatever's bothering you, I want you to know I'm always here to listen."

I stroked his arm through the coat.

"I know. It's just not something I'm ready to talk about yet."

Or ever. How many years had it been, and I'd still gone into a panic at the slightest reminder?

David was silent for a moment, the sound of a siren in the distance blending with a car backfiring at least a block away.

"You don't like feeding from humans?" There was a question in David's voice, like he was struggling to figure me out, and I didn't like it. He was getting too close to the truth. My arm tightened around his.

"No." My single word answer hung between us, and I could feel him waiting for me to explain. Expecting it.

Clearing his throat, David patted my hand.

"I have an idea."

Quirking an eyebrow, I peered up at him and found him grinning back, his eyes twinkling merrily.

"You have the day off tomorrow, right?"

"Yes."

He nodded to himself. "Good. I have something I want to show you."

Curious, I waited for him to elaborate, but his grin turned mischievous.

"I'm not going to tell you. It'll be a fun surprise this way."

"Mmm," I mumbled in agreement, curious what he could be planning. I enjoyed the comfortable silence as we made our way back to my apartment. The usual sense of anticipated loss washed over me when the tall grey building came into view.

"Are you sure you're okay?" he asked gently, turning to face me and tucking a stray curl behind my ear. Reflexively, I turned into his touch in a silent beg for more. He obliged, cupping my face, his thumb caressing my cheek.

"Yeah," I said, leaning forward, pressing my mouth to this.

I would never tire of this. His lips moved against mine, and I deepened the kiss, making it wetter and hotter as I pressed my tongue past the seam of his mouth, the needy ache in my core desperate for more than mouths and hands. I moved to his neck, kissing where so many other lips had been this night. By the time we parted to gasp in a breath of air, I was a trembling mess, my fingers buried in the folds of his collar.

"Do you want to come up?" I cursed myself as soon as the words were out of my mouth, freezing as I anticipated another excuse.

"I think the blood sharing has left me a bit tired, actually."

Nodding, I swallowed down the disappointment, trying not to let it show on my face. But David could read me better than anyone, and he frowned down at me.

"I'm sorry." David's voice was filled with remorse, but it didn't make pulling away any easier. Even expecting it had done nothing to dampen the loss I felt at the lack of contact. The tension wound my body tight, and I knew I'd find release at my hand tonight, that the sheets would be slick with my sweat by the time I was done.

"I'll see you tomorrow. Goodnight." My voice sounded shaky, even to my ears, and I cleared my throat, forcing my kiss-swollen lips to curl into a taunting smile. His eyes laughed back at me.

"Goodnight, Sarah," he said, turning and looking back over his shoulder at me. I stood there helplessly as I watched him walk away, the air around me feeling colder the further he got. David looked back over his shoulder at me, his brows pinched, and I swear he felt the same. That he could feel the separation as keenly as I did, that he hated it just as much.

He continued to glance back, as if compelled by the same force that left me rooted to the stone stairs. It took me a long time to leave the steps and return to my apartment, and when I did so, I moved in a haze, my system still revved up. The apartment was quiet, and I didn't bother with the lights, navigating the sparse furniture with the memory of a hundred such dark nights when I'd been returning from a hunt and unwilling to face myself in the light.

I shut the door to my room quietly and leaned back into the thin, paneled woods, letting my fingers drift into the crevices for comfort. My mattress was still on the floor, and I wondered if the dream really would stay away, and if I should get a proper frame now that I wasn't at risk of rolling out of bed. A bit more height would offer a lot more position possibilities, and I looked at the bed, filled with longing that David had said yes. That he'd come back here with me, his breath still in my ear, his large hands gripping my hips.

Gasping with neediness, I imagined he was there, a wall of warmth behind me instead of the cold wood. It was cruel the way he held himself back to me, willing to join his soul with mine, his mind, but not his body. Never his deliriously tempting body.

All I had were my fantasies and in them, David wrapped his long fingers around my hand and gently pulled me over to the bed. I laid down and stripped off my leather pants. They clung to me like a second skin, and I'd been hoping he'd notice. That he'd come home with me so I could show him just how great my ass looked in them. But he hadn't.

In my head, he liked them. He liked it better when I stripped them off, and he settled on top of me, his heavy warmth enveloping. I imagined what it would be like to explore him without resistance, to feel the sensation of my touch echoing in his mind the way it did when we kissed. He didn't pull away, didn't trap my hands to keep me away. No, he was just as ravenous as I was.

The pants came off with a final kick, and I trailed my hands up my torso, lingering on the peaks of my sensitive nipples, grasping them roughly like I imagined David would do in his haste to take me. His breathing would be as ragged as mine, his cock hard as he fought to take off his own pants. Then he was back, all over me, drowning me with his scent, his electrifying touch until the need grew within me. I barely recognized the desperate, breathy moans escaping my lips. My hand drifted lower in place of the man who wasn't really in the bed with me, and I set a punishing rhythm. Once he touched me, once we felt each other, neither of us would be able to hold back. There would be no slowly easing into it, just feral need and pure carnal satisfaction as it was met.

The thumb I used to circle my clit became more frantic as I pushed my fingers deeper, the way he would, letting the tension within me build until I was bucking into my hand and biting my lip to keep from calling out his name. An explosion of tension tore through me, and my back arched off the bed.

The relief didn't last long. It never did, and as soon as the waves of pleasure had abated, I craved their absence all the more.

It was going to be a long night.

When I awoke, I was stiff, the muscles in my thighs sore from wringing release out of my tired body. At least no dreams had haunted the scant amount of sleep I'd managed, and I tried to focus on how positive that was. How great the dream had stayed away even without David's soothing presence, but when I reflexively stretched an arm out to the side where David had slept next to me over the past week, a hollow feeling filled my chest when my hand met the cold sheets.

Was he still in bed, staring longingly at the pillow I'd occupied? I still couldn't understand why he hadn't accepted my invitation to come up, and that excuse.

He was tired.

Yeah right. No, he wasn't. His breathing had been just as ragged as mine, and he'd had to tear himself away violently enough to leave me feeling like he'd left an open wound in his wake. We could be so good together, and my mind drifted back to last night at the way he so effortlessly set my body on fire before leaving. Frowning to myself, I fingered the pillow beside me. My stomach grumbled, and with a sigh, I shook out the tangled mess I'd made of my crimson curls and threw on my usual pajama shorts. I only wore shorts no matter how cold it was in case the dream took me, and I needed to keep my legs as free as possible, but now? Maybe I could try something different.

A smile tugged at my lips, but the sight of an empty fridge, save for a cylinder of cold pig's blood, stripped it away. Normally, I wouldn't think twice about the meal. Food was food, and I needed it to carry on with my day, to do what I needed to do, but after David had made me those blood patties and completely transformed the blood meal, my stomach turned at the thought of choking down cold blood.

David's blood patties had spoiled me. The flavour of them, the warmth, the way they'd melted on my tongue. I popped the plastic container, hoping the sight and smell of the blood would stimulate my appetite. It had partially congealed on top, creating a layer of crust that wasn't the least appealing, and I gave it a delicate sniff, trying to remember that I was hungry.

Heating it up in the microwave didn't help, and I stirred the blood around miserably without eating any of it. With a sigh, I went to check our pantry and found some oregano. I thought David had said pig's blood paired well with oregano, but I couldn't remember. He'd excitedly told me about a number of combinations, and it had been a lot to take in at once. I decided it was worth the gamble. I sprinkled a few flakes and hesitated before adding a bit of pepper for spice. The taste was much better, and I hummed with satisfaction, nearly dropping my spoon when the phone rang.

I lurched for it, chiding myself and covering the receiver before bringing it to my ear.

"Morning." David's honeyed voice met my ears, and a smile curled my lips.

"Morning."

"How'd you sleep?" He sounded tired, and I fiddled with the phone cord, wondering if it was possible he'd been as worked up as me.

"Fine," I purred. David barked a laugh.

"Yeah, me too. Slept like a baby, actually."

I swear I could feel him wink at me through the phone.

"It's a bit of a trek out where we're going. You ready to leave in an hour?"

I checked the clock and was shocked to find it was nearly eleven. I knew I'd slept in, but this late? It was like my body was trying to catch up for all the proper sleep I'd been missing for the past decade.

"Yeah, absolutely. Sorry I hadn't realized it was so late." I rubbed at my forehead, embarrassed, but David chuckled on the other end of the line, and I could imagine the way his eyes would dance with amusement. A shiver wended its way down my spine, and I crossed my legs against the flood of arousal.

I should be sated. I'd spent enough time making sure I would be today, but just hearing him on the other end made my nipples strain against the top I still wore from last night. Counting to five in my head, I fought to turn my mind towards the mystery of today.

"Okay, I'll meet you out front in an hour, and we'll take a cab from there?" David asked.

"Yes, please?" It came out as a question, and I hated the husky neediness in my voice. But I was needy, and he'd spent enough time in my mind to know how much I enjoyed being around him. There wasn't anywhere to hide when every thought and emotion flitting through your mind was shared. No, I was sure David knew how much I missed him after even a night apart, how much I wanted him.

"See you soon," he promised smoothly before the line went dead, and I pulled the receiver to my breast, not caring about the way it dug into the tender skin. There was time for a quick shower, and while I knew nothing short of the man himself would rid me of this clawing, aching need in my core, I was determined to avoid being a shuddering mess at whatever mystery location he planned to bring me to.

I found release by my hand twice in the shower, my fingers shuddering against my abused clit, knowing I was only taking the edge off.

David had the cab driver take us to the outskirts of the city proper. I grew more curious the farther we went, but all my questions were met with the same response. You'll see, and a twinkle of mischief.

It was only after directing the driver down a dirt road that we stopped. David stepped out of the vehicle and waved off the driver with a warm smile, but he waited until the cab was out of sight before turning to me. It was a beautiful spring day. Warm enough that David had worn a short-sleeved shirt that gave me a glimpse of his deliciously thick forearms.

"Okay, what the hell are we doing here?" I asked with a frown when he began to toe off his shoes.

"You've told me about The Shades and how you drink from humans, and now I want to show you my way."

"Your way?" I asked with an eyebrow quirk.

He grinned. "There's a cattle farm just up the road from here, about a mile out."

"So why didn't we have the cab drop us off there?"

"Because it's been too long since you and I have raced, and I want to see if you can still beat me." He winked, his eyes alive with excitement.

"Race?"

"Yeah, race!" he said playfully, standing next to me and nudging my arm with his elbow. "You don't remember, but we used to race all the time when we were kids." He looked over at me with a sad smile that pulled at my heart. It was easy to forget we had a whole history I couldn't remember.

"And the shoes?"

"I've never worn shoes while racing before, and this road is clear of rocks and branches. You should take yours off, too. It'd make it more fair." With a nod to himself, he fixed his gaze down the road ahead and rolled his shoulders.

"No thanks," I said, stretching my arms to the sky. I'd always loved to run. I wondered if this was why, if some part of me remembered racing through the woods with David. My mind took me back to the dream for a moment, the terror I'd felt running through that twisted jungle with its large and imposing trees and the vines reaching out to grab me. Surely, I'd had happier days there on the island, running down paths, skipping merrily around the bends and teasing David for being slow. My lips quirked up into a grin, and I glanced over at him, covering my mouth to stifle a giggle when I found his expression dead serious.

He really didn't like to lose.

"Ready. Set. Go!"

He gave me almost no notice before taking off with a cloud of dust. With an irritated huff, I waved to clear the air and leapt forward, setting a punishing pace. My legs burned after a minute of flat out running, but I forced in a deep breath, pushing myself harder. The dream terror threatened to resurface, but I reminded myself I was safe now. I was with David out in the bright midday sun. Distracted, I stumbled and almost fell when he skidded to a stop in front of me. Hands on my knees, I panted as I fought to catch my breath, annoyed to find that while he was flushed and breathing hard, he wasn't nearly as winded.

"We're here!" he said, graciously ignoring his victory and gesturing to the cows roaming lazily across the rich green pasture in front of us. He casually hopped over the low wooden fence acting as a visual barrier for the placid animals within. I was close behind, watching with interest as he strode towards a cow.

It was a beautiful animal, large and broad. Its brown fur glistened in the sunlight and long rough tail slowly flicked from side to side to ward off the insects. Big brown eyes stared calmly at David as he approached.

He held his hand out palm first and whispered to the animal. I couldn't make out what he was saying, but the cow didn't seem troubled. In fact, it was mesmerized by him, leaning into his offered hand in an almost affectionate gesture, and I watched as he moved to scratch it behind an ear before gently placing his palm on the flat patch right between its eyes. With his fingers, he probed its neck before giving it a pat and moving his mouth down to the spot. A flash of fangs and then he was drinking. In a panic, I watched the scene unfold, eyeing the animal warily for any signs it would lash out.

David was strong, but the cow was huge. If it decided to rear up, if it didn't like what he was doing—

But the cow didn't startle, didn't run. The pasture remained peaceful, the animal totally content. There may have been a slight tremor when David had broken its skin, but otherwise, the cow appeared unaffected. He drank for a long time, longer than I would have drank from a human. Finally, he pulled away, spoke more words to the cow and touched his forehead to it once more. He placed his hand over the wound, leaving no trace of it when he turned to me.

He'd healed it.

No mark, and the animal seemed wholly unconcerned with what had just transpired, gazing at David placidly. He offered it some grass. Its broad tongue swiped out to accept it, and David patted its cheek as it chewed.

With humans, I'd always called them over and talked to them. Batted my eyes at the men. Asked the women if I could borrow their lipstick; it was easy to get close and something always seemed to happen naturally when my lips moved to their neck. They would moan with pleasure while I drank, although I wasn't aware of anything conscious I had done to make it so.

The cow's ear twitched away a fly, and it bent its head back to the ground for another mouthful of grass. David loped over to me.

"Your turn," he said, gesturing to the other cows lazily roaming the pasture.

"Oh, I can't do that," I said nervously, thinking how lucky David had been not to be trampled. But of course, he wouldn't be. He was showing me *his* way. He was experienced, but me? I had no idea what I was doing.

"Yes, you can, and I'll help you." His confidence was touching, and I gave him a watery smile. My eyes fixed on a cow with a darker patch of brown on one side as I tried to remember the way he'd approached, of the peace he'd brought to the animal. How was I supposed to do that?

"Is the one with the patch okay?" I asked, my mouth nearly too dry to form the words.

"Yes, she'll be fine." There was an evenness to David's voice that almost calmed me, but couldn't quite reach the fear settling low in my belly.

"Wait, you know it's a female?" Incredulous, I looked over to find him watching me with pinched brows.

"Of course I do." His arm came up to rest on my opposite shoulder. "It's in her mind, Sarah. You have to feel for her mind, just like any of the humans you've fed from."

I drew in a shuddering breath. Except I hadn't known what I was doing. It had been natural. Maybe my body had relied on pure instinct to feed, but this was too intentional, and while I knew how to approach people, what did I know about cows?

My gaze drifted over to the cow. She was beautiful, the dark spot making her distinctive among the rest.

"I'll hold her mind for you, and you can feel how I do it. You show them you do not intend harm, and thank them for the gift of their blood." He looked wistfully at the animals as he spoke. It pulled at my heart to think of how gentle he was, and I understood why he chose not to eat meat.

David casually walked up to the cow and laid his hand on her neck. He smiled down at her for a moment before extending his free hand towards me and gesturing for me to come forward.

I could feel David's connection to the cow as I approached and through it, I found her. The cow's mind was different from a human's, but there were similarities, and now that I could feel her mind humming, I was shocked I hadn't been able to before.

Heavy, hot snorting breaths greeted me, but the animal didn't react beyond that. Reaching out to her with my mind, I could see what he was doing—soothing her to allow for my approach. Frowning, I tried to touch her mind, and found David welcoming me in. He reassured her of our good intentions. All the while, he stroked the rough brown fur on her neck, using his nails to scratch an itchy patch.

Large brown eyes watched me as I tried to connect my mind to the cow in the same way David had.

Peace. Calm. Reassuring. I tried to use the same strategy he had, but the moment I connected, the cow ducked its head, and all I could think about was how large she was, and how easily she could hurt me. My arm shot up for protection. But then David was there, calming her. He laid a hand on her head, meeting her unblinking gaze.

"It's okay, Sarah. She won't hurt you. Drink," he said gently, stepping back while maintaining eye contact. I leaned into the warm heaving neck of the cow, admiring the thick hide and wondering how my fangs would penetrate it. Her neck pulsed, and I tried to probe at it with my fingers the way David had done. When I thought I'd identified a vein, I leaned forward to carefully sink my aching fangs in.

I touched her mind gently and carefully, wanting to connect with her the way I had seen David do, reassuring her she was safe as her hot, rich blood poured into my mouth. She was such a refreshingly large animal to drink from. Strong, and with blood to spare. Crying at how good it tasted to drink hot blood from the source again. No human faces from my past pulled me away from the cow's throat, and I drank until I was sated. I checked in the cow's mind occasionally to confirm she was okay, that I wasn't taking too much.

I wasn't. She was fine. Content even.

Sated, I pulled away, my fangs retracting. I swiped blood away from my mouth and held my hand over the wounds I'd left in her neck, sending my energy to heal the wrongness. I met the animal's eyes, laying a hand over her forehead to enhance our mental connection, thanking her for the gift of her blood.

I released her mind and felt David do the same. The cow kept eye contact with me for an extra moment, entirely unbothered, before turning and lumbering off as though nothing had happened. She joined a group by a thick clump of grass, pushing into a gap and taking her share.

She was fine. Not harmed. Perhaps slightly weakened from the meal I had taken, but nothing permanent. A tear slid down my cheek as I watched her graze, and I angrily swiped it away before turning to follow David over the fence.

We walked back in silence for the first few miles, my mind consumed with the faces of my past. How much pain had I caused, believing there was no other choice?

This had been so different—peaceful and freeing.

David took my hand, twining our fingers before bringing them to his lips and kissing my knuckles. He understood I needed the quiet, that I hadn't been ready to talk until now, and gratitude swelled in my heart with each passing moment until I began to calm.

"How was it?" he quietly asked.

"It was perfect." I didn't meet his eyes. I could only manage a whisper. So much remained unspoken, but I couldn't find the words. Not ready to discuss my past or deal with the shame I felt at having hunted humans all these years, I lapsed into silence again.

That *voice*. My father's voice. How long had it been since I'd heard it? Since it had tormented me? With this experience, I shut it out for good.

I wasn't a predator.

I didn't *need* to drink, to kill. I could live differently.

I didn't have to be my father's daughter anymore.

The hold he'd had over me through our shared blood was gone, and with this peaceful feed, the last remaining vestige of the hunt.

David held my hand at his side and squeezed my fingers. I leaned gratefully into his warmth, breathing in the fresh country air and the peace of the day.

"We'll go again. Next week." He nodded to himself and smiled over at me.

It was a long walk back, and it quickly turned dark. He tried to engage me in conversation a few times, but I still didn't feel like talking, and after a few failed attempts to discuss our upcoming graduation, he started telling me more about the ancients.

"We have cows on the island. They're big animals, and it's easy to take a large amount of blood without impacting them too much. I told you I was a scout, and that's another part of a scout's job—noting animals and human developments that might benefit the island. It was a scout who brought back the first cows so we could start a herd of them on the island. We tend them, of course."

I imagined David being held up as a child to drink from a cow—of me doing it as a child. No wonder he felt so comfortable with them.

"But kept animals don't satisfy those of us with a more predatory animal, and we still do hunts to satisfy the need to chase. Hunts allow us to flex those instincts and give us a slew of wild animals to drink from. Those are cared for and released back into the wild when they are well enough."

Humming my understanding, I rested my head on his arm as he launched into the different animals he'd caught over the years, and some of the herd animals they raised. All the while, he rubbed my stiff fingers and looked down at them occasionally with a frown on his face.

"Are you okay?" he murmured. "Maybe taking you out there was too much?"

"No," I said, suddenly anxious that he had mistaken my silence for unhappiness. "No, David, it was great. I'm so glad you took me out there it's just—I've hunted humans for so long, and I've always believed that was the only way to survive. This was just—you just showed me a new way. A kinder way. I loved it." I met his worried eyes, so he'd know I meant what I said. "It's just a lot to wrap my mind around, is all."

We reached my building, and I turned to kiss him goodnight before heading inside. Sensing my mood, he kissed me lightly, his fingers tracing a curl as he studied my expression worriedly.

"Goodnight, Sarah."

I didn't know if I could sleep after realizing such profound truths about myself and my past, but I nodded reassuringly.

"Goodnight."

With a parting kiss on the cheek, David turned to go, but I couldn't help watching the familiar sharp lines of his body until he rounded the corner, his spiky blonde hair disappearing from sight. Sighing, I headed inside, feeling a little more lost and lonely now that he was gone.

Chapter 12

The cow's blood was still singing in my veins when I woke up to Nina pounding on my door.

Blinking blearily at the red lights on the nightstand, I sat bolt upright at the time.

It was two a.m.

"Nina, is everything okay?" I shouted, already extracting myself from the blankets and stumbling to the door as the last of the sleep faded away.

Nina's pinched face greeted me. Mid-knock, her arm was still raised, and her small fist poised to strike. She wasn't wearing makeup, and her short black hair lay flat on one side. She barely looked like herself, and I took in the gooseflesh creeping up her bare arms and disappearing into the sleep camisole she wore. My alarm spiked.

"What's happened?"

Her lips twisted before she opened her mouth, the words pouring out in a rush. "It-it's The Bones. They've called a challenge for tonight. They're already assembled on our border. We had no notice and"—her eyes widened further, and she reached out a cold hand to grip my forearm—"they've got weapons."

Awkwardly, I pulled her forward into a hug, and she pitched herself into my arms with a sob.

"Hey, it's all right. We're going to be okay. You go get changed into something warm. I'll call David to meet us there."

She gulped and nodded, putting a self-conscious hand to her hair and smiling sheepishly back at me.

"Right, yes. We have to be strong. I'm the second, after all." She huffed out a laugh, and I felt a momentary stab of pity knowing Nina had never wanted the position. Her strength didn't warrant it, but it was tradition for the leader's partner to be his second, and she'd accepted the role.

At least she'd accepted it in times of peace. Now we were at war. Nina trudged down the corridor, her thin shoulders hunched forward under the burden of responsibility.

Now that she was spurred to action, I took a minute to process the situation. Calling a challenge like this when they knew we weren't prepared was an act of aggression. I only hoped Adam was right about David acting as a deterrent. If he couldn't scare them off, there was every chance they'd wipe us out.

I grabbed some jeans and a top, carrying them out into the main area so I could dress while phoning David. Tugging on my jeans with one hand, I dialed his number, relieved when he picked up after two rings.

"Hey, sorry to wake you, but we're being challenged, and Adam is calling you in to give a display of strength."

"Tonight?" David's voice was tight, and I didn't blame him, but we didn't have time to deal with it. If The Bones were already assembled, there was no telling how long they'd give us to be ready before they attacked.

"Yes, meet me at the clan house?"

David murmured his acceptance just as I secured the zipper of my pants. Throwing on the top, I turned to find Nina ready. She hadn't put on makeup, but she'd managed to run a brush through her hair, smoothing it into a silky black cap. We hurried out the door to hail a taxi.

I needed to get there, to talk to Adam and understand what was going on. Challenges happened, but it was customary, honourable, to give the other clan enough notice so it could proceed fairly.

Of course, The Bones wouldn't give a shit about honour. My blood boiled as I burst in the door, my eyes scanning the group inside before landing on Adam. He looked terrible, his brow permanently furrowed, a nervous energy coming off him. Nina ran to him, and he enfolded her in his arms, closing his eyes for a moment and mumbling something quietly to her before turning to me.

"Sarah, thank fuck. Where's David?" Adam released Nina to clap me on the back and lead me further into the room.

"He was asleep at your place, but he's on his way now."

Adam nodded thoughtfully, ushering me into the common area where all two dozen of our members were shifting around anxiously.

David entered a few minutes later, his expression tight. He dropped a quick kiss on my lips before taking my hand and standing with me.

There had been subdued chatter in the room, but it cut off when Adam cleared his throat, his height giving him the advantage of not needing to stand on anything to be seen clearly.

"We know what The Bones are capable of, and how they're always looking to expand. Tonight, we'll let them know we aren't weak. That we'll defend our territory." His eyes flickered to David's, and I saw something like respect pass between the two men. Anxiety churned in my stomach like a living thing, and I squeezed David's hand to center myself. "They're out for blood tonight, but we have a secret weapon." Adam nodded at David, and I heard someone at the back, who might've been Tom, whoop. David's lips pressed into a tight line at being called on, and I squeezed his hand reassuringly.

They'd called the challenge for an open alley two blocks south of our clan house. It was near the border, leaving them the opportunity to retreat to their own territory should they choose.

David's hand was heavy in mine on the way down, and I could feel the tension in his stiff movements.

By the time we got there, The Bones were already gathered in neat lines. Their clan was composed of some of the biggest, most ruthless vampires around, and I took in their brawny appearance, knowing the gaggle of kids we'd brought couldn't compare.

Sure enough, they carried the weapons Nina had spoken of. No guns. Those would make too much noise, draw too much attention. But a tall man with a heavy brow and alarmingly thick arms held a steel pipe fixed his eyes on Adam menacingly. The vampire beside him, wore a studded leather jacket and held an open switchblade in a clenched fist. *His* gaze shifted from person to person as though unable to settle on a target, and it made him all the more terrifying to watch, like he would attack without warning and lose the madness I could see gleaming in his eyes.

We had Adam, myself, and a few others who could hold our own, but many of the adults had moved away over the years.

It was painfully obvious that we were the weaker clan, and those kids were relying on us to keep them safe. I drew a shuddering breath, wishing we'd found some way to spare them from this.

We lined up opposite The Bones, and David stepped forward, beginning to remove his clothes while Adam spoke.

"This territory belongs to The Shades. To question it is to question our right to exist."

At Adam's announcement, a man stepped forward. His head was shaved tight to the skin, and a number of face piercings gave him an intimidating look. He had forsaken a top despite the chill of the night, intent instead on showcasing the swirls of black ink covering the meat of his broad chest.

"You're weak, Adam. We know it, and you know it. Give us your territory, and we'll let you live. Fight and"—he smirked, and the streetlight glinted off a bit of gold in his mouth—"we'll leave no survivors."

The teenager beside me gulped, and I gave her a firm look at her display of fear. She mouthed a quick, "sorry."

"We're not weak, Simon." Adam gestured at David, who had stripped and stood two feet in front of the line. I watched with shock and awe as he transformed, falling to his hands and knees, orange and black fur sprouting across his body. A tail sprang free at the base of his spine, and his back cracked into place with a sickening snap.

At last, he stood before us as a tiger, and the girl on my left, who had gasped earlier, grasped my arm tight enough to embed her fingerprints in my skin. The majority of our members hadn't witnessed David transform, and it was as much of a shock to them as it was to The Bones.

We should have shown them before, let them get used to David's other form, but there had been no time. David prowled the area between our two clans, his hackles raised before coming to flank Adam and let loose a roar so deep and powerful that the sound trembled in my very bones.

The leader of The Bones was unphased. His only reply was to smirk and nod at the man with the steel pipe who had shifted his attention to David the moment he'd stepped forward. Those cruel eyes were now fixed with rapt attention on the animal before him. Letting the pipe fall to drag ominously on the ground, he advanced, and those on the sides moved forward subtly to flank David. He stood his ground, growling and snarling at their approach, but refusing to move. But there were so many, and I couldn't imagine a scenario where he wasn't overwhelmed and brought down.

Visions of David on the ground while they kicked him tore through my mind, but he didn't flinch. Instead, he stood with his hackles raised and roared again—the sound echoing into the night. The men paused only a minute before continuing forward.

He needed help.

I could help him.

But it would mean exposing myself, both to my clan and theirs.

I had to stop it.

With trembling hands, I pulled off my long coat and tugged off my clothes until I was down to my underwear. The girl beside me stilled, no doubt tracking my movements. She'd been so scared at the start. It came off her in waves. Once I'd stripped, I turned to her and offered a reassuring smile.

"It's going to be okay."

Her mouth hung open in shock. She was a kind-looking youth with long brown hair and wide doe-like eyes.

Someone worth protecting.

Closing my eyes tight, I turned inward to find the tiger within and embraced, wishing I'd forced myself to practice. Embracing the tiger should have worked like it had last time, but I was too panicked. My mind filled with fear, and though I could feel the tiger within me, it slid out of my grasp when I tried to hold on to it. I shook my head to dispel the growing panic, but it remained. I couldn't stand keeping my eyes closed, knowing David was in danger, and I cracked an eye to find the man with the pipe inching closer. The muscles in his arms tensed as he prepared to lift the weapon.

No.

My mind cleared into sharp focus, and this time when I went to embrace the tiger, it didn't slip away.

The first time I'd shifted, I felt nothing. Now, fear coursed through my veins, forcing my eyes open to watch the approaching danger.

The world swirled around me, my body turning nebulous, and when it came into focus again, I was lower to the ground.

Anger replaced the fear, and I growled low in my throat. Outraged at the audacity of this man, I charged forward to stand beside David. A roar tore through my throat, and satisfaction swelled in my chest as the man with the steel pipe took a wary step back, his thick eyebrows drawn up in surprise.

How dare they come here to threaten us? I let my rage pour into the sound I was making, my roar blending with David's until the night air filled with deadly promise.

Uncertainty flashed in their leader's eyes. With a snap of his fingers, he called his men back to fall into line beside him.

Without a word, he nodded at Adam, turning and heading back down the alley. Those beside him flanking, and others moving to stand behind him and protect his exposed back.

We stayed still as stone, watching as they rounded the corner and disappeared into their territory.

We'd done it.

The Shades were safe, but now my clan knew what I was, and they didn't know me. How many times had I shrugged off their friendly advances, preferring to be left alone with my pain? To face the shadows alone?

They weren't my friends, were barely my family, but for the blood bond between us. Would they turn hostile? Demand answers that weren't mine to give?

I turned and found a sea of shocked faces. More than a few were tear stained. Then someone at the back let out a whoop and those frozen expressions broke. Now everybody was cheering with joy and rushing forward. Hands landed on me, disappearing into my fur and feeling oddly good as they rubbed against the grain.

"Thank you, Sarah."

Words of gratitude warmed my heart as never before, because now the clan saw me and not one of them turned away in disgust or fear. How long had I spent thinking of myself as impossibly different from them thanks to the horrors of my past?

But now?

No one turned away, and I twisted to see nothing but shining faces. Even Adam wore a small smile, like he couldn't help the bit of joy slipping through the cracks in his facade. His hand clasping Nina's, who beamed beside him, he watched over us all with a sparkle of pride in his glistening eyes.

David had been dislodged from his place at my side, forced to contend with his own array of admirers, and I pushed my way through the crowd to him, not surprised when they realized my intentions and parted to let me through. Then I was staring at him, truly able to take in the breathtaking beauty of his tiger form.

Thick, luxurious fur rippled across four hundred pounds of pure muscle. The blue of his eyes had been replaced with the molten gold of a tiger's eye, and I studied this new version of him with awe.

The crowd around us thinned. A few stragglers remained when we padded over to where our clothing lay in piles somebody had kindly neatened up.

I shifted, not caring for my nakedness. I was disappointed when my vision cleared and I found David with his back to me, already in his human form and wearing a pair of jeans.

He was faster than I was, and I guess it made sense since he was more experienced with shifting. At least I had a chance to admire the rippling muscles in his back and the v of his waist before he slid on his shirt. Our clan mates had vacated the alley to give us the privacy we needed to shift. There was no reason for David to keep himself turned away, but he did so, his hands fisted at his sides.

My skin pebbled in the chill air. His scent drifted over to me on a gust of cool wind, and I gulped it down greedily. The near fight had left my blood pumping with adrenaline, and now that the danger had passed, and I was alone with him, it only stoked the fire between us. I drifted over to him with an outstretched hand.

"Sarah, it's not a good idea. This has been a long night, and I think we should just go home." His voice was tight, like he was speaking through gritted teeth. His shoulders were stiff with tension, and his back was in knots. I'd been stepping carefully, not making a sound on my approach, but he'd sensed me.

He was just as attuned to me as I was to him, even if he didn't openly admit it.

"Why?"

"Because it's been a long night, and we should get some sleep."

It was a stupid excuse, a pathetic excuse. The knuckles on his fisted hands grew whiter with each passing moment.

I took another step towards him.

"Why?" I asked again, and was pleased when he floundered.

"I'm tired." The lie was thick in the air. I was close enough now to let a hand drift around his waist as I leaned into the warmth of his back and inhaled.

"No, you're not."

He was a steel rod, and I sought to soften him, running my hand across his abdomen to hook into the seam of his jeans.

"Yes, I am. Now can you please put on some clothes—"

Before he could utter another ridiculous excuse, I slipped a hand into his pants to take his hard cock in my palm. My hand skated along his shaft, learning the feel of him. David shuddered, and my body responded with a surge of need strong enough for me to hook a leg over his hip.

"What are you doing?" His voice was accusatory, but he didn't move to stop me as I took a firm grip of his shaft and pumped him in a slow rhythm. My thumb glided over a drop of pre-cum, and I slid it along the head of his cock, before roughly pulling along the length of him.

With a pitifully raspy cough, David pulled away.

"I don't—Sarah, it's—we've got to get back. I'll wait on the street for you to get changed."

Dumbfounded, I could do nothing but stare after him as he headed back to the mouth of the alley and disappeared from around the corner.

Irritated and aroused, I had no choice but to begrudgingly get changed, coming around the corner to find him leaning against the brick. His brows were pinched in concern.

"Hey. Sorry, it's just that it's pretty late."

All I could do was nod along like he hadn't been about to explode in my hand, just as desperate for release as I was.

"Can I walk you home?" There was a request for forgiveness in his tone, and I hated the vulnerability of it.

"Yeah, let's go." I took his hand in mine, imagining his long fingers teasing my clit. Neither of us spoke during the walk back. I expected a halfhearted goodnight peck on the lips when we reached my apartment, but David spun me towards him, his hands taking hold of my hips in a bruising grip as he pulled me flush against the hard line of him. He was still hard, and his length pressed painfully into my belly as he claimed my mouth. He kissed me like it was the first and last time—every bit of emotion and passion poured into it, and I whimpered when his hands stayed on my hips. When they refused to wander, no matter how I tugged at them.

But then he buried one in my hair, tilting my head to give him better access until he broke the kiss to draw in a ragged breath. He nuzzled into my neck, huffing in a breath like a man starved for air in a display of a need so powerful, I couldn't begin to understand the amount of control necessary to contain it.

At some point our minds had joined, sensation and need flowing back and forth between us like a burning river. I gasped when he nipped at the skin of my neck, and the delightful sensation shot right to my aching core. Whimpering in a needy voice I barely recognized as mine, I squirmed helplessly against his hold, and I tried desperately to roll my hips against his hard length. But he held me firm, and it was so cruel I wanted to cry.

He wanted me. None of this made sense. Brows drawn, I let myself explore his frazzled mind, searching for an explanation.

But as soon as I began to search for an answer, he pulled away both in mind and body, leaving me breathless and only able to stare up at him in shock. In the brilliant blue of his eyes, I saw a world of sadness that I struggled to understand. I wanted to tell him it was okay, to pull him back down into our embrace until all thought had melted into sensation, but it was painfully obvious there was something he was keeping from me.

I'd tried to ignore it, to excuse it away, to pretend the reasons he gave for avoiding my touch were valid, but now? There was something else to it, something I'd missed.

"Goodnight." His whispered words were a dagger to my heart, and he seemed just as defeated as I was when he pulled his hand back to hang dejectedly at his sides. His gaze burned into mine, and I thought he would take me back into his arms. But he took a single step back, and then another, his eyes never leaving my face. At last, I was the one to turn away, no longer able to stand the way he was leaving me again—aching for him and knowing another sleepless night awaited.

Chapter 13

"Maybe he's gay?" Nina said with a shrug before pulling out a bottle of azure nail polish from her pocket. The frazzled woman from the previous night was gone. Nina's hair was styled with curlers that were busy setting and wearing a polka dot bathrobe. She'd done some kind of skin treatment on her legs, and the scent of citrus and jasmine tickled my nose mercilessly. Still, as much as she'd hate to admit it, the confrontation had left its toll, and I noted the dark circles under her eyes peeking through the layer of foundation she'd applied.

This talking thing was new for me. I'd always been content to let Nina fill as much of the silence with her cheery voice until it rubbed off on me, if even just a little, but not this morning. I'd woken after a few hours of broken sleep, my body still on fire from the night before, and hadn't been able to resist asking her advice.

The moment I'd started speaking, she had gone quiet like she'd been waiting for me to share, and dared not say a word lest it scare me off. It had been enough to leave me with a sense of guilt at not opening up to her sooner, and relief that she was someone I could talk to about what was going on with David.

"No, he's definitely not gay." There was too much that told me otherwise. What I'd seen in his mind. The way his body reacted to mine. The way he looked at me. The way he kissed me like I was the air he needed. Frowning, I watched as Nina dragged the polish over her thumb nail, squinting at it and turning her thumb in the light as she tried to decide whether she liked the colour.

"What the hell, then? Guys are always tripping over themselves to get with you. You're like model gorgeous." She held both hands up for emphasis. I watched the saturated end of her brush with trepidation, relieved when it didn't spill onto our already bedraggled couch. She returned to her nails, holding her hand out and wiggling her fingers while she admired her work. Only two nails were done, but I could already tell the colour complemented her peach complexion perfectly.

Sighing, I tipped my head back again, crossing my arms over my chest. I didn't think I was 'model gorgeous,' but I'd never had trouble with a man not being interested in taking me to his bed. Emotionally, I might have been unavailable, but physically? My sex drive had made the physical side of things easy, and it should be easy with David, because of how right it felt when he touched me. Only it wasn't and I didn't know why. Blowing out a frustrated breath, I slumped back into the threadbare couch.

"Maybe he's just nervous? David seems a bit." She paused. "Sheltered. Maybe he hasn't dated a lot?"

He'd definitely led a sheltered life, but I knew he'd dated while he traveled. He'd hinted at it even if he hadn't outright told me. Besides, he had half the waitstaff at the Sticky Spoon smitten with him, and he hadn't had to do a thing.

Even the gay line chef had started to peek his head out of the kitchen when word of David's arrival reached him. It couldn't be just that. Then there had been that block I'd felt in his mind, like something was holding him back, and he hated whatever it was just as much as I did.

"You know what you should do? Take control. Maybe he's just shy." Nina shrugged nonchalantly, like it was the obvious solution, and I rolled my eyes in response. My gut told me it was more than that, but what if she was right, and David just needed a push? He could be waiting for me to really show him how ready I was to make the next move. Maybe that was what the block was—nerves on his part and a fear of taking control. That would be very much like him; wanting to be sure that I was ready for something before doing it.

Tomorrow, I'd show him just how ready I was to move forward. With a self-satisfied smile to myself, I twisted my head and waggled my eyebrows at Nina, who smiled delightedly back. I really needed to work on being more present with her.

"Want to go shopping?"

DAVID

I'd never understood the human concept of hell with its fire and brimstone. The idea of eternal torment had sounded ridiculous. Only now, I was starting to understand what it would feel like. How I'd found the inner strength to walk out of that alley, knowing Sarah was stripped bare and filled with the same need that had begun to define my time with her, was beyond my understanding. Groaning, I pushed my head back into the pillow. I'd spent the remainder of the night remembering how my cock had fit so perfectly into her small hand. How her breathy gasps had followed the rhythm of her tentative pumps like she was dying to join me.

I wanted more, had wanted everything since the moment our eyes first locked on that fateful blind date. There was a rightness to being around her, and it had only grown stronger the more time we'd spent in each other's company. Until that craving—that need to claim her in this irrevocable act—was overwhelming my every thought and impulse.

The only way to combat it would be to stay away, but there was no chance of keeping myself apart from her now, of playing aloof or pretending I just wanted to be friends. Not when she'd seen my mind and knew how hard she made me.

How hard she still made me after I'd found release by my hand often enough to leave the skin sore in my grip. It didn't matter. Just the thought of her and her pouty smile had me shuddering with need and stiffening again. At some point, I'd need to get up, eat something, get changed. Hell, I'd need to see her again, and I wanted to.

Badly. There was a tightness in my chest that only eased when she was close, and it grew worse the longer we were apart until I could barely breathe through the need to seek her out. How the hell was I supposed to do this? It was too much, and I was too weak. The only sane thing was to find some way to extract myself, to break the ties between us and release her from this living flame binding us together in agony.

Only I'd lost all sanity where she was concerned. I could never do it. So long as she wanted me, I was hers—would be hers—and it was growing increasingly difficult to convince myself that there was a chance she wasn't really mine. That the elders were right, and what she felt was a fabrication.

If I gave in now, if I let myself give into the indescribable strength of my need for her, I'd risk losing her for good. And while my body begged me to relent, my heart couldn't take the possibility of her loss. It squeezed in my chest, leaving me weak with worry until I'd found the courage to walk away. Because as much as I wanted to fuck her, to claim her and make her mine in body and soul, it couldn't just be for now.

When I took her, it had to be forever.

SARAH

Nina and I both had the morning off, and after I made her my rendition of David's spiced blood, we headed out to go dress shopping. The store I had in mind was a bus ride away. It'd take most of the morning, but it'd be worth it.

"Did you talk to Adam after last night?"

Nina gave a tentative bob of her head as we fought our way through the crowd to exit the bus.

"And how's he doing?" So long as we avoided mentioning vampires or anything supernatural, we could talk freely, but I still glanced around to see if anyone on the bus was paying attention, and I breathed a little easier when we stepped out into the open air where there was more than an inch of space between us and listening ears.

"Well, you know, he's…" Her brows puckered with worry, and I reached out to squeeze her arm. She looked up gratefully at me before giving a weak smile. "Nervous. Last night was unprecedented, and I think it made him realize how vulnerable we are. He told me last night that he's going to look into joining our clan with The Lucky Draws."

My mouth hung open.

It'd mean giving up power, control, all the things that Adam relished. She nodded knowingly at my expression. We'd stopped walking, forcing an irritated man with a suitcase to dart around us.

"Yeah, I know. It's a big step, but if you and David hadn't been there…"

I squeezed her upper arm.

The Bones would've slaughtered them. Every. Last. One.

"Any word from them this morning?" At my query, Nina snorted.

"Yeah, if you can call two drugged women with bags over their heads being dumped at our border as a peace offering 'hearing from them'." She rolled her eyes. "Don't worry. Adam saw them home safely. Fucking Bones."

I nodded my agreement, and we started walking down the street towards the shop. Those vicious assholes thought they'd show their respect for us by dropping off those women like they were prime cuts of meat?

The idea turned my stomach, and I was glad Adam was interested in joining with The Lucky Draws. I'd heard only decent things about them, and they were a large clan at eighty strong. If we joined them, we'd be reasonably safe.

Lost in thought, I almost walked past the thrift shop, only pausing when Nina grabbed my elbow. "Wasn't this the place?"

I grinned up at the hole in the wall shop with its baby pink sign.

Rosetta's Rags. But inside, nothing was a rag. The proprietor was a short middle-aged woman who favoured florals and prided herself on a collection of the most scandalous vintage and modern dresses. The jaw dropping kind. They were the sorts of things one would wear if they were looking for a one-night stand, or to entice their reluctant boyfriend into the bedroom.

We hurried in, and I eagerly ran to the racks, sifting through the selections until I had a handful to try on. Nina was in her element, and she had an armful picked out for me by the time I had found a change room in the back.

After going through more dresses than I could count, I finally settled on a black number with a low v neckline, showcasing the swell of my breasts and triangular cutouts in the sides. It was Nina approved with a short skirt and low back. The dress emphasized my waist, giving me more of an hour-glass figure than the willowy one I possessed, and revealing entirely too much skin.

Grumbling about the price given just how little fabric I was getting, I paid and we headed home. I'd speak to David and set up a date with him after work tonight. Nina had taken the day off, and she was delighted when I told her she could help me get ready.

Tonight was the night.

I refused to take no for an answer.

I stared at myself in the mirror, eyeing Nina's work. She'd added a hint of blush to my high cheekbones and a dark shadow skirting above my eye, making the brown colour standout. We'd left my riot of crimson curls loose and flowing down my back.

She'd wanted me to tie it up to show off the delicate nape of my neck, but I hadn't been able to shake the feel of David's hand tangling in the tresses to pull me closer. I wanted him to do that again, to have that handhold. Blushing madly, I'd somehow convinced her it looked better down. I looked about as well as I ever would, meaning there was nothing left to do but head over to David's.

He'd agreed to us spending the evening at his place. Nina had asked Adam over to ours. There was nowhere to go, nowhere to hide.

I barely processed the trip to David's building. The last time I'd seen him, the tension between us had been thick. Would it be the same this time?

Would we even say a word to each other, or would he take me in his arms the way I longed for him to?

Nervously, I rapped three times on the flaking paint of his front door. David wore a dark blue button-up shirt that emphasized the pale blue of his eyes, and I drank the sight of him in eagerly. White flour dusted a spot on his black pants, and I imagined him noticing it and being annoyed at having chosen the dark colour. I wasn't, though. He looked spectacular in black.

Taking my hand, he pulled me across the threshold, greeting me with a quick peck on the lips and a vaguely alarmed perusal of my outfit.

"Hey. Is it a special occasion?" He eyed my dress warily, and I laughed.

"Not really," I said with a mysterious quirk of my lips.

David moved into my side, his hand grazing across the exposed skin of the cutout as he pulled me close and kissed my temple. His scent nearly overwhelmed me at the unexpected closeness, and last night swam in my mind. I leaned into him, eager for more of his intoxicating touch, more of his warmth, but he pulled away. His eyes clouded with worry at my reaction. With a small smile, he turned to head back into the kitchen.

I unhooked my heels, padding after him, and sniffing the air eagerly. Whatever he was making smelled delicious—the spices wafted over to me as he shook two different pans and stirred something in a pot. I loved it when he cooked. I came up behind him and wrapped my arms around him. The nerves as I'd been getting ready and knowing what I'd planned for tonight seemed to disappear now that I was here with him.

This was David. I couldn't be nervous around him. His mind shone like a beacon, and I gently reached out to touch it, eager for his warmth. He wrapped my hands in his and brought them up to kiss along the knuckles. Our minds were connected and content for a moment as we basked in the togetherness after a day apart. At last, I released him and moved to the table when it became increasingly obvious that I was preventing him from tending to the food.

Taking a seat at the card table overlooking the kitchen, I wondered what our mental connection would be like during sex. When we kissed, I could feel it from both our perspectives, the desire and sensations emphasized through the experience. But sex? I could only imagine how it would be when it echoed.

Relaxing into my seat, I sat back and admired the way David moved expertly around the kitchen, his lean, broad-shouldered frame bending and twisting, tracking with smooth, quick movements like he was lost in a dance. My core tightened with need the longer I watched him, but I only smiled when he turned to me, a question in his eye.

Dinner was as delicious as it smelled, and I hungrily dug in, lamenting the cow's blood I'd shared with Nina earlier. I'd tried my best to heat it and add some spices, but it never compared to the way David cooked. I felt a swell of pity for Nina, who had raved over the dish, but never tried the real thing. Tonight, he'd made the blood into something resembling meatballs, and he served it next to flat bread with a red sauce.

After we'd finished eating, we moved to the lumpy brown couch, and I remembered that night, when I'd come here looking for answers after seeing him in the dream, how gently he'd walked me through my missing past. Cuddling into his arms, I thought about how much I cared for him, how he'd brought so much light and laughter into my life.

And how badly I wanted more.

David's arm draped across my shoulders, and I played with his fingers. He shifted beside me, and I noted the way his breathing picked up. We were hardly touching, but that need between us was always present. He felt it as keenly as I did, an ever-present tortuous pull.

Turning to him, I found him watching me with a half smile, and a question in his eyes. I'd kept my thoughts private, but he still knew I was planning something. We were too in tune, and I couldn't stop myself from giggling at the absurdity of it.

There were no secrets between us, and that should terrify me, but I had a marrow deep trust in David that made the vulnerability of the experience freeing.

"What?" he asked, grinning and leaning forward to lightly press his lips to mine. "What is it? Are you going to let me in on the joke?" He breathed the words against my lips. I loved this, loved him, and I groaned against his mouth before creating the necessary distance to gather my thoughts and answer him.

I stared into his beautiful eyes, the ones that had captured me from the second I'd first seen them, and that indescribable shade of blue I could get lost in. My hand shot up to rest on his cheek, and the smile tilting his lips slipped as things between us turned serious.

"No joke. I love you." I let those warm feelings, the depth of them, flow to David and his face cleared, the blue of his eyes darkening.

"I love you, too," he whispered, like it was obvious. The kind of thing you didn't bother saying, like the sky was blue and the grass was green.

You knew it without saying it. Eyes pricking with tears, I tugged the front of his shirt, pulling him closer so I could nibble on his delectable bottom lip and suck it into my mouth.

His taste, his presence, the way his hands shot up to lightly graze the skin of my exposed back, all of it was nearly painful in its intensity. The smallest taste of an addiction that didn't take the edge off but left me wanting more, like a drop of sugar on my tongue when the candy jar was right there, and I only needed to reach out and grasp it. I moaned into his mouth, and let myself sink into the sensation fully.

Every other time I'd done so, he'd pulled away, and I'd been left frustrated, but tonight…

I refused to be sent away. Need flowed through my veins, thick and sweet as honey. David groaned against my mouth, and the feral sound of it sent a new bolt of arousal straight to my core. Whimpering, I turned my head, giving him access to my neck. He fell upon the spot that always brought me to a frenzy, circling it with his tongue mercilessly as I helplessly arched my back into the sensation.

"Sarah," he said, arms coming up to grip my back.

I touched my forehead to his, increasing our connection and letting our hot breath mix. He spoke as if he wanted to say something, but I didn't want to talk anymore. This wasn't the night for talking. So I captured his lips before he could say another word, losing myself to the rhythm of our mouths moving against each other as my hands ventured lower to explore him. His fingers trailed helplessly up and down my back, but they turned rough when I straddled him.

He was as hard as I had expected, and he gripped me tight to his chest, groaning against my mouth and sending delicious shivers through my lips. There was no sign of pulling away this time, and I rolled my hips into his, craving the friction of his cock straining against his pants.

"Mmmm." He let loose a low animalistic growl, moving into my neck to kiss the sensitive skin there. My mouth found his, and I let the taste of him overwhelm my senses, but it wasn't enough. I wanted everything from him tonight, and I intended to take it.

But at some point, after I'd moved onto his lap, our minds had brushed against one another, and I sensed a flare of hesitation as my hand snaked down his torso. He still kissed me, but more gently now, and I could feel him mentally rein himself in. His hands relaxing and his grip on my back turning from feral need to tenderness.

Refusing to allow him to pull away, I found his mouth and kissed him hard, letting my tongue tangle with his until he was groaning against me again. Never had I slept with someone who had held out like this. I fought to slip the straps off my shoulder, to pull my dress down until my breasts were exposed.

"Sarah." Eyes wide, he stared up at me with awe in his lust-clouded eyes, and it was the most beautiful sight I'd ever seen. Then he was kissing me again, his hand falling to my breasts, those long fingers I loved so much pinching an erect nipple. With his other hand, he gripped my back, and I rolled my hips into his straining cock. The friction of it sending delightful shivers through my soaking cunt. Our hot breath mingled when we parted to take a panting breath. My heart pounded against his, and I pressed my palm against his chest.

He inhaled sharply as I moved to his neck, gently sucking the skin where I'd bitten him during his initiation. It was a spot I cherished, revered even. The first sharing of blood between us. I drew my tongue lovingly across the spot.

We'd be a little bit married. He'd said it, and I believed him.

I was his, and he was mine. I let the feeling of it, the certainty, flow from my mind to his, but instead of the joy I expected at my desire for our togetherness, I found an endless sea of fear.

"Sarah, stop."

The moment the word stop was out, I knew it was over. The urgency behind that one word left me sitting back in confusion. He wanted me. I could feel how badly he wanted this. Just like I wanted it. When he didn't say anything more, I moved back into the circle of his arms, sucking and nipping at his lips.

He was shy, scared. That was the problem, and I felt some confirmation in his mind. Brows puckered, I peppered kisses along his jaw.

"Shhh...it's okay," I said between kisses.

He relaxed against me, trailing his fingers up and down my spine, and I shivered at the bursts of pleasure his touch sent skating along my nerves. Then he was there at my neck, gripping me tightly again, and I groaned my approval. But a flare of that same endless fear broke across the surface of his mind again, disrupting the perfect moment between us. Pulling back to look at him, I kept my hands on his forearms and studied his expression. His brows were pinched, his eyes begging me to understand.

The way he looked at me was heartbreaking, and I frowned down at him, my hand reaching up to cup his cheek.

"Hey, it's okay." But my soothing words did nothing to calm the wild panic in his eyes.

"Sarah, I can't. I can't do this," he said, taking my hand from his cheek and kissing the palm. His voice was broken. Shattered.

"Why? What's wrong?" My heart still pounded. I needed him like I needed air, but something was terribly wrong. "Why can't you? I don't understand. I know you love me. I know that, and I know you want me, so why? Why keep this distance between us?"

And he had kept a distance between us. My mind conjured every occasion when he'd pulled back, when he'd restrained himself. He'd put this wedge between us on purpose, and looking into his eyes now, I knew it to be true. I hadn't wanted to believe it before. I'd convinced myself he was just nervous, but there was more to it, and I knew without a doubt he wasn't going to take me to his bed tonight.

My eyes stung with unshed tears as I moved off of him and turned away, my needy cunt protesting as I moved farther from what I needed. Just another night where he refused me. I was a fool to think that I could seduce him. I pulled my dress back up, securing the straps over my shoulders, and smoothed down my hair as I fought to compose myself, to push down the hurt so I could be strong. David's eyes followed every movement. I could feel them on me, but I didn't meet his gaze. This rejection felt worse than all the previous ones.

There had been no pretending, no reason to stop.

"Sarah…" he began, his tone pleading.

I stayed turned away, pretending to smooth out nonexistent wrinkles in my dress.

"You know how I feel about you. I love you, and I think you're the most beautiful woman in the world. Of course I want you. God, I want you so badly sometimes that when we're just sitting together, I can't stop thinking about it. I could die from how badly I want you. It's not about that. I promise. Sarah? Please look at me."

The raw emotion in his voice tugged at my heart, and I couldn't help but look. His eyes shone with worry even as he begged me to listen to what he had to say.

"I'm sorry. I didn't—" He blew out a breath, sitting up and straightening his shirt. "There's something I haven't told you." He licked his kiss-swollen lips before gently taking my hand and staring down at it, smoothing over the skin of my knuckles as he spoke.

"When I left the island, the leader of the elders approached me in private. He knew how I felt about you. Even as kids, I'd had a crush on you. I was never very good at hiding my feelings." He smiled down ruefully at my hand, playing with my fingers nervously.

"He told me that when I found you. I needed to bring you back to the island right away. I wasn't supposed to pursue you romantically." David took a deep, shaky breath, and my heart clenched right alongside his.

"He explained to me that you hadn't been around other ancients in so long. You'd been apart from other ancients for most of your life. Seeing a man of your own kind after so long, that…It was very probable that you would have a certain level of attraction towards that man. That you might be confused through no fault of your own."

My mind turned over his words, trying to comprehend what he was saying, this fear that haunted him.

"David, I've dated vampires and even a witch once—"

"That doesn't count. Sarah, at this point, any vampire, witch, or shapeshifter you've met may have had an ancient ancestor five or more generations ago. It's not the same. There are pheromones that you could never be prepared for. I was supposed to stay away from you, to bring you home, but I couldn't, and I'm sorry for that. This would've been simpler if I'd been a stronger man." He shuddered, bringing my hand up to his lips, holding it there. His next words vibrated through my hand, and my traitorous body responded. "From the second I saw you, there was no way I could stay away. Not from you—from this." Every one of his words echoed in my bones.

I couldn't stay away from this either, but I'd never wanted to. This thing between us was fire and magic. It was more than I'd ever expected, and I wanted it so badly it hurt.

"Everything we've done so far is forgivable. But that. Sex? Sarah, I can't do that to you. Not knowing that you might be confused about your feelings for me. So, you see, it's not about how I feel about you. None of this has anything to do with my feelings or just how badly I want you." His eyes glistened as he hazarded a glance at my face.

I was stunned into numb silence, my heart frozen into stillness. What he'd said had been worse than anything I could have imagined.

There had been a reason he held himself apart from me, and it had nothing to do with his feelings. No, those were just as vibrant as the ones I held for him, and while I wanted to take that knowledge and draw comfort from it, I couldn't, because what he had said was almost worse. This wasn't about love or desire.

It was about trust.

He didn't trust how I felt about him.

He didn't trust me.

David didn't trust me.

I pulled my lifeless hand away. It didn't feel like part of my body anymore, and David watched it fall frozen to my side, his expression pained at the loss. Swallowing hard to keep myself from crying, I stood up and headed for the door.

"Sarah, wait!" he shouted, rushing ahead of me to block the exit. "I'm sorry. You know I love you. Please understand, this wasn't what I wanted."

Anger like I'd never known before brewed in my chest, demanding a release. This thing between us was the greatest gift I'd been given in my life, and he dared to question it. To question me?

"You love me, but you don't trust me? You think what I feel for you is some kind of physical infatuation?" I shouted into his shocked face.

His mouth hung open. The words may as well have been daggers, but before the pain in his eyes could sway me, I pushed my way past his stunned figure, barely managing to hold the tears back until I was out the door.

David with his small smile and laughing blue eyes. He was brilliant, kind, funny, and intense all at once. Before he'd come into my life, I'd been purposefully closed off from other people. Even the men I'd dated since moving to the city had been kept at a distance. Not even Adam. Other than Nina, friendships had seemed impossible, but since I'd started seeing David, I'd managed a few conversations with the other waitresses at the diner.

It had all been because of him, because of the intoxicating way he believed in me.

All the pain and doubt that I'd held onto for so long melted away when he was around, because he saw me and loved me unfailingly.

Only he didn't trust that I felt the same.

I thought of all the days when we'd been too busy to see each other and how much I'd missed him in every way possible; his smell, his touch, his mind, his voice. How could he believe our relationship was based on a physical infatuation caused by my lack of exposure to other ancients as an adult?

It was like a knife to the heart.

The day wore on and I made a point of reading the chapters I needed to catch up on. He didn't call, and I wasn't sure if he would. Not after seeing how hurt I'd been the night before. He knew I'd need space to work through things, but it didn't stop me from missing him.

I badly wanted to see him. To feel his arms around me and talk with him, laugh with him, and forget the events of last night. Did he really think I was leading him on? That this soul deep obsession was the result of some hormonal deficit I'd been suffering from? That it wouldn't matter who had come to me here, I'd have fallen in love with any ancient who had found me first?

It was absolutely ridiculous, and the sheer disregard for what lay between us twisted in my heart like a dagger. How could he not understand what he'd meant to me these past two months?

But how could I convince him? He loved me and he wanted me, but he needed to protect me?

Bah, I put down a plate of scrambled eggs a little too hard, startling an older woman who blinked up at me through thick glasses.

"Sorry," I muttered, offering her a tight smile.

I could think of no way to convince David of my genuine feelings towards him. I'd trusted him with my heart so completely.

Me, who trusted no one.

I'd been helpless from the second I'd laid eyes on him.

Most of my shift was spent looking over my shoulder, hoping he would show up. Confusion clouded my mind. I didn't know what I would say, but my eyes were hungry for the sight of him.

Those meddling elders had done this. They'd made him believe, put these doubts in his mind. A fresh wave of hate rose in me towards those shadowy figures.

I loved David, and he loved me. Desperately. But he didn't trust me.

That was a problem.

After work, I ate a bowl of cold blood for dinner, not having the heart to heat it or add the spices that reminded me of David's cooking. I'd only heated it on the rare occasion before meeting David. My whole life had been that way, doing only what must be done to survive. Anything more hadn't been worth the effort. I blinked back tears as I stared down at my half-eaten meal.

It had only been a day apart, and already I felt like I was missing a limb. I couldn't stay away from him. Pushing back the cheap plastic chair with a loud squeal, I stood up decisively to grab my coat. He didn't have any lectures on Monday. With any luck, he'd be home. I just hoped Adam wasn't there.

David's stunned face greeted me when the door opened. He looked terrible. His skin was pale and dark circles lined his eyes.

"Sarah." His voice was rough and gravelly, unused.

As much of a wreck as I'd been, it was clear he was suffering, too, and my instinct was to hold him, to comfort him. I hadn't known what I was going to think, to feel when I saw him, and I was overcome with emotion. As frustrated as I was, I greedily drank in the sight of his lanky frame in grey sweats and a loose white shirt, his hair tousled madly. Without knowing what I was doing, I launched myself into his arms, my mouth finding his. He wrapped himself around me, enveloping me in his warmth.

His taste, his scent. I felt like I hadn't seen him in weeks. My body had missed him, and every part of me sang that I had come home.

"I'm sorry, Sarah," he murmured against my lips. But I shushed him as I pushed him further into the apartment, guiding him over to the couch.

We sat down together, kissing and running our hands over each other, and I let his touch soothe me from the time we'd spent apart. Such a tiny amount of time, but it was too much.

A minute was too much.

"I love you," he whispered, nuzzling my cheek and taking great gasping breaths against my skin. Like he was trying to soak me in just as much as I was trying to with him. He loved me. Wanted me just as badly. The feeling was liberating. He wasn't shy, wasn't nervous, he was scared.

His mind reached out to mine, and his need to connect to comfort himself was desperate. I breathed an inward sigh of relief as our minds connected.

He was open to me now. There were no more secrets, even if the one he'd been harbouring had been damning enough. Hungrily, I took in the warmth of his love, letting it soothe the pain in my mind.

I moved to deepen the kiss and press myself against him as I had the night before, finding him painfully hard. His eyes were hazy with lust and longing. Lost to it as much as I'd ever been. My mouth drifted to his, but when I moved to straddle him, he held me back with a hand on my shoulder.

"Sarah. Please. I can't do this. I told you. Anything but this." He looked so worried and honest that it hurt anew. We had just shared our souls with each other, yet he could still doubt me?

He was mine, and I was his.

I gently shifted off him and sat on the couch, resigned.

"It's not just what the elders said, Sarah. It's…" He sighed. "I can't lose you. I can't. You're everything to me and if we do this, it changes us. Our relationship would be forever altered, and there'd be no going back. What if we go back to the island and you discover that these feelings you've had for me were because you hadn't met another ancient in so many years? I don't think I could just be your friend again. No, I know I wouldn't be able to. I'd lose you and I can't…" He looked so lost and worried that it broke my heart.

"David, you're not going to lose me," I said, taking his hand in mine. He looked so haunted as he stared off into space. "I'm not a child, and I know my own mind. I know that I love you, and I know that I want this."

He turned to meet my eyes. "I still can't take that risk." He gently stroked my face, and I sighed into it. "Okay, so what do we do now? I won't go back to the island, and you believe that I'm unable to think clearly where you're concerned."

"I don't know." His brow puckered. Somehow, seeing him acting so anxious put me at ease, like we were in this together, and I couldn't help but smile.

He was trapped by what the elder had told him. I just had to break his resolve. He gave me a small cautious smile in reply, sensing a change in my demeanor. I moved closer to him, kissing his shoulder and reaching out with my mind. I'd break his resolve, but for tonight, I just wanted to be close to him; to be surrounded by his presence and relax into his embrace.

Chapter 14

"Are you sure you want me to stop?" I purred, dragging my tongue along the shell of David's ear. He shuddered beneath me. With our minds joined, I could feel how hard and needy he was for me, and I relished in my power. There was no question of his desire anymore. He shared it all with me, and the things he wanted to do left my throat parched and sent a furious blush up my neck.

"Yes, we should stop." But his words had no strength to them, and I smiled against his ear before trailing kisses along the sharp edge of his jawline.

"Mmm, we don't have to, though." The taunt landed, and David's hands moved to cup my ass. He ran his hands over my jeans, and I wanted to rip them off so I could feel his fingers dig into the tender flesh. But that wasn't how this game was played. Over the past three days, every time I'd removed an article of clothing, he would hesitate, the elder's words driving him to gently set me aside. And I'd let him. But there would come a time where he wouldn't be able to stop, and I could be patient.

The reward would be worth it.

So I kept my clothes on, moaning my approval into his ear when his hand ventured lower.

"Sarah, please, we have to stop."

Hearing him beg was what I wanted, and I only pressed myself tighter to him, taking one of his hands and placing it on my breast in encouragement.

His hand flexed before he pulled it away, and that told me everything. Slowly, I was breaking his resolve—little cracks appearing.

But I wanted more. Sitting up on my knees, I pressed his face to my chest. My nipples were hard as diamonds, and I knew he could see them through the thin fabric of my tank top.

"Sarah, no." Gently, but firmly, he took a grip on my shoulders, and pushed me back to sitting. "I told you before. I can't do this." He shook his head sadly, and I sighed before climbing off him.

I didn't want to rehash the same argument, so I sat down next to him on the couch and adjusted my clothing, steadfastly avoiding his eyes and pulling out the chemistry textbook I'd brought over. As if I could concentrate with arousal still pumping through my veins. I shifted uncomfortably, trying to dispel the wetness soaking my panties. I didn't need to look over to know his eyes were trained on me as I tried to refocus my attention. Finally, he sighed and pulled out his matching textbook.

"What page are you on?"

"Seventy-seven."

He flipped through his book and reached out his mind to me. Gratefully, we synced up, reading the same part. He was quicker at picking up things than I was, but I tended to understand concepts on a deeper level, and our learning styles complimented each other.

At least I'd get through a few chapters, even if I would much rather be doing something else.

Breakfast rush was busy on the weekends, with the previous night's party goers lining up for greasy breakfasts to soothe their stomachs. But it was better when David showed up soon after opening.

"Hey."

"Good morning."

He smiled and my mind drifted to the previous night when his control had started to slip, and I'd nearly won.

"Sarah, they need you at table four. Something about a special diet."

Shit. I gave David an apologetic smile before leaving him with Cheryl.

The dietary restriction turned out to be an extreme allergy to shellfish, which, thankfully, wasn't on the menu. By the time I had settled things with the relieved young woman, David had been seated in Cheryl's section, and I tossed my fellow server a warning look as she brought him a fresh coffee.

She looked back and winked at me, her blonde ponytail bouncing when she tilted her head. It was stupid to be jealous when I could still visit him as I was doing rounds with the coffeepot, but I knew she had done it to get under my skin, and when it came to David, everything got to me.

The day was long. Breakfast rush gave way to brunch, late lunch, and finally dinner. David stepped out only once by midafternoon. I tried to remember if he had a lecture, but he was back in an hour and a half, with a set of new textbooks and a warm smile.

"Busy day?" he asked once he was seated. When the day was done, I'd change out of the sweat-stained uniform and take a shower to wash away the grease, but for now, it was growing increasingly uncomfortable and there wasn't much I could do about it.

"Yeah, it's been busy. The crowd is finally dying down." I rolled my aching shoulders.

"I've been meaning to talk to you about that, actually."

"About what?"

"Well, I'm a scout and as part of being a scout in the human world, ancients are given money for their living expenses. I know you're not officially in that role, but I know the elders would agree that the money also belongs to you."

I stared at him, dumbfounded.

Their money. The ancients. Snorting, I lifted my pad of paper to my chest, pen poised to take his order.

"No thanks. I'm not interested in their money." But I couldn't stop the possibility from conjuring images in my mind.

No more diner.

School paid for.

Maybe even rent.

With a shake of my head, I dispelled the fantasy.

I wanted nothing from them.

"But Sarah, it's not their money. It's ours as a community, and—"

I didn't want to get into the island and my issues with the elders. "That place is not my community, David. I've told you this. I don't want their money. I don't need their help."

I just want you. I knew he'd heard me by the tightness in his eyes.

"You want a slice of apple pie and coffee or something different?"

Sighing, he leaned back into the booth.

"Just the pie and coffee. Thanks."

With a nod, I scribbled his order and table number on the pad, as though I would forget them, and went to tell the kitchen.

It was another two hours before my shift finally ended, and David walked me home, leaving me with a very tame goodnight that left the craving for him stronger than ever before.

The lacy lingerie was itchy under the loose sweater I'd thrown on, but I knew I wouldn't have to wait long for it to come off. David invited me in, the blue of his eyes already darkened with lust, and we moved to the couch. He turned on the TV, but neither of us so much as glanced at it. Barely a moment passed between us before I moved into his lap to straddle his waist, and his arms came up to hold me in a bruising grip. I waited until his hands were like claws on my back and his breathing ragged before I pulled the sweater over my head.

His eyes skimmed every curve, taking in the lace trim patterned across my breasts with a strip leading down my torso to disappear into my leggings. The back ended in a thong I couldn't wait for him to discover. But instead of ravishing me the way I'd imagined, David sat back on the couch, his eyes darting across my exposed flesh like he didn't know where to look, but couldn't turn away.

"Sarah, this is too much." His face was flushed, but his voice was resolute, and I deflated under the determination I saw there.

He wasn't going to do anything. I could tell. Flopping back down beside him with an exasperated sigh, I mulled the problem over how to get through to him. I reached out to his mind, studying his thoughts.

He was worried—no scared. If we did this, he could lose me. That's where this came from.

"You're thinking too much about this. Sex is—well, not that big of a deal. It's not something that is going to break us the way you're thinking. Really, it'd be nothing but a good thing," I pleaded with him to understand. Even knowing how serious a step he considered sleeping together, the desire raging through my body urged me to try.

"It is a big thing, Sarah. It's a very big thing. I can't just take that from you. I can't take advantage of that. I won't risk you hating me."

"And I'm telling you, it's not such a big deal to me!" I said, gesturing with my hands. "Even if we were to have sex and some mysterious realization comes over me when I meet another ancient, I wouldn't hold it against you. I promise it wouldn't matter." The idea of me meeting someone else and wanting them more than him, rejecting him, was ridiculous, but if it helped him to imagine a scenario where it would be okay, I'd meet his fear straight on. But my attempt had the opposite effect, and David turned to me, aghast.

"How can you feel like it's no big deal? I don't get it. It'd be a new experience for the both of us. You can't possibly know how you'd feel about it until after."

Silence followed his heated words, and in it, understanding passed between us.

David was a virgin. Somehow this gorgeous man who enraptured everyone he met had never done this. That's why he'd been so resistant, so worried. He was a virgin, and he'd assumed I was, too. But now he understood I wasn't, and he wasn't able to shield me from the flare of hurt and betrayal in his mind at the realization.

Jaw tensed, he stared blankly at the TV.

"It's no big deal to you because you've done it before." He spoke the words more to himself than to me, as though he needed to hear them, to process them.

"Yes," I replied in a hushed tone, still reeling from the stab of hurt and betrayal coming from him. It was there in his eyes when he turned to me now—a flash that he was helpless to suppress.

David stood and paced the room while I studied the floral pattern of the couch, tracing each petal with my eyes and letting the task calm my frazzled mind. I could feel his eyes on me for a moment before he grabbed his jacket and walked out.

I burst into tears the second he was gone. I'd never been ashamed of sex before—it was just another physical need, like eating or exercising. I'd never thought of my virginity as something I should have kept secret and safe for the right person.

But David had.

I barely slept that night, and my eyes were puffy from crying the next day when I went to work, the chilled morning air unable to cool the heat still staining my cheeks. I nearly dropped the carafe when David appeared a few hours later, lining up for a table with the rest of the customers like usual.

He looked haggard, and even the smile he gave to the hostess was strained, the gesture tugged at the skin around his eyes. He hadn't slept any more than I had, and my heart clenched at the sight.

I brought him coffee and a slice of apple pie without taking his order, setting the plate and the cup on the table in front of them. He stared down at the food wordlessly before meeting my gaze. His eyes cleared as they studied my face, taking in the puffiness under my eyes. I moved to leave, but he grabbed my wrist, trapping me at the table long enough to hear his words.

"Hey, can you take a break soon so we can talk?"

I nodded, swallowing a lump in my throat. A cheerful girl named Kimmy, with a tightness across her bust and a bounce in her step that spoke of future plans outside the diner, offered to cover for me.

Like everyone at the diner, she was invested in my relationship with David, and my face had been a topic of conversation all morning. This time I'd remembered to bring a change of street clothes, and after I got dressed, we headed out. He held the door for me as we left, but kept a distance. I wasn't sure that was a good sign.

We walked in silence for a while, the cold wind blowing against my face. My hands stayed tucked in my pockets.

"I'm sorry for how I reacted last night. I didn't have the right to act that way. I know things are different here in the human world, and it wasn't fair of me to act so wounded."

We walked on for a moment before he sighed and continued, "It's just. I've dated before, but I've never been close to anyone, and it never felt right…"

I could feel his eyes on me, but I wasn't ready to meet them. I stared straight ahead as we walked on.

"It's not fair of me to expect that you wouldn't have done those things. I guess it just always felt like something really important to me. I didn't know what I was waiting for really until I met you and realized that I was always waiting for you," he said, his voice thick with emotion.

Glancing over at him and taking in his flushed face, I didn't know what to say. There were so many things about me he didn't know. I'd shared so much but not any of the darkness that lay in my past, and it wasn't that I didn't trust him, it was that I didn't want to relive the moments that had left such deep scars.

But now. I'd always feared that if he knew what I'd been a party to, he'd walk away. There were things about me he didn't know, couldn't know, because I hadn't told him.

Hadn't told anyone.

I'd been closer to David than to anyone else in my life. I needed him to know me.

To know everything. Anything less was unacceptable. I didn't want any distance between us anymore, and as much as I'd been able to pretend that my past hadn't created that divide, it had. It did.

I needed to explain things, to share, and I had to do it sooner than later while I could still survive if he decided it was too much. That I was too much. Having been faced with that very real possibility the night before had emboldened me to lay myself bare before him. If he left me, if he chose to walk away, I'd find my way through the pain.

"There are lots of things about me you don't know, David. I haven't purposefully kept anything from you, but it's just some stuff is hard to talk about. There are things that haunt me from my past that I've never told anyone. Like my first time." I sucked in a deep breath. "I have to finish my shift, and it's a long story. Can we talk about it after I'm done?" Stopping, I turned and met his gaze head-on. Whatever he saw on my face surprised him, and he leaned forward to gently kiss me on the cheek.

"Of course." He took my hand, and I gave him a halfhearted smile as we headed back to the diner.

The rest of the afternoon passed without incident. I wasn't nervous about telling him about my past. Not anymore. Spine straight, I moved through my day with determination.

I was exhausted from the fear and worry of those days coming back to haunt me, and pretending they hadn't happened wasn't working. I just wanted it done, and it was strangely liberating to know he'd soon know all my dark secrets.

If he rejected me, so be it. He wouldn't be the first person in my life to let me down, but he would be the most important.

My shift finally ended, and we headed out together. We walked a little apart as we had done before, my hands firmly in the pockets of my coat. I didn't want to hold his hand or feel connected to him for this; I just needed to get it out.

I stared straight ahead as we walked in silence. At least the streets were mostly deserted, and we didn't have to dodge around pedestrians. Boston didn't sleep, but it did doze. There was just David and me in the dark of the night, walking together side by side, our paces perfectly matched. A pair.

But for how much longer?

He glanced over at me occasionally, waiting. Adjusting my jacket, I began.

"There are things you don't know about me that might be too much for you to take. They're things that I haven't told anybody." I drew in a shaky breath before continuing. "The first question anyone asks a runaway is why they ran away. I've never really answered that question before." I didn't dare meet his eyes.

"I'm telling you this because it relates to what we talked about last night. The people I thought were my parents were vampires, as you know. What you don't know is that they were murderers."

David's head shot up, and he stiffened beside me.

If only there wasn't so much more to say.

"We lived in a large family compound outside of the city, with aunts and uncles and cousins all living in separate large houses on the same property. It was quite elaborate. My father was the leader, and my mother was content to drug herself into a stupor, going along with whatever he said." I could see her in my mind's eye, a small mousy woman who kept herself apart from the rest of the family. She hadn't had time for me, hadn't cared for me. She'd let my father raise me the way he deemed best. "Like all vampires, my family believed that we needed human blood to survive, but they also felt killing was part of it. That pain and suffering were necessary."

My lips twisted on the last word as images of my father and his stern, self-righteous face flashed through my mind.

Monster. The word came unbidden to my mind. He was my monster, and he'd made me like him. Sucking in a breath, I fought to steady myself through the onslaught of memories.

My Aunt Becky's self-assured expression sprang to mind. She'd been a devotee of my father's teachings, and certain killing humans was the 'natural order.' That they were our prey. They'd tried so hard to convince me. Every time I closed my eyes, I could see my father's stern face glaring down at me when I'd refused to harm even so much as an animal. No daughter of his would be so weak. He'd made it his mission to harden me and make me 'strong.'

The memories threatened to pull me down into a panic, but I needed to get through this.

Swallowing hard, I continued. "My family was affluent, owning a lot of property in the surrounding cities. They would invite whole families to the compound for barbecues where they would slaughter them: men, women, children, babies. It didn't matter. They were human, so they were our prey. It was as simple as that. I don't know how they managed to keep it under wraps. Car crashes were the official story or sometimes house fires. They did it at least once every two months." The haunting images filled my mind, the screaming and shrieking as I hid in my room trembling, hiding under my covers.

"I-I couldn't do anything to stop them. I wasn't brave. I hid when it happened and tried to stay in my room so that I would never have to see their faces. Of course, my father tried his best to force me out of the room, to fo-force me to watch." My lips trembled, and I pressed them together. "That was the worst. He would force me to join them for the 'festivities' at the start of the event. Watching all the humans laughing and mingling with my family. Everyone was always in a great mood then. The humans because they were being taken under the wing of such a well-known family, and my family because they were anticipating what was to come."

Faces flitted across my mind, my father shouting at me to join them as the blood frenzy started, watching the humans who escaped the initial attack cower and hide, their eyes filled with horror and understanding. Once my father was preoccupied with the slaughter, I'd escape back to my room.

"The rest of the time, they were kind to me. Showering me with gifts and attention, although my father would take me out to 'toughen me up,' hunting livestock on the grounds."

The streetlights were bright, and I took a moment to look up at the city I called home.

My city.

This was my home, not that place so saturated with blood it permeated into every memory. Had there been moments of joy in my old household? Of love?

I couldn't recall a single one.

"My Aunt Becky homeschooled me so that I never left the compound. I had a tutor come once a week for supervised visits, and that was my life."

But it hadn't been a life. Just surviving from day to day, living with the fear and guilt of knowing it was going to happen again, and I had no way to stop it.

The next part was particularly hard to explain, and I swallowed the lump in my throat. It wasn't such a cold night, but I felt a chill, rubbing my arms and shivering. "At one of the slaughters, there was a boy my age. He came to talk to me, and I got this idea in my head that maybe I could save him." I frowned. My logic at the time had been fuzzy, nothing but a childish dream. "I pulled him away from the gathering and took him to my room. I thought if there was a reason to bring him to my room, a reason to stay with me, maybe I could hide him there. I put on some music when the killing started and convinced him to stay. My family was accustomed to me hiding in my room and thought nothing of it. Of course, they discovered us the next morning, and the boy was killed." I looked away, tears filling my eyes, not able to find the words, to speak through the pain and describe what had happened to Ryan.

Afterwards, I'd cursed myself for the foolish nature of the attempt. How would I have been able to keep him safe? I still remembered his face the next morning when my father slammed open the door and saw him. Ryan probably thought my father was furious with him for sleeping with his daughter. The truth was he was furious with his daughter for not killing him.

Breathing through the turmoil the memories brought up, I forced myself to get the next part out.

"He took Ryan outside and made me watch." My breathing quickened as the memories washed over me. His face had been filled with fear and horror as my father's fangs had extended before him. My father liked to see that they were afraid. They all did. But the worst part of it was the way my father had grabbed hold of the back of my neck and forced me to reveal my own fangs. The way Ryan had turned and tried to run, not just from my father, but from me.

"I was fourteen years old when that happened," I said shakily, trying to get myself under control. "At fifteen, I stole some jewelry from my mother, took one of the cars, and drove as far and as fast as I could to get away from them." I still didn't know where I'd found the courage to leave them behind and enter the world alone, but I had. "I managed to figure out how to sell things, and I sought out other supernaturals. The Witches of Stain took me in and cared for me in exchange for my abilities. When I was settled, I called the police and made an anonymous tip about my family."

A shaky breath rattled its way out of my throat. "I told them where they could find the bones." I watched the news that night, and while they'd found the graveyard, my family must've been tipped off because they'd fled. Where they were now, I had no idea, and the thought haunted me. Were they killing again? Had they searched for me?

I blew out a breath, the release of tension at having finished the tale leaving me helplessly weak. "So now you know the deepest, darkest secrets of my past. You know all the terrible things I've done."

I'd told him everything, laid myself bare. But now that I had, I couldn't stand to find out what he thought of me—certain I'd see Ryan's expression mirrored in his eyes. All that was left was for him to realize I was a monster and turn away.

Tears pricked my eyes, and I stuffed my fists more firmly into my pockets, trying to find some warmth on a night that felt ice cold.

Too long. The silence had gone on too long, and though I could feel David processing everything I'd told him, his mind humming along beside me, I felt more alone than I ever had. More than when I'd left the compound. More than when I'd discovered the witches were using my power for nefarious purposes.

It had always been just me, and this thing with David, this fantasy, hadn't changed that. I was a monster, deserving of the empty life I'd embraced.

David stopped short, his arm coming up to block me and keep me from continuing. He took my opposite hand and pulled me roughly, forcing me to turn and face him. I kept my eyes averted, my hand cold and clammy in his.

"Sarah, you can't tell me you really blame yourself for any of that? You were a child. You weren't responsible for what happened to those people. Sarah. Look at me." Urgency dripped from his words, but I kept my eyes fixed on the metal zipper of his coat. He waited patiently until I found the courage to look up, and it was there I found my answer.

In his expression, I saw nothing but concern and love. I hadn't scared him off.

It nearly broke me, and I swiped away a tear.

"You did everything you could for those people. You were a child in an impossible situation. I know you, know how good and kind-hearted you are. How terrible that must have been, and I'm so sorry that happened to you. Because it shouldn't have happened. None of it should have happened." His voice was thick with emotion as he gently rubbed my arms through the coat, like he was trying to warm them through the thick material.

His mind brushed mine in the lightest touches, and I let him see it. Experience what I had. The horror of my past, how certain I'd been of him leaving. Eyes widening, he gripped both my arms more fully and gave me a small shake.

"You really thought I'd leave?"

My tongue was numb, and tears pricked at my eyes no matter how I fought to blink them away.

"That I could leave? That I'd want to leave over this?" He shook me again, his blue eyes wide with incredulity. "I'm never leaving. Never. The only way I would leave is if you asked me to."

At that, the tears finally spilled over and I let them, burying my face in his chest as sobs shook through my body. I clung to him, and he wrapped his arms around me, his hands tenderly stroking my back.

"I can't believe you've been holding onto this for so long," he murmured into my hair. "It's okay. You did what you could for them. You tried when others would have let it destroy them." The conviction in his voice was a balm to my soul. But had I tried enough?

"I didn't," I said against his chest. "I could have fought back. I could have found a way to reach out to someone who could stop them. I should have done something. If I could have just saved one life." I choked on the words, the last dissolving into a sob that dipped my head forward.

He held my shoulders firmly until I was forced to meet his eyes.

Clear. His eyes were so clear. He was so certain.

"Sarah, I want you to listen to me. You tried. You were a child, and there were a lot of them. You couldn't do anything or save anyone. All you could do was save yourself and you did that. You got yourself away from those people, and you reported them. No one could have expected more of you." I tried to look away, but he held me firm. "I'm proud of you."

His words rang in my ears.

Proud? I was reeling. How could he be proud of me for what I'd done? The part I'd played by being a piece of that family unit.

"No, David, you don't understand. I was part of that family." Squeezing my eyes shut, I could hear my father's voice chiding me for failing to live up to his legacy.

"Sarah. You are not responsible for the things they did. For the way they are. You are responsible for yourself." His words wormed their way into my mind, bringing with them a sense of closure.

"Shit, Sarah. Was this why you weren't eating properly when I first found you?"

I hadn't known he'd noticed, and I fiddled nervously with the cuff of his coat.

"It was hard to feed on humans, and I thought I had to. That I needed their blood to survive. Was it so obvious?"

David sighed. "Well, I knew I wasn't supposed to be able to count your ribs." His arms tightened around me, and I relaxed into his embrace.

He was the first person I'd ever spoken to about my vampire family, and for him to react this way—to be proud of me. I'd let myself be overcome with guilt for so long, hated myself for being weak, but maybe David was right. I *had* been a child. And while I'd failed to save even a single soul, I'd tried.

I hadn't realized until that moment how badly I'd needed to hear that.

"Come here," he said, wrapping me fully in his arms and tucking my head under his chin. A few more tears flowed down my cheeks, but the worst was over.

Because he was still here.

He hadn't turned away from me. Didn't think I was a monster. Instead, he loved me just the same, and the fractures in my heart from those early years felt as though they were healing. David's mind hummed with warmth and acceptance, beckoning me in, and when I reached out to his mind, a peace settled over me.

After a few minutes, he pulled back to look at me. "Better?" he asked gently.

I smiled and nodded. "Yes." But there was something else still there between us, and we needed to let it out into the open air so it could breathe.

"Do you understand now why I can't go back to the island? The elders left me with those people. They left me there with those monsters. How can I go there and face them? To place my mind and my life in their hands?" Shaking my head, I willed him to understand. "I can't do it, David. I'm sorry. I don't ever want to see them again."

"I understand," he said, frowning at me. "But you know that it's not just going back there, it's the unfairness of what they did to you. They took your childhood when they took your memories. To remember that you were loved, and you had a different family before you went to live with those assholes. You had parents. You liked papayas." His frown deepened.

"And you used to laugh and run and play like any normal kid. They took that from you, Sarah. It's time for them to give it back. There was no death and pain in your childhood, and after hearing your story, I feel even more sure that you need to go back there and have your memories restored. Memories of the island, of us." He gently stroked my cheek before tucking a loose curl behind my ear. "Just think about it."

I smiled and nodded. We wandered the streets until exhaustion pulled at my steps, and I steered us towards my apartment.

"Can you stay over tonight?" I pleaded, cringing when he hesitated. "Just to sleep," I interjected before he could say no. He studied my expression, and I was painfully aware of how pitiful I must look. How I was too fractured, too raw to even know how to make an expression anymore. He nodded solemnly.

"Of course."

DAVID

Sarah lay across my arm, and I watched her sleeping face, hating the pucker still clinging to her brow. All this time, all these years, she'd been tormented by her false family. I'd known there was something in her past she'd kept from me, something horrible, but this? It was so far beyond what I'd been expecting. Those years spent with those people had nearly broken her.

No wonder she hated the elders. I'd hated them when they'd sent her away, and again when they'd erased all means of finding her, but now...

I didn't know if I could forgive them for placing her in such a terrible environment, for looking into the minds of those people, and deciding she belonged there. Sarah whimpered in her sleep, and I pulled her onto my chest, her red curls spreading out behind her and trailing across my arm. She didn't wake, but the fisted hand she'd held to her mouth relaxed, her fingers splaying out against my chest. I wished I could feel the gentle touch of her fingertips against my skin instead of through my shirt.

How stupid I'd been for reacting like an asshole when I'd discovered she wasn't a virgin. Of course she wasn't. I hadn't met anyone else in their mid-twenties who was a virgin like I was. It was foolish of me to assume that she was one, and the way she'd lost that virginity...

I'd seen him in her mind. There hadn't been passion or much interest in the act itself.

She'd been too terrified for any of that. Blowing out a breath, I hugged her closer, wrapping both arms around her. She sighed against me, her breath easily penetrating the thin fabric of my worn-out shirt, and tickling the skin beneath.

She'd known nothing but cruelty from the people who were supposed to love her, to care for her, while her own parents had nearly gone mad with worry. The elders had done it all. Torn her away and left her to those people. Screwed her up enough that she'd expected I would leave her over it.

My eyes stung at the memory of it in her mind. How certain she'd be that I would pull away and forsake her the way everyone else had. I wanted nothing more than to reassure her of my permanence in her life, to take every last step forward with her until we were merged at a cellular level. Nothing else would do. I pulled her up higher, tucking her into my neck, her position on my chest no longer close enough.

There was one possibility, one way to resolve the elders' concerns without Sarah returning to the island, but to do that to go there would mean facing my own demons.

For now, I was content to hold her in my arms and offer whatever comfort I could.

Chapter 15

SARAH

Nina had been right about Adam's plans, and once he'd decided to join our clan with The Lucky Draws, things had happened quickly. There wouldn't be a clan known as The Shades anymore. Adam would have to relinquish his authority, dropping to take the position of second to The Lucky Draw's clan leader, but we'd be safe. The Draws had four times our number and most of them were capable adults.

I was proud of Adam for having made the sacrifice, and with The Shades now more secure, they'd be less wholly dependent on David and me for protection. Which was how David and I found ourselves in a crowded bar filled to the brim with old and new clan members. It was supposed to help solidify our merge, but I couldn't help feel the tension and notice how cleanly the lines were split, the familiar faces of my own clan congregating together.

Leaning back into David's warmth, I closed my eyes, settling into his embrace when his strong arms came up to encircle my waist. He kissed my temple, and the stir of arousal at the touch brought with it a reminder of his lack of trust. Things between us had been easier since I'd shared my family history, like the extra layer of intimacy had soothed the need for us to grow closer, but David's fear of my feelings being fabricated stayed lodged in my chest like a bit of shrapnel left behind from a bullet long removed. Ever present and occasionally making itself known, but impossible to dislodge.

Every time I thought of it, I felt the sting anew.

Frowning, I rubbed at the spot on my chest where I imagined it was lodged, willing the pain to leave me alone, if only for tonight, so I could help Adam to integrate the two clans. We stood next to the bar with Adam, Nina, and a small group of what had originally been Shades. Tom had become something of a protégé to Adam and stood at his side.

Shots of an amber liquid were passed around. A quick sniff told me it was a decent quality whiskey. Wordlessly, Adam raised a glass and gestured around to us.

"To The Shades."

There was a murmured agreement before we all slung back our shots. The whiskey burned like hell going down, and I coughed to ease the sting.

"You okay with being the second?" Tom asked with the bluntness of youth, but Adam remained unphased.

"Of course. As a leader, I know I must do whatever the clan requires to be safe, and this is what the clan requires of me." It seemed so painfully obvious to him, and I envied the ease of his convictions.

Of course, Nina had to chime in.

"Well, I was named second purely because I'm your girlfriend, and it's not all bad. Sure, it's not like you have the same power as a leader, but you're relied on. You'll still be running hunts."

Adam nodded thoughtfully before dropping a kiss on Nina's slicked back hair.

She giggled, setting the sequins on her dress to dancing in a glittering array nearly as bright as her eyes, when she peered up at him with a toothy grin. "Besides, Sarah was forced into that role back when you two used to date, and it wasn't too bad for her. She's stronger than you, plus an actual fucking tiger, and she was still okay taking the back seat, right, Sar?"

David stiffened behind me. Frowning, I tried to look over my shoulder to understand what had triggered such a reaction.

"Sarah? Hello?" Nina was relentless, and I turned back to her with a glare.

"Yes, it was fine, and yes, I guess I am stronger, but strength alone doesn't make you a leader." Nina went to reply, but David stayed frozen behind me. I reached out to him mentally, but his mind was closed to me. "Excuse us," I muttered, taking his hand, and pulling him further down the bar, where we could speak more freely.

His face was rigid, his expression blank.

"You okay?"

His jaw tightened a fraction, and he nodded, but I could tell he wasn't. I pressed my palm against his cheek. "Are you feeling okay?" This wasn't like him, but for the life of me, I couldn't think of what could have happened or been said to cause such a reaction.

Jaw tight, he nodded. But then Nina was grabbing my hand and pulling me out onto the dance floor, and I was forced to leave him standing at the bar, staring at nothing. I extracted myself after two songs, leaving Nina surrounded by the others, and climbing Adam like a tree.

David startled when I approached him at the bar and took his hand.

"Hey, what's wrong?"

He studied my face and smiled, but it didn't reach his eyes. I could tell by the tension still set in his jaw that it was forced. Twining my fingers with his, I squeezed his hand.

"Let's leave. Adam's got this." Once we were far enough from the bar, the music fading to a distant thrum, I stopped, turning towards him and taking both his hands in mine.

"What's wrong? Will you talk to me now, please?"

He fixed his gaze on our clasped hands.

"It's just—why didn't you ever tell me you dated Adam?" He glanced up, and I caught a flicker of pain in his eyes.

"Oh," I said, realization settling in. "Oh, I guess I never told you that, did I?" It hadn't felt important. My time with Adam had been before I'd met David, and it'd been over for so long. But I could tell it was important to David, and I squeezed his hands.

"David, I'm sorry, it's just—we dated so long ago. It didn't occur to me that I should tell you. It wasn't really working between us and when he met Nina, I bowed out. I could see that they were meant for each other."

He pulled his hand away. "He's my roommate, Sarah. We live together. Don't you think I'd want to know about that?" His sharp tone caught me by surprise, but I detected the hurt beneath it, and he was right. I should've told him. And why hadn't I? I'd barely thought of my history with Adam since I'd met David.

Never had I shared myself or my life with him the way I did with David. Adam had been a boyfriend who'd become a close friend, and who was now dating my best friend. Nothing about that relationship compared to what David and I had, but instead of telling him and reassuring him, I stayed silent. The words stuck in my throat.

"Did you sleep with him?" David's eyes burned into mine, demanding an answer.

"Yes."

He shook off my arm and stormed away, his coat flap flying open. Sighing, I let him go, knowing he needed some space to calm down. The jealousy I'd felt when David had told me how he'd dated while moving around doing correspondence school had been intense. Even knowing it wasn't the same for him, that he hadn't slept with anyone, hadn't helped. I could imagine how finding out someone he was close to now was a former partner.

The jealousy would drive me mad.

DAVID

Adam and Sarah had dated.

They'd been a couple, and by the way they still shared the occasional knowing glance, they were still close. She'd been his second, his partner, had shared everything with her.

And they'd slept together.

Jealousy tore me apart from the inside until I couldn't think straight, until I'd had to pull myself away from her and leave.

I regretted it instantly. The pain of her absence was in no way worth the brief reprieve from dealing with the knowledge of her history with my roommate.

Adam, who'd once caged me like a tiger, who left his socks in the hall for me to trip over, who I had begun to respect and admire as a leader. All this time, he'd been Sarah's former lover. I should be able to push all the rage and jealousy aside, but it was this situation, the knowledge that he had done those things with her, while I couldn't. It tied me in knots until I walked so far and so long, I didn't know where I was and had to stop and ask for directions home.

Sarah, she loved me, or she felt she did. Had she loved him? Had she needed to coax him into the bedroom?

Of course she hadn't. I imagined how easy it must've been between them. How he'd had no qualms about taking her to his bed and fucking her senseless.

I wanted to yell, to break something, but I settled for kicking a metal garbage can, hissing at the sharp stab of pain. Cursing my own thoughtlessness, I tried to flex the foot, and winced at the attempt. I'd need to heal myself later.

Everything I'd shared with Sarah, every moment, every touch, it was driving me insane wondering how much of it had been the same with Adam. Had she laughed with him? Did he meet her after work the way I did?

But more than anything, I hated how he'd been in her life before I had. How he'd been there for her. How she'd shared herself with him. How he'd known her in a way I hadn't. Knew what she felt like beneath him. What she sounded like when she found release. The unfairness of it churned in my stomach until I found myself outside of her apartment, staring up at the great grey building.

I'd kissed her here, more times than I could count. Claimed her mouth the way I wanted to claim her body, and even when she'd offered it so willingly, when she'd begged me to take her, I'd kept myself back.

For what? Honour? Fear? I didn't care anymore, and with that lack of caring came the freedom to launch myself up the stairs.

SARAH

Exhausted but unable to sleep, I switched on a comedy, settling into the couch and trying not to think of the bits of David's intoxicating scent still clinging to the ratty fabric. The sitcom jokes were just starting to get a reaction out of my tired mind when a firm knock at the door caught me by surprise.

Nina wouldn't knock.

Neither would Adam.

Frowning at the door, I threw off my blanket and hurried to answer it, my steps stuttering when another heavy hand fell into a furious round of pounding. I opened the door to reveal David. He looked terrible, his frame riddled with tension and his eyes haunted. Without saying a word, he moved inside and slammed the door behind him. He stared at me, his lips slightly parted, like he wanted to say something.

Before I could speak, he pressed forward to claim my mouth, one hand snaking up my back to hold me in place. He pulled back, just far enough for us to look each other in the eye. My breath hitched when he kept his lust-darkened eyes on mine, removing his coat to take me in his arms and crush me against his chest. There was no hesitation in the way his hand fell to my breast, playing mercilessly with the nipple through the fabric of my nightgown until I was moaning against his mouth. This had been what I needed, just this. The wild abandon of it.

David's hand tangled in my hair, tugging at the roots as he rained kisses across my face before touching our foreheads together and pausing a moment, our heavy breathing the only sound in the room.

Then he was taking his shirt off, and my hands eagerly sought the bare skin. I fumbled with the edge of my nightgown, relieved when his hand found mine, and together we wrestled me out of it until my breasts were bare before him.

"Beautiful," he muttered, his mouth descending on my collarbone to nip and nibble at the skin. Shocks of pleasure tore at my system. Everything he did went right to my core, leaving me needy. Gasping, I wrapped my arms around his neck and clung to him. He pushed me back as we made our way to the couch, the length of his hard shaft pressing into my stomach.

He'd held back for so long, and for him to be ready—to let loose—it was everything I wanted. But I had to know if he was leading me on again, if I could trust him not to stop. I forced myself to pull away, to meet his eyes, and ask him the question.

"Are you sure?" I was breathless, my body a live wire in his grasp.

"Yes," he said. His gaze was even, and his eyes were clear. He was serious this time. There was no teasing in the brilliant blue of his eyes, and my eyes rolled back as I hitched a leg over his hip, putting my entrance level with his cock. Kissing him gently, I took a moment to appreciate that he was finally letting go of the foolish notion that I didn't know my mind. The distance his worry had put between us had been hurtful, but now...

His hand grasped the nape of my neck as his hot mouth moved against mine. He pushed me down on the couch in one forceful motion, and I went without a fight. He watched me, his pupils blown, the blue of his eyes deliciously darkened by a lust so thick I could practically taste it. I was ready. Slick and hungry for him, and I opened up my mind to show him how badly I wanted him to ravage me, to lose every ounce of that control he'd kept between us.

But it was as I lay naked before him, showing him my wants, my needs, that his expression changed and he looked away. But not before I'd seen it—the pain and fear in his eyes.

"I'm–I'm sorry, Sarah. I-I can't do this..." His voice broke, and I didn't know what to say.

He'd come to me ready for this to be the night where all the walls he'd built up between us would crumble. I'd forced myself to stop and ask him, and he'd said yes.

He was ready. I'd seen it in his eyes. My chest was tight with disappointment, and I sat up to stiffly, searching out my nightgown and slipping it over my head.

David sat down heavily on the couch beside me, dropping his head into his hands.

"I'm sorry. I know I keep hurting you. I know that my coming here tonight wasn't fair. I'm sorry. I—just seeing you naked and so beautiful, I can't do it. It would change everything for me. Please understand. If there's even the smallest chance I could lose you over this, I can't." His voice was thick with emotion, and I softened towards him, reaching out to cover his trembling hand with mine. But tonight had made something clear to me, something I hated to admit.

I wouldn't let there be any secrets between us.

"David. I know you're worried, I do, but this isn't good for us." Because what did it mean for our relationship when he didn't trust me, when he couldn't trust himself around me?

He squeezed his eyes shut and threw his head back, staring at the ceiling.

"I know. I hate it. I hate worrying about us and keeping myself in check around you. You have no idea how many times I've wished I could forget everything the elders told me." The thought sent shivers trailing up my arms. I wanted him unleashed, untethered, so badly I could taste it. "Then tonight, finding out that you and Adam had dated. That you'd slept together, something we haven't done yet—"

"Not for lack of trying on my part," I muttered.

"Oh, I know, it's my fault, not yours," He glanced at me apologetically. "I don't suppose you've changed your mind about going to the island?"

I shook my head, looking down. "You know I can't go there. I told you why. I'm not sure if I'll ever go back." I sighed heavily and met his eyes again. We were at a stalemate, and I could see no way forward. The thought choked me, but somehow, I found the words.

"Where does that leave us, David? If I can't go back there, and you can't trust what's between us?" A deep exhaustion settled in, my limbs heavy, my mind tired. Outside of this one issue, we were inseparable and everything was perfect; we were happy and in love. But his lack of trust in my feelings for him would eventually destroy us. I could feel it starting to poison our interactions, and I stared at him imploringly, willing him to understand that he had to set aside the elder's warning so we could move forward.

He watched me a moment before answering. "I may have a solution. I haven't wanted to consider the possibility, but if I can ask you to go back to the island" He trailed off, leaning his head back wearily against the couch and staring at the ceiling once more. Frowning, I moved a little closer to him. He tensed, probably worried I was going to continue my advances, but the tension in his arm settled when I sat back on the couch at his side. "Remember how I told you that when my parents died, I was passed around from household to household? How I never belonged to a single household because the ancient families were too jealous of one another to allow anyone to actually adopt me? Well, all that happened because I didn't have any family members. If I'd had any family, that person would have had an undisputed claim to me. I didn't have any family members on the island, but I did have an uncle who left the island to be a scout in the human world. I was very young when he left and don't remember him at all, but he was my father's brother, Nicholas. He still sent a note yearly with information for the elders, so we knew he was alive, but he never left an address for anyone to contact him.

"When my parents died, there was no way for the elders to let him know what had happened. There was no way for them to let him know about me." David snorted. "He was an irresponsible asshole who never thought to leave a return address in case of an emergency. I could have had a home with him and stayed in one place, but he never cared enough to come visit the island. Not once, in all those years, did he ever come back. As a kid, I used to wish that he would come back one day, sailing in on a great big boat." He gestured and a faraway look came over his face. "Everyone said he looked just like my father, and I used to wish that he would come home and it'd be like having him back." He sighed. "But of course, he never did. Just before I left after my last visit home, he finally did send a return address. I brought it with me when I came back, and it's maybe a five-hour drive from here."

"So you're saying you want to see this person?" I asked, not really understanding the relevance.

He looked over at me. "I'm saying that I never want to see that man in my life, but I want *you* to see him. He's an ancient, Sarah, a full-blooded ancient." He sighed and sat forward, licking his lips. "I'm saying that I'll see him for you. If you agree to meet him, I wouldn't have any more reservations."

I considered what he was saying. My thoughtful silence filled the air between us. "Okay. But you have to promise me that after I go with you, this is the end of it. I'm not going to hear anything more about you doubting me. Never again." I said the last firmly, searching his eyes.

His reply was a warm smile, and he leaned over to kiss me tenderly, his lips brushing mine again and again before he pulled back to look at me, love shining in his eyes. He brought up his hand to stroke my cheek.

"No more doubts."

CHAPTER 16

We planned our trip for the following weekend using David's scout funds to rent a car and a hotel room in Syracuse. Eager for things to be settled, I was in a haze all week. After visiting David's uncle, we'd stay overnight at the hotel. Just the thought of seeing the version of David that had visited me at my apartment prickled my skin and spread warmth, radiating from my core. But this time, there would be no reason to pull away. No tentative hold on his control.

What would it be like when he let go of his inhibitions? I was drooling just thinking about it. He'd held himself tightly in check since we first met, but not anymore. Hands twisting in my hair, the way he'd held my neck firm with his mouth, worshipping every inch of my exposed throat.

Packing my bag was a challenge. No part of me wanted to pack clothes, but I begrudgingly threw them in for the return trip. David pulled up in front of my apartment in a crimson rental car. The inside was just as garish, with tacky wood paneling and cheap faux leather seats. It might not be pretty to look at, but it would get us there, and that was all I cared about. Loading my duffel into the trunk, I slipped into the bucket seat beside him, smiling cautiously in greeting.

He beamed back, his eyes twinkling. We shot off into traffic with an alarming start that squashed me into the seat. David put on the radio. The drive was long, and I dozed through most of it, the chittering radio and his presence soothing my tired mind. I'd been having trouble sleeping again.

It was the stress of not knowing what was going to happen next. We just needed to get through this trip—to put it behind us so we could move on.

I glanced over at David when we passed the sign for Syracuse, expecting him to be pleased the drive was almost over. But he stared straight ahead with furrowed brows, his grip on the steering wheel white knuckled.

This trip was nothing but positive for me, but while I was looking forward to meeting Nicholas and dispelling David's irrational fears about my feelings, he was about to confront someone he'd harboured resentment towards for years. I laid my hand on top of his and squeezed his fingers.

I didn't bother to reach out mentally. He wasn't usually this closed off with me anymore, and I sensed he needed the quiet of his own mind. My worry would only distract him, and he'd feel compelled to reassure me. Still, I couldn't stay silent. Everything in me screamed to somehow make this experience better for him.

"It'll be okay," I spoke in a hushed tone, but he jumped, glancing over at me as if surprised to find me there.

"Yeah, I know. I just have a lot of anger towards my uncle for never checking in. For letting so much time pass without giving a care for the people he'd left behind." David's eyes hardened, and his hand tightened further on the faux leather of the steering wheel, straining the fabric hard enough I wouldn't be surprised if an imprint was left behind. He glanced over at me, letting his hand drop to the gearshift between us in invitation.

"I know." Nodding, I studied the dust peppering the dash. I took his hand, twisting our fingers together until they were almost knotted. Inseparable. Like we'd always been meant to be.

We pulled up to a low-rise brown brick apartment building. A car alarm was going off in the distance, and the street was flooded with pedestrians. We parked in a paid lot around the corner. David paid for the minimum one hour, and then we were there, standing in front of the building where his uncle lived. Sucking in a deep breath, he stared up at the building, his hand cold in mine.

"I'll be with you the whole time," I promised.

He looked at me gratefully, and I gave him a reassuring smile.

"Keep your mind open to him and really reach out with your senses while we're here," he pleaded. It was a reminder to make this encounter worthwhile, and I nodded my solemn agreement.

David's uncle lived on the fifth floor, and we took the rickety elevator up to find a brown door with chipped paint and a brassy knob. After blowing out a breath, he knocked firmly on the door. We waited for what felt too long of a time, and just as he was raising his hand to knock again, the door opened. The man looked like a shorter version of David with a slightly larger nose and a wider mouth. He had the same flashing blue eyes and spiky dirty blonde hair, but he cropped his in the front short, with a streak of it flaring down to the middle of his back. A friendly grin split his face when he saw David.

"Michael!" Nicholas shouted, pulling David into a tight hug.

Michael. That was David's father's name, and I froze, watching in shock as Nicholas clapped David loudly on the back. Nicholas pulled me into his arms next, squeezing me tight and rocking me from side to side before giving me a sloppy kiss on the cheek.

"So good to see you. Come in, come in," he urged, gesturing wildly for us to enter.

David and I shared a look before stepping inside. This was starting off differently than either of us expected. I'd known David resembled his father, had seen him in his memories, but for his own brother to mistake him? With an encouraging pat on his jacketed arm, I stepped over the threshold, David following behind.

Nicholas gestured to a solid-looking oak dining table in the center of the room, and we took our seats. The sturdy piece of furniture was at odds with travel knickknacks and sports paraphernalia covering every surface. Shelves of stuffed mascots proudly hung opposite the table, and I tried to puzzle out which sport and team they were from. But then I looked over at David to see him watching his uncle, his jaw clenched so hard I could see the muscle twitching through his cheek, and all thoughts of the strange decor were forgotten.

I squeezed his hand gently before turning my attention to the man puttering around the cramped kitchen. Travel teaspoons hanging on the wall clattered when Nicholas yanked open the door on his sticky fridge.

"Hey, Michael!" he yelled over the sound of clinking bottles as he rummaged around his fridge, his voice muffled. "You're in luck, buddy. I have exactly three beers left. What are the chances?" With a chuckle, he re-emerged with our drinks, popping the tops with a well-practiced movement before smiling broadly at us and pulling up a chair at the head of the table. He passed two beers to David, who handed me mine without looking, nearly spilling the frothy beverage.

"Thanks," David began, swallowing hard. "But I'm not Michael. I'm Michael's son. David."

Nicholas's mouth fell open, and he squinted at David.

"Well, I'll be damned if you aren't the spitting image of your old man, son." He barked a laugh, leaning over to clap David on the back, and I couldn't help noticing the twitch in David's jaw when Nicholas called him son.

Nicholas gave David another hard clap on the back, hard enough to rattle his shoulders. "How the hell are you? I haven't seen you since you were about two feet tall!" He smiled warmly at him before glancing at me. "And you. I know you." He waggled a finger at me like I'd been trying to disguise my identity. "David was always palling around with you! Morgan's kid. Sarah, is it?"

Morgan. My mother. It could only be her name. I hadn't had the courage to ask for more details about my parents. Not knowing I was unlikely to meet them again. Morgan was a woman I would never know. A woman I was denied even the memory of. Giving Nicholas a watery smile, I nodded. But there was a tension between the two men, and I could tell Nicholas didn't understand it. Brows furrowed, his gaze flitted between the two of us.

"How is my brother, anyway? It's been a while since I've been back," he said, his eyes glazing over as he stared off into the distance for a moment.

With a deep breath, David began the story of what had happened to his father and mother. I was proud of how clearly his voice rang out. The joy in Nicholas' eyes was replaced with shock and grief, and his shoulders hunched forward as he was faced with the reality of his brother's death.

While David told him what had happened, I focused on the purpose of our visit. Following David's instructions, I opened my mind to Nicholas, reaching out to him gently. He looked up at me, but said nothing, so I probed more gently and was hit with a blast of pain.

Poor Nicholas had truly loved his brother, and with ancients living such exceptionally long lives, the news of his fluke accident was devastating. Apparently, the gentle way I probed his mind was common among ancients, as it enhanced communication by allowing them to sense the emotions of one another. David had promised it would be completely acceptable in the current situation, but I still watched him hesitantly as I reached out to see if the intrusion was unwelcome.

Trying to subtly blow out a breath, I reminded myself of why I was doing this. David needed to know I had connected and been completely exposed to another ancient. I would prove to him that his silly fears were unfounded.

Nicholas' mind was so different from David's. It was naïve and filled with extreme emotions. He was warm-hearted, but had a hard time understanding things. I watched him struggle with the news of his brother's death, the knowledge of it failing to settle in. He didn't want to believe what he was hearing, and perhaps he wouldn't have believed it if David wasn't sitting here in his apartment, a doppelgänger of his deceased brother, and telling him it was true.

I investigated Nicholas with all my senses. I closed my eyes briefly and let his scent flood my nostrils. It was similar to David's in that it had a wildness to it that had made it hard to place before I'd met any other ancients. But it wasn't the same, not at all, and I frowned as I puzzled out the differences and similarities. Nicholas' scent lacked a certain spice, and I didn't find myself the least bit intoxicated by it. I listened to his heartbeat and focused on his voice, finding it all normal.

No undue attraction at meeting another ancient washed over me in the way David had worried. I was myself as I had expected to be.

I didn't crave Nicholas, didn't want him.

Only the man at my side mattered.

What a ridiculously unfounded fear that had caused so much trouble. David reached the end of his tale, and I watched as the light in Nicholas' eyes went out, the truth of his brother's death finally beginning to sink in.

David's voice turned bitter when he turned to his own childhood and what had happened to him after his parents' death. "None of the families would accept anyone taking me permanently. You know how they are, so terribly jealous of one another, and with no living family around, the elders had no choice but to have me shuffle among the family houses. I had no true parents ever again. You never came to check on us, on anything. Never came to see if you might be needed!" His eyes burned like blue steel.

Nicholas was stunned to silence, looking down at his hands and rubbing at his finger calluses. He liked working with his hands and never bothered much to heal the discomfort away. I'd effortlessly picked up the information from his mind, and I stared down at the rough skin in wonder. He bowed his head. With his shoulders hunched forward, he looked so unexpectedly pitiful.

"I'm sorry. I had no idea. I should have gone back. I should have been there for you—for Michael. Maybe I could've helped." He cowered in his chair, wringing his hands.

"Yes, maybe you could have." David glared at him, but I could feel him softening. He hadn't expected a sincere apology, hadn't thought his uncle would be so broken by the news of his brother's death. "It's in the past," he finally said in a quiet, tired tone drained of all emotion. "It doesn't matter anymore."

Nicholas could have been a father to him, should have been a father to him. He had made a tremendous error in not returning to the island sooner, and David had suffered the price. But there was nothing the man before us could do to change any of it, and I knew it wasn't in David's nature to cause undue suffering.

David stood up, his chair screeching against the tiles. "Thank you for the beer, but we have to go now," he said. Both our beers remained untouched on the table. I understood, not wanting to stay here any longer than he had to. It was uncomfortable being in this stranger's presence, knowing that he could have been a son to him. I smiled politely and stood to follow David out the door.

But Nicholas was right there with us.

"Can't you stay for a while longer? We could watch the baseball game. Hang out." He came around the table to take my arm, his fingernails biting into the flesh. But his eyes were on David. I'd just been a closer target. David gave a tight smile, gently pulling me towards him and extracting me from Nicholas' grip.

"No, I'm sorry, but we have to go now."

I couldn't blame David for not wanting a relationship with this man, but Nicholas' grief was so fresh. Desperation flared to life in his eyes. He wanted a relationship with his only remaining family. Maybe someday they could reconnect, but I didn't think so. David had spent the course of our relationship denying the pull between us rather than bring me to meet this man.

On impulse, I pulled Nicholas into a tight hug. I wouldn't force David to stay and build a bond with him, but at least I could offer him some comfort, and by the way he clung to me in return, it seemed like I had succeeded.

Would he have returned to the island if he'd known what had happened to David's parents? What I'd seen in his mind told me he would have. He was just a man who had made a mistake.

A costly one, but an error that was in no way malicious. Taking advantage of the way Nicholas leaned into me for comfort, I took a deep lungful of his scent, hugging him tight enough for the collar of his shirt to tickle my neck.

There wasn't a trace of attraction or infatuation, and this is what I wanted David to see in my mind later, so that he would truly believe me when I told him I loved him. I needed to make this visit count. Nicholas smiled gratefully as we pulled apart, his familiar blue eyes shining with unshed tears.

"Take care," I murmured politely as we turned to go.

David's hand was like a stone in mine as we left the apartment and headed back out to the street, and I rubbed circles on the back of it with my thumb in an effort to soften it into something resembling flesh. But he didn't say a word as we headed back down the elevator and out to the car. It was only when we were inside the rental that he spoke to me. We'd found a spot near the back.

"That was damned hard." Sighing, David leaned back in his seat, tipping his head back into the headrest.

"I know," I answered, rubbing his arm in soothing circles.

"He's been here all along. Living his life, not aware of anything that happened. Never thinking about anyone he left behind."

I rubbed his arm some more and took his hand, opening his clenched fist and trailing my fingers lightly across his palm. Realization dawned on him as though he was just remembering why we'd come, the reason we'd done this difficult thing, and he turned to me, his frame rigid with tension.

His beautiful face was so desperately hopeful.

"Sarah," he began, licking his lips nervously and searching for the right words.

"David. You know the answer," I said, staring hard into his eyes. "You know. You don't need to ask." I swallowed around the lump in my throat. After this visit to his uncle, I understood why he'd never been able to shake what the elder had told him about me; part of him was still a sad little boy, abandoned by everyone he loved. It was hard for him to trust that I was his, and that I wouldn't abandon him the way so many people had. Perhaps as hard as it had been for me to open up to him, to believe that people were worth connecting to.

In the end, we were both a little broken.

Him perhaps more so than me.

Piercing blue eyes shot to mine, and I stared back, meeting the intensity. His expression broke when he found his answer, and he let out a strangled sound before twisting towards me and touching his forehead to mine. The sounds he made as he kissed me were pure animal joy and relief. Little grunts and moans as he claimed my mouth the way I wanted him to claim every aspect of me. Until there was no him or me, only us.

His mind screamed yes, begged for that closeness, that oneness.

I shared my love and desire for him openly and felt the beauty of him truly accepting it for the first time. There were tears of relief and joy in his eyes, and they fell between us as his hands explored my face, relishing the feel of it as though it were brand new to him. He marveled that I was his, and I wanted to slap him for thinking otherwise. That part of him that wouldn't let him believe someone could love him suddenly found that it could be true.

I pulled away for a moment to meet his eyes. I knew myself to be in danger of getting hurt again, and I needed to be very clear about this before I lost myself in him once more.

I searched his eyes, clouded over with emotion. There was hurt in his expression, and he stared up at me cautiously, not understanding why I had pulled away. But as much as I wanted this to be it, I needed this last thing between us to be settled.

"No more doubts?" I asked him firmly.

He shook his head, pulling me back into a kiss.

"No more doubts. Never again. I swear it." David's eyes were clear and filled with a promise. He would never do something this hurtful again. He had his answer now. It was over. Relief hit me in a wave of euphoria and I laughed, falling into him.

I was amazed to find we were both crying at the release of tension between us, our tears mingling into a salty mess that tasted thick on my tongue. There were no more barriers. All the doubts that had divided us were gone in an instant. I'd told him I was his for months now, but it had never fully reached him. Now he could understand what he meant to me, and I would never let him feel abandoned the way he had as a child.

Never again. We touched foreheads, losing ourselves and finding each other.

Chapter 17

By the time we pulled into the hotel parking lot, the sky was darkening into a haze of pinks and purples. The sign out front was worn down with rusted red flakes gathered in the corners and the "y" of the vacancy sign blinked in and out. No one would describe the See You Soon Motel as glamorous, but I didn't care so long as they had beds. There were no more barriers between David and me, and my heart soared when we slowed to turn down the bumpy gravel driveway.

David scooped up our bags, smiling shyly back at me as he did. It was almost like the night we had first met. The tension in the air was palpable, and I found myself too jittery to hold his hand as we approached the hotel office to check in. Instead, I planted them in my coat pockets.

The pimply-faced adolescent at the front desk had an unfortunately long nose and greasy brown hair plastered to his forehead. When he saw us approach, he leaned forward to leer at us as he took our reservation details from David and handed him the key.

"Have fun." He smiled knowingly.

We didn't say a word to each other as we headed up to floor three in a tiny elevator with an old-fashioned faux metal grill at the front, but I caught him stealing a glance at me and we both chuckled at the strange awkwardness of the moment. Tucking a curl behind my ear, I studied the elevator's circular buttons, noting the cracked plastic around the edges. David's hand brushed mine in the crowded space, and I jumped.

Blood pounded in my ears as he fumbled with the keys, finally opening the door with a click and flipping on the light switch to illuminate a room with a neat bed covered in a red plaid comforter. A pair of quaint wooden lamps with yellowing lampshades lit the room with a warm, welcoming glow.

I sucked in a deep breath and turned to him. He was studying me so intently, his eyes darkening with lust. I wanted them dark like that all the time—wanted to stain them that colour until he couldn't be rid of me. The nerves from the elevator were forgotten and neither of us looked away. Slowly and without breaking eye contact, I moved further into the room. He followed me, his eyes trailing my figure with rapt attention as I began fumbling with the buttons of my shirt, my numb fingers sliding uselessly against them. He remained frozen in place as I slipped out of my jeans. His pupils dilated, and his breathing was uneven. But he didn't move, didn't advance. He'd seen me naked before, but this time was different. This time, he was free to act.

The bags dropped from his shoulder, and he pulled his shirt over his head, exposing an expanse of lightly sculpted muscle, like the artist who had made him had known anything more would have been criminally beautiful. His pants went next, and my eyes fixed on his erection, tracing the thick veins with my eyes the way I wanted to with my tongue. He was as beautiful as I'd always known he would be, and he was mine. My naked flesh quivered with anticipation as I drank in the beauty of his form.

Broad shoulders tapered down to a v, and I moistened my lips as I considered taking him in my mouth and how he would choke me. How I wanted him more than I could remember wanting anything else.

At last, I looked up to meet his eyes to find his pupils blown out. He cupped my cheek, and just the light touch and the promise of it set me off.

I clasped his hand to my cheek, groaning and turning my face to kiss his palm. I took one of his fingers into my mouth to suck.

A shudder went through him as I worshipped the digit, dragging my teeth across the pad. He snapped, gripping my hips with both hands and crushing his mouth to mine. The tangle of our tongues was hot and needy, and his hand snaked around to fist my curls and hold me in place.

My own hands explored up and down his chest and the taut muscles of his back. Before I could venture lower, he twisted my head to trail kisses along my jaw, nuzzling into my neck, sucking and nibbling until I gasped for breath. His length pressed into my stomach, even as his mind reached out to mine, seeking to join us more completely.

He wanted nothing more than to lay me back onto the bed and claim me for his own, and the sheer violent strength of the need left me stunned. It had ravaged his mind, driving him to near madness when we were together. I had nearly broken him. I saw the truth of that in his mind, how he wouldn't have been able to stand being so close to me while holding himself back for much longer.

But as much as I wanted him to take me the way I'd seen in his mind, this was his first time, and our first time together. Everything was new to him. I gently pressed my palm against his hard abs, my eyes rolling back at the delicious twitch of the muscle beneath my hand.

I leaned forward, tilting my chin up.

"Let's take it slow. We have lots of time." My voice came out husky, and he looked away, his brows drawn and lips pressed into a thin line.

"Sorry, Sarah. This is—" He was at a loss for words, and I understood why. This thing between us had been building for so long now. Twining my hands behind his neck, I pulled him down and into a slow, deep kiss, letting my tongue press lightly against his until he kissed me back with more force. The heat of his cock pressed into my hip bone.

I took one of his hands, drew him over to the bed, and stood in front of him. God, he was beautiful. I lightly pushed on his chest. He took the hint and lay back on the bed. Trust softened his expression as he relaxed back into the mattress.

But I wasn't anymore prepared for this than he was. I'd shared my body with others before, but love? This level of feral need? No, this was a new experience, even if I did know the mechanics better than he did. Straddling him, I positioned myself in front of his cock, reaching a hand back to take hold of his shaft. I savoured the way his shudder vibrated through the delicate bundle of nerves already sensitive in anticipation of his attention.

David groaned as the head of his cock, slippery from pre-cum, pushed eagerly into my hand. The silky smoothness of him glided across my palm, and it was almost too much for me. No part of me wanted to take this slow, to ease into things, even if it was what he needed. Only the desire to make this a good experience kept me from impaling myself upon him and filling the aching void in my core. David's hands moved lightly up and down my back, even as his mind begged me to end his suffering. I kissed along his jawline, enjoying the tingling pleasure in his mind as I did so.

He was lost to it, to me, and I reveled in the way he let himself succumb to the need. His hands fell to my ass, massaging the cheeks to the same rhythm I was using on him.

"Sarah, Sarah." My name was a gasping plea, and I fucking loved it. I claimed his mouth, swallowing the words. His hand snaked in front of us. Maybe he didn't have much experience, but thoughts and feelings flowed between us. His deft fingers fell to the delicate bundle of nerves at my center, testing the way his touch made me react until he found the right pressure, the right swirl of his thumb.

A cry tore from my throat at the shiver of pleasure driving me higher. And then he lost it, sitting up and crushing me to his chest, burying himself in my neck. He lifted me with one hand and positioned himself at my entrance. I was so wet, so lost to my need for him that he met no resistance, sinking to the hilt in one movement that left us gasping into each other's mouths. The invasion was so shocking, so sudden, so welcome, and I fought to adjust to the glorious stretch, to the way he filled me so completely. It was almost too much, and I clung to him, scoring his back with my nails as I adjusted.

We fit together as perfectly as I'd imagined, and when he gave a tentative thrust, I panted into his neck, the tension already coiling in my core. I wouldn't last long. Not like this, not with the very thing I'd been craving offered up to me on a silver platter. I rained kisses on his face, pulling myself upwards and sinking back down onto him. A needy squeal escaped me when the movement brought the barest moment of release.

A taste of the heaven that was to come.

David moaned at the noise, and I could feel just how incredible this was for him, how tightly I gripped him. How wet and hot I felt. He moaned and the throaty sound shot right to my tightening core. Feeling his pleasure echoing my own was a new experience, and it was enough to drive me further into a frenzy.

More. I needed more. More of this. More of him. I lifted myself to the tip before slamming down against his shaft in an effort to drive him impossibly deeper. Because it would never be deep enough, never long enough.

Never enough.

Our moans intermixed, and a primal need grew in his mind. What he wanted, the control he wanted, was almost enough to send me tumbling over the edge. The way he wanted to claim me, to bite me, to take everything I was so willing to give. Internally, I was screaming yes, and he heard me. My consent was all he needed, and I whimpered as the last ounce of his control, the fear of taking me too roughly, of taking more than he should, was stamped out.

Because I wanted him rough, wanted him to take everything from me until I was a fractured shell crying out for more.

Gripping my shoulders, he flung me down roughly beside him, barely breaking contact as he took hold of my wrists with one hand and pressed them into the wood of the headboard. His mouth fell heavy to my breasts, sucking and nipping mercilessly as I groaned my complaint at his absence. I was aching, empty. In need. My hips bucked helplessly in his grip. As if remembering himself, he looked up at me, and I was struck dumb by his beauty, by the feral need twisting his features into an expression I'd never seen before but would never forget.

He claimed me in a single stroke, driving into me with his weight forcing him deeper. My eyes rolled back, but he didn't give me a moment to adjust to the newness of the sensation. His thumb found my clit, and he pounded into me mercilessly.

Our minds became completely incoherent—nothing more than a stream of pleasure and sensation drifting from one to another. He moved to my neck, his hot breath falling there rhythmically in time with his thrusts, and I tangled my hands in his hair as the tension built higher.

I could feel it building in his mind, the tension between us as taut as a deadly wire that must snap, must break. Tears streamed down my cheeks as the first powerful wave of pleasure tore through me like wildfire, consuming every nerve ending.

But it was more than a release. David followed me and that connection flared to life between us. We were one being. Whole. Something deeper than minds and bodies. More profound. A soul-deep connection I could hardly comprehend but for the pleasure it brought.

A strangled animal sound ripped from my throat as I shattered, pulsing around him as his warmth spread through me and waves of pleasure sent me higher. My knees closed reflexively, trapping him inside of me. Stars clouded my vision, and my muscles spasmed. It was all I could do to gently rock my hips against him, to prolong the moment for as long as possible.

It wasn't enough.

I needed more. Had to have more. Even fresh from release, with David moving down my body to lay his head against my heaving breasts, all I could think about was having him again. Of how impossibly good he had felt. And that connection between us, the sheer joy when we'd shared a climax. He moved to lie beside me, his lips seeking mine with the utmost tenderness. Our hands roamed each other's bodies. Things had happened so quickly, and I longed to memorize every detail of him.

Without the immediate need overwhelming our mental connection, I shared the deep contentment I felt. How perfect it was that we were together. Because we belonged together—right together—with no barriers between us. Our bodies twined as though we were two threads in a piece of yarn, perfectly fine on their own but stronger as a pair.

Thinking back to how it had been before, all the mental anguish we'd both experienced over this one simple, animalistic act, was painful. Laughable. All that worry, all that fear, for what?

Why had we waited so long when this was how we were always meant to be?

We lay like that, exploring each other's bodies, appreciating all the curves and valleys of each other, feeling sensations and emotions echoing in each other's minds. It tickled when I brushed his leg, right near his waist. I stored the information for future use. His mental chuckle made me smile.

But then it happened, as it always did with me, the need rising up again despite how languid I was, how hard I'd just come. I hated how I couldn't just enjoy this moment. How my ridiculous sex drive always left me craving more. Even as I thought it, I realized David had pulled back to study me.

There was amusement in his mind at my reaction, and frowning, I fought to explore the feeling. Words didn't belong between us, not tonight, but he showed me the source of his amusement, and I gasped. Because he wasn't done either, and just as the need was rising in me, that craving coming back stronger than ever, it was the same for him. Tangling a hand into my mass of curls, he held me in place as he kissed along my jaw, his mouth wet and hot on mine.

The night became one long cycle of sleeping and waking to the feeling of tension building between us and the release that came with our joining. We should have been sated, but it was never enough. The fire in my veins pulsed in time with our movements, again and again, before we lay back together to rest.

When next I woke up, I found the room bright with daylight. David's mind hummed along beside me as he slept, and I turned to study his sleeping face, tracing his features. The long nose which gave him such a strong profile. How he had trailed it across my body even as he peppered kisses along my fevered flesh. His strong jaw, and how he liked it when I nipped at the area in front of his ear. His lower lip was slightly larger, and I found myself obsessing over the way I would suck on it later.

I thought about waking him, but something made me hesitate. The night before had been unreal, and I wanted so badly to hold on to it, to make it last just a little longer. Neither of us had spoken a word the whole night, letting our mental connection do the communicating for us.

It had been a profoundly deep experience, and I could feel how much things between us had changed. If only I could live in a world where it was only him and me together in the dark for a little longer.

His eyelids flickered, and he stirred. Yawning, he stretched, cracking an eye in a flash of pale blue that made my heart squeeze.

"Good morning," he said, raising his arms and stretching. His voice was heavy with sleep.

"Good morning," I replied, unable to keep a grin from setting in. His eyes twinkled with amusement, and he rolled over to claim my lips before pulling me into his arms, his breath tickling my ear.

"I think I forgot to say I love you last night," he said, stroking my hair.

"You didn't have to." The words barely came out around the lump in my throat.

And it was true. The force of his love was apparent. It was in everything he did, every gesture, every touch.

He loved me.

I was loved, and for the first time, I realized just how important it was to me that I had someone in the world who cared as much as he did.

I pulled back to look at him.

"I love you, too. So much." Tears welled up in my eyes, blurring his features, and I angrily swiped at them. I had known that sharing physical intimacy with him would be important to both of us, but I hadn't been prepared for the closeness that sharing minds during the act would be. There had been so many emotions flowing between us the night before, and they were catching up with me now.

"Hey," he said, gently kissing me and tenderly wiping away a stray tear with the thick pad of his thumb. He gently touched our foreheads together, his mind waiting for me to reach out. I touched his mind with my own, and he soothed me through our connection. His love and warmth offering me the peace I needed, the promise of just how much more than one night we would be. He kissed my lips before moving to my neck, nuzzling in playfully, and I laughed at the graze of his lips against the sensitive skin.

But his playful tickle turned serious. His nose trailed up along the column of my neck, and he sucked at the skin just under my earlobe. I drew in a sharp breath as he hardened against me. He rolled me onto my back, twining our fingers together, and kissed down my neck and across my breasts, lingering to trail his tongue slowly over a nipple.

Just as I was about to beg for his mercy, to pull my hand free so I could touch him, the phone rang. Its shrill, insistent chime reminded us that there was a world outside of the bed where we had shared our souls. David chuckled, steadfastly ignoring the phone and continuing his ministrations. It wasn't long before I was squirming and mewling beneath him, my hips bucking uselessly in a silent demand for him to pay attention to my needy cunt.

David might be unpracticed, but with my mind so readily available to him, he was quickly learning exactly what I liked. And with a devilish smirk, his hand fell between us, circling the raw bundle of nerves at my center with enough pressure to leave me a weak, pliable bit of putty in his talented hands.

It was almost unfair how he knew what I wanted, what I liked, and it wasn't long before he replaced his hand, and we made love to the music of the phone. It rang at least four more times with a polite break in between before the final waves of pleasure worked their way through my system, the stars in my vision fading. David spent an extra moment nuzzling into my neck before prying himself away. He grabbed the receiver just as it began to ring anew.

"Hello," he said breathlessly. "Oh, I see. Yes, my apologies. We slept in." David smirked at me, and I grinned right back. We certainly hadn't lingered in bed to sleep. His jaw ticked. "No, no need for that. We'll be down very soon." He hung up and turned to me.

His eyes danced in the way that made my heart beat fast, and I clenched my legs together against the resulting wave of arousal. I was already imagining having him between my legs again. "Apparently, we missed checkout by an hour, and they aren't very happy about it."

Oh.

Staring at him in shock, I marveled for a moment at his lack of reaction, before hopping off the bed and rapidly sorting through the mess of clothes on the floor. I threw him his pants, and was just turning to get dressed, when he grabbed me playfully about the waist. I could see him in the dresser mirror, hugging me from behind, his arms encircling me. My bare skin tingled where we touched.

"David, we have to go. There's a charge for late checkout, and—"

His breath tickled my ear, and his hard cock pressed into my hip. Just knowing he was hard again was enough to have me melting back into his chest.

"I don't care. I'll pay whatever it is. Last night was incredible." Damn him and his husky voice.

"This morning wasn't too bad either," I cooed, molding his hands to my waist and forcing myself to move away from his warmth. But I missed him the second we were apart, and I turned to lightly kiss him on the lips before giving him a stern look.

"But we really should get going." If we didn't get out of here soon, we'd end up back in the bed, or the shower. Thoughts of the shower, of the cold tile pressed against my body as he took me, left me salivating, and too late I realized he'd seen the image in my mind. Pupils blown, he grabbed my arm even as I placed a trembling hand on his chest and tried to stem the flow of arousal.

"We have beds back home, too," I promised, trying and failing to keep my tone light. I turned to pull on my underwear, but he caught me, banding an arm across my waist. This man would be the death of me.

He turned me towards the bathroom, easily taking control of my body as if any part of me wanted to stop him. Swallowing hard, I let him guide me into the shower on legs still weak from the force of my release.

This was going to be a very late checkout.

The man at the front desk was considerably older than the boy from the night before. His dour face regarded us without an ounce of remorse as he informed us we were indeed being charged. But David only chuckled in a mad way that made my cheeks burn. He made his payment, and we headed out to the rental car.

How different it felt to slide into the seat next to him. Like I was a different person from yesterday. He retrieved a cooler of frozen blood we'd left to defrost overnight, and we drank it without warming it, though David scoffed at the temperature.

After a night spent where sleep came in spurts, I fell asleep for the first part of the drive. When I woke up, it was to his hand on my knee, his thumb making lazy circles across the cap. Growing uncomfortably warm, I willed his hand to drift between my legs and find my nub. But instead of taking his hand and placing it where I wanted, I cleared my throat.

"How are you doing after everything with Nicholas?" It had been a difficult encounter for him, and we couldn't exactly do what I wanted with him driving. He peeked over at me in surprise before returning his attention to the road. But he pulled his hand away from my leg to place it on the wheel, and I felt a sense of loss at its absence. David's jaw muscle twitched, and I regretted bringing up Nicholas.

"It was hard, Sarah, but it was worth it," he said, the tension in his jaw easing. He looked over meaningfully at me, and I knew what he was thinking even if he didn't say it or think it to me. My heart warmed.

I was worth it.

We were worth it.

The things we'd done were worth it. His hand dropped to the armrest between us, and I placed mine on top. Shit, the things we'd done. Now that I'd thought about it, I couldn't think of anything else, and I shifted awkwardly in place at the flood of arousal soaking my panties, adjusting my old band shirt in an attempt to disguise the movement.

Face flushed, David switched on the radio, and I played with his fingers. His mind hummed away beside me as he concentrated on the road. I'd brought some reading to catch up on, but my thoughts kept drifting back to the night before, until I slammed the text shut in annoyance and chucked it into the backseat. He quirked an eyebrow at me, and I shrugged.

"I don't feel much like reading." I returned to toying with his fingers, imagining his hands on me. How good he'd felt, how right. How damned quickly he'd learn to play my body like an instrument he was born to. He must've caught the hint of my smile because he glanced over with a grin.

"Okay, what is it?"

"Just thinking about things,"

"Oh yeah, what sort of things?" He laughed, guessing what I had on my mind and rubbing my thigh. *Just a few more inches to the right.* My god, but I wanted him again. How crazy it was that my body could even respond after last night. I'd even had him just this morning, rough and wicked under a stream of water hot enough to scald my skin. Yet his hand on my leg was all it took to leave me a mess, just as needy for him as I'd ever been. He knew what he was doing to me, his fingers drifting a few inches closer to my center before returning to draw small circles.

Bastard.

My hand tightened on his, and I tried to pull it closer to my needy clit, screaming out for his attention, but he pretended not to notice, returning his hand to my leg. I could feel his touch so clearly through the chiffon skirt I wore, the soft fabric moving over my helplessly trapped leg. This was torture, and we were only about halfway home.

My breathing came in fast little gasps, and I tried unsuccessfully to push his hand away. Laughing, I batted at it.

"David, stop," I begged.

But his response was just to smile at me. The next thing I knew, we were pulling over on the side of the highway, and David was parking the car. As soon as he shifted into park, his deft fingers sank between my legs, and I groaned. I gripped his wrist to hold him in place as he worked me. He withdrew his hand, and I whimpered, but then he was slipping past the elastic waistband of my skirt, and I threw my head back with a moan when he found my needy nub and began to circle it.

"Come here."

I looked up to find David's eyes dark. His pupils expanded as he watched, and he pulled his hand free to drag across my lip, letting me taste myself. Shuddering, I licked the salty mess from my lips.

I tasted like him, and it was no wonder after last night.

The thought of our tastes mingling so completely made me ravenous for more.

"Come here," he repeated, but I hesitated. Cars swept past us in an angry parade. "Don't worry, we're off to the side and everyone is driving faster. Nobody will notice."

I didn't know if that was true or not, but with the lust swirling in the air, heavy with promise between us, I decided I didn't care.

"Now, come here." This time his tone brooked no argument, and I hurried to comply, sliding my skirt and panties off in one movement and awkwardly climbing over the armrest between us to sit on his lap. After fighting with the zipper of David's jeans, he was released, and I sank onto him gratefully, the stretch exactly what I'd been craving. Neither of us lasted long once I started moving up and down against his length, and I clung to his shoulders as pleasure tore through me, an endless sea of waves crashing upon the shore until at last they began to ease. We were both breathing hard when I moved back to my seat, and I self-consciously peered behind us at the passing cars, worried that someone had seen us and would turn around to come confront us and convict us of some crime.

The scent of sweat and sex was heavy in the car as we set off, and after a while, I struggled to fight off the need for him again.

This was too much. How many times did we have sex last night? I had no idea. The whole evening was a blur.

"About last night." I caught a flash of blue as David peeked over at me before fixing his eyes back on the road. "I've never... Well, it's just I've never been so caught up with someone physically like this before. I mean, really, we should be more than satisfied now, and all I can think about is how badly I want you to pull over again." I laughed it off like it was a joke, but my voice came out strained and breathy.

A flush crept up his neck, and his hands tightened on the steering wheel like he was struggling to keep them in place.

Like he knew exactly what I was talking about.

"Do you remember how I told you that all the scouts are required to read the old scout's notes on humankind and human society?"

"Yes."

"Well, other scouts took human or supernatural lovers while they were out traveling, and they all said the same thing. Ancients have a much higher sex drive."

"Really?" All those times I'd taken a lover and was left wanting. I'd always thought it was me, some symptom of my trauma or a physical failing. Even with Adam, I'd gone to sleep hungry for more.

"No, Sarah, there's nothing wrong with you. You're perfect." He smirked. "Probably something wrong with me. We'd never leave the bed if I had my way. Even now." His grip on the steering wheel tightened, and the sight of him already filled with need sent arousal singing through my veins. I ran a soothing hand down my legs, but it did nothing to ease the rising demand within me.

We could pull over again. It was hours yet before we would be home, but if we stopped as many times as I wanted, we'd never get there.

David turned thoughtful, his eyebrows knitting together. "I suspect the high sex drive has to do with how difficult it is for us to produce children. The more time we spend in bed, the more likely it is that we'd be able to have kids. It makes sense really, and it can still take ancients hundreds of years to conceive a child."

I was surprised to see that he'd thought so much about it, but I shouldn't have been. He was a scientist and had probably considered all angles. It wouldn't surprise me if he'd done extensive research on the subject.

"Well, that's interesting," I said, staring out the window at the passing cars to distract myself from the rush of heat creeping up my neck. After a while it worked, and I was able to fall asleep, waking up in surprise to find we were already back in the city. David pulled up to my apartment building and stopped, but I turned to him in alarm.

Were we really going to say goodnight now? He didn't meet my eyes, and his shoulders were tight as he stepped out of the car and retrieved my bag from the trunk.

"Everything okay?" I asked when we reached my door. Surprised, he shrugged.

"Yeah, of course it is. It just feels strange to be apart so soon after last night."

I nodded thoughtfully.

"You could come in. Stay the night."

His eyes drifted across my face, lingering on my lips.

"I have to return the car, and you have work in the morning. Something tells me if I stay over, we won't sleep."

I couldn't argue with him, and found myself nodding along glumly.

"I'll see you tomorrow?" I clasped my hands behind his neck and leaned forward to kiss him, wishing I could argue with what he'd said. But the reality of life was upon us again, and he was right.

We'd see each other tomorrow.

"Night," I whispered, giving him a final quick kiss before turning to head inside. Sighing heavily, I looked around my empty apartment, switching on the light. Had the past few days really happened? It already felt strange not to have David close enough to touch. He wouldn't be home for at least an hour, but I already had the urge to call him just so I could hear his voice.

I would see him tomorrow, and the thought brought me comfort as I readied myself for bed. David always came by the diner to study so long as he wasn't in lecture. The way he would walk in, eyes only for me as he was shown to his usual bench seat, filled my mind as I drifted off to sleep—his twinkling eyes and quiet smile featuring prominently.

CHAPTER 18

David showed up at the diner just as the doors opened, and I looked up when the bell jingled, knowing it would be him. He grinned at me, and the anxiety that had been slowly building in my chest eased. But I could see the dark circles under his eyes and knew I matched him.

At first, sleep had come easily, but I'd woken in the night and reached for him. When I didn't find him beside me, ready to fulfill the need screaming through my veins, I'd had to find my own unsatisfying release. Now that he was here in person, my nipples hardened as I approached his table and took in his intoxicating scent. I'd thought it was hard to be around him before, but now that I knew what it was like between us.

It was torture.

A deep ache settled between my thighs, and I fought to ignore it as I watched Cheryl lead him to the booth he favoured. Near the kitchen, I would have an excuse to pass by him the most often, and I swallowed hard. If this was what it was like so damned early on, it was going to be a long day. He slid onto the bench, pulled a biochemistry text out of his satchel, and looked up at where I stood three tables over, the customer's order I'd been taking completely lost.

Offering my apologies to the frazzled woman having breakfast with an equally harried friend, I took her order and made a point of dropping it off in the kitchen right away, brushing by David without saying hi. If I did, I'd be delayed further.

Once it was placed, I went straight to his table, stopping short when he peered up at me with a twinkle in his eyes and a smirk on his lips.A flush crept up my neck, and my face burned. Because I knew that look, knew exactly what he was thinking, and wanted every bit of it. Instead, I cleared my throat and tried for normalcy.

"Good morning. How'd you sleep? I slept great." There, I'd done it. Only my voice was husky despite my best efforts, and I shifted in place to dispel the ache at being so close to him. David just grinned back, and by the twinkle in his eye, he could tell I was lying.

"Yeah, me too." He hummed deep in his throat, his gaze straying lower to where my uniform buttoned above my breasts.

I swatted his arm with my notepad, hoping the lighthearted jab would break the thick need already demanding I seek the privacy I needed to have him, but doing so only reminded me of how those powerful arms had easily lifted me into a new position that had left us both spiraling towards ecstasy. He knew it, too. Chuckling, he met my eyes.

Visions of the night we'd spent entwined together danced in my mind, and the urge to grab him by the coat collar and drag him into the bathroom was strong enough that I was forced to take a step back lest I act on it.

"You want the breakfast special?" My voice was squeaky, and I coughed to mask it. Chewing on my lip, I tried to think about anything other than how good he felt and how badly I wanted a bit of his addicting taste.

Just a quick kiss. Surely we could manage a quick kiss. I could duck behind his menu and pretend to be helping him make a selection. My gaze drifted down to his mouth, until I was moments away from acting on the impulse, when his voice interrupted my thoughts.

"Sure."

My eyes shot to his, and I stared at him dumbfounded until I remembered I'd asked him if he wanted breakfast. The smile slipped from his face, and the colour of his eyes darkened just a shade. I realized he was just as close to losing control as I was.

My heart squeezed painfully with regret as I offered him a watery smile before heading back to the kitchen and placing his order—the breakfast special, no meat. Pressing my back to the kitchen wall, I fought to control the arousal trying to take hold. But how could I when he was sitting out there, when he wanted me as badly as I wanted him?

It was all I could do to make it through my shift, with his eyes following my every step. I barely stopped by his table, and felt a stab of guilt at not refilling his coffee. Luckily, I was able to beg Cheryl to take over the refills, but just knowing he was there proved challenging.

It was harder than I'd imagined having him so close, but not be able to talk to him and share my mind. He was always so adorably absorbed when he focused, and I wanted to listen in.

When my shift finally ended, I changed into a shirt and jeans before coming out to meet him. He was already waiting outside, leaning against the doorframe, his face a mask of stone as he took my hand in his. The tightness in my chest eased at the physical contact, and he guided me down the street before tugging me into a dark alley two buildings down.

Twisting my hand in his hard enough to hurt, he turned me and pushed me into the brick wall. His mouth fell to mine, claiming me and saturating me with his taste. He trailed kisses along my jaw before nuzzling into my neck to suck and nip in a way that had my legs falling open. The ache in my core flared to life until I was moaning and turning my head to give him better access.

Oh, how I'd missed this. It had only been one day and my body had missed him. We fit perfectly together, his hands venturing down to roll my hips into his. David's mind brushed mine and all the emotions and longing from the day flowed between us. I was home. One hand brushed my cheek, and all thought left me. I shivered beneath him, but I jolted in alarm when an older woman bundled against the cold coughed and glared down the alley at us. She gripped her shopping bag and hurried past, like we were diseased and it might be catching.

How were we going to extract ourselves from this?

"I bet we can make it over to my apartment before lecture," I whispered, his mouth still at my neck. "It's closer to campus." I gasped when he pressed his length against me, cursing the layers of clothing that prevented him from sinking in.

We rushed to my apartment, dodging around a woman with an armload of groceries. David's hand was tight in mine as we ran giggling through the street until we reached my apartment building. We stumbled up the stairs, pushing through the doors and hurrying down the hallway to fling the apartment door open.

Thanking whoever listened that Nina was out, I turned to him the second the door was shut. We stood and stared at each other, reminding me of the way we'd stood frozen on our first night together.

But I broke it before the moment could stretch any longer, crashing into him and claiming his mouth as we thumped against the closed door. Taking hold of my hips, David kissed me until my breath came in helpless squeaks as I pawed at my clothing.

He kissed up my jawline, his hand slipping beneath the waistband of my jeans to find my nub. Biting my lip to keep from screaming out, I rolled my hips against his hand, wanting more. I'd been desperate for him in the night and my hand had been a poor substitute.

I worked the button of his jeans, crying out when the rough pad of his thumb circled my nub, and the tension within me built higher. Yes, this is what I'd been missing. At last, he sprang free. With a groan, he caged me in against the door, pushing my face aside to inhale deeply at my neck.

"Do you know how badly I wanted you all day?" The rough edge of his voice made me shiver, even as the way he worked my nub drove me closer to ecstasy. "All day, every minute, I was sitting there. All I could think of was this."

Words escaped me. I could only moan my agreement, unable to explain how I'd had to force myself to stay away. How the muscles in my back were sore from the tension.

He pressed hard against my clit, and I gasped when he tugged my jeans over my hips in one movement and hitched up my leg to position himself at my entrance. Then he was sinking deep, and we both groaned. I reached out, eager to feel the sensation echo in his mind. God, his mind. I'd missed it almost as much as his body, and I filled myself with him, knowing it would never be enough.

Cupping my ass, he slammed me into the wall as he worked his way in and out, stretching and filling me hard enough to make my teeth chatter. I broke when he did, his guttural yell driving me over the edge to the place of soul togetherness. Waves of pleasure lingered between us.

I was already lamenting that it was over.

"It's never over." The raw edge of his voice left me whimpering in his grip.

Brushing a curl off my cheek, David found my lips and claimed my mouth, and I was lost to the taste of him. His hand gripped my hip, and I could feel him already hardening inside of me.

It was all we could do to make it to the bedroom and shut the door.

Rather than question if I would invite him in at the end of the night, it became a matter of whose apartment we would be staying at. After the first night when we'd been apart, it became an unspoken agreement between us.

Being apart wasn't working. It left us both feral with need the next day. Even after spending the nights in each other's arms, I found my craving for him growing stronger each day. It was tolerable when we'd spent hours locked in an embrace, but barely.

The lab exam we had together was uncomfortable. The lab coat was rough against my erect nipples as I fought to keep my mind on mixing and titrating. He always found an excuse to brush up against me. The careful measurements were hard to manage, and I knew my performance was suffering.

Every minute when I wasn't in a lecture or at work, we were in bed exploring each other with a furious need that never settled, never rested. Sleep was forgotten, as was eating. All else paled in comparison to the heights of pleasure and a desire to live on that other plane together.

But by the end of the week, I was struck with an unusually powerful wave of melancholy. I spent the day at work trying to understand the source of my mood. David hadn't appeared yet, giving me some rare time on my own, although the thought of him still asleep in my bed was enough to leave me flustered without his distracting presence.

David. This had to do with him somehow, but I couldn't understand why. I was in love with a man who loved me. We were happy. The sex was incredible.

So what was wrong with me?

I was starting to think maybe I couldn't be happy, like the trauma I'd experienced at the hands of my vampire family had stolen the ability from me, but then David showed up to distract me from such thoughts, beaming and taking his usual seat. My heart soared at the sight, and I chuckled into my hand when Cheryl disappeared in the kitchen soon after, no doubt going to alert the rest of the waitstaff that their favourite regular had arrived.

Only he was my favourite regular, and standing there watching him quietly pull out his book for the exam he had on Friday, I realized the problem.

We'd barely talked in ages. Things between us had been so hot and heavy that we'd spent the entire week completely caught up with the physical aspects of our relationship. Gone had been the playful banter and long walks late into the night.

We'd spent more time together than ever before. Our bodies and minds joined on a soul-deep level that left me dizzy with gratitude, but through it all, I missed him. Staring at his spiked hair, at the way he smiled to himself while reading, I missed him so damned much my heart hurt. The emotion was powerful enough that he must have felt it because he looked up with a frown, cocking an eyebrow at me in question. I turned back to the dirty plates I was clearing in the hopes of disguising the way I'd openly been staring at him across the restaurant.

The idea seemed ludicrous, but there it was. It bothered me. When I finished my shift, I was determined to broach the subject with him. We walked outside, but before he could take the initiative, I pulled him towards me and kissed him tenderly on the lips.

Not passionately, just tenderly, my lips pliant against his.

He pulled back to watch me carefully, a frown puckering his brow, and I hated how I was worrying him. How to broach this subject tactfully had been on my mind all afternoon, and somehow, I'd come up with nothing.

"Can we take a walk together?" I asked in a small voice. Brows furrowed, David slowly nodded.

We walked in a comfortable silence—me enjoying the feel of his warm arm in mine and him looking around as though he was interested in all the shops on the busy street, all the while his attention was focused on me as he waited for me to speak. I took a shaky breath before reminding myself that this was David. I could tell him anything.

"I feel strange saying this, but I realized today that I've been missing you." The silence stretched between us, and I hated it. How I longed to take the words back, but they were there between us now, and I knew he was mulling them over, trying to think of a way to help.

Whatever he'd been expecting me to say, this wasn't it.

"It's just that, I feel like we haven't spent much time together just talking or enjoying other things together lately. I can't remember the last time we went out to a restaurant or a walk that wasn't us trying to get back to one of our apartments." I sighed, hating this the more I spoke. "It's stupid. I'm sorry. I know I'm not making much sense."

He stopped walking and pulled me around to face him.

"Hey, it's not stupid. Maybe we got a little carried away," he said, giving me a teasing smile. "It's just—" His eyes wandered, searching for the words. "It's hard to think about much else." He met my gaze, and I let out a sigh, because I felt the same way. I wanted to lie with him in bed for a week. If we could do that, maybe there'd be more time to talk, to do other things, but the time we spent together was always so short, so squeezed.

I needed both sides of him.

All sides.

The man I'd fallen in love with, and the animal he became when we were behind closed doors.

"You're right, we need a bit more of a"—his lip curled up into a smirk—"balance."

"You really don't think it's ridiculous?"

He looked at me, his eyes narrowing.

"I think you're probably right, and it's my fault."

"No, David, I—"

He held up a hand, and I was relieved to see him grinning over at me. "So what do you want to do tonight?"

I couldn't help but smile back.

"I just want to walk together like we used to. To talk and get lost wandering the streets," I said, beseeching him with my eyes. I knew he would do anything for me, would happily do this, but I wanted him to understand, to tell me I wasn't crazy.

He didn't answer, but smiled and held his hand to me. I took it gratefully, and we started off, not having a destination.

I had no lectures tonight. We were free to wander, free to let our feet guide us, and talk the whole night away if that was what we wanted.

It was exactly what I needed, and while I still felt that need for him, I knew there would be time for that later. Our feet would eventually lead us back to one of our apartments, and we would find a bed to lie down in together.

We walked a while in silence, talking about our future. It was both of our last year in school, and we'd talked many times about what would happen next. We both planned to work in research, but here in Boston? Somewhere else? Wherever we started, we'd be climbing our way up the ranks for years until we could run our own research projects. We wandered the streets hand in hand until we did eventually find our way back to my apartment.

After that night, we made more of an effort to find a 'balance' in our relationship. We went out for meals together. We watched TV. We went out on double dates with Adam and Nina, but the physical part of our relationship was still very real and ever present. At the end of each night, we both knew that we would fall into each other's arms.

Chapter 19

Extracted from digitalis leaves, gitalin is a water-soluble mix of glyco-sides used to treat heart failu–

The words on the page were wiped from my mind when David dropped a kiss on my neck. My breath stuttered, and I tilted my head to give him better access.

"Sorry," he muttered, before sitting back on his knees to continue kneading the tension out of my upper back. Still aching from where he'd hitched my leg over his shoulder and taken me not five minutes ago, we should both be sated, but I knew it wouldn't last long. For now, David's hands on my back were what we both needed to stay sane.

His mind was loosely connected to mine as he listened in on my reading.

Just one day left.

"I promise I'll be good."

But I caught the stutter in his voice, and it was enough to pebble my skin. Breathing deeply, I returned to the text.

Heart failure. Gitalin is also used to treat auricular fibrillation, and studies have shown–

His hands drifted lower to cup my ass, and I was lost. Turning to stare at him in accusation, but what I saw took my breath away.

He was rock hard, his eyes clouded with a familiar haze of lust that darkened the blue and blew out his pupils until his eyes were almost black.

My heart pounded as he reached around, his hands drifting across my abdomen before gripping my hips. His eyes followed the path with reverence.

"Sorry." He shook his head as though to clear it, and I sat up.

I hated it when he apologized, especially when all it took was one look at his face to leave me in the most delicious agony only he could save me from. Hands clasped behind his neck, I kissed him, moving up and down his length to coat him with my slick. But he broke the kiss, his hands shaky with need against my back.

"We're supposed to be studying for the exam."

We were, and I knew it was important, but I couldn't remember why anymore.

"It can wait."

It couldn't, but it would have to. Hands braced on the back of David's neck, I took his hand and guided it to my soaking entrance.

He threw his head back, my name a prayer on his lips as I sank down onto him, stretching as he filled me.

Leaning forward, I clung to his neck, and he thrust up to meet me, grabbing my hips to push and pull at the fast rhythm we both craved.

But it wasn't hard enough, deep enough for either of us, and with a groan, David cupped my ass and lifted us. He moved us to the floor beside his bed, pressing me into the laminate as he sank in fully. I gasped at how damned good the stretch of him felt. His thumb found my nub, and I squirmed beneath him, wanting more. Needing it. Needing him. Stars exploded behind my eyes, and he came a moment later with a roar, massaging my hips as the last of the waves of bliss dissipated.

Careful not to put his weight on me, he covered my body with his, his forearms on either side of my face.

"So what was that about Gitalin?" I laughed, and he nuzzled into my cheek, kissing and nibbling.

"We really should study, though."

"Yes, I know." His breath tickled my ear, and I sighed contentedly. It wasn't the first time we'd both wanted the roughness of the floor, and it wouldn't be the last. But I found myself missing a soft pillow for my head. David kissed my cheek noisily, and went up on his knees at the bed, returning a moment later with one clenched in his fist. Laughing, I hit him in the arm with an open palm.

"Hey, no peeking." Our minds hadn't been joined, but he'd clearly had a glimpse of my thoughts. He beamed back unapologetically, and I smacked him again.

"I can't help it. When we're like this, it's hard not to just connect automatically." He was right, though I hadn't reached out and let him in, I hadn't been blocking him, and the physical closeness emphasized our mental connection.

Grinning, I reached out a hand. "I'll take my pillow now, please."

But when he made to give it to me, I took the opening to throw myself at his chest, wrestling him to the ground.

His hands were on me in an instant, finding the area of my ribs where I was most sensitive and using his deft fingers to tickle me mercilessly. Consumed by laughter, he easily rolled me over to pin me beneath him. I could barely breathe through the forced mirth, and I slapped him on the back.

"Stop, Davey, stop!"

He went still in an instant, pulling back to look at me. Frowning, I studied the serious expression on his face.

"What's wrong?" Alarmed, I sat back up to look around us, wondering if someone had knocked and I'd somehow missed it.

Eyes bright with excitement, David grabbed my upper arm.

"You used to call me that when we were kids. Not all the time, but if you were ever particularly exasperated with me." He laughed and the hope flaring to life in his eyes was hard to bear.

Swallowing, I laid a hand on his arm. With us growing closer, it was easy to forget about our shared history, but now he stared at me with such raw joy.

I hated how I needed to crush it.

"I'm sorry, David. I wish I remembered." And I did wish I remembered that time in my life when I had been a carefree child with David.

"I wish that, too."

And there it was, the one thing that still came between us. He looked away, hiding the pain from me, but I could see it in the tightness of his eyes, had known what it felt like in his mind. He badly wanted to share those memories with me, but it just wasn't possible with my amnesia.

Sighing, I turned to sit up, but he stopped me with a hand on my shoulder.

"We could still go back there, Sarah. It's home."

But I was already shaking my head. Tears threatened as a familiar pit of dread yawned open in my stomach.

"But they aren't really like that, Sarah. It was a nightmare, not reality. The elders are flawed, but—"

"You know what they did to me. What happened after they left me with those people. I'm sorry that's your home and your family, but it's not mine."

"Yeah, I know that," he answered wearily, and I looked up when I felt a deep well of sadness in his mind. Alarmed, I cupped his cheek.

"I'm sorry," I whispered, and I badly wished I could say yes. That I had the courage to face the elders, to confront them, and take back what was mine.

He understood as only he could, turning to kiss my palm.

"I know it's important to you, but those people. David—" Biting my lip, I tried to think how to say this, how to voice the fear I'd harboured ever since I'd learned about my past. "They could do it again."

As much as David tried to reassure me otherwise, he couldn't dispute that they had the power to strip my memories away, to take everything I'd built and force me to start anew who knows where and with who. Lost and without the people I loved. Adam and Nina—gone. David? I wouldn't even have the memory of him. Shivering, I hugged myself.

"Sarah." David's arms came around my back, and he pulled me into his chest. "I'd never let that happen. I'd die first."

Nodding, and fighting the tears that were forcing their way out of my eyes no matter how I squeezed them shut, I curled gratefully into his chest. Wrapping my arms around him, it reminded far too much of the glowing figure from my dreams—the figure that had once been the only trace of him left to me.

DAVID

Davey. She'd called me Davey. How long had it been since I'd heard my nickname on her lips? I knew how it affected her when I reminisced about those days, how quiet she always grew when her missing memories were brought up, but I hadn't been able to help myself. Not when I'd heard that one word squeak past her breathless lips.

Now she frowned down at her text, and I could hear her struggling to read in her mind. The focus she'd had before I interrupted her was completely lost. I resisted the urge to reach out a hand and smooth the divot in her forehead. Had we really been laughing and joking a few minutes ago?

The air was thick with unspoken words.

Come home with me. I wanted to comfort her, to assure her until that terrible fear she'd shared with me was gone, but there was no resolving it. And while I would've given up on returning to the island, put it aside for her, I couldn't.

Not when I was forced to go back there.

Already the upcoming separation felt like too much. The two feet between us, where she sat cross-legged on the rug, much too far. I needed to hold her, to feel her soft skin against mine, to let her tinkling laugh burn into my ears until it would never leave me.

She couldn't go back there, and I understood. I did, but I wasn't able to make that choice for myself. Like the coward I was, my lips quirked up in a smile when she looked up at me, and I hated myself for it.

Energy flooded my system with the need to do something, and I stood up abruptly, disturbing her from her reading. She stared up at me with such trust shining in her warm brown eyes. I couldn't bring myself to tell her how I'd be leaving after our exams were done.

Instead, I leaned down to cup her cheek, my breath tight when she melted into my palm. The powerful way she reacted to my touch felt like a gift, and I drew in a shuddering breath, my pants tight. It took so little for me to grow hard around her. Just the sight of her was enough.

I'd live inside her if I could.

"I'm going to go out for a quick run." She frowned up at me, and I smoothed out the crease in her forehead. "Not for long. I'll be back soon." I let the promise in my words soften the air between us. I couldn't resist dropping to my knees and kissing her temple, but I held myself back from pulling her into my arms.

As much as I hated it, I needed to get outside, to have some distance from her so I could think through what to do next.

"Soon. I'll be back soon, okay?"

She nodded against my hand, her soft crimson curls tickling my wrist. The promise had been for her, but it was also for me. I wanted to spend every free moment with her, in her mind, touching her body, or just in her presence. Leaving to do something alone took some convincing.

But I couldn't stay here and look at her right now, not knowing how devastated she'd be when she learned of my return. I forced myself to stand, to walk over to the door, to smile back at her perfect face, and take a moment to admire how her tangle of wild curls framed it so perfectly before leaving.

The cool breeze soothed my anxiety almost immediately, and I took a deep breath, imagining the fresh air of the woods and birdsong of the island instead of the human scents and sounds of the city. Sarah's vampire parents had lived out in the country, but I was sure she couldn't remember the peace of the island—of the nights there, how the birds and animals sang as if mourning the loss of the day before lapsing into silence.

If only there was a way to convince her to return with me. I'd love to blame her for it, to think she was being unreasonable, but her fears weren't unfounded, and I could never claim they were.

She'd been through so much, and it was wholly the fault of the elders. If anything, her hatred for them was less than what I'd expect. Hell, I hated them for what they'd done to her, and I hadn't known the extent of it until recently. So much pain, so much torment, and why? Because she'd awakened near the body of a murdered fisherman.

The elders had made their assumptions and damned her without evidence. It took weeks of searching before we found the panther and proved her innocence. If the elders had only done the search themselves, or mobilized the community. But they hadn't cared. They'd cast Sarah out into a nightmare of a life. Away from her parents. Away from me.

What would it have been like to grow up together? For this force between us to have slowly developed as we matured instead of roaring into life when we'd met as adults? The crush I'd had on her hadn't compared.

She was pretty

She was my friend.

Of course, I loved her. What would it have been like for those tender feelings to develop naturally into the soul rending bond it now was?

Frustrated, I rolled my shoulders. The streets were quiet tonight, and while I'd been too worked up to change out of my jeans and into pants with more stretch, I'd run in slacks once. The pinch of fabric at my hips was uncomfortable. I took off at a slow jog.

Our last exam was tomorrow.

I had to tell her.

I was running out of time.

I had to tell her.

I increased my pace, but kept it at a human's speed. I ran like that until my tight muscles loosened from sheer exhaustion, and only then did I return to the apartment, drinking down two glasses of water and showering off the sweat before I allowed myself to open the bedroom door.

Light from the window slanted across her sleeping face where she lay curled on our bed, her hand outstretched and resting on my pillow. Her face was smoothed by sleep, and I took a moment to admire her. The pout of her lips. The way her lashes curled, and the delicacy of her cheekbones. The white sheet draped across her sleeping form showcased the swell of her hip. She was so beautiful my heart ached just looking at her. The need to touch, to claim, overpowering any remaining thoughts of my impending trip.

We had our exam tomorrow. She needed the sleep, but I knew it was kinder to wake her now. There was no chance of sleeping through the night when we were so close to each other. Either I woke her up now, or she woke me up later. I slid under the covers, already hard, my hand coming up to pull her into my chest as I kissed her pouty lips and felt her stir.

"Mm?" She cracked an eye, and I kissed her more deeply, pushing my tongue into her mouth, eager for a taste. Groaning, she turned towards me. Her arms came up to hold me back, to venture between us, and find how hard and ready I was. But sleep still clung to her, and I moved lower, sucking and nipping along her collarbone. I wasn't surprised to find she'd gone to bed naked.

Clothes got in the way.

Clothes were an inconvenience. If I could have her naked all the time, her body on display for my hungry eyes, I would.

I paused at her small, round breast, worshiping the left even as my fingers mercilessly pinched the right. She squealed, arching her back into the sensation, and I lightly brushed her mind so I would know how it was affecting her.

She loved it. She'd tried to stay up, to wait for me, but had succumbed to sleep, wishing I would do this very thing whenever I returned. She'd lain here craving me, and I'd been out doing—what? Running? The stupidity of my decision struck me, and I smiled ruefully, pressing a cheek to her heaving chest. Her hand came up to hold me in place in a silent plea for more, but I pulled away, trailing kisses down her stomach and across the line of her hips before I reached her cunt.

She was wet, and I sank a finger into her heat, marveling at how drenched she was. My cock twitched uncomfortably when she bucked her hips against my finger, urging me to sink them deep. And who was I not to oblige her? To deny her a single thing I could give?

I sunk two fingers to the first knuckle, burying my face in the taste of her sweetness until I discovered her nub. With my other hand, I pumped my aching cock to the rhythm of my fingers inside of her, twirling my tongue across her clit the way I knew she liked. I barely needed the confirmation in her mind anymore. Her breathing quickened to panting gulps, and she pressed against my head to drive me deeper.

But this wasn't what she wanted, what either of us wanted, and I couldn't wait any longer. I broke from the heaven of her taste, making my way up her torso to find her mouth and tangle my tongue with hers. I let her taste herself on me, to know how sweet she was. How perfect. I nearly came when her delicate fingers curved around my cock and pumped me roughly.

She groaned into my mouth, and I growled in reply, pushing her legs open and finding her wet heat with my eager fingers. She was past ready, letting out the little whines and moans that were my new favourite sounds, and I positioned myself between her thighs, pressing eagerly into her softness.

Heaven. There was no other way to describe the way she gripped me, the intoxicating blend of her taste and smell, or the way it saturated me until I thought I would die without it. She panted beneath me, thrashing against her pillow and wiggling her hips to provide a taste of the friction she needed, but I held back from giving her what she wanted.

This moment. The way we fit together. How well we matched each other. I would never tire of it, and I stared down at the place where our bodies joined in wonder, before pulling out to the tip and slamming back into her.

Her eyes rolled back. She was close, as close as I was, and I couldn't wait any longer. Need overwhelmed thought until I was hammering into her, lost to the sensation—to the way she gripped me—the pain mingling with pleasure when her nails dug half-moons into my back. Her lips parted, her back arching nearly off the mattress, and her cunt pulsed around me as release took her to a higher plane.

The sight of her eyes wide, her lips parted in awe, sent me over the edge, and I clung to her. Filling her, giving her everything, and letting my release shudder through me and bring with it that moment of sheer joy and togetherness. Sated, I lay back beside her, and she cuddled close to press her face into my neck.

"I love you," I murmured into the tangled mess she'd made of her hair.

I couldn't make out the words she mumbled in reply, but I peeked down to see a smile curving her beautiful lips. The hum of contentment in her mind was soothing, and I drowsed beside her. For tonight, everything was perfect. The island had kept for thousands of years.

It could wait until after the exam.

Chapter 20

SARAH

Somehow, we made it through final exams. Neither of us had felt like much of a celebration or attending graduation with our peers, but after a lot of prodding, we'd agreed to go out for dinner with Adam and Nina.

The place Nina had suggested was one step above a diner, fine porcelain plates at odds with the paper napkin wrapped cutlery. Nina already had her choice ready by the time the waitress came around.

"Tacos. Two of each type."

I couldn't help but eye my tiny former roommate, wondering where all that food was going to go, but she just gave me a toothy grin before leaning back into the shelter of Adam's arms. "What? It'll make great leftovers."

I rolled my eyes at that, placing an order for their soup of the day.

"What'll it be, sir? Sir?"

David stared at a drop of condensation drifting slowly down the side of his water glass, seemingly oblivious to the exasperated waitress, and I nudged him with my arm.

"Hmm?" He looked up at me, not her, and I tipped my head in the waitress' direction, knowing I'd be frustrated in her situation.

"Oh, sorry, um, yes. I'll have the—" He snatched up the unopened menu in front of him. "Nachos, please. No beef."

I'd been growing steadily worried about whatever was going on with David, but it became painfully obvious by the time our food came that something was distracting him, and with exams out of the way, I had no idea what it could be.

He barely spoke the whole night, and by the time we said goodnight to Adam and Nina, I was wracking my mind. The only thing I could think of was how I'd called him Davey the other night and the resulting discussion. I'd always known how badly he wanted to take me back to the island, and how my refusal bothered him, but this seemed extreme.

We walked the streets on our way home, and I settled into the familiar pace, letting my head drift to his arm. Only once the taut muscle relaxed beneath my cheek did I speak.

"You've been acting so distant tonight. Is everything okay?" I softened my tone and rubbed his cold hand, smoothing out the long fingers I loved so much. "Whatever it is, you know you can tell me."

He turned to me with a frown. "It's nothing, Sarah. Don't worry about it. I'm fine."

But he wasn't, and we both knew it. I squeezed his arm.

"No, something is wrong and you need to tell me what it is so I can help."

Sighing, he turned to face me fully, taking my hand and playing with my fingers as he tried to find the words.

"It's almost been a year since I've been away from the island." He looked up at me like he'd made a huge revelation, but I had no idea the importance. Sighing, he broke eye contact. "Scouts are required to check in after a year of time away. Otherwise, it's assumed that something happened to them, and they're mourned. I can't do that. I can't do what my uncle did to me, Sarah. I need to go back." Before I could interrupt him, he held up a hand. "And I know you can't. I know that, and I don't want you to. This is something I need to do."

His words sank in, and panic rose in my chest.

His time was up.

He needed to go back.

Go back…to them.

He turned over my numb hand, gently staring down at it a moment before looking up beseechingly at me.

"It wouldn't be for long. Just a week. I need to communicate my findings to them, and I've been arranging my work so I can do it as quickly as possible. I'll make it as short a trip as I can, I promise."

His words reached me, but I was disconnected from them. He had to go back. Back to that place with those people. All the worries I'd had that the island would somehow tear us apart sprang to life in my mind once more.

What if they did something to him when he was there? What if he never came back? I wouldn't even know how to find the island or where to go. The thought was nauseating. They could do that. Do anything. But then his uncle hadn't been there in years.

"David, your uncle—you said he sent them notes. Couldn't you do that?"

David sighed. His brow furrowed as he met my pleading gaze.

"Even if I could figure out the magic to transport a note there—that is what he did, Sarah. He sent his little notes every year to say he was alive and convey all the information he'd gathered, but he never checked in. He never found out if everyone back home was okay. He didn't even know his brother was dead until we went to tell him about it. I can't be like that. I need to make sure that everyone there is okay, that no one needs me."

I need you.

I wanted to scream the words at him, to shake him until he agreed to stay away from that place, to stay with me. But how could I do that? As much as I hated the elders for what they'd done, these people were David's family.

"I promise I'll be okay. I'll go there, communicate my findings, and come back just as soon as I ca—"

"I don't want you to go back there!" The force of my words disturbed the quiet of the night, and he looked at me in surprise. Taking a deep breath to steady myself, I continued more quietly, not meeting his eyes, though I could feel them on me.

"They could do the same thing to you, or maybe they wouldn't let you come back again. If you put yourself in their power." My voice trembled, and I cleared my throat to settle it. "What if they decided that I'm bad for you and just kept you there? I wouldn't know how to find you or how to even communicate with you. You'd just be gone."

I looked up, tears welling in my eyes as I fought to be heard, to find the right words to make him stay. There was this feeling. This terrible feeling whenever I thought about that place, like it was just waiting to ruin my life. Like going back there would ruin me completely.

"I can't lose you." Because that's what it came down to, and the irrational part of my mind insisted that's what would happen if he went there. His eyes filled with concern, and he gently wiped away a stray tear with his thumb.

"Sarah, you won't. I would never let them keep me from you. Do you understand me? Never." His eyes burned with conviction. But how could he stop them? I believed he would try, but they were strong. They were a group, and he was one man.

I nodded because I didn't want him to worry. I wanted to put this behind us. But I wasn't reassured. Far from it.

"No, Sarah. Look at me," he said firmly. I raised my eyes slowly to meet his.

"I would never let that happen, and if we were somehow separated. I'd find you again. I'll always find you." His voice was clear and firm, filled with the certainty I needed.

Leaning into his chest, I let him pull me into a tight embrace. He held me tenderly, his hands light on the back of my coat as he dropped kisses on the top of my head and gently rubbed my back.

"It'll be okay. I promise," he whispered into my hair.

I wanted to believe him, wanted to let his conviction override my doubt, but every time I thought of him going back there, fear turned to ice in my veins until I could scarcely breathe.

"Why don't you just go with him?" Nina asked me in typical Nina fashion as she busily packed a box. Her hair was pinned back to keep it out of her face, but she'd managed a full face of makeup. She shrugged her thin shoulders and put her hand out for the tape. Everything was so simple to her and part of me hated how easy it sounded.

Sure, just go with them. Take a little trip to a magical island and have my memories restored. One week and we'd be back after a vacation, and I'd be returning whole, my memories intact.

Only, it wasn't simple. The elders made everything complicated.

"Because I don't want to see those people. I don't want to risk them doing something to me again," I muttered, barely loud enough to be heard.

Nina knew some of the truth, enough to understand what I meant, but not the details of what my vampire family had been like.

She bit through the tape and secured the end before turning with her hands on her hips to stare me down.

"If you stay back, you'll just worry about something bad happening to him. At least if you go, you'll be together. What's the difference? Just go. Make a little vacation out of it. God knows you could use one. There are beaches there, right?"

Beaches. Would they look like they had in my dream? Pristine white and soft as butter. How could I go there, to walk those wooded paths where, in my dreams, I had raced with fear pounding in my head?

Nina drummed her acrylic nails on the counter, quirking an eyebrow at my silence. I drew in a shaky breath. If I went, I would be with David. We'd be able to face them together. And then there was the way he felt about bringing me back, what it would mean to him. It'd be like he'd rescued me the way he'd always dreamed.

The rest of the afternoon was spent on lighter topics. Adam and Nina's new place was a one bedroom on the border of what had been The Shades and The Draws. Moving would be good for their cohesion, and it wasn't as though our apartment had been a prized peach. There were enough spider-webbed cracks in the window to leave it drafty in the winter.

Rather than taking a taxi, I walked back over to the apartment I now shared with David. If I went back with him, I could at least help protect him from any danger, but it would mean facing the people who had left me with that terrible family. Who had taken me from my true home and stripped me of my memories. They'd left me adrift in the world without knowing who or even what I was, and they could do it again. The thought was terrifying, but my chest became unbearably tight whenever I thought of David going there alone.

I knew how warped their judgment was. How they'd passed David around like a commodity rather than give him the stability he'd needed.

They thought they knew best, and what happened if they decided David and I being together wasn't for the best?

By the time I returned home and headed upstairs, I'd come to a conclusion. David was lounging on the couch, his long legs stretched out and crossed at the ankles. A copy of *Moby Dick* flopped open on his lap. It was such a beautiful scene. I almost didn't want to disturb him.

Toeing off my sneakers, I padded over to the couch and squeezed myself into the gap between him and the armrest. He moved over to give me more space, slinging an arm across my shoulder, and leaning forward to kiss my temple.

"Hey, how'd it go?" His breath ruffled the hair at my temple, and all I could think about was the very real possibility of losing him to the island, of what the elders might choose to do.

I couldn't let it happen.

Wouldn't let it happen.

"It was fine." I breathed him in, letting the peace I found in his presence soothe my agitation even as his scent excited me.

"David." My serious tone caught his attention as he waited patiently for me to continue. "I've been thinking a lot about your trip, and you're right. I am worried."

He started to protest, but I held up a hand.

"The thought of you going there and not coming back, well, it—" I got choked up and stared straight ahead to steady myself. "I want to go with you." The words came out in a rush and as soon as they left my lips, the tension drained from my body.

"Really?" There was a note of vulnerability in his voice that choked me with emotion, and I pulled back to meet his gaze head-on.

"Yes, I don't want to, but I can't—" I shuddered out a breath. "I can't let you go back there alone."

David's grin spread from ear to ear, and he crushed me to his chest so hard I could feel his heart pounding with excitement. A smile curved my lips at his unabashed joy.

"Oh, Sarah, that's—this is going to be fantastic. I promise there's nothing to worry about, and I'll be there with you the whole time. We'll just stay at the house. You don't even have to meet anyone. You'll get your memories back, and we'll head straight back once I'm done communicating my findings. Nothing bad is going to happen. It's going to be perfect!" His excitement was contagious, and I let out an irrepressible squeal when his lips tickled my neck.

I wished I could share his excitement, his joy, but the island and its people had been a source of terror for as long as I could remember.

And that was why I'd never been able to let him go alone, to walk into danger without me there to protect him. He might fulfill a dream to bring me home and complete his original goal in setting forth for the human world, but I knew not to trust everything to run smoothly.

David had come here to find me, to save me. Now it was my turn to be his protector. To trust we were strong enough together to face whatever waited for us, and come back out again.

The End

ABOUT THE AUTHOR

Faye writes the kind of narratives that give her strength and courage. You can expect dark themes, high stakes, true love, and fierce heroines who struggle through their broken pasts to find human connection and salvation. Her works are best described as dark fantasy with strong romantic subplots featuring non-human characters with entirely human feelings and weaknesses.

She shares her writing space with a wildly supportive husband who regularly leaves her 'cofferings' (coffee offerings), three tiny humans who provide just the right amount of distraction, and a former Egyptian street cat who warms her lap to the purrfect writing temperature.

When she's not writing, you can find her traversing the outdoors and photographing everyday moments, changing her perspective and finding the hidden beauty in ordinary life.

The best place to find out more about Faye's future projects is on her socials.

https://www.tiktok.com/@faye.knightly.writer?is_from_webapp=1&sender_device=pc

https://www.instagram.com/faye_knightly_writer

Or check out her link tree to see everything in one place and join her newsletter for book perks!

https://linktr.ee/faye_knightly_writer

Also by Faye Knightly

The Breeders series by Faye Knightly is composed of interconnected stand-alones set in a post apocalyptic dystopian world where mates are forbidden and pack loyalty is prized above all.
You can find the Breeders series on Amazon and Ingram Sparks.

https://mybook.to/AGsRt

Read on for a peek at Breeders (Book 1)

"It's no big deal really. You just breathe this in and lay back on the bed." The breeding program coordinator sounded almost bored, his voice droning on tonelessly as he informed me about the safety protocols. His thick glasses gave him a bug-eyed appearance further emphasized by the lack of hair on his barren head. He wore a long lab coat that went to his ankles. I guess that made sense—he'd be fully protected from any fluid mishaps.

My fluids.

With a gulp, my eyes drifted to the central feature in the small room—a cramped twin bed with a black waterproof mattress and uncomfortable-looking black straps hanging off the sides. Soon, I'd be strapped to the thing waiting for man after man to come and fuck me for the glory of the pack.

The rest of the small room was surprisingly homey and designed to help the breeder relax, with two nightstands on either side of the bed and a painting of rolling country hills on the wall. But the cozy flower-patterned lamps barely gave off enough light to call the room dim, and I knew it was intentional. Wouldn't want me to see any details of the would-be-fathers of my children. Or smell them. Wrinkling my nose with disgust, I looked around the room for whatever was pumping out the obnoxious floral scent invading my nostrils and found a white plastic cylinder secured to the ceiling. A pile of water bottles in the corner had me rubbing my bare arms against the chill of the room. Right, that was in case any of the men became thirsty after exerting themselves.

They weren't for me though. It was said when you went into heat you didn't get hungry. Or thirsty. Or want anything other than sex, sex, sex. I swallowed hard, trying to imagine being that far gone. Those black straps hanging haphazardly from the bed would be locked onto my ankles soon, helping to keep me from thrashing my way off when the heat madness took hold. Shiny metal rails were slid under the bed right now, but I knew they'd be pulled up and secured in place once we began. Yet another safety measure for poor sex-crazed Cassie.

Sex-crazed Cassie. It was hard to believe I'd soon be reduced to an animal needing to be strapped to a bed lest she harm herself. Coughing nervously, I frowned down at the freckles peppering my fair arms. At five foot four with hardly any breasts to speak of, green eyes, and straight dirty blonde hair with a tendency to frizz— would I measure up to their expectations? And if I did, would I be able to perform my pack duty and go through with this?

Say the heat madness took hold, and I became the lust-filled creature the pack wanted me to be, what of the men? I hadn't seen a boy my age since they separated girls and boys at puberty. The boys I'd played soccer with and who had helped me jar fireflies at dusk were completely different creatures who watched us from a distance with a predatory gleam in their eyes, their round boyish features replaced with hard angles and gangly limbs teeming with thick muscle. They were enigmas with deep, rumbly voices and broad shoulders.

A new fear emerged. Would they find me attractive enough, or would they see me lying on the bed, and turn to leave—water bottles left without use, my entrance slick, my body desperate?

I wanted to call the whole thing off, to say that the signs of my heat coming must be false. The feverish chills and dry mouth, the restlessness all a part of my imagination, but I couldn't back out.

Not when this was the only way I would ever be a mother.

I'd always wanted that, always, and my heart had swelled with pride when the scholars had looked into my genealogy and assigned me the role of a breeder instead of a worker. I would be a pack mother, like I'd always dreamed. Younglings had always trailed after me, begging me to tell them more of my stories or to play some of my made-up games, and I wanted to have my own little ones someday to do those things with.

It was in the weeks leading up to my heat when the reality had started to sink in, and all those good feelings had turned into fears and nerves so powerful I could scarcely eat or sleep. I wanted this. I was meant to be a mother, but as much as I told myself it would all be okay, I was a mess by the time my heat started showing signs of starting.

To fulfill my dream of motherhood, I'd have to go through at least one heat cycle with a lineup of men visiting me in this strangely homey room, fucking me senseless in the hopes their seed would take root. Supposedly, I would enjoy it, but maybe I'd be terrible at sex.

I fiddled with the white cotton shift I wore, trying to stretch it over my exposed thighs. Even the coordinator was making me nervous. Was there hint of lust swirling in his hazel eyes? Maybe he was in the breeding program. Shit, shit, shit. For all I knew, he would don a mask and take a turn.

Maybe he was here to get me warmed up. Tension churned in my stomach as I assessed him. He was older, around fifty, but that didn't mean he couldn't be used as a breeder—not if the record keepers found him to be a good match for the woman. But he was wearing glasses, and the record keepers did hate to tarnish their perfect breeding program with hereditary issues that could impact a wolf's ability to defend the pack.

They could look past it though, for the right genetic combination.

The air became thin, and I wheezed, nearly jumping when the coordinator reached out a calloused hand to pat my shoulder fondly. I managed to meet his eyes and saw only kindness there.

"You're going to do fine. You've practiced, right?"

Practiced? Oh yeah, I'd practiced. I nodded, lowering my head and fixing my eyes on the hideous black ankle strap. All the breeding females were permitted to take a first when they first started showing signs of their heats starting. We were instructed to choose a man to have protected sex with so we would be prepared for our breeding days. We were supposed to practice with them as much as we wanted. They wanted us as comfortable as possible, but the whole experience had been so sweaty and unsatisfying that I'd only been able to do it twice.

At least the man had been eager enough. I hadn't dared to ask anyone outright, but my mother had found a gentle older man named Reg who had asked about me when I'd turned twenty-two and started showing signs of my heat. Wildly overweight, sex with Reg had been sticky and loud. I could still feel the slap of his belly against my back when he'd taken me from behind, and the throaty grunts by which he'd made his pleasure known. It hadn't hurt but it was unappealing, and now I was going to have to put up with that for however long it took for my heat to die down enough to regain my sanity.

"Just climb on up here and get comfy. You'll need to remove your nightgown. We don't want to risk you getting tangled up in it." He smiled, gesturing invitingly at the mattress. Get comfy? Was he serious? His hand remained extended expectantly, and the silence stretched between us until I couldn't stand it anymore.

With a shaky nod, I climbed up on the bed. The mattress crinkled noisily as I did, and I stripped off my cotton nightgown, dropping it on the nightstand just within reach. A button with a long cord sat on the table just in case I needed to tap out. I stared at the shiny red button longingly then turned my attention to the simple white door where my breeding males would enter once my heat started.

It took me a moment to realize I was trembling. I ran my hands up the gooseflesh of my arms, startling when the coordinator clicked something into place. A handrail. Right. They'd used these beds in hospitals, and the shiny metal grips were integrated into the bed. The coordinator gave me an apologetic look before moving to the next one and securing it.

Almost ready.

www.ingramcontent.com/pod-product-compliance
Lightning Source LLC
Chambersburg PA
CBHW030936120726
47906CB00002B/596